Also by Linda Broday

Bachelors of Battle Creek
Texas Mail Order Bride
Twice a Texas Bride
Forever His Texas Bride

Men of Legend
To Love a Texas Ranger
The Heart of a Texas Cowboy
To Marry a Texas Outlaw

Texas Heroes
Knight on the Texas Plains
The Cowboy Who Came Calling
To Catch a Texas Star

Outlaw Mail Order Brides
The Outlaw's Mail Order Bride
Saving the Mail Order Bride
The Mail Order Bride's Secret
Once Upon a Mail Order Bride

Texas Redemption
Christmas in a Cowboy's Arms anthology
Longing for a Cowboy Christmas anthology

a COWBOY *of* LEGEND

LINDA BRODAY

sourcebooks
casablanca

Published by Sourcebooks Casablanca, an imprint of Sourcebooks
P.O. Box 4410, Naperville, Illinois 60567-4410
(630) 961-3900
sourcebooks.com

Printed and bound in Canada.
MBP 10 9 8 7 6 5 4 3 2 1

Author's Note

Dear Reader,

I'm off on exciting adventures with a new series called Lone Star Legends. This series features some of the adult children of Sam, Houston, and Luke Legend, so you'll still get glimpses of them and the Lone Star Ranch.

It's also a new time period. All of these will take place around the turn of the century. Things are a lot different. The country is changing so fast. Automobiles, electric lights, and reform issues pose challenges. Industrialization brings economic growth. Women are fighting for the right to vote and stand up against inequality and the sale of alcohol.

Grace Legend, the daughter of Houston Legend, is right in the thick of things. She's joined the temperance movement and is bound and determined to shut down as many saloons as she can because she's seen firsthand how liquor destroys marriages and families.

Owner of the Three Deuces Deacon Brannock has spent every waking moment trying to make his saloon pay off but fears the worst when he finds himself in the crosshairs of the temperance women. This is a war he has to win. Lose the saloon, and his dream of buying some land and returning to the life he loves is dead.

I'm sure you have ideas about this. I can see both sides. I've lived with alcohol all my life and have seen how it can sometimes change a person. Yet I also know what it's like to be dirt poor and have a dream I couldn't reach.

I hope you enjoy this story and the rest of the series. Next up is *A Cowboy Christmas Legend* with Sam Legend Jr.

Happy Reading,

Linda Broday

One

"DESTROYER OF MEN'S SOULS! BEWARE THE PITFALLS OF THE devil's brew!" Grace Legend held up her sign and directed her loud yells into the murky interior of the Three Deuces saloon.

A gust of wind delivered the stench of the nearby stockyards up her nose and a swirl of dirt into her eyes. She blinked several times to clear the grit as the two dozen temperance women behind her took up the chant, banging drums and shaking tambourines. They sounded impressive.

A surly individual went around her and reached for the batwing doors. Grace swatted him with her sign. "Get back! Back, I say. This den of iniquity is closed to the likes of you."

Built like a bull and smelling like the south end of a north-bound steer, the man narrowed his gaze and raised a meaty fist. "This here's a free country, and I can go anywhere I like."

Gunfire rang out down the street, and a woman screamed. Grace was glad she'd stuck a derringer in her pocket. This section of town saw killings every day, even though the citizens cried for someone to clean it up and make it safe.

She wanted to take a step back from the surly man more than anything. She really did. He had meanness rolling off him like rancid, thick snake oil. But giving ground wasn't in her makeup. Not today and not as long as she was alive. She had a job to do.

Grace sucked in a quick breath, shot him a piercing glare, and parked herself across the doorway. "I bet your wife would like to know where you spend your time when you should be working. Shame on you wasting your money on whiskey."

"I earn it, and I'll spend it however I see fit. Now step aside." He snarled and raised a fist.

"Or else what?" A voice in Grace's head warned that this course of action could be dangerous, but she never listened to that boring bit of reason. No, she saw it as her right and duty to make a difference in the world, and make it she would. She couldn't do that sitting on her hands like some timid toad, afraid to utter a sound.

At least a half dozen gunshots nearby rent the air, and people ducked.

A crowd had begun to gather and pressed close, as though sensing a free show. Some of the men got into a heated shouting match with her ladies.

Before she could move, the quarrelsome fellow barreled into her, knocking her sideways. Grace launched onto his back and began whopping him with the sign. However, the handle was too long for close fighting, and none of her blows landed. Hell and damnation!

She released a frustrated cry and wrapped both arms around his head.

"Get off me!" he roared.

"When hell freezes over, fool." She heard a door bang and the footsteps of someone new.

Masculine hands yanked the two of them apart.

"Hey, what's the meaning of this?" The voice belonged to a man she assumed to be the saloon owner.

Breathing hard, she jerked at the bodice of her favorite royal-blue dress, straightening it before grabbing the immense hat that barely clung to one side of her head. She blew back a blond curl that had fallen across one eye, blocking her view. Only then did she get a glimpse of the gentleman whose livelihood she meant to destroy, and the sight glued her tongue to the roof of her mouth.

He presented quite a handsome picture with his coal-black hair and lean form. Who could dispute that? Yet his physical attributes paled in comparison to his assertive bearing. Confidence surrounded him like music from a songbird, yet there was none of the arrogance she'd seen from others plying the same trade. A Stetson sat low on his forehead—a cowboy? Grace did a double take. Saloon owners wore bowlers, not Stetsons. She was unable to move her gaze from his piercing eyes that reminded her of smoke, shadowed by the brim of the hat. The stormy gray depths warned of the danger of crossing him.

And more. Oh my!

Aware that her friends were watching, Grace took in his appearance—the silk vest of dark green belonged to a gambler. Combined with tailored black trousers, he appeared a profitable businessman, the hat aside. Until she looked at his worn, white cuffs and boots in desperate need of repair. Had he spent everything on the window dressing with no thought of footwear?

Her gaze rested on a well-used gun belt slung low on his hips, complete with what appeared to be a long Peacemaker. By now, most men left their firearms at home. However, having grown up with weapons of all kinds on the Lone Star Ranch, she understood the need to sometimes keep a gun handy. Although crime in the notorious area had begun to decline, running a saloon at the edge of Hell's Half Acre was still a risky business and called for protection of some sort.

She patted the small derringer in her pocket to make sure it hadn't fallen out.

"I asked what's going on here," the owner repeated.

Smelly glared, wiping blood from his forehead. So she did get a lick in. "This churlish fishwife assaulted me when I tried to enter, and I demand that you do something."

"Churlish fishwife? Why you!" Grace swung her sign again—only it caught the tall saloon owner instead, knocking him back a step.

Towering head and shoulders over her, the man snatched the sign from her hand, broke it over his knee, and pitched the pieces aside. His eyes had darkened to a shade she'd never seen before and had no words to describe.

"Care to explain why you're running off my business, lady?"

The question came out silky and wrapped in velvet, like her father's did when he wanted to put the fear of God into someone. That frightened her far more than yelling. This cowboy saloon owner was someone to reckon with.

Although quaking inside, Grace drew herself up and thrust out her chin, praying her group of women were behind her. Although the quiet failed to reassure her. "I'm asserting my God-given right to free speech."

"You tell him, Grace!" one of the women yelled.

"Free speech about?" he snapped.

"The evils of drink. It's destroying the fabric of our society and wrecking homes."

"And it's your duty to straighten us men out?" he barked.

His dark glower shot a shiver of alarm up her spine, especially when he edged closer. Why couldn't she have been born taller? She felt like a bug he was about to step on. He was every bit or more the height of her six-foot-three father.

How come she didn't hear a peep from her ladies? If they'd left her...

She inhaled a deep breath to steady herself. "As much as I'm able. I cannot turn a blind eye to hungry kids and wives bearing the scars of abuse. It's a sin and disgrace. I'm their voice." She clasped her hands together to hide the tremble. Her parents—and many others—had warned that she'd go too far one day. Dance to the music, and eventually she'd have to pay the fiddler. Anger flashing from his eyes said this might be the time when she'd have to pay up.

The belligerent clod inserted himself between them. "You gonna stand here and jaw with her all day, Brannock? Send for the sheriff. She's breaking the damn law."

Brannock shifted his attention to the ill-humored patron, the tense set of his shoulders reminding her of a rattler coiled to strike. "You telling me my business now, Cyril? Go home. I have this under control."

"I came for my beer. You know I come every afternoon."

Brannock flicked his annoyed gaze to Grace, a noise rumbling in his throat. "The saloon is temporarily closed. You'll have to come back."

"Just wait until the others hear about this. We'll ruin you." Cyril stomped away.

"You'll have to get in line!" the saloon owner shouted, then bit back a low curse and swung his icy grays on her. "I don't want to throw you in jail, but you'll leave me no choice if you continue down this dangerous path, Miss—"

"Grace Legend." She smiled sweetly. "I have a—"

"God-given right to free speech," he finished for her. "I heard the first time. Didn't anyone warn you about the danger of coming here?"

"I don't listen to things of that nature."

"You may regret that one day." His deep voice vibrated across her skin. "I have a business to run, and I intend to make money at it. Do I make myself clear?"

"Perfectly." She glanced up into those dangerous eyes, and before she could release a scathing retort, someone latched on to her arm.

"There you are, sis. In trouble again, I see."

Irritated, she glanced up into her brother Crockett's face. "Yes, here I am. I haven't turned to a pillar of salt, landed in jail, or shot anyone." She glanced around to find that her group of women had indeed disappeared, left her to face the owner by herself. She realized then that if she was going to do this, she'd have to do it on her own. Just as she'd usually had to.

"The day's young." Crockett's grin faded when his gaze went from her sign lying in splinters to Brannock. "I'm sorry about the mess. I'm Crockett Legend, Gracie's brother. I hope there's no hard feelings."

The air spewing from Brannock's mouth said there was plenty of ill will to go around. "Keep your sister away from my saloon or I won't be so forgiving next time." The cowboy bit the words out like they soured on his tongue, then whirled and went inside his establishment, slamming the wooden doors behind the batwing swinging ones and slid a bolt just as a woman's scream sounded a few doors down.

One of those newfangled automobiles drove by and backfired loudly. The disappointed crowd began to disperse, grumbling at the lack of bloodshed.

Grace jerked her arm from her brother. "Not until I get my sign."

He bent to help. "Watch out for the sharp pieces. I don't know why you keep getting into these scrapes. Pa's ready to throw up his hands, and Mama's wondering where she went wrong. Gracie, you don't have to get on everyone's bad side. Just do the right thing."

It irritated her that he kept referring to her babyish name. She'd long adopted the more adult Grace, yet her family refused to abide by her decision.

"I am doing the right thing. I'm living my life my way, on my own terms." She suppressed a yelp when a jagged piece of wood slid under her nail. She wouldn't cry out. Remaining calm, she juggled what she'd picked up and pulled the fragment out, then wrapped her bleeding finger in a handkerchief Crockett quickly supplied.

"Give those to me." He took the mangled sticks from her. "What happened?"

"I was marching peaceably when a man tried to prove he was boss." As they moved down the street, she told him about the fight with Cyril and how Brannock had snapped the sign over his knee. "The nerve of him. He's very ill-mannered."

Still, she grudgingly had to admit that he was also a little intriguing. He was different from the men she was used to seeing in the lower end of town. Though he was angry, he hadn't brushed her aside like a bothersome fly and had sent the drunk on his way.

"Stay away from him, sis. Deacon Brannock has a reputation for showing no mercy."

"What does that even mean?" Was he a cruel man? She didn't feel that from him.

"Do I have to spell it out? He's ruthless. He crushes people. If a man doesn't pay his tab, Brannock takes him into the alley and they settle up one way or another."

"How would you know?"

"I hear talk."

Grace cut a glance at her looming brother, who at age twenty so strongly resembled their father, Houston. They shared not only the same dark hair and eyes, but muscular build and toughness. Houston once drove two thousand head of longhorns up the Great Western Trail, battling cattle rustlers and bad weather the entire way. Though she'd been just a babe, Grace had gone along with her mother. The harrowing stories of near-death situations were ingrained in her.

She'd survived for a reason. Wasting her life in foolish endeavors like needlepoint and cooking wasn't her idea of living a meaningful life. No, she had a purpose to fulfill—doing important work that changed lives.

Grace could see Crockett doing something like that too. And succeeding. By all accounts, he made a good living as a cattle buyer and kept a home in Fort Worth as well as on the Lone Star Ranch. Her brother seemed to have a forty-year-old mind in a young body. His life was set, and Grace envied that. She moved from one thing to another, never satisfied.

Crockett laid the mangled sign down and opened the door of his home. "Sis, you have to stop getting in these fights that you can't win. You're worrying the family, especially Mama."

Her parents called her their crusader, always fighting against injustice of some sort. First it was saving her baby pig from slaughter. She'd made signs and sat in its pen until her father relented. That graduated to armadillos, the favorite tree where she sat to read, children's rights, and protesting the sale of wild horses and burros. You name it, she'd been involved. But this was different. Images of the battered women and children she'd tried to help over the past year flitted through her mind. Ava, Hilda, Beth Ann, and May. Beaten bloody and crying, but in the end staying with the only life they knew and preserving their marriages at such a great cost to them and their children.

The silent face of Libby Daniels frozen in death followed the endless line of those beaten. Grace stilled, recalling her best friend who'd married a charming man with a violent side and a taste for whiskey. She and Libby had gone to the ranch school together from age six. Libby had been the daughter of one of Grace's father's hands and had fallen in love with a drifter Houston hired to ride fence.

Less than six months after the wedding, Grace found Libby lying dead in the snow a few steps from headquarters.

Her vacant eyes staring heavenward still haunted Grace's sleep.

Grace blinked hard and whispered, "I can't stop. Lord, I wish I could, but I can't."

Her brother put his arms around her. "I don't understand what drives you. Go home and accept one of the dozens of marriage proposals you've gotten."

Not on a bet. Grace rolled her eyes. Her family was constantly trying to marry her off. On Sundays, she'd never known which cowboy would be sitting at their table, so she stayed away from the ranch as much as possible. She just couldn't take the cowboys' hound-dog eyes.

She laid her head on her brother's shoulder. "There's more for me than marriage and kids, Crockett. I have things I have to do."

He was silent for a long moment. Finally, he let out a long sigh. "Please be careful. Promise me."

She'd finally found the one cause that lodged in her gut, that she was unable to shake. She was done with burying friends and acquaintances due to abuse. Shutting down these saloons and the flowing liquor would help save so many lives, marriages, and families. This would be her life's calling. This would settle the restlessness in her bones and bring calm and much peace to her soul. This would define her life.

"I'll do my best." She pulled away from Crockett and glanced through the window in the direction of the Three Deuces Saloon.

Deacon Brannock didn't scare her…that much.

Two

DEACON STORMED UP TO HIS QUARTERS ABOVE THE SALOON. Glaring down at the street, he massaged his right hand that had gone numb during the altercation with Grace Legend.

Damn his rotten luck!

Why had the fight three years ago that broke his arm damaged tendons and left him in this shape?

After patching him up, Doc had shaken his head and murmured that he should be grateful to have an arm of any sort hanging from his sleeve.

Grateful? Deacon gave a snort of disgust. Damn this new turn of events. Just when things were finally, finally going his way, and his establishment had begun to turn a slight profit, up popped this temperance movement and the group of women determined to destroy him.

He couldn't win for losing. If this saloon went broke, he'd wind up with nothing.

Deacon strode to a glass decanter on the table and poured a drink. His life seemed to always be one step forward and five back. He rolled the glass of amber liquid across his cheek. Anger rose like thick, black sludge, choking him. The Legend woman, or another like her, ignited with the need to whip the world into shape, would be back. He could lose every single thing he'd worked tirelessly for.

Damn fate! When would he catch a break?

The long mirror in the corner caught his reflection. Pain and anger strangled him.

He flung the glass into the mirror, shattering both—and the image of the miserable bastard staring back at him.

The door swung open, and a young woman hurried in, her eyes wide. She stood, clutching her hands over her swollen belly, as though afraid to come closer. "I heard a crash. Your arm?"

"I'm fine, Leah." The lie slid out easily enough.

When she rushed forward to pick up the glass, he snapped, "Leave it."

"I don't mind. You've done so much."

Deacon softened his voice. "I don't need you to clean up after me."

Leah stretched to her full five feet. She looked more child than woman at sixteen and should have still been playing with dolls. She chewed her lip. "Is it Seth? Has he found me?"

"No."

"I don't want to cause you trouble. I'll leave before that happens."

Deacon stepped over the mess and took her arm. "I'll hear no talk of leaving. You're supposed to rest. Let me clean this up, and I'll challenge you to a game of backgammon. How's that?"

Her smile tugged at the scar still healing on her cheek. "You know how I love to play. Thank you for taking me in, Deacon."

"You needed someone to care. This is little enough." He helped her to the door to her room, then returned to his black thoughts and the liquor that promised to numb him. What would happen to Leah if the temperance women closed his place down? To her child? There was more at stake than simply him and the survival of the Three Deuces.

He swept up the broken glass and mopped the mess, the man in the broken mirror watching him. Maybe he should get what he could for this place and move to more peaceful climes.

Only where would that be?

The movement sweeping the country was happening everywhere. And Leah needed him. Her rotten husband was searching high and low and had vowed to kill her when he found her. One of

Deacon's regulars, Seth Pickford, was twice Leah's age and prone to uncontrollable rages. Deacon had intervened during the last beating that had taken place in the alley behind the saloon and hid Leah upstairs. No man would beat a woman near Deacon and him not stop it. He would never tolerate wife- or child-beaters, although the law gave a man the right to do as he wished with both.

A low growl rumbled in Deacon's throat. The damn law needed to be changed. No wonder the women were up in arms. He really didn't blame them. They took the brunt of their husbands' drunken rages.

He would like to help more women like Leah, but he didn't want to beat a damn drum either.

Still, he ran a respectable place and threw out anyone who had too much. Even so, they just went down the street to other saloons, so his efforts didn't accomplish anything. His conscience pricked him. He could see how he added to the problem. Little he could do, though.

But was that true? Hell! To close his doors would shatter his dream of bettering himself.

If the women would just leave him out of their war and let him keep making a living.

The broom and mop put away out of sight, he poured himself another drink and sat in thought. Despite everything, Grace Legend had piqued his interest. Her brother had called her Gracie and the storm that had built in her dark-blue eyes told him it rankled. Deacon chuckled. The pretty lady had a hell of a temper. She'd sure made Cyril toe the line—no easy task.

With a cloud of honey-blond hair and the bluest eyes he'd ever seen, he was sure the spitfire attracted her share of attention wherever she went. Certain kinds could be dangerous. For a moment, he felt a little protective of her until he remembered why she'd shown up at his door.

The Legend name nibbled at the edges of his memory. He'd heard it before. Where? But try as he might, he couldn't recall.

Finally, he finished his glass and strolled down the hall to Leah's room. Through the open door, he saw her at a small table with the backgammon board already out. She glanced up with an impish smile. "There you are. I thought you might be afraid to come. I'm going to beat you this time."

Leah's brown eyes appeared large among her other more diminutive features as she studied him, reminding him so much of his little sister. It was Cass's face he'd first seen in the alley that had sparked a fierce protectiveness. They bore a startling similarity. Leah's hair, the color of a newly plowed field, glistened in the light from the window. She needed a woman's companionship, not a crotchety man like him with a bum arm that didn't work right.

"You and what army?" Deacon slid into the other seat. "Prepare to lose."

Her smile faded. "Are you feeling better?"

"Everything's fine." He arranged the fifteen playing discs in their correct places, keeping his gaze lowered. If he'd lifted his eyes, she'd have seen the chaos inside and worried. He wasn't her problem. "You go first."

Leah rolled the pair of dice, moving her discs on the board. Although the moves made little sense, he complained that she was out for blood. As he'd intended, she giggled.

Gunfire broke out down the street again. Both froze, listened for a moment, then resumed play. It was such a regular occurrence, they rarely paid it any mind. This was the price of living in what amounted to a war zone, and once darkness fell, all bets were off and you took your life in your hands. He hoped Grace wouldn't be so foolish to still walk these streets. Hopefully, she'd go back to what seemed like a nice, orderly life.

He let Leah win the first game out of three, and they set the pieces up again. Deacon found it difficult to keep his mind off the silence down below and the fact that the longer his doors stayed locked, the more money he would lose. Even so, he won the second game.

Halfway through the third, it hit him. He'd seen Houston Legend in Medicine Springs, Texas, at the trial nine years ago. Grace's brother, Crockett's, resemblance to Houston was strong, and Deacon figured they had to be his kids. Few others carried a name like Legend.

Leah broke into his thoughts. "Your turn, Deacon."

"Right." He rolled the dice and made his play, his thoughts returning to the man he'd looked up to back then. Without Houston, Deacon would've ended up in a worse mess. No question.

"Your heart isn't in this game." Leah folded her arms across her large belly. "Tell me what's wrong. I know something is."

Deacon blew out a breath and put his head in his hand. "Just thinking about something."

"Those women marching outside the saloon?"

He jerked his head around. "I've warned you about opening the door."

"I didn't. I saw it all from up here through the window curtain. Are you worried?"

"Some. But my mind is on a man I crossed paths with ten years ago."

"Will he come after you, Deacon?" she asked softly.

"No." Not unless he messed with Houston's daughter, if in fact she was. Deacon really wouldn't relish a fight with the big, muscular rancher. "Forget them and let's finish. I see you're about to beat me."

The girl laughed. "For once. It's not every day I catch Deacon Brannock sleeping."

"You haven't won yet."

In the end, he let her win. It was only right. She had so few reasons to laugh.

"Deacon, what's going to happen when I have this baby? Who will help bring it into the world?"

"I'll get a midwife." Dammit, he should've already made

arrangements. He'd put it off due to the fact that Seth was keeping an eagle eye on the place, which prevented Deacon from leaving Leah alone. "I'll take care of that soon. I promise."

"I'm kind of scared. Who will hold my hand?"

Deacon cleared his throat and went for something light, but the words came out raspy anyway. "I will. I'll be right here by your side."

"Like family?"

"Absolutely. Don't worry your head about anything. I'll get you through this."

Leah blinked back tears and whispered, "Thank you, Deacon."

The truth was, she had no close family left. They all died during an epidemic, and that's how she ended up married to Seth Pickford. The only kin she had remaining was an old maiden aunt in Atlanta, Georgia, and Leah swore that was the last place she'd go.

Deacon tucked a curl behind her ear. "You're going to be okay."

"I know. I'll rock my baby and tell it all about my mama and papa and brothers. And I'm gonna love it and never let anyone hurt it."

In the ensuing silence, Deacon went to the window and stared out at a group of cowboys trotting down the street. They must've brought some cattle to the stockyards. He clenched his jaw. He'd open up for the night crowd come hell or high water. One bad day would put him under, and he meant to hang on as best he could—even by a thumbnail.

An idea was forming that just might work. At least for tonight. It would call for black paper and a lot of word of mouth. He'd have to find Izzy Anthony, a ten-year-old kid who often hung around. Deacon had come to care deeply for the poor urchin who had no one.

Keeping to his habit of late, he scanned the lengthening shadows of the buildings across the street for Seth Pickford's stout body. In the man's younger days, he'd probably been all muscle, but thirty years of laziness and drink had turned it to flab. Deacon saw no sign of him.

Or Grace Legend and her group of do-gooders. Still, it was early.

"Deacon?" Leah asked.

"What?" He let the curtain fall and turned.

"If you close the saloon and leave here, will you take me with you?"

The question jarred him, although it shouldn't have. Leah always seemed to sense his thoughts. What would he do with her if he chose to sell out? Maybe some preacher's wife would take her and the baby in. He could give them a little money for her keep.

But take her? The inhospitable land he had in mind where a man could disappear was too dangerous.

He turned, the sight of her tears twisting his heart. "Honey, I'm not going to leave unless it's the only solution left." He opened his arms, and she flew into them like a little lost bird. Deacon propped his chin on the top of her head, glad to have someone who gave a damn about him.

Yes, they were family—all each other had.

❦

Crockett went back to the stockyards, and Grace flew into a tizzy making herself another sign. Her brother would have a fit that she'd gone back to the Three Deuces, but she couldn't afford to waste any time. Tomorrow she'd give a report at the temperance meeting.

She'd joined the movement several weeks ago after hearing a talk by Mrs. Carrie Nation. Oh, how the woman's words had thrilled, and Grace knew she had to take up and carry the banner—no matter the hardships and pain—for every woman of all stations of life.

"How much discomfort are you willing to suffer for your fellow sisters? How many slurs? How much missed sleep?" Mrs. Nation had asked.

"As much as it takes to win!" came the answering shouts.

This was a fight in which they had to be victorious, and there was no backing down.

It consisted of a lot of aspects. Educating the world of the evils of alcohol, protecting the vulnerable women and children, equality, and the crown jewel—gaining the right to vote.

A shiver raced through her at the thought of being able to cast a ballot, open up her own bank account without having her father or brother sign for her, or perhaps one day holding office. Women elected to Congress could make laws and be sure they were fair for everyone, not just a few. A thrill shot through her heart.

This fight was also for her eleven-year-old sister, Hannah, so she wouldn't have to suffer the same indignities as Grace.

With a strike of the hammer, she nailed the handle onto the sign, thinking about what to paint on it. What was the engrossing line Carrie had said at the last temperance meeting?

Oh, yes. *Living for a higher purpose is as honorable as dying for it.*

This was what Grace had been born to do. She knew it, and maybe Carrie Nation did too. Deacon Brannock had best take heed. She had social injustice in her sights, and she meant to make a difference.

After the meeting, Mrs. Nation had pulled Grace aside and told her she was a born leader and women would follow her all the way to the finish line. Right then, Grace vowed to do her best.

With the handle secured on the sign, she grabbed the paintbrush.

Alcohol Destroys Families. Stop the Bleeding. Protect the Innocent.

There. She stood back. Perfect. She hurried up to the room she kept while staying with Crockett and made quick work of changing clothes and fixing her hair.

With luck, she might run into her cowboy again, and she wanted to look her best.

One might never know when she'd need to. Her pulse quickened.

She really shouldn't care about her appearance, but a part of her couldn't help acknowledging that she wanted him to see that it wasn't just old women and spinsters who cared about this reform. If she could just convince Brannock that alcohol destroyed lives, he might listen to reason. And closing just one saloon would be a victory.

Her father's warning sounded in her head. *I don't care what cause you take up. Whatever you do, keep the family name out of your activities. I mean it. Don't sully our name, our reputation, that we've worked hard to protect.*

Guilt crept past her zeal, and she swallowed hard. Staining the honored family name was something she swore to never do. Her grandfather Stoker had fought for Texas independence and received the land the Lone Star Ranch sat on from Sam Houston himself. Her father and uncles had fought equally hard since against outlaws, rustlers, fire, drought, and everything else to build on what her grandfather started. Now, the ranch covered six counties and measured five hundred thousand acres.

Crockett was right. Darn, darn, darn! They were going to be madder than a herd of scalded cats. And disappointed in her. That was the absolute worst part.

But only if they found out. Grace brightened. What would a little harmless marching do? It wasn't like she was hurting anything. Plus, she had her battered women friends to consider. She filled her lungs with good old Texas air. This was for Libby Daniels. She'd been unable to save her friend, but she could get others out of that situation.

This was only the start of something with real meaning.

Her other secret, she'd guard with her life. She had safeguards built in to prevent the family finding out. Thank goodness she'd taken the name of Sam Valentine for that work.

Still, this cause might cost her dearly. Shaking off the niggling in her head, Grace picked up her sign and headed for the door.

Three

THE THREE DEUCES APPEARED DESERTED WHEN GRACE AND her posse of women arrived as twilight settled in. From sunset on was the busiest time in Hell's Half Acre. You wouldn't know it by Brannock's dark saloon. She stood there a moment, then rattled the stout wooden doors behind the swinging batwings and found them locked tight. No sounds came from inside, as best she could tell.

It downright took the air from her righteous zeal.

Maybe she was early. She glanced around nervously. All the other saloons on the street were going strong with liquor flowing and music blaring. And would continue 'til midnight or later.

An older woman named Hazel lowered her sign. "What's going on, Grace? There's no light inside."

"I haven't a clue." Grace tried peering in a grimy window that had probably never been washed and discovered someone had painted the panes with black paint. Was it like this earlier? The fight with Cyril and meeting Brannock had occupied her attention, so she couldn't say.

She glanced around but caught sight of no one heading toward the establishment. A twinge of disappointment shot through her. What was the use of marching in front of a deserted building when there were plenty of others?

"Well, I'm not wasting my time here," declared another woman.

"Me either," a voice chimed in. "It's spooky all closed up like this. Could be haunted."

"Or a trap." Esther looked right and left, her eyes wide, hands jittery. For good reason. They'd had rotten eggs, rocks, and mud hurled at them.

Hazel sidled closer and sniffed. "You're wearing perfume. This may seem an odd question, Grace, but why did you change to fancy clothes? We all kept our old ones on."

They never wore their Sunday best to march in because of the things thrown. One time, a man had showered them with kerosene.

"I just thought… I mean…" Grace inhaled a deep breath. "You know, that's not important. Our work, our commitment is what matters, ladies, and I suggest we get to it."

"The sinful Deacon Brannock had nothing to do with getting gussied up?" Hazel pressed.

"No, absolutely not. I just wanted to look nice in case I get thrown in jail and there's a photographer." Grace forced herself to meet the older woman's gaze and saw that she didn't buy that.

Hazel snorted. "Yeah, makes as much sense as anything."

Though irritated, Grace smiled sweetly. "Why don't you ladies go on down the street and I'll join you? I'll stick around a few minutes longer. Be very careful and stay out of the line of gunfire."

As though on cue, a flurry of gunshots erupted, followed by loud shouting. The women huddled together.

She wouldn't put it past Brannock to pretend to be closed and open up once they'd left. No, she wouldn't put any trick past the cowboy saloon owner.

Saying they wouldn't march long, the group went down to the next saloon, banging their drums. Grace was glad she hadn't had to explain something she didn't fully understand herself. There was simply something different about Brannock. He didn't have the cruelty about him of other saloon keeps.

To feel better about her task, Grace marched back and forth in front of the Three Deuces for a few minutes but didn't find the heart to yell anything. Deflated, she sat on a step of the boardwalk.

Tinny piano music drifted on the breeze, along with rounds of off-key singing. The men seemed to be drunk already. She should go join her group of ladies, but the thought held no appeal. The Three Deuces was where she wanted to be. Where smoky-eyed Deacon Brannock had set up shop.

A boy around ten years old wandered up and sat beside her. "Whatcha doin', lady?"

"Waiting."

He peered up from beneath a long shock of red hair that fell forward. "What for?"

"For this place to open."

"You mean Mr. Brannock's? He's closed. Might never open again." The boy paused, then added, "Might sell out."

Guilt raced through Grace that she was the cause of putting him out of business. She hadn't really meant to. She shook herself. *Yes, she had planned to do that very thing.* At least she had to be honest with herself. She *had* wanted to shutter the saloon. But not run him out of town.

Just make him change his profession. Which was what? He looked like a cowboy, but he wore the clothes of a saloon owner. Confusing.

The boy shook back his long hair. "I'm Izzy. What's your name, lady?"

"Grace." She stuck out her hand and shook his. "Pleased to meet you, Izzy."

"It's short for Israel. I hate that name, so I made up this one." He picked at a scab on his hand. "Did you know you can make up new names if you don't like what they give you?"

"Of course. Makes it harder to find people." *Especially those with a need to disappear.* Grace smiled. In her case, it made it easier to do things she didn't want her family to know about.

He grinned. "I might change my name every week until I've gone through them all."

"I hate to poke a hole in your plan, Izzy, but you'll be an old man by the time that happens. Besides, folks add new ones all the time so you'll never run out." She motioned to the large scrape he was picking at. "What happened there?"

"Aw, ain't nothing to fuss over. Got in a fight with some bigger kids on the next street. They don't like me and cuss a blue streak. These streets are dangerous. Maybe you should go home, Miss Grace. They's killings ever night. Lots of people die. Do you have a gun, lady?" Izzy glanced up, the freckles marching across his nose caught in the fading light.

"Yes, I do." She patted her pocket. "I can defend myself."

Izzy's hand inched to her skirt. He rubbed the fabric. "I sure hope so, Miss Grace." The boy was silent a moment. "Why are you so mean to Mr. Brannock? What did he do to you?"

The question threw her. She straightened her shoulders. "I mean Mr. Brannock no harm. He's a lovely man. I just object to him selling alcohol, that's all. Any other time, we might be friends. Say, how did you know about our fight earlier?"

The kid's face reddened. He hopped to his feet. "Gotta go. Just remembered something."

Before she could even tell him goodbye, he was off like a flash. Very odd. Had Brannock put Izzy up to saying those things? He must've, or else the boy had witnessed her clobbering the saloon owner with her sign and overheard the rather heated words they'd exchanged.

The scoundrel. She wouldn't put anything past Deacon Brannock. He'd been mighty furious at her and the women. It was almost like he'd sent this kid. For what reason? To discourage her? What had Izzy said? Oh, yes. The place was closed and might never open, that Brannock might sell out. It stuck in her craw that the grown man would stoop to using a boy to do his dirty work. The disreputable tinhorn. Just wait until she saw him again.

Her stomach rumbled, reminding her she'd missed supper. She knew a café in a better part of town, but first, she went to meet her fellow marchers.

Grace was sure the Three Deuces would be open when she returned. But what if it wasn't? What if he meant to stay closed until she and the women left for good?

She gritted her teeth. Emerge victorious she would. She had right on her side.

⁂

Deacon stood in the deep shadows across the street. His gaze was riveted on Grace Legend and Izzy. He let a smile form. She hadn't seemed to take the darkened saloon well. Had the boy remembered what to say? Izzy was a bright kid, though, and his eyes had glowed at sight of the nickel.

It was worth every cent for the street urchin to stand on the corner with a sign for customers to use the back entrance. Though early yet, the saloon was having one of its best nights.

The blackened windows, with paint, then black paper, blocked out the low light and had completely fooled the temperance women and Grace. Now, if only the men kept the noise down.

All of a sudden, Izzy jerked to his feet and sped off. What had happened? He'd have to find the boy and ask. Just then Grace rose and went down the street to join the other women. She didn't look one bit happy to Deacon. A soft chuckle broke free.

Round one went to him.

Yet he knew this was only temporary. She wasn't the sort to give up. This lady had the tenacity of a bulldog, and when she sank her teeth into something, he feared she wouldn't turn loose. If she did, it would mightily surprise him. No, the pretty Grace Legend had grit and sass.

The look in those startling blue eyes had spoken of staying power, especially when she thought herself to be in the right. Which would likely be pretty much all the time.

In a way, he admired that. To feel that passionate about

something so fully and completely shot her above other women. If she didn't pose such a threat to his business, he might like to get to know her.

He had a feeling she'd be one hell of a backgammon opponent.

Too bad he would never find out. Friendship with such a woman was dangerous. She wouldn't bat an eye about using whatever information was at her disposal against him.

Just then a drunk stumbled to the front door of the Three Deuces and banged on it, hollering. Deacon pushed away from the side of the building he was leaning against and hurried across the street. "Hold the noise down, mister. Can't you read?"

The customer turned toward him, wrapping both arms around a post to keep from falling. "R-r-read what?"

Clearly, the man was beyond both reading and understanding. The drunk, his shabby clothes full of holes, had probably never learned his letters. Reeking of cheap whiskey, he loosened his hold on the post and would've gone down if Deacon hadn't grabbed him.

He held the man upright. "This saloon is closed. Go on down the street."

"I-I-I w-would, but this ship is in rough water, mister. It's about to c-capsize. I'll d-d-drown. Are you the captain?"

"Let's go find you a dry dock." Deacon aimed him toward a dark section of boardwalk midway up the block and told the man he was home. The drunk curled up in a ball and began to snore almost immediately.

Deacon hurried back to the Three Deuces just as a group of drovers arrived with money in their pockets and he let them in the back. "There's a three-drink limit tonight, gentlemen." Any more than that and the men would get rowdy and give everything away.

One stared and released a curse word. "You got any women upstairs?"

"No. Just selling liquor tonight. Sorry."

"Not as sorry as us." The cowboy made a lewd comment to his friends and laughed.

"Maybe you should just mosey on down to another watering hole." Deacon watched their hands through narrowed eyes. They were young and probably weren't a bad sort when the liquid courage he smelled on their breath wasn't so strong. Deacon met his barkeep's eyes and shook his head to the unspoken question of needing help. Harry Jones returned to serving drinks.

Harry had come to him about a year ago in need of a job and hadn't asked for much—just the back room where he could fight his demons alone. Deacon had never questioned the tall, ponytailed beanpole about where he came from or his story. That was a man's private business.

When the three cowboys decided to find more hospitable surroundings and left, Deacon climbed the stairs to check on Leah. He found her in her room, rocking and humming softly.

She glanced up with a smile. "Sounds like a quiet crowd tonight."

"For the most part. Need anything?" He thought she looked tired.

"Nope. I'm fine. Just thinking about my baby and how I can't wait to hold it."

All women in her condition probably got anxious for the big day. Leah wafted between fear and excitement on any given day. On the other hand, Deacon was dreading it and wondered how well he'd be able to help her through this.

"Deacon, I've been thinking about how I can help repay some of your kindness."

"You don't owe me anything," he answered gruffly.

"Still, there are things I can do. For instance, I can make tamales for you to sell out of the saloon. Meat pies too. Drinking men like to eat. I learned that from Seth. But they don't always want a meal. They can eat these with one hand, without a fork, and they're real easy to make."

"You don't need to be wearing yourself out and standing on your feet for hours. No." He admitted she did make a good point, and it would bring in more money, but he couldn't ask that of her. Growing a baby took enough energy.

Leah stood and glared. "I'm fully capable of doing something. I have to feel useful."

Deacon turned to leave. "We'll talk later."

"I want to talk now. Don't brush me aside like a child. You do that all the time." She crossed the space and rested a palm on his arm, softening her voice. "You need the extra income, and this will help. Plus, I need something to do besides stare at these four walls. I'm going crazy. Put yourself in my shoes."

He studied her earnest, brown eyes. "All right. We'll try it for one week."

"Thank you." She kissed his cheek.

Deacon grunted. "Don't think you can wrap me around your finger. I need to go back down for a bit in case Grace Legend returns. Get your rest."

"And get to bed early and be sure to brush my teeth and comb my hair and lock my door. I know all that. For God's sake, stop, Deacon." She slapped his shoulder. "You're not my mother!"

He flared. "You need someone to look after you!"

Leah's voice softened. "I just need a friend. That's all."

"Sorry for going overboard. I'll try to refrain." Actually, he was grateful she set boundaries. He didn't need to get more emotionally involved with her than normal because leaving was looking more and more probable. The temperance movement grew stronger by the day, and sooner or later they'd run him out. Some of the other owners told him they'd tried to pay them off to leave them alone, but he didn't have enough to make it worth their while. Might be best to cut his losses and emerge with something at least.

Several heartbeats passed before he spoke. "Make a list of what you'll need to make tamales and meat pies, and I'll send Izzy after them tomorrow."

"I will. Thank you again for letting me help."

"Of course." Forcing a smile, he gave her a peck on the cheek and went down to ride out the night with the drunks. Or maybe he'd slip outside for some cool spring air and ponder his dilemma in silence with a bottle of his best bourbon.

❧

Grace wound through the streets, her stomach full of pot roast and potatoes plus a big slice of blueberry pie. Though the berries weren't in season until much later in the year, the big cities could ship in about anything you could want anytime you wanted it. That still amazed her.

A three-quarter moon had risen and shone down on her, and that released a big wave of homesickness for the Lone Star and family. She could picture her parents; sister, Hannah; and brother Ransom, sitting down to eat. Her father and seventeen-year-old Ransom would try to talk ranching, and Mama would give them her famous look with a slight shake of her head.

Grandpa Stoker would probably be taking meals with them. At eighty-one, he still rode a horse every day and worked alongside the men, but his cook had passed on, and he hadn't hired another—at least that she'd heard.

Oh, how she'd love to see them and smell the fresh air of the ranch. Soon, she promised.

She rounded a corner and pulled up short. The Three Deuces was still dark. Questions swirled. Had he already picked up and moved on?

What if he had? Wasn't that what she wanted? A strange feeling settled in her chest that she might've taken away Deacon Brannock's livelihood. Well, if he'd stick around, she could help him get into a different business.

Where was Izzy? She doubted that anything happened in this part of town without the boy knowing. Yet what could he add to the bit he'd already shared? Maybe something.

After dodging drunks and getting ready to give up, she finally spied him and hollered.

He came running. "Hi, Miss Grace. Need something? Tonight's real busy." He pulled a handful of change from his short britches. "I almost have enough here to eat on for a whole week if I'm real careful and skip a few meals."

"So you're working?" Her chest ached for the boy with too-long hair.

"Hafta if I don't wanna starve."

Was his family so poor they sent Izzy out to work in this bad part of town?

"Isn't your mother worried?"

Izzy glanced down at his feet, where a big toe protruded from his shoe. "Ain't got no ma. No pa either." He raised his eyes that revealed heartache and sorrow. "Got no fam'ly. Jus' me."

"Where do you sleep?" She scanned the stream of saloons and businesses of ill repute that offered danger and death for a young boy. She swallowed hard, pain piercing her heart.

"I gen'rally bed down under the boardwalk by the mercantile."

How many times had she complained that her bed didn't have enough feathers or the water wasn't hot? Shame washed over her that she'd taken everything for granted. She hadn't been raised with luxury, but they hadn't gone without either. Izzy had nothing at all nor people to love him. She swallowed hard, feeling humbled.

"I see. About this money you make. What kind of jobs do you do for people?"

"Runnin' and totin' mostly. Do you need me for something? If not, I gotta go work some more."

"Let me get this straight. You fetch and carry?"

"Lady, that's what I was trying to tell you, but I do whatever anybody needs no matter how stinky or dirty." He turned and took two steps.

"Wait." Grace fumbled in her pocket and pulled out two quarters, pressing them in his grimy palm. "I need some information."

Izzy's eyes lit up. "Gee thanks!"

"Tell me what happened to the Three Deuces and Deacon Brannock."

"He's gonna be real mad." Izzy stared at the two shiny quarters, then raised his head, resigned. "Hunger is a powerful thing. A man's gotta do what a man's gotta do."

After listening to Izzy spout Brannock's plan, Grace set her jaw and marched down the street to the darkened saloon. Her anger rose higher with each step she took, and by the time she arrived, her temper was nearing the explosion stage. Just wait until she got through with him. No doubt he was laughing his head off.

That hurt worst of all.

Seething, she marched around back, where muted voices drifted through the night.

Four

THE BACK OF GRACE'S NECK TINGLED BEFORE SHE MADE IT halfway around the dark saloon, shooting a warning to her brain. Thick night shadows closed around her, and Crockett's dire words echoed in her head: *Deacon Brannock has a reputation for showing no mercy. He's ruthless.*

No one knew where she was. She could disappear and never be found. The air teemed with frightening noises that made her jump out of her skin.

If the man scared Crockett, who wouldn't hesitate to fight a grizzly, maybe confronting Brannock wasn't the brightest idea. Still, she kept walking, albeit a bit slower.

A loud gunshot followed by a scream rattled her nerves. She yearned to spin around and leave, but Carrie Nation's words from her last talk stopped her. "We have to be strong and willing to give everything inside us to find a more peaceful life. God is on our side!"

Amen. She would not run like a ninny. She sucked in a sharp breath, pulling her shoulders back.

The black inkiness seemed to have long, thin fingers that reached for her.

What had happened to the dim light that she'd seen through the open door?

A small animal leaped onto her shoulder from up high. She screamed, flinging her arms and dropping her sign. Finally, she processed the feel of short fur against her neck and a cat's long claws. Several long minutes passed before her racing heart settled back into an even rhythm.

Before she could lift the feline off, it jumped to the ground and vanished like a flash.

A voice, low and deep, came from somewhere near. "What are you doing skulking about?"

She jumped, unable to see the owner of the voice. "I'm not skulking. Show yourself." Her voice didn't sound as firm as she'd tried to make it.

Silky words left the man's mouth as he emerged from the shadows. "You should've heeded my warning."

The gloom sharpening his Stetson-wearing profile made him appear mysterious and deadly.

A shiver raced through her. "Deacon Brannock," she whispered.

"Whatever you're planning, I mean to stop you." He stepped closer, silently, into a thin shaft of light coming from the partially open back door.

Grace moved back and picked up the wooden sign. "I'll...I'll hit you if you don't stay away from me. I swear I will. And your attack cat too."

Brannock snorted. "Attack cat?"

His dour, ill-humored attitude was in keeping with his ruthless reputation. She yanked her spine ramrod straight. "Yes, your cat attacked me, and I bet you trained it."

"I didn't, but that's a thought. Aren't you out late, princess? This part of town is dangerous. Folks have been known to, uh... how shall I say this? Disappear."

The way he said *princess*, like it was something distasteful, made her yearn to run, but Grace forced herself to stay rooted and quiet—waiting.

Brannock took two more steps, a growl rumbling in his throat. "Why are you trying to ruin me? I think I deserve an answer."

"It's nothing personal."

"Isn't it?" He flung the question at her like a hailstone.

"I just have a problem with the alcohol you sell. It brings out pure meanness in men, and their wives and children catch the brunt of their rages." She kept her tone even and didn't raise her voice. She'd learned long ago that once a man felt threatened, he stopped listening. "My best friend, a girl I grew up with, suffered a beating at the hands of a drunk husband and died. She was kind and thoughtful, never hurt a flea, yet she succumbed at her drunk husband's hands. Other women, acquaintances, have too. I'd like to take every drop of whiskey and dump it in the river." Her voice shook with anger.

"Did this man get drunk here at the Three Deuces?" he asked quietly.

"No."

"But you wish to punish me for it."

"Not punish."

"No?" He barked a laugh and half turned.

"I know that one instance wasn't your fault, but other wives and children might suffer at the hands of some of your patrons." Grace met his piercing gaze unflinching.

"Might? So I'm responsible for the future? I run a clean business. We stop serving to men who've had enough, and we don't serve to any who wander in barely able to stand."

"Other saloons do."

"Then take this matter up with them, Miss Legend, and stop lumping us all together. Sounds like a fairer way to settle the score." He arched a brow. "Or do you care about fairness?"

"How do you suggest us women find them? It's easier for you to go into another line of work," she countered hotly. It made perfect sense to her.

"Do you have one picked out for me? Shall I sell rugs or mustache combs? Or perhaps toothbrushes and boot polish?" The lines around his mouth tightened. He was not amused.

"You're mocking me. Be serious. You could open a mercantile or dry goods store." Slight movement at the door drew her attention. It appeared to be a…woman? Before she could focus her eyes on the mere shadow and see more clearly, it vanished. Did she really see a person, or was it her imagination? She didn't know.

Yet the thought that he might be keeping working girls upstairs soured her stomach. She'd wanted him to be more noble.

Deacon pinched the bridge of his nose and sighed wearily. "I'll escort you to a safer part of town."

"And if I refuse to go?" she asked softly.

"Ahhh, princess, you really don't want to test me on this. Now, bring your sign and come along." He took hold of her elbow and placed his mouth against her ear. "Or else I'll have to signal my attack cat."

"You probably would, scoundrel that you are."

"You should heed my warning. I may not be this sociable next time."

"Sociable? So that's what this is? I wish you'd have told me." Grace lapsed into silence as he led her through a maze to a street brightly lit with gaslights. When they stopped under one, the sizzle reminded her of buzzing insects. And the smell was putrid.

She removed her hand from his arm. "Cowboy, don't think this is over. Not by a long shot."

His face darkened, and his silver-gray eyes turned as stony as his voice. "It is for tonight."

She clutched her sign and gathered her pride. "Good night, Brannock."

"Sleep well, princess."

Grace tilted her head to look up at him. "Why do you keep calling me that?"

"It fits. You seem to feel entitled. It's in the words you use, your bearing, your…" His gaze slid slowly down her body. "Every part about you screams that you were raised with those who have plenty. You're nothing like me—one of the *have not* folk."

The open scrutiny made Grace squirm. No one had ever looked at her like he did. But his accusation hurt. "You're dead wrong."

Brannock shrugged. "Time tells all."

He stood with his legs braced wide as she moved toward Crockett's residence. His gaze burned between her shoulder blades, and she wanted to turn around for another glimpse of this man who was more than able to match wits with her, but she kept her body pointed toward home.

Deacon Brannock was proving to be more than a simple purveyor of liquor.

She kept her eyes peeled for Izzy, praying the boy was safe and warm. She was *not* one of those snooty, rich heiresses with little care for others. Ask anyone.

∽◦∾

Deacon admired Grace's shapely backside and waited until she vanished from sight before he swung toward the Three Deuces. It was a safe bet that she was finished for the night.

The winner of round two was yet to be determined. He thought he'd made a great rebuttal to her flawed logic though. Not that she was wrong about all of it. Too many saloon owners cared little beyond the almighty dollar. They sold to anyone at any time—even young boys still in short britches.

Back at the saloon, he picked up the ugly, one-eyed stray that had started hanging around after Harry began feeding it.

"You're earning your keep well. Nice work." He scratched the feline between the ears, chuckling. "I never had an attack cat before. Stay on the job long enough, we'll have to name you."

The solid black animal yawned and stretched as though bored with the whole subject. Deacon set the cat on a barrel and went inside.

His brown hair pulled back in a ponytail and tied with a leather strip, as it always was, Harry strode over, a white apron hanging to his knees. The man spoke low. "Boss, the men at the table in the back have been huddling together and talking about some kind of plan. Sounds like they're plotting something against those temperance women."

The quiet warning tightened Deacon's chest.

"What else, Harry?" This would for sure be the last straw for Grace. Especially if she found out they'd hatched their plan in his saloon.

"Not much. They're pretty quiet about the details. Every time I go near, they hush up."

"All right. Thanks for telling me." When Harry turned, Deacon called, "Wait. You may have to name your feline buddy. It looks like we have ourselves an attack cat."

"Oh yeah?" Harry grinned.

"He stopped one barrage tonight already."

Harry rubbed his bristly jaw, a flicker of a smile curving his mouth before it vanished. "I'll call him Sarge after the meanest man I ever knew."

Deacon rested a hand on his friend's shoulder. "I think there's a story there. I'd love to hear it sometime."

"I'm not much for talking, you know that."

"I do."

Once the man went back behind the bar, Deacon took a slow turn around the room, eyeing the roughly dressed troublemakers. All five were the seedy sort, the ones always quick to start trouble. The one doing most of the talking seemed to be the leader. He looked to be in his late twenties. Long, shaggy hair spilling from a hood gave him the appearance of the grim reaper.

Deacon caught the words "meet at noon tomorrow" and "do-gooders" before they saw him and stopped talking. Shortly after, they stood. The leader adjusted his hood, and they clomped out. Noon tomorrow didn't tell Deacon much, but he assumed it would be somewhere along the street. Whatever they had planned, he'd try to be there to stop it if possible. Just follow the gaggle of women.

It occurred to him that letting it proceed might eliminate his problem, but as bad as he hated their intention of driving him out of business, he couldn't let anyone hurt them.

Especially one blue-eyed blond who carried the fresh scent of sun-dried sheets. The light, clean fragrance had given him a heady sensation when he'd placed his mouth at her ear. The sheets he'd slept on as a boy had smelled that way after hanging in the sunshine to dry. At least the few times they'd gotten washed. He'd counted himself lucky when his mother had taken the time and energy to see to such things. Love for her surged, and he blinked hard.

Other memories of sad longing crowded in through the hole he'd opened. He quickly pushed them back, blocking out the images. Like Harry, he too had his share of demons to fight.

Although he was tempted to get a bottle from his private stock and drain it, he resisted. One hard-and-fast rule of his was never to drink while the Three Deuces was open. It was too dangerous. In this business, he never knew when he'd need to draw his gun, and nothing boded well for a drunk trying to handle a firearm.

Harry slid a drink in front of him, and Deacon waved it away. "Just coffee for now."

"Sure thing, Boss. Probably wise." Harry poured some coffee.

A lady of the evening sauntered in. After looking everything over, she took a seat next to Deacon. "With that Stetson, you look more like a cowboy than a saloon keep."

Her words stirred long-hidden memories of cattle drives, open range, and bronc busting. That was the life he loved, but here he sat in a saloon he'd won in a poker game, trying not to lose his rear.

He took in her painted face, weary eyes, and low-cut dress. She probably wasn't that old, but the hard living had taken a toll. "Never judge a man by what he's wearing. What do you need, ma'am? If you're selling, I'm not buying."

"A job. I don't see any working girls about."

"Nope. I have no need of any. Sorry."

"Makes two of us." She rose and went back out into the night.

The memories she'd stirred had to stay buried. Deacon sat at the bar until closing time, thinking about the woman and the difference between her and fresh-scented Grace Legend. If he could start over, he'd give anything for someone like her.

After Harry locked up, he filled the money bag from the register and handed it to Deacon. "We survived another night, Boss. About average, I'd say. I've seen worse."

"I've found that's the way life goes. Like cattlemen, always between hay and grass. Never flush." Deacon locked the money in his safe. One more task left before he could climb the stairs. He watched Harry gather up Sarge and head for the back room. Things were a lot less complicated for a man in Harry's shoes. Maybe Deacon should get a cat and forget about a lost life and sweet-smelling women.

"Nope." He shook his head, thinking about Grace. She was a lot more entertaining than a mean, one-eyed cat, especially when she had her dander up.

He went out the back door to make his usual patrol and locked it behind him.

Sleep wouldn't come until he made sure it was safe for Leah. It was far too easy for Seth Pickford to toss a match into the dry timber of the building and rid himself of his wife. The mangy bastard meant to make good on his vow to see her and her child dead.

❧

Grace laid her sign on the porch and slipped into Crockett's house, praying he was still out. She didn't want to have to explain where she'd been, especially to her brother. The foyer was dimly lit, as well as the rest of the quiet first floor. Just inside, she removed her shoes and padded toward the stairs in her stocking feet.

"Where have you been?"

She jumped a foot high at the unexpected male voice and turned to see Crockett emerging from a shadowed doorway. "What are you doing? You scared me out of ten years of my life."

"Good. So I'll ask again. Where have you been?"

"Out."

"I can see that, Gracie!" Crockett ran his fingers through his dark hair and stood it on end, exasperation on his face. "Pa told me to keep an eye on you, but you aren't making this easy."

"Look, I'm twenty-two years old and long past the need for a nursemaid. I'm able to look after myself without my kid brother watching my every move." She linked her arm through his and padded into the parlor, where she dropped into an overstuffed chair. "For your information, I went back to the Three Deuces; only, it was closed." She didn't tell him any of the rest, and especially none of her conversation with Deacon. No, that was her secret to keep. "My stomach objected to not feeding it, so I stopped in a café." When he opened his mouth to object to her eating in Hell's Half Acre after dark, she quickly added, "A café in a better part of town. I'm not a half-wit, little brother. And I had my derringer."

"Oh, that of course makes it all right." He rose and paced back and forth, looking so much like her father, she had to blink twice. "I'm responsible. You get hurt, I'll catch the blame."

"I don't know why I can't have my own house where I can come and go as I wish. Just because I wear a dress, I have to have a keeper, like a batty patient in some asylum."

"I'm sorry, but that's the way it is."

"Then I mean to change it. Stop pacing, you're making me nervous," she snapped.

Crockett stopped and faced her. "I told you to stay away from Deacon Brannock. Remember that time I warned you about old man

Arnold's wolf dog and not to go near it, but you insisted on trying to pet it anyway, and it bit you? I was right then and I'm right now."

"I can't help it. I have a sworn duty to help the movement. Every saloon owner we can put out of business is a strike for the good of all womankind."

Although she hadn't tried that hard, truth was, she couldn't forget him. The memory of his warm breath against her ear, his lips so close, stirred something strong inside her. She hadn't been the same since meeting him. Those flashing, gray eyes that could see everything she tried to hide had issued a challenge, much like a gauntlet thrown at her feet, that she couldn't ignore.

From as far back as she could remember, she never could pass up a dare, no matter how hard she tried. It was something she'd been born with that awoke a fierce desire to win.

"That's what concerns me. I have to tell Pa. You leave me no choice."

Grace quashed the angry words she wished to say and stood. "As a wise, young boy told me tonight, 'A man's gotta do what a man's gotta do.' Good night, Crockett."

"I'm not trying to be mean. I'm protecting you."

She faced him, shaking. "I'm damn tired of it too."

Without another word, she collected her shoes and headed up to her bedroom to become Sam Valentine. She had an article due at the newspaper, and writing those bland stories about the ranch for a small weekly column on the back page had become boring and lifeless. After six months of writing them, she was running out of stories about her family to tell. Her editor had given her three days to come up with something else or he'd fire her.

This called for a serious article with teeth.

Carrie Nation had issued a call for women to use whatever gifts they possessed to advance their cause. Grace was a born writer. This piece would be powerful and hopefully lead to meaningful change. Plus, she'd keep the job she loved.

Then, she'd focus on Mr. Deacon Brannock. Why was a cowboy living in a saloon?

She could smell a story a mile away, and the man was hiding something. At the first opportunity, she'd begin a search to uncover the truth, possibly hidden somewhere in the newspaper files.

Five

Deacon was mulling the evening over as he kept to the shadows along Rusk Street, away from the other saloons and brothels still open. He was in a strange mood. Part of him yearned to whistle a tune while the other half wanted to find a reason to pound his fists into someone.

The night air whispered around him. He couldn't recall when his emotions last felt this conflicted. However, the first time remained as clear as a cool stream winding through the Rocky Mountains.

The night he'd gotten up enough courage to kiss a girl he'd been sweet on.

Then up had jumped the devil to spoil his happiness when a few hours later, he'd held his best friend's head in his lap and watched him die.

Who would spoil it this night? He didn't want to know.

The lower end of Fort Worth carried many names, of which Hell's Half Acre was only one. Sodom on the Trinity appeared in newspapers regularly. No gaslights could be found on these streets. Only a few dim lamps through the windows lit the way.

Pretty Grace Legend had to have the same grit as Mary Porter to come down here at night. But then, she would fight a saber-toothed tiger to get where she wanted to go. Yet underneath all that fierce determination lay softness and compassion in the way she treated Izzy and in remembering her dead friend.

How her eyes had flashed blue fire when he'd accused her of being entitled. A smile curved his lips. A bit of truth sparked. He enjoyed riling her—and calling her "princess."

By all that's holy, how could he wage a war with such a woman? The lady fought dirty.

Deacon put aside thoughts of pretty Grace to sharpen his attention on his surroundings. Men with their heads in a fog often got their throats cut or shot.

Here, all was dark and still. This was his part of town. This was where he belonged. Not Grace Legend's world, where the lights were bright and smartly dressed folks walked about in clothing Deacon could never afford.

It was necessary to remember that. Her world and his mixed like oil and water.

The green silk vest, white shirt, and dark wool trousers he wore were all the nice clothes he owned, and he saved them for nights when he needed to appear the profitable businessman. A friend had once told him about the importance of having one set of *impressing clothes*.

Not that these would impress too many with a discerning eye.

The door across the street at Mary Porter's establishment opened, and the madam herself stepped out, pulling her shawl close. She ran one of the high-end brothels, and Deacon could only imagine the cost of a night spent with one of her girls. But he admired the pretty woman with nerves of steel who pushed back against those foolish enough to try to run her out.

They were speaking friends, and she'd been known to pay the Three Deuces a visit from time to time. He'd never be a paying customer at her place, and she didn't try to persuade him.

Her gaze found him, and she smiled, nodding. He returned the acknowledgment.

The faint scuff of bootheels sounded, and a warning rippled just under the surface of his skin. Deacon rested a hand on the butt of his pistol, sharpening his gaze, scanning the street.

No cat could've made that noise.

He melted against the side of a closed laundry, barely breathing. His gaze roved from one doorway to the next.

A flash of movement came from the corner of his eye, and Mary Porter yelled, "Watch out, Brannock!"

He turned in time to catch a blow with his raised arm. The tall, burly assailant, who reeked of whiskey, had huge hands, but Deacon had muscle and his wits. He gave the man a right uppercut, followed by a left.

A loud grunt that followed told Deacon he'd delivered pain. But the drunk whipped out a knife with a four-inch blade and brandished it. "I want my wife!"

This close, Deacon made out the features of Leah's husband and jumped back to avoid the slashing, sharp metal. However, the flash of silver caught his vest, leaving a large rip. Deacon grabbed Pickford's wrist and forced his arm up. He hammered the man's knife hand against the side of the building until the weapon clattered to the ground.

"You'll never use your fists on Leah again. I swear on my life!" Breathing hard, Deacon slung the man to the dirt. "Never."

Seth wiped his mouth with the back of his hand and glared. "She's mine."

"Not anymore."

"I know you're hiding her in the Three Deuces, and I mean to find her."

Deacon picked up the knife, wiped the blade, and closed it. "The only thing you'll find is a grave, and that, I can guarantee. If I were you, I'd be looking at Leah's aunt. Leah's as likely there as anywhere."

"That old battle-ax lives over in Georgia." Seth rubbed his jaw. "I cain't very well trot over there to see, now can I?"

"Life's tough. Now, get up and go home, or that grave could come sooner than you think." Deacon hoped the man bought the suggestion about the aunt. That would be a blessing for Leah and it wasn't likely to put the old woman at risk. Pickford, broke on any given day, was too damn lazy to go across town, much less make a long trip to Georgia.

Seth pulled himself to his feet, weaving like a drunken sailor. "I'll have my knife."

"I'll keep it for now."

Two hefty men from Mary Porter's strode over, guns drawn. "Need any help, Brannock?"

"You're a little late, fellows. Tell Mary thanks, though."

Seeing that the tide had definitely turned against him, Seth gave up arguing and staggered off, his once-appealing features now bleeding.

Relief filled Deacon. He was glad it had been he and not Leah tangling with the bastard. He stuck the knife in his pocket and straightened his clothes, frustration shooting through him at sight of the slash. Dammit! He didn't know if the vest was salvageable or not. Buying new would cut into his profits. He thanked the two bodyguards Mary Porter had hired and strode toward home.

Halfway there, Izzy caught up with him. "Boy, you can sure fight, Mr. Brannock."

"Isn't it a bit late for you to be out?"

"Nope. I set my own hours. Gotta earn a living."

Deacon drew up short and scowled. "I've got a bone to pick with you."

The kid ducked his head. "I didn't mean to tell Miss Grace about you having customers go in the back way. Honest. But she gave me two whole quarters, and I really, really needed them bad. I'm saving up for a wagon that'll help me make more money by hauling things." Izzy glanced up. "I'm sorry I told. She smelled really nice, and she smiled at me."

Deacon's heart turned over at the dirty face staring up at him. He'd been in the urchin's shoes. "I understand, but let that be the last time you talk when I ask you not to."

"I promise. I really do." The worry on Izzy's face vanished.

"Good. Now, in the morning, I need you to fetch these things to me from the mercantile." Deacon handed him the list for Leah's cooking then took out enough to cover it and pressed the money in the boy's hand. "Don't dawdle. These are important."

"Yes, Mr. Brannock. I won't mess up again. But you think Miss Grace is pretty, don'cha?"

"Yeah, she's all right." Deacon itched to say more but thought better of it. Izzy would probably go tell her and that would make things much worse. Clearly, the boy was taken with her. Maybe she reminded him of his mother. Deacon didn't know what had happened to Izzy's folks. He should've asked. Dammit! He could be more caring. Yet to learn more would mean that he had an obligation to help. And he couldn't take the boy to raise. He had enough to handle.

"Well, I like her. She tries to make people think she's mean, but she's real nice. See you tomorrow." Izzy put the money for the purchases in his pocket.

When the boy started to walk off, Deacon called, "How much money do you need for that wagon?"

Izzy turned. "A dollar fifty. Why?"

Deacon took two dollars from his pocket. "Here. I don't want you to be tempted to talk about our business dealings anymore."

The kid's eyes widened as he took the sudden windfall. "Wow, thank you, Mr. Brannock!"

"You're welcome. Good night."

"Good night, sir."

Deacon watched him hurry down the street, glad he'd helped the orphan like the man who once lent him a hand. His heart burst to do a bit of good, even though he didn't have the money to spare. He glanced down at his vest. No new one now for sure, but he'd live with that. Sometimes a boy needed to know that someone cared about him. Especially when all he saw were the angry glares of snarling men who'd sooner kick him as not.

∞

Hours after she'd climbed the stairs, Grace put the finishing touches on her article and leaned back. She was happy and felt she'd done her best writing. She'd told her friend Libby Daniels's tragic story. The beatings Libby kept quiet about and the chance she'd had to escape her husband, only to stay because she'd seen no other real options for her. Grace spoke of the embarrassment and shame of living with an alcoholic, the fear of never knowing what would set him off.

Now, to get her editor to run it. That would take a miracle.

Pemberton gave all his juicy articles to the male reporters, confirming her belief that the newspaperman didn't think highly of a woman's skill with a pen. In fact, he seemed to think she belonged in a kitchen at home and had said as much. She'd show him different.

Yawning, she stretched and glanced at the clock that read midnight. She dressed for bed and slid between the sheets, but her mind wouldn't shut off. Thoughts of Izzy living beneath the boardwalk circled like a flock of hungry buzzards. He had no one to make sure he was warm and fed, no one to make him go to school. A young boy needed an education. He needed love. He needed hope.

What could she do to help?

She thought and thought but decided she should talk to Crockett and pick his brain. Flopping over, she shut her eyes tight, but this time Deacon Brannock's scowling face appeared. He seemed determined to be disagreeable. The man probably thought his imitation of that grumpy, old cat of his frightened her, but tonight she'd felt his gentle touch that slid over her arm like dove's feathers.

His warm, fragrant breath had fluttered the strands of hair at her ear.

Her stomach flipped upside down. What would it be like to press her lips to his full mouth? Heat flooded over her. Why was she thinking about something that would never happen?

She threw back the covers and got up to open the window to let in some cool air.

Why was she so interested? Maybe it was the hat. That black Stetson made him different and sparked questions. Had he once been a cowboy, or maybe he was still a cowboy and the saloon was a side venture? It was hard to figure him out, but she enjoyed a challenge.

Who was he? Morning couldn't come soon enough. The *Fort Worth Gazette* had over three hundred articles about people in the city. And Pemberton might've heard of Brannock. She'd ask everyone she could think of. If he'd made the news, the *Gazette* would have something.

All she knew was that he was contributing to something she staunchly opposed.

Cooled off, she turned up the gas lamp and flipped open a notebook, jotting down everything she knew about him, which was very little.

A knock came at the door. "You still up, Gracie?"

"I'm having trouble sleeping. You?"

"Can we talk?" Crockett asked.

Grace closed the notebook and let him in. "Something on your mind?"

"I want to apologize. I'm sorry for the angry words I said." Her brother met her gaze. "I don't like fighting with you. I just care about your welfare and don't want anything to happen to you."

"I know. I'm sorry too. I hate cross words. Forgive me?" Grace wiped crumbs from his mouth. "I love you, you know."

"All's forgiven." He pulled her into a quick hug. "Working on something?"

Guilt swept over her, but she couldn't tell him the truth. She searched for something that would be logical yet safe. "I'm making a list. I'm going to fix you fried chicken for dinner tomorrow night just like Mama's."

Crockett laughed. "You'll probably have us both homesick and blubbering in our gravy, you know that?"

"Probably. I miss them. Maybe I'll make a trip back soon." Just for a short visit.

"We can go together. I have some business to attend there with Pa in a week or two."

"Sounds wonderful. It would do us both a world of good." She could afford to be gone a few days, but not for long. She had her work to do.

"Good night, then." Crockett went out and closed the door behind him.

Grace turned off the lamp and sat at the window, staring at the millions of stars. Somewhere out there were the answers to everything she sought. All she had to do was find them.

Come hell or high water, she sure meant to give it her best and solve the nagging puzzle. Not because he had a nice smile, saw to her welfare, or possessed a touch that sent heat up her arm.

She could never be drawn to a man of his type.

Six

Come morning, Grace was walking from the house to the *Fort Worth Gazette* newspaper office when a friend and fellow temperance marcher, Celia Ann Turner, ran toward her, crying. "What is it, Celia Ann?"

"My Leonard didn't come home last night," she sobbed. "I just peeked inside the Blue Star Saloon, and he's sitting there like a fat slug, swilling whiskey with a half-naked woman. Will you come with me to get him?"

Grace glanced down at the article that she'd written so painstakingly in hopes of keeping her job and tucked it into a satchel. "I'll help you, Celia Ann."

A few more hours wouldn't hurt anything, and Lord knew her friend had a big problem.

They linked arms, and Grace did her best to calm Celia Ann. "At least you know Leonard's not dead and lying in a hole somewhere."

"I guess. But my twins have come down with chicken pox, and my little one sliced her hand open, and the doctor said we have to pay our bill or he won't come anymore." Celia Ann's waterworks burst, and she sobbed even harder. "I need Leonard, and he's stinking drunk. Bet he spent every cent we had in the Blue Star."

Grace patted her arm. "I'm sorry. You sure have trouble. I think we should round up some of the other ladies to come along. Just in case Leonard gets mean."

"Good idea. He'll be mean all right."

By the time they collected six other women and made it to the Blue Star, over an hour had passed. The Blue Star was quiet, and

Leonard Turner still sat inside with two or three other men and several saloon girls.

Grace turned to her friend. "How do you want to proceed, Celia?"

"We'll all go in together, grab him, and pull him out. If anyone tries to interfere, we'll have enough to fight them."

"Wait. Does he have a weapon?" Gwen Morris asked.

"He always carries a forty-five," Celia answered. "I'll try to grab it first."

Feeling about as confident as an auctioneer with laryngitis, Grace took Celia Ann's hand and pushed inside the dim saloon. No one glanced their way, which gave them an advantage of sorts, but the moment Celia saw Leonard with a saloon girl's arm around his neck, she released a loud shriek and raced to them.

"You low-down, chicken-livered, rat-toothed excuse for a husband!" Celia Ann clawed him with her nails, the bag on her arm flying left and right. She didn't limit her attack to Leonard either, turning on the woman. "You're nothing but a grimy Jezebel." Her words drew everyone's attention.

Grace didn't know exactly what to do next except grab the gun Leonard had pulled. She applied a firm grasp and wrestled him to the floor where the other women sat on him. One woman bit his arm in an attempt to get him to release the weapon.

"You two-bit tramp! Get off me!" Leonard roared.

Guttural yells, shrieks, cussing, and name-calling filled every inch of the Blue Star until Grace could hardly think. Afraid of what would happen if Leonard managed to keep the gun, she grunted and pulled until she broke his hold; however, in the process, he fired the weapon.

She jumped back, dropping it, scanning the bodies for the sight of blood. "Is anyone hit?"

Since no one claimed to be injured, Grace tossed the gun over the long bar and grabbed Leonard around the neck. She inhaled a deep breath and yanked him toward the door. By the time they finally emerged from the saloon, Leonard wore half a shirt and had women hanging on him like barnacles to a ship's hull.

Celia Ann delivered a swift kick. "I told you, you'd better not lay out all night in one of these sinful places. We got sick kids that the doc won't see, and our youngest with a hand sliced open. Then I catch you with a half-dressed alley cat. How could you? Don't you love me anymore?"

"Stop, woman!" Leonard pulled himself to his feet, his eyes burning with rage. "No, I don't love you. I don't think I ever did. Now, leave me the hell alone." With that, he stumbled back inside.

Celia Ann stood there, tears creating rivers down her face. Finally, Grace put an arm around her. "Let's go home. I'll give you money for the doc to treat the kids."

Gwen Morris patted Celia's hand. "We'll figure this out together."

They had neared the Three Deuces when a group of two dozen men blocked their path. They all carried buckets. The two slouchers in the front had cold, mean eyes. Grace turned to find another way past, only to find that blocked also.

The angry men struck cold fear inside her, but she refused to give way to it.

She thrust her shoulders back and straightened. "Let us pass."

The women pressed close to her.

"Hear that, boys? These hell-raising bitches don't even know how to say please." The speaker wore a hat pulled low and a long duster. "I think we need to teach the do-gooders a lesson and make them think twice about coming down here where they don't belong."

"Yeah."

"Let's run them out of here. This is our territory."

"Go home, you do-gooding Bible thumpers!"

The volume of noise frightened Grace enough without the

threatening rhetoric. One of the mob tossed a bucket of animal entrails at them, catching Grace's dress and shoes. Another slung his bucket of white paint, splattering Celia Ann. Screams echoed up and down Rusk Street.

A sudden rifle blast rent the air, and everyone ducked, the men included.

"Let's make this a little more even, boys." The deep voice came from above.

Grace glanced up to see Deacon Brannock, legs braced wide, on the upstairs balcony of the Three Deuces. Dangerous and deadly, he held a short-barreled rifle in one hand and a pistol in the other. To her, his mannerisms appeared close to how her father and his brothers looked in her mind when they'd encountered rustlers on the cattle drive to Dodge City.

A shiver danced up her spine and she inhaled a deep breath.

"What the hell are you doing, Brannock?" yelled Mr. Duster. "You have more reason than anyone to get rid of these women. They're trying to run you out of business."

"I will never condone violence against women. There's a right way to do things, and it's not this. Now, set those buckets down and everyone clear the street."

"And what if we don't?" The speaker's hand inched toward his holster.

Deacon fired his short-barreled rifle, the blast ripping the toe out of the smart-mouthed rabble-rouser's boot. "The next shot will be into flesh. Do you really want to challenge me?"

"All right, all right!" The men suddenly began to find other things to do than harass the women.

Grace glanced up at the confusing saloon owner. She never knew what to expect from him, and that constantly kept her off balance. "Thanks, Brannock. We appreciate what you did."

He tipped his hat and, without a reply, stepped back inside the saloon, rubbing his arm.

A thin-ribbed dog ran out and started lapping up the animal entrails.

"Let's go get cleaned up, ladies." Grace turned from the empty balcony. "Celia Ann, I'll make arrangements for the doctor to come to your place. I want to help you."

The woman's hollow eyes filled with sorrow. "I can't believe Leonard said those things. I know he had feelings for me before that woman came along. I know he did."

"Of course, dear." Grace patted her friend's shoulder. "He'll come to his senses when the alcohol wears off."

"Maybe. But I don't want anyone who treats me like yesterday's garbage." Celia Ann lifted her chin. "I'll raise my children by myself."

Unable to find a reply, Grace nodded, and her ladies moved toward the better part of town. She still had time to bathe and go to the newspaper office. After seeing this new side of Brannock, she itched more than ever to unearth everything she could about him.

Seven

A BATH AND CLEAN CLOTHES PUT GRACE IN BETTER SPIRITS. She made her way downtown that afternoon and pushed through the doors at the *Fort Worth Gazette* a little over an hour later, dressed for success in a tailored, navy-blue dress devoid of frills. She was all business.

Smiling and nodding, she went straight to Pemberton's open door and knocked.

The fiftysomething editor parted his hair in the center and combed it to each side, where it did a little flip. Barely Grace's height, he kept his weight under control. Or maybe the missus took the credit for that, since she strictly monitored his sweet tooth.

Her boss stood behind his desk and glanced up with a frown before waving her inside. "Who are you today? Legend or Sam Valentine?"

"Valentine, sir." She pulled her neatly written article from a folder and handed it to him. "I have just what you've been looking for, and I think it'll resonate with readers."

Pemberton grunted, his suit looking as though he'd slept in it. "That remains to be seen."

The clock above his desk ticked loudly as he read it. Grace whispered a prayer, clasping her hands to still their shaking.

Finally, he glanced up. "Not bad. Not bad at all."

"You'll run it?"

"Only if you can guarantee others that are similar." Horace Pemberton flipped open a box of cigars and removed one. "We're living in an age of reform. The citizens are demanding change. Bring me stories of corruption, greed, and wrongdoing that address our readers' concerns, and I'll keep printing your articles."

"Thank you, sir."

The baggy-eyed editor lit the cigar and puffed. "You have quite a nose for smelling stories, Valentine, and can write a good sentence." He shook a finger. "Don't let it go to your head. You still have a lot to learn."

Happy tingles danced along her body. He never gave praise.

"Yes, sir. Thank you for giving me another chance."

"I'm keeping you on notice until I see more." Pemberton sat in a squeaky chair. "Do you have anything else?"

Izzy's situation crossed her mind, and also the factories where children worked from daylight to dark for pennies. "Yes, sir."

"Your next assignment is due in two days." Pemberton met her gaze. "Any problem with that?"

"Not a bit." Grace gave him one of her widest smiles.

He turned to a stack of papers, then noticed she hadn't left. "You can go."

"May I ask you a question? I promise I won't take up too much of your time."

"What about?"

"Are you acquainted with Deacon Brannock, the owner of the Three Deuces Saloon on Rusk Street?"

Pemberton froze. He slowly placed his cigar in the heavy glass ashtray on his desk, his face a mask of alarm. "I only know what I've heard. Brannock is a shadowy, dangerous figure. Don't tell me you've crossed paths with him."

Her boss's words and manner struck a measure of fear inside her. That everyone seemed afraid of Brannock had to mean he was someone to avoid.

Grace wet her dry lips. "I have had some dealings with him, and that's why this curiosity. Please tell me what you know."

"He's trouble. Stay away from him," Pemberton barked.

"Has he appeared in the newspaper? Just tell me that much."

"I ran an article a year or two ago. Some fight at the saloon that ended in a killing. Now, if you don't mind, I'm busy." The editor opened a desk drawer and lifted a file. "Go."

Grace left and headed straight for the room that held the archives. Two hours later, she rolled her shoulders and stretched, disappointed that she'd found nothing. Clearly, this would be a painstaking process.

In need of help, she strolled to the oldest reporter's desk. If anyone knew of Brannock, it would probably be the intimidating Ned Cross. The man's dark, piercing gaze and stern features had kept her at a distance. Now, she'd brave the lion's den if she had to for answers.

"Hi, Mr. Cross. May I ask you a question?"

Ned glanced up and lodged his pencil behind one ear in his dark brown hair. "I wondered how long it'd take you."

"For what?"

"To ask for my help. I've been watching you, and although at times you appear to be over your head, you muddle through by yourself. Your writing is decent enough, I admit."

"Thank you, sir." She wasn't sure if that was a compliment or not. "I learn more by doing, I guess. It wasn't any slight against you or the others."

Streaks of gray woven through the hair at his temples suggested Ned Cross was not a young man. She guessed him to be fortyish.

He tilted his chair and placed his hands across his stomach and the cheap, blue vest. "What do you want? If it's to waste my time, run along."

Grace unclasped her hands and anchored them on Cross's battle-scarred desk. "I was searching for any files in the archives about Deacon Brannock, but I'm having trouble finding anything. Pemberton said he appeared in an article a year or two ago."

Ned suddenly shot up. "I wrote the article, and a more surly man you've never met."

"What happened?"

"A fight in the Three Deuces between two patrons. Both pulled guns, and one ended up dead. Brannock shot the live one's ear off and booted him out into the alley. The man also turned up nailed to an outhouse door the next morning, a bullet in his skull."

"Oh my!" Crockett's warning that the saloon owner settled things in the alley shot into Grace's head. "Did the sheriff arrest him?"

"Couldn't without proof, but the sheriff questioned him extensively. Why are you digging into this, if I may ask?"

"Our paths recently crossed, and I want to know more about his character." She tried to swallow, but her mouth couldn't even conjure up a drop of spit. "Do you think he murdered his patron?"

"Let's just say I wouldn't put it past him. Deacon Brannock isn't anyone to trifle with, and forgive me, but you don't appear strong enough to take a man like him head-on—even if you are a Legend."

Powerful misgivings inched up her spine until she could barely draw breath. "In here, I'm Sam Valentine." She turned to go.

He caught her arm. "Look in the files under October 22, 1897."

Almost two years ago.

"Thank you, Mr. Cross. Do you think he's in other articles as well?"

"Doubt it. I don't think he lived here prior to that. If you pursue this, be prepared to take the risk." Ned softened the warning with a half smile. "Be careful. It'd be a shame to lose a pretty woman like you. These offices would be awfully dreary if you didn't brighten them."

The compliment caught her by surprise. Ned Cross had never acknowledged her presence. Not once. She'd thought he hated having her in the office.

"I'll do my best to stay alive." But she'd not quit in pursuing leads despite everyone's dire warning. Deacon Brannock had best be ready for the truth to rain down on him.

❧

Deacon had barely put his rifle and handgun away when he caught a rap on the back door of the saloon. Rubbing his damn arm that had gone numb again, he opened it to find Izzy with his shiny, red wagon and Deacon's purchases.

"I got it, Mr. Brannock." Izzy's grin stretched across his face.

"I see that. It's sure a pretty color." Deacon made a show of admiring it and testing the hard rubber wheels before turning his attention to the packages in the wagon. "Is this my order?"

"Yep. Got everything you asked for." Izzy pulled some coins from his pocket. "Here's your change."

"Thanks." Deacon halfway expected the boy to try to wheedle his way into keeping the leftover money and was surprised when Izzy didn't.

The boy lifted each item he'd bought and brought it all into the dark saloon. His curious gaze circled the room. "I don't know what you plan to cook, but I hope you let me have some when I come back around. I don't eat much."

"You can have some," Deacon said gruffly, ruffling the urchin's hair. "Now be off with you. I got work to do."

A noise from above jarred Izzy's head around, but he asked no questions. Leah must be restless. Well, he had a cure for that. As soon as Deacon let the boy out, he hurried upstairs.

Leah stood at her chest of drawers, fully dressed. "Who was that?"

She looked radiant but tired. Maybe the baby's doubling growth wasn't letting her sleep well. Deacon thought it must be awfully uncomfortable.

"The boy Izzy. He brought everything you'll need to make the tamales and hand pies."

A grin transformed her face. "Excellent. I'll get right on those."

"Whoa! After you eat some lunch first, young lady."

Leah pouted. "You're such a stickler about—"

"Your health. Yes, I am. I want to keep you hale and hearty and give your child the best start possible."

"And I thank you from the bottom of my heart." She crossed the room. "Thank you for all you're doing, Deacon. I found my guardian angel."

He frowned. "Stop. I'm no angel. A devil is more like it."

"You like to make people think you're real bad, but I know different." She laughed lightly. "You haven't fooled me."

"If you promise to bolt the doors and let Harry keep you company, I'll go out for a bit. Need to talk to Mrs. Adams, the midwife, and make arrangements for you."

"I promise. I would like to get this settled so I'll know what to expect."

That made two of them. "And so you will. I want the best for you." He left with a smile and went to rouse Harry. The sooner he finished with this birthing business, the better he'd feel. While he was out, he'd look for the gang who'd threatened to put an end to Grace and her temperance army.

❧

The afternoon sun shone like gold when Deacon issued last-minute instructions to Harry, buckled on his gun belt, and strode out the back. So far, no sign of the temperance women, which suited him fine. He prayed they'd stay away and let him have some peace. However, logic told him this was only a slight reprieve. They'd return.

Especially Grace Legend. She was persistent.

Deacon moved swiftly, keeping a sharp eye out for Seth Pickford. The man would be looking to get even after the thrashing Deacon had given him.

Three streets over and four blocks up, he approached a house made of rough-hewn planks painted forest green and knocked on the door. No one answered, so he knocked again.

"Hold your horses!" a woman hollered from inside.

The door swung open, and Deacon stared at a gray-haired grandma wearing a bloody apron. "Mrs. Gretchen Adams, the midwife?"

"You're looking at her, mister."

Somewhere back in the recesses of the green house, a babe cried its lungs out. Mrs. Adams swung around. "State your business. I have my hands full here."

She didn't offer to let him come in.

"I want to make arrangements for you to attend my...niece's childbirth. I'm told you're the best around."

"How far along is she?"

"I don't know." Sweat popped out on Deacon's forehead. He pulled out a handkerchief and mopped it up. "Leah is about this big." He made a circle with his arms to show her.

"Any spotting?" Mrs. Adams asked.

"What?" Deacon had a feeling that was important, but he had no idea what it meant.

"Spotting. Blood."

He swallowed hard. "I don't know." Leah hadn't mentioned anything about that.

"How old is she?"

Deacon frowned. "Sixteen. Can you come to check on her?"

"If I have time. A lot of expectant mothers are in line ahead of your niece, but I'll do my best." The infant's crying in the background became more insistent. "I really have to go, mister."

"But what'll I do if you can't come, Mrs. Adams?"

"Best learn the basics of birthing a baby is all I got to say." With that, the woman slammed the door.

Deacon stood there in stunned silence for a full sixty seconds.

Surely there was more than one midwife in the area. He couldn't be expected to deliver the baby himself. To see Leah's private parts. The blood and fluid. The fragile life that he'd have to hold in his hands. He gulped.

Sick to his stomach and legs shaky, he returned to Rusk Street, a world he knew like the back of his hand.

Breathing a huge sigh of relief not to run into the scum with their rank buckets of animal guts, Deacon moved on to the Three Deuces. Luscious smells wafted from the back of the saloon, drawing him forward. He opened the door and stepped inside.

Face flushed, a strand of hair stuck to her cheek, Leah glanced up from her boiling pot. "You're back. Did you find her?"

"I certainly did. Everything is going to be all right." He didn't have the heart to tell her the truth. Besides, he'd find some qualified help if it he had to scour every inch of Hell's Half Acre. "You've nothing to worry about."

"Thank you, Deacon." She wiped her hands and curled her arms around his waist. "You're like an older brother. I'm happy we made our own family."

"Me too, kiddo," he said softly, soaking up the feeling of belonging to someone.

She stepped back. "I'm almost finished with the tamales, then I'll start on the empanadas."

Deacon glanced around. "Where's Harry? I told him to stay close."

Just then, the slender bartender came from the storeroom, his arms full of woven baskets of all shapes and sizes.

"I told you not to leave Leah." Deacon hated the coldness of his tone but couldn't help it.

Harry's spine stiffened. "I was only gone a moment. Leah asked me to get these."

"It only takes a split second for trouble to call. I gave you instructions not to leave her."

"Deacon Brannock, stop it." Leah raised her voice. "Harry did nothing wrong. If you can't talk to us in a civil tone, go back out and stay gone until you can."

"I'm real sorry, Boss." Harry backed toward the room he'd claimed.

Anger was slow to leave, and minutes passed before Deacon could speak in a quiet tone. He didn't like Leah having to remind him to be more understanding with those around him, something he forgot on occasion.

He pinched the bridge of his nose and sighed. "I apologize, Harry. It scares me because I know how quickly Pickford could bust through the door and take Leah. Regrets are too late. On the other hand, I understand that no one likes a person breathing down their neck every second."

"Especially me." Leah rolled a tamale and added it to the pile on a plate. "I simply won't abide it."

Although he disliked the dressing down, he admired the strength she had shown in the few months she'd been with them. He had a feeling that Seth would have a hard time finding a punching bag now.

Harry took the opportunity to slip quietly through his door, and that hurt something inside Deacon.

But for now, he shot Leah a look of admiration. "You're feeling stronger." He glanced away for a moment and lowered his voice. "I had an encounter down the street with Seth last evening."

Color drained from her face. "What happened?"

Deacon left out a good deal in the retelling, but Leah seemed satisfied. He turned the conversation to another topic. "I don't suppose you've glimpsed the temperance women?"

"Not yet. Why?" Leah reached for more corn husks.

"No reason. Just checking." He wondered if Grace had made it out of the lower end of town all right. Part of him, admittedly a rather big part, missed their sparring. Surely the pretty woman with grit wouldn't give up this easily.

That would be a real disappointment. He frowned. He was losing his damn mind.

He went to unlock the doors. A few regulars waited. And a friend he'd not seen in a while. They shook hands. "Come on in."

Will Bonner stepped into the dim interior and glanced around. Deacon hadn't spoken to the rancher since he won the saloon a year ago. Somewhere in his late forties, Will hadn't changed much—still long and lanky, a little more frost in his dark hair, the same gray eyes that seemed to see more than Deacon wanted. Mustache was new. Looked good on him.

They sat down, and Harry came from the back. Deacon motioned him over. "Two beers, Harry. This is an old friend of mine, Will Bonner."

"Nice to meet you, sir. I'll bring those beers." Harry went behind the bar.

"Been a long time, Deacon. I hated to see you trade ranch work for selling liquor. You have a gift for breaking horses." Will stretched out and locked his hands behind his head, staring at Deacon, who shifted uncomfortably. "I've never seen anyone gentle a horse the way you do, and it's a beauty to behold."

"I love horses, and I was happy working for you, but my life took a new direction when I woke up from a two-day drunk and found myself the owner of the Three Deuces."

"Not much to look at, but whatever's cooking is making me hungry. You married now?"

"Nope." Deacon glanced down. "I heard about Mrs. Bonner. I'm sorry to hear she passed."

"Thanks. She couldn't breathe. Her lungs were too bad. I sure miss that woman."

Harry brought their beer, and they sipped in silence for a bit.

"How's the ranch doing?" Deacon finally asked.

"It's still there—which you'd know if you took a ride out once in a while. Those ten miles haven't grown any longer."

How did he tell Will the memories choked him, and the smell of the land penetrated too deeply into his soul to get out? It was better to live in the city than on something that would never be his and have it tease him with every sunrise. Might not make sense to some, but it did to him.

Deacon took a drink, eyeing Will over the rim of the mug. "This keeps me pretty busy, you know."

Will grunted and glanced at the other two patrons. He'd already seen through the lies. The rancher pulled his legs in and leaned forward. "I have a proposition if you're interested."

"Yeah? What's that?"

"I've got this wild mustang the boys caught a month ago. Some of the best horseflesh I've ever seen, and they can't break it. I know you can. I'll give you five hundred dollars."

Five hundred could buy Deacon a nice spread. His breath hung in his throat.

His own land. That was huge. Until the saloon, he'd never owned anything except the clothes on his back. Taunts of being so poor his mother had to make his shirts from her dresses rang in his ears. And chants of others of being a bastard child. He shook himself.

The dream he'd had as a boy and now as a man glittered within reach. Unless fate had a say.

Unable to resist the temptation, he stuck out his hand, and they sealed the deal.

∽

Grace found the article Ned Cross had mentioned and pored over each sentence. Several times the word *uncooperative* came up, and she grinned. Nothing described him better. Apparently, he'd known one of the two inebriated patrons, and they'd had angry words even before the fight. A bystander reported that the patron had called Deacon a murderer and yelled that he'd gotten away with killing more than one man. When that drunk had turned up dead, fingers pointed to Brannock. The article was pretty much as Cross had described.

Well, if Brannock had killed others, there should be a record, but after spending the entire afternoon digging through the files, she had to admit defeat.

Next, she went to the telegraph office and sent a message to her uncle Sam, who had served as the sheriff of Lost Point, Texas, for almost twenty years. If anyone could find out more about Brannock, he could.

Yet when the answer to her telegram arrived late that night, it chilled her bones.

> *Can find no sign of anyone named Deacon Brannock in the State of Texas. Stop. I'll keep searching.*

Eight

SHE MADE GOOD ON HER PROMISE TO CROCKETT AND SET OUT a meal of fried chicken, a large bowl of white gravy, and another of green beans. She served them up with homemade biscuits.

Though she stayed busy, her mind kept going to her uncle's telegram. How could Brannock have erased all record of himself in Texas? Why? What was he hiding?

The man did exist, only the question remained: Under what name? Who was he?

Her brother glanced across the table at her. "Thanks, Gracie. This is almost as good as Mama's. This feels a little like home, you know. I really miss them. Ransom is probably as tall as I am now, and little Hannah is almost twelve. We need to set a day for the trip."

"We'll try to do that soon."

"No, tonight. Right now, or we'll never do it," he insisted.

"You're a pain in my behind." She got the calendar and stabbed it with her finger. "Two weeks from today." She hoped she had nothing important come up at the newspaper.

"Fine. Thanks for humoring me."

Grace told him about the article she had found dealing with Brannock. "Have you heard talk of any of this down at the stockyards?"

"Some. Almost everyone believes he's a killer." He forked more food in his mouth.

"I telegraphed our uncle Sam and got him to try finding out more about Brannock, and guess what?"

"What?"

"He can't find any record of the man. He's like a ghost."

"I told you to leave him alone. It's not your puzzle to solve, Gracie. Get that?"

"But I can't let it go. It's like he's dangling a carrot in front of me. Taunting me."

"Then eat the carrot and move on to something else. I mean it. Drop it now."

If only it were that simple.

That night, Grace dreamed of handsome, gray-eyed saloon owners and a voice that kept taunting her about finding the man whose name he'd stolen. She tossed and turned before finally rising and getting ready to meet her friend, Carrie Nation, in a few hours.

With little sleep, Grace ate a light breakfast. Yawning big, she closed the door behind her and found her way to Carrie Nation's porch. The petite, heavyset woman was dressed in her usual black attire. "We need to step up our attacks, Grace. We're not getting results." Carrie's cool blue gaze pierced Grace. "I don't think you're very committed to our cause."

"What do you mean? I'm doing everything I know."

"Take a hatchet and march right into those saloons and break every last bottle of whiskey." Carrie's heavy jowls shook with the passionate words. "We have to get the owners' attention and make them listen. Are you in? Or out?"

An image of her destroying Deacon Brannock's Three Deuces played in her mind. He'd be enraged. A direct attack on his business could push him over the edge into violence. She swallowed hard, thinking about his dangerous reputation—his dark tendencies. There was only one reason she could think of why he didn't exist in Texas under his current name.

A shiver ran up her spine.

"I don't know, Carrie."

"This is no time to be squeamish. I thought you had guts, Miss Legend. Passion. Drive. Persistence."

Grace did but… She swallowed past a lump. "All right."

"I'm glad to see you came to your senses." Carrie reached into a barrel and pulled out a short-handled hatchet, handing it to her. "Get your ladies and go do the Lord's work."

Grandfather Stoker was going to be anything but thrilled about this, not to mention her father. *Don't disgrace the family name.* Feeling a bit green around the gills, Grace hid the hatchet in the folds of her dress and hurried to gather her group. Maybe she could talk them out of attacking Brannock's place first. They'd move farther in and work backward.

Yes, that might be best.

They made it to Rusk Street a little before noon, but the women halted at the Three Deuces and refused to budge. They attacked the locked wooden door with their hatchets and marched behind the shiny oak bar. So far, there was no sign of anyone.

"Come on, Grace, let's get busy. Where's your hatchet?"

"I—I must've dropped it." She stood frozen as her friends swept a row of whiskey bottles in various degrees of fullness from the shelf. The noise of breaking glass crashing to the floor could've waken the dead.

"Here." Celia Ann thrust a hatchet into Grace's hand.

"Hey!" Brannock charged down the stairs. "Stop! You're trespassing."

The women scattered, and Grace looked around to find herself the sole one remaining. Again. And she held the raised hatchet. Brannock raced straight for her with murder in his eyes.

Trembling, Grace swung. "Come a step closer and I'll use this. I swear."

"You wouldn't dare, you little troublemaker."

Spit dried in her mouth, and she narrowed her gaze. "Oh, but I would. Try me and find out how fast I can swing this."

His eyes blazed, flames shooting from their depths. "What's wrong with you? This is private property. My home. Have you no respect? No decency? No upbringing?"

Suddenly, Libby Daniels's cold face frozen in death no longer provided justification for anything, least of all this. Shards of glass glittered from the amber liquid on the floor. This was a bad, bad idea, and she knew how damning it looked for her. When Brannock lunged, she darted around him, her heart hammering. He missed her just barely but managed to wrench the hatchet from her hand.

Too busy evading him, she didn't see a second man until the collision jarred her. She struggled to get free of the strong arms. "Let me go!"

"Not on your life. Brannock, what are we going to do with her?"

"I don't know, Harry, but I'm not going to give her another chance to finish wrecking this place."

Just then, Grace squirmed enough to break Harry's hold, and she wasted no time in racing for the stairs. A woman at the top screamed. Grace made it halfway up before bands of steel wrapped around her.

"No you don't!" Brannock lifted her off her feet from behind, his arms around her waist. He carried her back down, keeping his arms wrapped tight, offering no chance of escape.

"Put me down!" The exertion of the flight and the struggle to escape made it difficult to breathe. She gasped for every bit of air she could find. Every warning she'd heard mentioned about Deacon Brannock buzzed in her head like hundreds of flickering, sizzling gaslights.

She was in big, big trouble.

His warm breath fluttered the hair at her ear. "Not a chance, lady. You and I have some settling up to do. You're going to pay for this mess."

"And if I don't?" she grated out between her teeth.

His voice slid over her like pure silk. "Oh, Miss Grace, I don't think you want to know the answer to that. Haven't you heard what I do to people who cross me?"

The soft warning that drifted between the words sent a shiver up her spine. Would Crockett ever know what happened to her? Or her parents? She could disappear and leave no trace. Gone in an instant. She had no doubt Brannock could make that happen if he chose.

"Like the woman upstairs? Are you holding her against her will?"

"Her and a dozen others," he snapped.

The saloon door rattled, then swung open. Harry entered with a man wearing a silver star on his chest. She swallowed hard.

"I didn't have to go far to find this deputy." Harry motioned the lawman forward.

Brannock's hard body tightened, bringing Grace so close, she could feel his thundering heartbeat. "Deputy, this woman broke into my establishment and smashed my whiskey bottles. I'm pressing charges against her."

"Gladly." The deputy's stare bore into her. "It's the only way to stop these women."

Brannock passed her to the lawman with a warning, "Be careful. She may have rabies."

This would be a black mark against the Legend name—Stoker and her father. Bringing shame to the family was everything she'd tried to prevent. She was going to jail.

Panic rose, and Grace tried to speak, but the words stuck inside her. She worked her tongue and finally managed, "What if I pay for everything?"

Deacon Brannock leaned to lift a tendril of her hair, clucking his tongue. "My dear Miss Grace, you scoffed at that notion. Remember? No, that's completely off the table now. Open wide and take your medicine. You'll remember the taste."

The deputy yanked her over to the destruction she and her

ladies had left, their feet crunching on the broken glass. "There's only one way to make a believer out of you women."

Grace sagged against the hands gripping her. If Pemberton caught wind of this, he'd fire her from the paper, and if her father learned of it, she'd be dead, not to mention Grandfather Stoker. He'd disown her. She'd made a horrible mess of things. She lifted her gaze to Brannock's. "I apologize for all of this. Believe me, I'm really sorry."

"Sorry you did it or that you got caught?" he asked.

"My folks raised me to respect people's property. Not this."

"I'll drop the charges if you come clean about who really did this."

"Is that true, miss?" the deputy asked.

The road to freedom beckoned. All she had to do was turn her friends in. Celia Ann's face swam before her. She had three sick kids and a rat for a husband. Gwen Morris took care of her sick mother. All the women of their group had problems they were dealing with.

Grace licked her dry lips. "No. It was me. I did it all."

"Let's go." The lawman led her out the door, and while his grip was strong, it wasn't bruising.

She sent one more pleading glance at Brannock's unyielding profile, but he didn't blink. She thought she saw a flicker of disappointment in his gaze.

A short time later, the deputy locked her in a cell. Grace gripped the bars, panic rushing over her in crashing waves. "Deputy, will you get word to my brother where I am?"

"Crockett Legend?"

"Yes. You can find him at the stockyards."

"I'll send someone."

"Thanks." Grace moved to the small cot and sat. Something stirred around her. The mattress ticking was alive with hundreds of bugs. Yelling, she hopped up.

A man in the next cell raised his head from the pillow. "Pipe down, lady."

"I have bugs on my bed! Oh God, oh God!"

"You'll get used to it, missy." He turned over and went back to sleep.

Grace doubted that. She moved across the small space. Why had she gotten herself in this mess? She should never have listened to Carrie, never broken into the Three Deuces, and never lied for her friends. Now she was dragging the Legend name through the mud. The worst shame she'd ever known wound through her. Brannock had stood up for them against the mob of angry men, and she and the ladies had repaid him by destroying his place.

The image of the woman she'd seen on the stairs crossed her mind. She took a deep breath. Maybe the woman heavy with child was his wife.

She had to stop this wild speculation. What difference did it make? She had no hold on Brannock. None. He was free to do whatever he liked.

Even if he did have working girls upstairs, it was none of her business, and she had to get that through her head. Who was she to judge?

Oh, if she could just get out of here, she'd stop forming these preconceived notions. Did she want Brannock to be a bad person? Good heavens, no. In some strange way, she sort of liked the man. However, she was a reporter, and that meant reporting the facts only. Period.

So here was a tally of where she stood in a nutshell. She'd let her friends drag her along to a place she didn't want to go. She'd lied to the deputy. And she'd blackened the family name.

Not her finest hour.

The outside door opened to reveal Crockett's familiar form as he strode into the sheriff's office. First, Grace wanted to weep that he'd come. Second, deep embarrassment rushed in its wake. She hated for him to see her in here, locked up like this.

Crockett's gaze searched the cells. He flashed her a smile, then marched straight to the desk. "Deputy, I'm Crockett Legend, and I'd like to see my sister."

The lanky young deputy with nice green eyes glanced up. "Legend, Legend. Grace?"

"That's right."

"I reckon you can see her for a moment. You'll have to leave your handgun here."

"Fine." Her brother laid the pistol on the corner of the desk, then hurried toward her. When he got there, he gripped the bars like he wanted to rip them out. She shrank away from the anger on his face. "What the hell were you thinking, Gracie? I told you to stay far away from the Three Deuces and Brannock. But did you listen? No, you did not. You always do whatever pleases you without a care in the world for the consequences."

"It's good to see you, too, Crockett." Her voice turned soft and contrite. She tried to still her quivering lip. "I'm sorry, okay? Thanks for coming. Will you see if you can get me out?"

"Already spoke to the sheriff before I came here, and he's going to make an example out of you because of our family's status." At least Crockett did seem distressed about her predicament. "I hate it, but you'll have to do some time."

She croaked, "How much time?" Like a year? Or maybe ten? She couldn't stay here that long. Panic set her heart racing. "What if you went to Brannock and asked him to drop the charges?"

"Tried that too. The saloon is locked up tighter than a spinster's pocketbook. He refused to answer the door." Crockett ran his fingers through his hair. "Gracie, there's nothing I can do right now."

"Thanks for trying, little brother. Do you think you could bring me a few things?"

"Sure. Name them."

"My journal and a pencil. That's all."

"Sure. Try to manage as best you can."

She swallowed past the thick lump in her throat but couldn't do anything but nod.

"Time's up." The deputy waved toward the door. "Let's go."

Her brother squeezed her hand. "Try not to worry."

Tears burned the back of her eyes. "I'm glad you came. Please don't tell Pa."

The deputy hurried Crockett out onto the boardwalk without giving him a chance to utter another word.

Grace had never felt so alone, so cut off from the world. "Deputy?" she called.

"Yes, miss."

She smiled sweetly. "May I please have a chair? I need a place to sit other than my bug-infested mattress."

"I might be able to do that."

Twenty minutes later, Grace didn't know how grateful she could be for just one chair. Her feet hurt from being on them so long. "Thank you so much. What's your name?"

"Coop Langley."

"That's a nice name. Do you have folks here in Fort Worth?"

"Yes, ma'am. I go to their place every Sunday for Mama's meatloaf."

"Coop, I've never been locked up before, and it's quite frightening. Do prisoner's get supper in here?"

"Maggie May's Café across the way sends it over about five o'clock."

She rubbed her arms against the chill.

Coop nodded toward her bunk. "Get the blanket that's on your bed if you're cold, ma'am."

She wrinkled her nose. "It's full of bugs. I just can't stand them crawling on me."

He winked. "I know what you mean. We've never washed them and some of our prisoners have never taken a bath before."

"I can believe it."

The rest of the day inched along like a waterlogged snail, and darkness finally fell. Crockett returned with her journal and pencil and surprised her with a clean blanket.

"Little brother, I could kiss you." After the deputy shook it out to check for smuggled weapons, she wrapped it around her. The soft warmth was divine.

Crockett held his hat in one hand and gave her shoulder an awkward pat. "I told you I'd be back. I wish I could provide more."

"That's okay," she said quietly.

After a moment's hesitation, he shifted and spoke. "A woman named Celia Ann came by the house asking for you. I told her you were here. Hope that was all right."

"Sure. She's a friend."

"She wanted me to pass along that the doctor is treating her children."

"Oh, good. I'm relieved about that."

Crockett pushed back a lock of hair from his forehead. "Her eyes were sad."

"Her husband left her for another woman."

Coop ushered her brother out, and a short time later the deputy was relieved by a sourpuss named Froman, who bit her head off if she tried to ask anything, plus he wouldn't bring her supper until after he'd let it grow cold. He wasn't a very nice man.

Loneliness, a rank odor, and dead silence cast long shadows in her cell. Wrapped in the clean blanket, she tried to sleep, but worry crawled along the inside of her eyelids.

At 3:00 a.m., Froman opened her cell to throw in a busty working girl falling out of her tiny dress, her face paint smeared to high heaven. Without offering a name, the lady of the evening walked to the bunk and promptly fell asleep. She kept muttering something about shooting someone called Braxton the next time she saw him.

Then an hour later, Froman threw in another soiled dove. The two fallen women instantly hated each other. Name-calling commenced, fists flew, and the hair pulling began.

"You low-down hussy! I saw him first!" The busty prisoner grabbed the other and backhanded her.

"He already paid me, Elephant Nose!" The two locked horns and landed on top of Grace. The chair broke, and they all went down, Grace at the bottom of the heap.

"Horse dung!"

"Donkey ears!"

If she ever got out of this mess, she'd walk the straight and narrow for the rest of her days. But the question remained of when that would happen and how many bruises she'd have before it did.

Nine

DEACON GOT LITTLE SLEEP AS WELL. HE KEPT THINKING about how he'd replace what the women had destroyed. He had a small stash in the storeroom but not enough to keep going for long. Maybe he should throw in the towel. But the dream of owning his own land beckoned like a beautiful lady crooking her finger.

Will Bonner's offer could get him what he desired more than anything.

When Deacon won the saloon, he'd envisioned it as a way to own a small spread. He thought he could get it running good and sell it. But the damn place kept losing money instead of making it.

And now, Bonner's proposition could also end in failure if he couldn't break the wild stallion.

Something always stood between him and what he wanted. Deacon let out a frustrated sigh and turned his thoughts to another beautiful lady crooking her finger at him. He felt bad for Grace Legend in a way. The severity of her actions had only sunk in after the deputy arrived. Dammit! Why hadn't she just told the truth? Yet he kind of admired her for not squealing on her friends. No one liked a rat.

There seemed to be more to Grace Legend than a pretty face. Or was he simply hoping?

The door to Leah's room was closed, and no sound came from inside. He stole down the stairs, lit a lamp, and sat. The flame created dancing shadows on the wall. Leah had already put baskets out for her tamales and empanadas for tomorrow. He'd open a little early in hopes that the food would make up for the low supply of whiskey.

Who knew? Maybe they'd start a new trend in the lower end.

Footsteps alerted him, and he glanced up at Harry. "Sorry to wake you."

"You didn't. My nightmares beat you to it." The bartender shuffled behind the bar to make coffee. "I figure we both might need this. You look worried, Boss."

"I am, a little. Maybe this is an omen to sell out and head for more peaceful climes."

"Are there any left? If so, I haven't found 'em."

"You're probably right, Harry." Deacon rubbed his chin. "Besides, Leah needs us."

"Yep, that little girl does." Harry put the coffee on to boil on the little one-burner stove and sat down. "It was nice of your old friend Bonner to drop by."

"He wants my help taking the wildness out of a mustang. I worked for Bonner before I got this saloon. He has a pretty little ranch outside of town."

"Are you going to do it?" Harry rubbed his eyes.

"Going to try." Deacon didn't mention the money. That might fall through like everything else in his life. "Told him I'd start next week. I'll need you to run things here."

"Sure thing."

Silence drifted like dense fog across still water. Two men haunted by memories too thick to keep buried. They sat side by side, alone in the dimness with the tick of a clock providing the only conversation.

"I've killed before." Harry's voice was so low, Deacon wondered if he'd only imagined it.

"I figured something like that." He didn't prod for more. Maybe Harry had nothing else to share, and if so, that was all right.

The bartender rose and moved beyond the lamplight. There,

he lit a cigarette. "Yeah, well the bastard deserved it." He blew out smoke. "Sometimes that's the only path left for a man."

Deacon nodded, knowing the truth of that all too well. "Hell will take care of him."

"He came into my shanty, ate my food, slept under my roof, made me think he was a friend." Harry's voice cracked. "All the while he…he plotted to kill me. Said I owed him, and he was collecting." Harry ran a hand across his eyes. "I didn't know what he was talking about. He said the claim I was working up in Cripple Creek rightfully belonged to him."

"You mined for gold?"

"For three years. It never amounted to much. I showed him the deed to my claim, but he pulled out this gun and fired. The bullet missed. I had no choice but to kill him. None."

Deacon shifted in his chair. "You did what any man would've done."

"I suppose. Doesn't make the nights pass any easier, though."

"How long has it been?"

"Two years. Sometimes I can wash the nightmares away with whiskey. Other times not." Harry went to check on the coffee. "The thing is, I still see his face. I dragged his body into a tunnel and sealed it with dynamite." Harry broke down and sobbed. "I never told anyone what had happened." His shoulders shook with sobs. "He's haunting me, and I can't get rid of him."

Shock went through Deacon. He had nothing to say, so he rested a hand on Harry's shoulder.

"He was older by a few years, and when he drank, he went out of his head. I did my best to keep him away from liquor. After that, I packed up and left my claim, my friends."

They sat drinking coffee until daylight, barely saying anything else. A handful of words couldn't ease a man's grief when the life he'd known had vanished.

Deacon couldn't change what had happened to Harry or to himself either, but they could choose how to spend the rest of their lives and make the years count. He went to the back door and opened it to look at the breaking dawn. The sky had the appearance of clabbered milk in pinks, yellows, and golds. A sudden thought of Grace Legend came into mind. He had trouble forgetting her, even though he'd like to wring her pretty little neck for putting herself in that situation in the first place. Clearly, she hadn't wanted to be there for the little smashing party.

Now what? Dammit, he couldn't just let her stay in jail!

❧

The next morning, Grace barely heard the sheriff's door opening from the street, but the voice brought her straight up from the floor where she'd spent the night.

"I want to see my daughter, and I want to see her now!"

Dear Lord, her father! She was going to kill Crockett when she got out. But that was for later, and facing her pa was nothing she could put off.

Houston Legend's large form filled the law office. She knew how cattle rustlers, outlaws, and thieves felt when he appeared. She glanced around for a place to hide, but the room was bare except for the two women who'd made peace sometime during the early morning.

Deputy Froman's cold voice reached her. "Just who might you be? I have three ladies locked up."

Houston gave his name, and Grace watched a bit of color drain from the hateful man's face. Served the swaggering deputy right. Her father had taken lessons on intimidation from Grandpa Stoker, who could put people in their places faster than peeled lightning. She tucked herself into a ball and pulled the blanket over her head.

Footsteps pounded on the floor, then her father spoke. "Gracie, you can come out now."

She slowly let the shield drop and let a bright smile take shape. "Good morning, Pa. Fancy meeting you here."

He grabbed the iron bars separating them with his large hands. For once, she was grateful to have the barrier between them.

"What's the meaning of this, young lady?"

"Oh, you mean me being in here?"

Houston snorted. "It's a little late to play dumb, don't you think? Yes, that's exactly what I meant!"

His thundering voice woke her cell mates.

"Hey, mister, lower the volume to a roar," one mumbled.

But he kept on like he hadn't heard the lady. "Gracie, care to explain?"

She rose and moved to the bars. "It's a long story."

He whirled, went to the deputy's desk, and brought a chair back. "I have time." He sat and made himself comfortable.

This was going to get ugly. Anger created two glittering spots where his eyes should be.

Taking a deep breath and twisting her hands, she started with Celia Ann and Leonard and finished with the mess left in the Three Deuces, leaving out the part about lying for her friends. Taking the full blame, she met his gaze. "I'm sorry I let things get out of hand. If only I could go back and make a different choice."

"Do you think destroying this Brannock's property was right?"

"No, but neither is he in the right selling whiskey. It's ruining families. Look at Celia Ann, left to raise her three children by herself. Two are sick right now and the doctor won't come unless she pays her bill. And what about Libby Daniels on our ranch, who was beaten to death by her drunk husband? That's not right. Pa, I just want to see change for us women."

Anger had left his face, but he remained silent.

"I want to be able to vote and help make laws. I want to walk into a bank and open my own account without you or Crockett telling them I can. And I want women to be safe from drunken rages."

Houston stood and reached through the bars to cup her cheek. "I understand the why. You should be able to do all those things, and it's not right that you can't. But don't think that I condone violence in my daughter. That's unacceptable. There are ways to get what you want without destroying property. I've heard this Carrie Nation talk and I disagree with her tactics. Force never works."

She leaned her face into his gentle touch. "I see that now. Thank you for understanding. Can we keep this from Grandpa?" Seeing disappointment in Stoker's eyes would kill her.

"I'll do my best. That's all I can promise."

"What do you think will happen to me? Can you get me out? I didn't get a wink of sleep and everything is full of bugs."

"Let me see what I can do." He turned stern brown eyes on her. "But only if you've learned something from this."

"Oh, I have, I have. Absolutely. Cross my heart."

"I'll be back then. Get ready to roll up your sleeves because you won't get off scot-free."

"Thank you, Pa." Tears filled her eyes as she watched him go out the door. She was so lucky to have a parent like Houston, who must've ridden through the night to get to Fort Worth by morning. In fact, she had the best family in the world.

Now, how was she going to make things right with Brannock?

❧

Deacon opened the saloon a little before noon, and the wonderful smells of tamales and empanadas lured men in by the droves. An hour later, they were still going strong. He and Harry sold as much food as they had drinks.

A large figure strode through the batwing doors, and Deacon recognized Houston Legend. He waited until the familiar figure sat at a table before going over. "What'll it be?"

Houston met his gaze. "I'll take whatever is creating that aroma and a beer."

"That would be tamales and empanadas."

"I'll take a dozen of both."

Deacon waited for recognition to dawn, and when it didn't, he relaxed. "Coming right up."

When he delivered the order to Houston, the questions started. "I'm looking for Deacon Brannock."

"You found him. What can I do for you?"

"I'm here about my daughter's role in what happened here yesterday. Sit, maybe we can make a deal."

"I'm sorry I had Grace arrested. Yesterday wasn't the first incident with her, but it was the first time she used violence. Or rather the women she was with. Frankly, I'm not convinced she took part. The others left her to take the blame." Deacon waited for the yelling to start. When it didn't come, he pulled out a chair.

"Maybe. But being there made her just as guilty." Houston unwrapped a tamale and ate it with his fingers. "Thank you for having her thrown in jail. It was the best thing to happen to her. Gracie has always been too headstrong for her own good. Telling her no was like waving a red flag in front of her. Pressing charges got her attention. Now, I want to see what it will take to get you to drop them."

Being offered a bribe by a girl's father was a first, Deacon had to admit. "I meant to go to the sheriff's office this morning, but as you can see, business was booming, and I couldn't get away. I don't want your money."

Houston unwrapped a meat empanada and stuck half in his mouth. "What if I replace every bottle of liquor that the ladies broke? Will that make it right?"

Every bottle. That would cost a pretty penny, as expensive as alcohol was.

"That would be sufficient, I suppose."

"Not entirely." Houston wiped his fingers on a napkin. "My daughter needs to do something to make amends. I see you swept up the glass, but perhaps she could scrub the floor—on her hands and knees."

"Do you not like her very much?"

Houston laughed. "I love her more than my own life. Still, she needs to remember this for a very long time, if you know what I mean."

For the first time, Deacon was happy he didn't come from money or privilege. People like that sure had a mess load of problems. So did he, but his were easier. Less temptation.

"Yes, sir. All right, I can manage that."

"You'll have a lot of dishes that need washing too."

"I will." Lord, Grace was going to be madder than a hogtied steer. A grin lifted the corners of Deacon's mouth.

Houston leaned closer and narrowed his gaze. "You look familiar. Do I know you?"

Deacon stilled. "I don't think so."

"Ever been to the Lone Star Ranch? I could've sworn we met. Maybe you worked for us."

"No. I must have one of those faces. They say everyone has a twin walking around."

"I've heard that. Well, accept my gratitude for reining Gracie in. Her mother and I have been trying to do that for years."

Deacon clasped Houston's extended hand. This was the strangest conversation he'd ever had with any girl's father. Most of them had held rifles when talking to him.

"I'm heading back to the ranch tomorrow. Do you mind if I stop by and pick up a batch of these tamales to take with me? Also, some of these empanadas. They're the best I've ever eaten."

"No, I don't mind. I'll have them ready to travel."

"Excellent. Expect a wagon of alcohol this afternoon to replace what you lost."

"Thank you, sir, but it's not necessary." What was he saying? Without more inventory, he'd go out of business, and there went all his hopes and dreams.

"It's only right. My daughter caused this."

That afternoon by three o'clock, a wagonload of whiskey and other spirits arrived. Twice as much as what Grace and her friends had broken. Deacon stared in amazement. Just when he thought he was done with trying and life couldn't throw any more surprises, he found out how wrong he was.

Then before he and Harry could unload, Grace appeared with her sleeves rolled up, and he had a hard time remembering that he'd promised to make things difficult for her.

The sunlight tripped through her honey-blond hair and sparkled in her blue eyes like colored diamonds. The memory of how her body, alive with a wild heartbeat, had felt held tightly against his chest teased the edges of his mind.

"Brannock, I'm here to work. Tell me what you want."

Grace Legend was trouble, and he wasn't altogether certain he was up to the kind she brought. The vibrant, passionate woman filled his dreams and whispered along the fringe of his sanity and, despite their differences, he wanted her.

Ten

GRACE KEPT HER GAZE LOWERED, WAITING FOR BRANNOCK'S orders. She yearned to be anywhere except in the dim interior of the Three Deuces, but her father had decreed otherwise with a strong threat thrown in of what would happen if she didn't. Her palms sweaty, she tightened her hold on a cloth bag that contained everything she'd need for the afternoon.

The smells drifting from somewhere close surprised her. Was he cooking?

Or maybe the cook was the woman she'd glimpsed on the stairs during the chaos?

His quiet reply barely reached her ears. "You can start with the floor, I suppose. It's a sticky mess. I assume your father told you what we agreed on."

"Yes." In fact, he did so in a rather loud voice, and now she had to comply with the other part that would fulfill the bargain the two men had struck. Though unable to see Brannock's eyes, she knew they would be as unforgiving as the rest of him. "I'm sorry for what I and the other ladies did. I'm not a destructive person."

"Why did you take the blame?" His voice held curiosity and something else…admiration? "I noticed that you stood by while your friends destroyed the place."

The hard profile of his face, partially hidden in the gray shadows, scared her. Sharp, prickly needles of danger crawled up her spine. If only the room offered more light. The dimness playing across his features sent her imagination into overdrive and reminded her of the rumors of dead men nailed to outhouse doors.

"I saw you," he repeated quietly after she took too long to reply.

A ripple of surprise ran through her. "What are you talking about?"

"This isn't your handiwork. The others in your...flock...did this."

The man noticed everything. Grace squirmed under his piercing gaze.

She licked her dry lips. "They couldn't afford to spend time in jail. Most have children. One has a sick mother. I have no one dependent on me. And like you said, I stood by when I shouldn't have let myself get caught up in this. I was wrong in not trying to stop them. I'm sorry, Brannock."

"I believe you."

"I'd like to be friends if you'll let me."

He was quiet for so long, she wondered if he'd reply. Finally, he gave a soft snort. "Friends? Is that possible. After everything?"

Grace didn't blame him for being leery. Maybe she should offer a compromise. "If we can't be friends, can we stop being enemies?"

Again, silence filled the space between them. This time he didn't speak.

"Think about it." She smiled brightly. "I should get to work." She whipped out a long apron from her bag and tied it around her to protect her dress. She'd get this unpleasantness over as fast as possible.

"You'll find water and soap behind the bar. A bucket as well."

Why not the kitchen where the smells drifted from? she wondered.

"Thank you, Brannock. I suppose you'll inspect my efforts when I'm done?"

"No, your father gets that task."

The sudden cheerfulness in his tone snapped her head around, and she found the broad-shouldered saloon keep wearing a wide grin. Darn the handsome devil! He was enjoying her downfall a little too much.

Gritting her teeth, she found everything she needed behind the bar and set about scrubbing the sticky mess from the floor. When she glanced up, he'd disappeared. Without his disturbing gray eyes on her, she could relax.

In the passing time, she scrubbed the filthy floor, cleaning it of snuff, spit, and disgusting vomit. She finished and struggled to her feet, placing a hand to her aching back.

"You missed a spot" came a quiet voice that sent shivers up her spine.

She jumped at the unexpected sound and turned to see him in the shadows. "Do you always sneak up on people?"

"Are you always so skittish?"

"Only when men lurk in the shadows." Was he watching the whole time? Probably. Sour thoughts filled her head as she searched the rough planks for the missed spot. Discovering he was right put her in an even darker mood. She quickly took care of the missed place. "Any others?" she asked sweetly.

Killing him with kindness would go further than animosity. Besides, if she got close to him, he might drop a clue about his mysterious past.

"You can wash the dirty glasses now."

"Thank you." She flashed a wide smile. "Perhaps I can do your laundry while I'm at it?"

"Don't be ridiculous," he snapped. "This is no game, so stop pretending otherwise, Grace. Or would you rather be back in jail awaiting the judge?"

Fire flashed. "I'm smart enough to know it's not a game! I also know how lucky I am to be free."

"Keep your voice down. Someone's trying to sleep."

"My apology." Grace almost bit her tongue half off wanting to say something scathing.

He stepped into the light, and she couldn't help the catch in her breath. Dark stubble covered his jaw, and his unbuttoned shirt added a roguish appearance. He was truly a devastatingly handsome—formidable—man. She couldn't deny how he affected her.

Grace closed her eyes for a moment, her heart racing. She couldn't deny a good many things. But most of all, she couldn't deny the truth...her skin knew his touch.

Knew his gentle hand on a dark night. Knew his arm holding her flush against him.

A breathtaking smile suddenly curved his full lips. "I hate to ruin the image you've gotten in your head, but the sleeper is my bartender Harry Jones. He needs some shut-eye before his shift starts."

A noise above drew her attention. "Whatever you say, Brannock."

"I've been thinking over your offer of being friends."

"And?"

"I'm willing." He turned away as though that settled everything.

"That just made my day," she muttered darkly.

He never heard her quiet words, and it was just as well. She had to finish and get out of there. Grace turned to washing the glasses, forcing herself not to swing around when he took the stairs, whistling a soft tune. She lifted her hands from the water to scan the area, her gaze landing on a short-barreled rifle on a low shelf—the right height for a barkeep to reach for if trouble called.

"Of course he keeps a rifle. Everyone in the Acre does," she muttered again.

She stole to a closed door and slowly turned the knob. Light shone through the crack, and she took note of a slight woman at the stove, cooking. When the person swung around to reach for a pan, Grace discovered two things—one, the female was heavy with child. And two, she was a young girl no more than seventeen or eighteen.

Grace pushed inside, and the girl smiled, completely unafraid. "I wondered who was creating these delicious smells. I'm Grace."

"I know all about you. Deacon tells me how much trouble you're making for him. He's thinking of leaving all this hassle behind, and I don't blame him. He's a good man." She scowled, reaching for a bundle of dried corn husks to wrap the tamale dough in. "He usually makes me stay upstairs, but I'm glad I get to come down and cook. I'm Leah." Still frowning, the girl stretched out her hand and they shook. "I get so lonely up there all day. I begged him to accept my help in keeping the saloon open by selling this food, and he finally relented."

Grace looked at Leah closely but saw no marks where she'd been tied up or beaten, and the fresh-faced girl appeared clean, her brown hair pulled back in a long braid. "Are you a prisoner here?"

Anger filled Leah's soft, brown eyes. "Deacon is a kind, decent man. He loves me."

"Oh, honey. A man like him knows the right things to say to make you believe them." He had to be at least twenty years older than Leah. Grace wanted to warn her about wily men like Deacon Brannock. "I can take you out of here."

"I'm not going anywhere. I'll stay with Deacon."

A door opened and shut somewhere in the saloon, and a warning slid along her spine. She had to get back out there before he caught her.

"Just think about what I said. You can escape this, and I'll help." Giving Leah no time to reply, Grace quietly left the kitchen and returned to her glassware.

Her thoughts were like a pile a leaves that a sudden wind picked up and whirled this way and that. Damn that man for holding Leah, telling her he loved her, filling her with his baby. She scrubbed the glasses furiously. That poor, poor girl.

Her father entered through the back door. "How's everything going, Gracie?"

The pet name had her gritting her teeth. "Pa, my name is Grace. Do you think you can remember that? Grace."

"I don't know how you expect me to remember that. I've

always called you Gracie, and I don't see why you're throwing such a hissy."

"It sounds babyish."

He kissed her cheek and grinned. "I know."

"Then please stop."

"Honey, if it upsets you, I will try to remember your new name."

"It does upset me a great deal. Thank you."

"Are you about ready?"

"I just have to dry these glasses." She could tell her father about Leah's situation, and maybe he'd fix it. That was a thought.

"Glad to hear it." He glanced around. "Where's Brannock?"

"I couldn't say. Last I saw, he was going upstairs, but he appears and disappears like some sour-faced magician." She set the last glass next to the others against the mirror and removed her apron, folding it.

Houston wandered to the floor she'd scrubbed and studied it. Finding it to his satisfaction, he nodded. "Good job."

"Then I'm done, I guess."

"I'm really sorry about the work, Gracie…Grace." He placed his hands on her shoulders. "I couldn't bear to see you behind bars."

"Is it true you replaced all of Brannock's whiskey?"

"I did. To save your hide, I might point out."

All their efforts in closing the saloon doors had been in vain. "Pa, you just undid all our hard work. Brannock will keep selling to drunks."

Houston's good mood vanished, and he held up a hand. "Stop. I'm well aware of your thoughts concerning alcohol, but my interest was in getting you out of jail. You broke the law. You're confusing the two issues. I'm only going to say this once. Get down from your high horse. On the Lone Star, we will have alcohol. End of discussion."

When she opened her mouth to speak, he added, "Not one more word."

Grace worked to keep a lid on her anger, and she managed to speak in a calm, even voice. "I see. I owe you thanks for my freedom. We'll just agree to disagree."

"That's exactly right. I want no part of this movement, nor does the family." His dark scowl lifted. "Let me take you to the Ashton for a nice dinner. Crockett can join us. I leave tomorrow, so this is our last chance to eat as a family."

The Ashton was known for its fancy decor and thick steaks. It would be wonderful to see a little more of her father and maybe fill him in on the Three Deuces. "Sounds good."

Footsteps sounded, and Brannock came from the storeroom. "Didn't hear you come in, Legend."

Darn the man! He really did appear like magic. When had he come downstairs? Grace wondered if there was another way down from above. Had he heard her talking to Leah? She noted he'd buttoned his shirt, covering that broad chest.

"Just got here. Did the wagon I promised arrive?"

"Yes, everything is as we agreed."

"Then our business is concluded." Houston shook Brannock's hand. "My children and I are having dinner tonight at the Ashton. Join us."

Grace choked and erupted in a fit of coughing. With Brannock sitting across the table, she'd be unable to take a single bite. The insufferable man filled a glass with water and handed it to her. "Thank you," she murmured.

"Don't mention it." Brannock's crooked smile did little to ease her coughing spell. He turned to Houston. "I appreciate the invitation, but I have previous plans, I'm afraid."

"A pity," Grace murmured.

Houston put an arm around her shoulders. "If you change your mind, you're always welcome to join us."

Brannock caught her gaze and held it for a long moment, and she found herself unable to breathe until he broke the spell. "I won't."

She pulled from her father's arm and hurried out the door, having had quite enough of Deacon Brannock for one day.

∽

A few hours later, Grace sat with her father and brother in Fort Worth's fanciest hotel. If things hadn't gone as well as they had, she knew very well she could be sitting in jail, dodging elbows and watching another repeat of a battle royal.

They ordered, then Houston sat back. "Gracie, your mother and I would like you to come home for a bit." His grim expression said it was more than a request.

"My name's Grace, and I have my work here. I couldn't possibly. I thought you understood how important this is to me."

"Just for a visit. I insist," Houston pressed. "Your grandfather isn't getting any younger. He misses you and Crockett."

Crockett's glance slid from her to their father. "I've been wanting to take care of some business on the Lone Star. What if Gracie comes with me?"

"Any idea when, son?"

"I think I can swing it in two weeks." Crockett took the beer he'd ordered from the waiter. "Let Gracie stay until then. I really need her here."

Houston appeared surprised. "I didn't know she was helping you."

Grace fumed at the way they took charge of her life and gave her no say, even after she'd explained all this to her father in the jail. Had he just pretended to listen?

"I thought I told you that she keeps my books, writes reports, and does all sorts of things." When their father wasn't looking, her brother winked across the table. "Two weeks is hardly any time, and we'll be home on the train. Meanwhile, I'll keep her out of trouble."

She jumped to her feet. "Stop it. Both of you. I'm right here, yet you're talking around me."

"Sit down, Gracie," Houston said in a loud whisper.

"Stop running my life. I'm sick of being treated like some simpleton." Diners at nearby tables stared. She finally slid into her chair.

Their food arrived, interrupting the conversation, and there was a long pause while they checked out their meal.

Finally, Houston cut his steak and forked a bite into his mouth. "Since you put it that way, son, I think we can postpone her visit for two weeks."

Though Grace wanted to scream, she sat there like the five-year-old her father tried to make her and had to swallow the words she yearned to say. She listened to him and Crockett, realizing he treated her younger brother like a man.

Finally, unable to take any more, she laid down her fork. "Pa, I was thinking of shaving my head. What do you think?"

Houston choked on his beer. "You can't be serious."

Grace shrugged, examining her nails. "Look at the time I'd save fixing it. I think I might start wearing trousers as well. Keeping the hem of my dresses clean is hard work and trouble I could avoid."

She finally had his attention.

"If this is a joke, I'm not laughing." Clearly, her father found the direction of the conversation not one he particularly enjoyed.

"I'm just trying to find some things I can decide for myself," she said quietly. "So far, you've taken over my life to where I hardly recognize it. On the other hand, my kid brother gets to be his own man. Can't you see how ridiculous this is?"

Houston sighed and leaned back in his chair. "All right. I have been a mite heavy-handed, I'll admit. I'm just trying to protect you. A father can't stand to see his little girl hurt."

"I know," Grace answered softly. "That's the problem."

The crash of shattering glass from a nearby table sent her back to the day she turned ten years old.

"*Well, lookee here. This is our lucky day, fellas. She thinks she's Houston Legend's brat.*" The dusty rider laughed and grabbed the reins of Gracie's new buckskin.

"*Look, Carl, old man Legend and his sons are hard on our tails. We ain't got time to waste.*"

"*Hey, I know all that. But this little girl is our ticket to safety. Besides, I got my own reasons for taking her.*"

Grace shook herself to send the memory back where it came from. She'd just celebrated her birthday when she was abducted by a group of bank robbers as she rode along the creek on the horse her grandfather gave her. That was the most terrified she'd ever been before or since. They held her for five days, giving her little food or water. She never cried—Legends didn't do that. Not even her uncle Sam when rustlers hung him from an oak tree. Luckily, his brother Luke had ridden along in time to cut him down.

Her hands trembled as she reached for her glass. She still remembered the day her grandfather and his three sons had ridden upon the four robbers, riddling them with bullets, and how she ran to Houston, sobbing. He'd scooped her up and made her feel safe and loved.

In the back recesses of her mind, she recalled something one of the dying robbers had hollered to her father. *Tell her about Yuma Blackstone and what he did to her mother! She deserves to hear the truth!*

The man might've said more, but Houston's Colt stopped him. What had the man meant? Who was Yuma Blackstone, and what had he done?

She'd asked over the years, but those who knew kept quiet. From time to time now, Grace had these flashes of memory and wondered if she'd ever know the truth. Would the newspaper have anything in their files about the incident?

Voices now jarred her, and she realized her father had asked a question.

"I'm sorry. What did you say?"

"How is your steak, honey?"

"Fine." She glanced down to see that she hadn't even cut into it. Maybe Brannock had taken Leah from her folks and kept her in the saloon. Maybe Leah's situation was similar to her own kidnapping.

Crockett nudged her. "Where did you go?"

"Just thinking." She turned to her father. "If you suspected someone was being held against her will, would you do something to save her?"

"You know the answer to that. Yes." He took a drink from his glass. "Who are you talking about?"

She told them about Leah at the Three Deuces. "She thinks she loves Brannock and won't let me help her."

"If this Leah didn't want to leave when you offered, there's not much you can do. You can't save someone who doesn't want to be saved." Houston's low voice held sadness. "I spoke with Brannock at length, and he didn't appear to be the kind of man who'd do something like that. Maybe you misunderstood the situation. Leah could be a relative. Or a wife."

"It's possible, of course." Her thoughts moved toward trying to be more levelheaded. If she wanted to develop as a respected journalist, she had to rein in her impulsive behavior and act responsibly.

If she wanted to have a grown-up name, she had to start acting more like an adult.

No more jumping from the frying pan into the fire at every turn.

But how did a girl find logic in the way her heart reacted when Brannock touched her?

Eleven

MONDAY MORNING EARLY, DEACON RODE OUT TO THE BONNER ranch. He stopped on top of a little rise and gazed at the peaceful scene below. The two-story, whitewashed house sat next to a big pond from which Deacon had once fished. A small dinghy bobbed at the dock, inviting him to come closer. Man, he could still taste those catfish cooked over an open fire and nights under the stars just the two of them.

He'd often thought that if he could choose a father, he'd want him to be someone of Will's even temperament and manner. Will Bonner cared about people and did them right. In the two years Deacon had worked for him, never once had Will raised his voice. That wasn't to say they hadn't had disagreements. They'd had lots but settled them by talking everything out. Too bad Will and his wife had never had any kids.

Deacon inhaled the fresh Texas air into his lungs. If he could have a parcel of land like Will's, he'd swap the saloon for it in a heartbeat. This deal he'd struck with Will was anything but certain. Maybe he couldn't coax the wildness out of the horse. Or maybe it would turn up lame or possibly die. That money was a long way off and nothing he could count on.

Will emerged from the house and waved to him, then strode to the big red barn. Deacon nudged his horse and rode down. Better get started.

He reined up at the house and dismounted, half expecting Mrs. Bonner to come out with a big smile on her face. It didn't seem right that she was gone. Shaking himself, he passed a large corral and went to the barn.

Will waited just inside the wide door. "Were you up there comparing this to saloon work?"

They shook hands. "How did you guess?"

"I know you like the back of my hand. I'm keeping the mustang in the round pen in back. He seems a bit calmer there for some reason. He's torn up everything I put him in. The other hands call him Diablo." Will pushed his hat back. "I think Devil fits him as well as anything. He's tried to kill everyone who's gotten in the corral with him. One of my men is barely hobbling, and another has a broken arm."

"You can't keep something that wants to be free," Deacon said softly. "We have to give him a reason to want to stay."

"That's your job. I sent the men out to round up strays, so you won't have any distractions."

"I remember where everything is. Will, where did you get this mustang? They've been gone from here for years."

"The men found a small herd way up in the hills where they were hiding out. I don't know how they escaped capture before now, but this one did."

"What kind of shape is he in?"

"A little scarred up, but otherwise fine. Come on, I'll introduce you to Diablo."

They left the barn and walked around back. The mustang's coat shone blue in the sunshine. Deacon had never seen a more beautiful horse. Diablo glanced up, watching their approach with wary eyes, pawing the ground. They propped their feet on the bottom rail and rested their arms on the top.

Diablo raced around the perimeter, snorting and flaring his nostrils. Several times on the pass, he tried to bite or kick.

Will watched for a bit, then said he had some work to do and left.

Deacon didn't try to go into the pen with the angry stallion. Too early for that. He stayed still, making eye contact when Diablo stopped running and stood in the middle, his large muscles quivering, showing the whites of his eyes. "Where is all this hate coming from? Huh? No one's taken a whip to you. I'm going to help you figure that out."

The horse seemed to find Deacon's voice soothing, so he kept talking about anything and everything. Each time he stopped, Diablo raced around the pen like he was possessed. After a few hours, Deacon climbed over the rails into the pen. He stood where he could dive out at a moment's notice. The mustang shifted and pinned his ears flat against his neck.

A warning shot into Deacon's brain a second too late. Diablo charged and caught Deacon's right shoulder as he dove between the rails. White-hot pain tore through him, and for a moment, he couldn't breathe, couldn't think, couldn't move.

Dammit! He curled up, cradling his arm, waiting for the spasms to subside.

When his legs could hold his weight, he stood. Holding his arm, he hobbled to a chair that someone, maybe Bonner, had set under an elm tree. He collapsed with a groan, checking his ribs for fractures. He didn't know what hurt worse—his body or his pride. For a long moment, Deacon sat, trying to remember why he was doing this.

The devil horse had the audacity to look pretty pleased with himself, calmly nibbling at some hay Bonner had placed in one corner.

Deacon glared, working his arm a little. It had gone numb, of course. Imagine that. He cursed the man who'd broken it, a man with no conscience and a taste for violence. Ross Santana and Diablo were two of a kind.

No matter his pain, Deacon wasn't done. He had serious money on the line, and he intended to claim it. Somehow.

∽

Grace and her ladies returned to the Acre on Monday, armed with signs, drums, and chants they'd memorized. This time they started at the other end of the street and slowly worked down. The owners of several saloons stomped out and got into a shouting match, but they couldn't be heard over the group of loud women and noise-makers. They finally threw up their hands and went back inside.

The women crusaders neared a corner when Grace spied three boys beating up on one and kicking him.

"Hey! Stop that!" Grace brandished her sign, and the hooli-gans scattered. She knelt beside the younger boy lying so still. She turned him over and recognized the wild thatch of red hair. "Izzy, it's Miss Grace."

Blood oozed from the boy's nose and lip. Tears wet his cheeks. "I'm scared."

Her heart broke for this child who tried to be so strong. Life was hard enough for those who had family and a place to live. She couldn't imagine how it was for kids not having anyone or anything.

Love for Izzy washed over her. She put her arms around him. "I know, honey. I'm so sorry you have no home. Did those boys hurt you?"

Izzy straightened, his chin quivering. "I'll be okay." But the next moment, he couldn't hold back the tears and collapsed, clinging to her.

Grace let him sob his heart out and found silent tears running down her face as well. No part of this was fair. Why hadn't she seen this before? Maybe because she hadn't wanted to, and until marching for the temperance cause, she'd stayed far away from Hell's Half Acre.

The Three Deuces was close by. Maybe Brannock would have what they needed.

"I wish I had Mama back. I miss her." Izzy plucked at the fabric of Grace's sleeve. "She was soft like you and kind. Sometimes

when I'm afraid at night, I close my eyes and remember her face."
He broke down in sobs again. "She talks to me some and tells me
to be strong."

"What happened to your mother?" Grace asked gently, rubbing his back.

But Izzy only shook his head, trying to be brave. Maybe the
boy didn't know, or maybe she died suddenly in an accident and
he never saw her again.

The world was a scary, confusing place to children who were
left to find their own way.

Grace wrapped her arms around him, murmuring comforting
words. If she ever saw those big bullies again, she was going to
report them to the sheriff. They shouldn't be allowed to run the
streets, doing whatever they chose.

When Izzy cried himself out, she got him up and helped him
hobble down the street. She knocked on the back door of the
Three Deuces, and Harry opened it.

"I'm not here to cause trouble, Harry. I need a place to clean
this boy up. He's hurt, and this was the closest place."

Harry's scowl vanished. "Come in. I'll see what I can do for him."

"Thank you." She and Izzy followed the bartender to the
kitchen that smelled like tamales. It was spic and span, and a large
cloth-covered plate sat on the small table. She pulled out a chair
for Izzy while Harry pumped water into a tin bowl.

The bartender set it in front of Grace, along with pieces of flour
sack that looked to be clean. "I'll get some medicine from upstairs
while you tend to him."

"Harry, I'm truly grateful." Grace touched his arm. He nodded
and left.

She went to work, gently cleaning the blood and dirt. Izzy also
had some deep scrapes on his arms and legs. Next, she checked
him for broken bones but found none. His leg was probably
sprained bad and accounted for his hobbling.

The tears had stopped, but his eyes held deep sorrow that bruised something inside her. To fill the silence, she talked about her own childhood some and how the world became a most frightening place at times. "I got into quite a few fights at school because I wouldn't let bullies hurt the other kids. I went home more than once with a black eye or bloody nose. One thing I will never abide is bullies."

"They're mean."

"Can you tell me what happened?"

"I usually hide when I see them, but the owner of the China Lady paid me to pick up some sugar and other things from the mercantile, and I was delivering them. Those boys took my red wagon and my customer's order." His lip quivered. "I don't know what I'm gonna tell Mr. Quincy. He's gonna be real mad and won't give me any more business. And Mr. Brannock will be mad I lost the wagon. I'm in a jam."

Anger blazed inside Grace. "Don't you worry. I'm going to get them back."

Izzy eyes widened. "No, Miss Grace. They'll hurt you."

She'd like to see those little snot-nosed brats try. "One thing about bullies is I've never seen any stand against someone confronting them. They all run like scared rabbits."

Harry returned with a brown bottle of mercurochrome and bandages. "This should help."

"You're a godsend." She took the medicine. "This will sting," she warned Izzy before dabbing it on his scrapes and cuts, then quickly blew on each place.

To his credit, Izzy only whimpered. He'd seemingly regained his stoic nature.

"You're really brave," she told him.

"Not always. I try not to cry though."

"Where's Brannock?" Grace asked Harry. "I don't see him around."

"He took a ride outside of town."

She'd never heard a more evasive answer. Clearly, he didn't want to say, or maybe Brannock had told him not to. What was the cowboy saloon owner up to? She'd give anything to know. "Fresh air is good for all of us. Harry, I'm much obliged for your help. We'll run along. I have a red wagon to find."

"Be careful, Miss Grace," Harry answered. "Anything you want me to tell Brannock?"

She thought a moment, then smiled. "No. I don't believe so."

They left, and Grace took Izzy down to the piece of boardwalk he'd claimed. "You stay here. Do not come after me. I shan't be long."

"I'm scared for you."

"I'll be just fine. Wait and see." Grace marched down the street, her hand in her pocket on the derringer. No one had better get in her way. She wouldn't pull it on a kid, but she wouldn't hesitate on a man.

It didn't take long to find the brazen, little thieves. A group of four gathered in front of a vacant building, talking. One sat in the red wagon. They didn't pay her any mind.

She cleared her voice. "I'll have Izzy's wagon and Mr. Quincy's order now."

The pimply-faced boy in the wagon glared. "Beat it, lady."

Grace calmly jerked up the wagon tongue before he could say more and dumped him out in the dirt. The other bullies laughed but sobered when she swung a hard gaze onto them. Some items wrapped in brown paper sat near them. Those had to be Quincy's purchases.

"Please put the man's items into the wagon." Her tone left no room for argument.

"If you want 'em, you'll have to take 'em." The belligerent voice came from a boy older than the rest. He was the same height as Grace.

She pulled the wagon around behind her, then marched to the speaker. "I asked you politely but since you ignored me, we'll have to do things a different way."

Though seething inside, she adopted an outward calm, bringing the heel of her shoe down hard on the boy's foot.

"Ow!"

While he was dealing with foot pain, she grabbed his ear and jerked him to the ground. "Put the man's purchases into the wagon. Now!"

The other boys hightailed it as fast as they could away from her. The one in fear of losing his ear quickly obeyed, then the second she released him, he raced off after his friends.

Grace dusted her hands and pulled the wagon back to Izzy. He threw his arms around her waist.

"Thank you, Miss Grace. Did they hurt you?"

"Nope. If you have any more trouble with them, let me know."

"I will. I'm glad we're friends."

"Me too." She smoothed his hair. "Izzy, would you like to come live with me?"

Surprise crossed his freckled face. He was silent a moment. "I cain't. I got a business to run."

"Think about it. And if you ever need me, here's the address of my house." She took a pencil and scrap of paper from her handbag, scribbled her address, and handed it to him.

"I wish—" Whatever else Izzy was about to say remained unspoken.

Grace hugged him and kissed his cheek. She fought back tears all the way home. There was something wrong with a world that left children to navigate the maze of surviving and growing up all by themselves.

Twelve

OVER THE NEXT WEEK, GRACE AND HER GROUP MARCHED peacefully with their signs up and down Rusk Street, avoiding the Three Deuces. Grace had a serious heart-to-heart with the ladies. No trying to prevent anyone from entering saloons. No engaging in any violence. And no trespassing. Their new rules angered Carrie Nation, but Grace didn't care. She'd learned her lesson and found staying inside the law preferable.

As her father had said: there was a right way of getting attention and a wrong way.

Brannock seemed to be avoiding her.

Celia Ann's husband, Leonard, had come crawling back, and she'd let him stay. At least for now.

"It's too hard by myself, Grace," she'd said. "I need his help with the kids."

Grace had put an arm around her friend. "It's your business, and you know what you can do. You don't have to explain anything to me. Not one single thing. This is your life."

"He said he's changed, but I know better. He'll do the same thing again one day." The shell of a woman had glanced down at her feet. "I wish I were strong like you."

Now Grace glanced over at her friend and smiled, trying not to judge. Her mother was fond of saying that no one knew what another was going through until they walked in their shoes. The painted women in the jail swept into mind, and she realized she'd judged them when she knew nothing of their circumstances. She'd really try to be more compassionate.

The day had clouded up, and it sprinkled off and on, which Grace was grateful for. The morning had been extremely hot, and she thought she'd die of heat exhaustion. Over the week of marching up and down Rusk Street, she'd kept a sharp eye out for the pregnant girl Leah but never caught a glimpse of her. The Three Deuces was doing a booming business though, since Brannock had started serving food.

Just as well that she hadn't seen Leah. Nothing could come of that situation.

Izzy had been strangely missing, and she prayed the kid was all right. Maybe he'd moved over to a different, more profitable street. She wished he'd let her help make things easier.

At night, she wrote her articles for the paper, and Pemberton had liked them. In fact, he pressed her to find other areas where reform was needed. She'd wanted to yell that it was all around them in every section of the city, but she stayed silent and nodded, determined to turn over a new leaf.

On Saturday, Grace and her group ended up outside the Three Deuces, which for some odd reason hadn't opened its doors. Twilight fell over them, and all the women left except for Grace. She couldn't have said why she stayed. Something just seemed to glue her feet in place.

She was deep in thought when Brannock burst from the saloon, his eyes wild, hands in his dark hair. "Grace! Quick, I need help."

Panic gripped her. "What is it? Is someone shot?"

He grabbed her arm. "You'll do. Come with me."

"Where?"

No answer. He pulled her through the saloon and up the stairs toward yells and heavy moaning. They burst into a bedroom where the young girl named Leah writhed.

"Help her!" Brannock ordered.

"Hey, I'm no doctor. Not a midwife, either." Panic raced through her. "Go get someone."

"I did!" he yelled. "You're it."

Oh dear Lord! Her thoughts whirled so fast, she had to grab on to the footboard. Although growing up on a ranch had taught her a little, Grace could almost put all she knew about birthing into a thimble. The naked truth was she had no real experience in midwifery save for helping her mother with her last one. However, no one had to tell her the baby was coming, and she was the only person the young girl had.

Grace quickly moved to the bed, rolling up her sleeves. "Hi, Leah, remember me? I'm Grace."

Leah grabbed her hand. "I don't know what to do!"

"Then it's lucky for you that I do," Grace fibbed. "Just relax, dear. Take deep, even breaths and let your body do the work." Though furious at Brannock for putting the girl in this situation, Grace set that aside for now. Compassion for Leah took precedent. She laid her hand on the girl's perspiring forehead. "You're going to be fine. Just fine."

She turned to Brannock and spoke through gritted teeth. "Go try to get a midwife again. There has to be someone in this town."

He pinched the bridge of his nose, calming down a little. "Everyone I spoke to is unavailable. There is no one but you."

Grace glanced at Leah's worried face. "I see. We'll need a pan of water and clean cloths. Can you get them while I check on the position of the baby? Oh, and bring some water for Leah to drink."

She felt like asking for a stiff shot of whiskey but thought better of it.

Breathing heavily, he pulled her aside. "Don't you let anything happen to her."

Anger that she could barely control flared to life. "Or what? Are you threatening me? Do you really want to do that right now?"

He ran a hand across his bloodshot eyes. "Just do your best. That's all I ask."

"I always do." She placed a hand on his arm and softened her voice. "I don't want anyone to die today, most of all Leah or this baby. Now go get me that water."

When he turned for the door, Leah cried, "Don't leave me, Deacon! You promised."

Wrestling with conflicted feelings, Grace followed his tall figure as he went to Leah, sat on the side of the bed, and tenderly pulled her swollen body close. She couldn't look away from his caring touch and the sound of his soft assurances. His gentleness surprised her, but not as much as how well he played the part of a devoted husband. She'd never expected that of the man. He must really love her.

His deep voice filled the room as he brushed damp tendrils of hair from Leah's small face. "I'm not leaving, sweetheart. I'm going for water, and I'll be right back. Listen to Grace and try to stay calm."

At Leah's nod, he kissed her forehead and left.

"Now, let's see what we have going on." Grace bustled to the bed and pressed around on the girl's belly, feeling the size of the baby. "It's in perfect position," she announced with a smile. "Do you mind if I raise your gown and determine how far we are?"

"I don't mind." Leah forced a smile. "I'm kind of glad Deacon left for this part."

That was a rather odd thing to say about a husband. Still, Grace knew some couples went throughout their marriage not seeing each other naked. Given Leah's age, she was probably shy about such things.

"Have you been married long?"

"You have it wrong. We're not married, ma'am."

That was far worse, but not a total surprise. In fact, Grace should've known the louse would want the milk without buying the cow.

The child had just barely started the process. This birth would take a while.

She patted the poor girl's hand. "Maybe he'll come around."

"No, ma'am. He wants no part of matrimony." A strong contraction hit, and Leah gripped Grace's hand, releasing a loud cry. "It hurts! Mama! Mama!"

After the contraction passed, Grace covered her patient. "Where is your mother, if you don't mind me asking? If she's nearby, I could send for her."

Tears filled Leah's brown eyes. "She's dead. I have no family other than one old aunt in Atlanta."

"I'm very sorry. You need to have someone with you."

"I have Deacon, and that's enough."

Grace's thoughts went to her mother. Lara had been a Boone before she married Houston, and from all accounts, very beautiful, except for the long scar that covered the length of one side of her face. Though only a thin white line now, it must've once been gruesome. Her mother had never spoken about it and changed the subject each time Grace had broached the subject. Had Yuma Blackstone done that to her? Was that what the robber had meant?

The door opened, and Brannock stepped inside, a bowl under his arm, a pitcher of water in hand.

Relieving him of the items, she shot him a black look of disgust. Her voice in a whisper, she turned her wrath on him. "How dare you take advantage of such a young girl! You don't even have the decency to marry her. What about your child? Will you even acknowledge it, give it your name, or let it go through life a bastard?"

Flames shot from his stormy gray eyes. "Stop right there. I don't know what it is you're thinking, but you got it all wrong, princess."

"Then you won't mind explaining your relation to Leah?" she whispered furiously.

He stepped closer, his granite face only inches from hers. "I'm protecting her."

If she hadn't been so furious, she might've been terrified of him. "Is that what you call it these days?"

"I'm saving her from her husband and his deadly rages," he grated. "Leah is just a friend. Nothing more."

"Deacon, I'm scared." Leah descended into the throes of another contraction, writhing and twisting on the bed.

He hurried to her and took her hand. "I'm right here. Just like I promised."

"I can't stand this horrible pain. It hurts really bad."

Was it true that Brannock really was protecting the girl? Had Grace only seen what she'd wanted? With the absence of other women in the living quarters, maybe the man spoke the truth.

Grace poured water into the bowl and wet the cloth. "Leah, just think about your baby and how holding it will bring such joy." She placed the cloth on the girl's forehead.

Leah glanced up at Brannock. "You are my family, aren't you?"

"Yes, we're family."

Though Grace had tried to act the professional to keep the girl from panicking, it suddenly struck her how little she knew. Two lives were in her hands, and the enormity of the situation held her in its grip. She tried to remember things the ranch women had done to help a birth along. *Think*. Her mind couldn't settle long enough to remember.

Brannock poured some water into the glass, handing it to Leah. He turned to Grace. "Shouldn't we be doing something?"

Just then, the fog in her brain cleared. "Get her out of bed, and we'll take turns walking her. That should help. Leah, when you have a contraction, lean over the footboard until it passes."

They walked Leah for hours it seemed, and it did appear to speed things along a bit. Grace and Brannock took catnaps in a chair through most of the long night.

Finally, in the wee hours of dawn, the babe made an appearance.

"You have a son, Leah." Grace tied off the cord, wiped the babe clean, then laid him in his young mother's arms.

"My beautiful little boy." Leah gave her son a weak smile. "I've waited a long time for you," she whispered, touching his face with her fingertips. "Isn't he pretty, Deacon?"

"He certainly is."

Apparent emotion made his voice raspy, and Grace noticed a sparkle of wetness in his eyes. A knock came at the door, and she opened it to see the bartender carrying a tray.

"My contribution," he said. "I thought you could both use some coffee, and Miss Leah a cup of chamomile tea, but I won't come in if it's a bad time."

"Nonsense. Come on in." Grace took a cup from which steam was rising. "I could kiss you."

Harry turned three shades of red.

"She didn't mean it literally." Brannock reached around Grace for the second cup, took a sip before setting it down and carrying the hot tea to Leah.

"We have a boy, Harry." Leah held up the baby. "He's pretty."

Harry grinned. "That's real nice, little lady. You did good. What are you gonna name him?"

"I don't know." Leah sipped on the tea and glanced at Brannock. "I don't want him to carry his father's name. Do I have to?"

The father must be a brute. Clearly, Leah wanted no part of him.

Grace cleared her throat and was the first to reply. "No. He can be whatever name you want."

"Absolutely." Brannock touched the baby's cheek with a fingertip. "A different last name will make it harder for Seth to find him. What was your mother's maiden name?"

"Madrid." Leah touched his hand. "I'd like to name him after you, Deacon. You've helped me so much."

"I'm flattered, but name him something else. Please."

"Maybe I'll name him after my father—Johnny. And I won't let anyone call him John. It'll be Johnny." She blinked back tears.

Grace didn't point out that it sounded like an outlaw name. "I like Johnny Madrid."

"It has a nice ring to it." Harry beamed. The smell of scorched bacon drifted up the stairs. "I'm burning breakfast." The slender man took off out the door and clattered down the stairs.

"That settles his name." Leah sighed happily and rested against the pillows Brannock had fluffed behind her. "Grace, I can't thank you enough for everything."

"Just settle my curiosity. How did you wind up here with Brannock? I formed all sorts of wrong ideas."

Brannock snorted. "I'll say."

Grace angled her head to search his handsome face. Was she also wrong to wonder who he really was and what he was hiding?

Leah told her how Deacon kept Seth Pickford from beating her to death, giving her a safe place to hide, and Grace felt like a fool. "I'm so sorry. I owe you both an apology."

"I didn't exactly help," he admitted, finishing off his cup of coffee. "I should've set you straight from the start, but I tend to guard things I consider my business with a heavy hand."

Grace collected the empty cups. "I'll take these downstairs and leave them on my way out. I have to be going."

"Will you come by later?" An expectant look crossed Leah's features.

"I think I can do that. Until later, then." Grace had a hard time pulling her gaze from Brannock. *He isn't married.* The words kept repeating in her head, and she feared she wore a silly grin.

The ends of his dark hair hugged his thick neck above the collarless shirt. A look she'd never seen before simmered in his eyes, sent heat rising up her neck, and she almost dropped the cups.

He got to his feet. "I'll see you out."

Her skirt swished against his pant legs as they moved down the stairs, and she thrilled at the sound. At the bottom, he took the empty cups and set them on a small table.

"A truce is in order, don't you think, Grace?"

"A truce? About? I haven't changed my position. I still think selling liquor is wrong."

"So it's to be that way, is it? I'm happy to keep locking horns with you." His voice was quiet. He slowly moved closer until mere inches away, so near she could hardly breathe. "I was talking about not being enemies anymore."

"Oh. Are you willing to be friends?" Why was she so breathless, for God's sake?

Brannock brushed the pad of his thumb across her cheek. Awareness rippled inside Grace, and she couldn't have tingled more if lightning had struck her.

"Hell, I might be asking to get swatted, but I'd sure like to kiss you."

The blood in Grace's veins raced at Brannock's quiet statement. She tilted her head in invitation and leaned toward him, eyes lowered, her heart hammering. He stood at least a foot taller and seemed like a giant tree when he placed a large hand at the small of her back. The touch of his lips to hers set her heart thundering against her ribs, and the faint scent of shaving soap floated around her like autumn leaves after the first frost.

She'd been kissed by a lot of boys and a few men, but none even remotely resembled this rugged, gray-eyed saloon owner who'd taken in a terrified girl and given her a safe place to hide.

Grace slipped her hand around Deacon Brannock's neck, wound her fingers in his hair, and prayed he wouldn't end the kiss and halt the delicious sizzle dancing between them.

For once, she had no intention of hurrying. Her job, the world, and sleep could wait.

Thirteen

THE DIM LIGHT IN THE SALOON SOFTENED GRACE'S PRETTY face. The light wisp of her breath feathered across his cheek and left Deacon with a tenuous hold on his self-control.

He tightened his arms around her, wondering what just happened. He had no idea what he was doing. For the first time in a long while, he didn't stop to consider the implications—he just followed his heart. Grace was the most irritating and difficult woman to understand, just like that damn mustang Diablo that still wouldn't let him in the pen. But there the similarity ended. One minute she was fighting like a wildcat, and the next was as soft as a kitten with its claws pulled in.

But he loved kissing her. There was no mistaking that.

The clean scent of her hair drove him to distraction. The strong florals of other women were all wrong for Grace. She parted her luscious mouth, and he slipped his tongue inside. The tangy sweetness of the kiss that reminded him of the unforgettable taste of summer peaches did nothing to dampen his desire. He moved a hand to her slender throat and rested it just beneath her jaw. The soft curves of her body pressed against him like the whisper of night, and he wanted to wrap his arms around her and never let her go. God, he'd missed this. It had been so long since he'd held a woman in his arms. Grace was soft, inviting, and he had trouble keeping his thoughts off more than a kiss.

She moved back a little and broke the kiss. "Goodness, Brannock, you sure know how to give a girl a sendoff!"

He studied her for a long moment, his eyes searching the

lines of her face before letting his mouth curve in a half smile. "Complaining so soon, princess?"

"Just wondering if being friends has gone to your head." She patted his arm. "Birthing business seems to have a strange effect on you."

"Never." He snorted. "I like sparring with you, Grace. You always improve my game."

Her slow grin did funny things to him, especially when kiss-swollen lips framed it.

"Me too. I can't sharpen my vocabulary without practice." The teasing glint in Grace's blue eyes faded, and she chewed her lip as her voice turned serious. "Who are you, Brannock?"

A jolt ran through him. How could she know about the fake name? Or was she only fishing? He recovered quickly and barked a laugh, determined to make light of the question and maybe throw her off the scent. "I believe you know that answer. My name has been well established. Is this some kind of game? Who is anyone? Who are you?"

"I'm… Forget I asked." She turned to go, then swung back around. "I was wondering…have you seen Izzy lately?"

"Come to think of it, I haven't." And it was rather odd. He should check on the boy.

"Does he have anyone who looks after him?"

"The kid has no one who gives a damn that I've noticed. Why the interest?" He wondered when Grace had taken such a shine to Izzy.

She shrugged. "I just care about him. Same as I would for any orphan. My heart goes out to youngsters alone on the streets. It's not right."

"I agree. I'll do some checking around and see what I can find," Deacon promised.

"Thanks." She moved toward the door and the early-morning sunshine.

"Leah will need checking on. You'll come back?" He held the door, hoping he didn't sound too pathetic. Truth was, the competent woman was growing on him. And Leah needed female companionship. Yes, he wasn't above using Leah.

"I'll return tonight to see how she's doing."

"She'll be pleased. Goodbye, princess."

Grace nodded and picked up her discarded sign from where she'd thrown it last evening. His gaze followed her shapely figure as she made her way down the street, dodging horses and horseless carriages. Just because he'd kissed her didn't mean he'd gone over to her side.

❧

Troubled by Izzy's disappearance, Deacon strode the length of Rusk Street that afternoon, asking every saloon owner and bartender if they'd seen the boy. Although he hadn't wanted to worry Grace, he admitted Izzy's absence had caused great concern. It wasn't like the kid to stop coming around. Not at all.

But no one had seen the ten-year-old. Deacon next went to the boardwalk, under which the kid slept. Although the ragged blankets, the red wagon, and a few belongings were there, Izzy wasn't.

A street-toughened boy approached him. "You looking for Izzy, mister?"

"I am. Have you seen him?"

The youngster glanced left then right. "Naw, I think a haint must've got him."

"Who?"

"A haint. They's lots of 'em around here. Ain't you scared?" The boy licked his bottom lip, his eyes still darting first one direction then another. "Sometimes I hear 'em prowlin' the streets, looking for kids."

Deacon knelt to get on eye level. "I don't believe in ghosts.

There's lots of other things scarier than that." Like evil men who hurt for the sheer fun of it. Seth Pickford for one.

"Haints took my ma and pa. I went to sleep in the loft, and when I woke up, they was dead. Bad spirits stole the breath right out of 'em."

The kid sure had a fanciful imagination "Why do you think it was haints?"

"My grandpa once told me that they was thick in the woods and never to go there. He said they'd steal my breath. Then one morning they got him," whispered the boy.

Deacon hid a smile and forced a serious tone to his voice. "You don't say?"

"I do, mister. I surely do. They took my friend Davey too," the youngster whispered as though he'd be next if he said it too loud. "He didn't have no fam'ly either."

"How come you didn't get taken?"

"I hid."

Could it be possible people were snatching up kids off the street? With all the talk of cleaning up the city, something with the street urchins could be happening. Maybe they'd scooped up Izzy and put him in a home. If so, he'd welcome that. Izzy was becoming old before his time.

Deacon stood. "You gotta name?"

"Simon."

"I'm Deacon Brannock." Deacon reached into his pocket and pulled out a few coins, handing them to the kid. "Get yourself something to eat. Come find me at the Three Deuces if you happen to see anything. I'll make it worthwhile."

"Thanks, mister." The boy raced down the street, dodging a horse and rider.

Deacon wanted to yell a warning to watch out for haints, but that would've been cruel. Clearly, the grandpa had invented the story to keep Simon from wandering too far from home, but fear wasn't healthy and could follow the boy all his life.

His thoughts on where Izzy had gone, Deacon returned to the saloon to help Harry, who was eyeballs-deep in tamales under Leah's watchful eye. The food wrapped in corn husks hardly resembled the ones she'd made. Some had too much stuffing and others not enough, and all were lumpy.

"Harry, try to use the same amount, like I showed you." Leah reached around him to remove a portion of the bulging mess.

"I'm a bartender, not a blasted cook," the ponytailed man grumbled.

Leah waved him aside. "Then hold the baby, and I'll take over."

Deacon wondered if this would go any better. Harry was all thumbs and almost dropped the little bundle. "Stop," he ordered. "It doesn't matter if we have any to serve the men. This is a saloon, not a café, for God's sake."

Leah kept working. "I'm almost finished with this batch. You'll be short, but you'll have some at least to entice your patrons with."

"You should be in bed, not in this kitchen." Deacon took the baby, and Harry gave him a smile of gratitude. Deacon glanced down into Johnny's tiny, sleeping face and wondered what kind of man he'd grow up to be. If he had any say in the raising, the boy would respect his elders, love his mother, and be kind to others.

"I can't lay up in bed when all this needs doing." Leah reached for another package of dried corn husks. "I'm perfectly able, and I don't have much left."

"Hmpf!" But he knew better than to scold too much. He turned the conversation to Izzy and told the bartender what the kid Simon had said. "Harry, did you ever believe in haints?"

"Heck, I never stopped." Harry rubbed his scruffy face. "I pity the little feller, though. Fear sure is hard to put to rest."

"I think all of us struggle at one time or another," Deacon said. He didn't mention how often it used to visit in the dead of night. Or the times he'd lain awake, praying for the dawn.

And when fear mixed with superstition, it became twice as bad.

Leah turned from her task, tears bubbling in her eyes. "Poor Izzy. Do you think he's all right, Deacon? I can't stand the thought of someone being mean to him."

"I wish I knew."

Her lip quivered. "Can you report him missing?"

"Fort Worth probably has hundreds of urchins, Leah. Who'll bother to look for just one?" No, this job was for him. Only one problem—Seth Pickford. Deacon needed somewhere safe to put Leah and the baby for the time being while he became the hunter.

A muscle in Deacon's jaw bunched. If anyone had stolen Izzy, they'd best run, because he was coming.

❧

Grace slept for a while in the quiet of an empty house, then rose about midmorning. No matter what she found to do, she felt Deacon's full lips, his warm breath mingling with hers like the hot, jagged lightning of a summer storm. She'd known he would be a good kisser but never thought he'd take the step.

Or her either, for that matter.

Kissing was a fine art in her opinion. Some were sloppy, some harsh as though the kisser could force the kissee to feel something, and still others' lips floated down like a downy feather that whispered to a girl's heart. Brannock fit in that last category. Although he wasn't the first she'd tasted, he seemed somewhat of an expert in the matter.

Now that he'd kissed her, she wanted him to do it again. But would they ever have another chance? She frowned. Maybe he was used to women who went around kissing all the time.

She'd check on Leah later that afternoon, happy to have an excuse to return. Who knew what would happen? Each time she and Brannock got together, they usually left with cross words. The kiss had been quite different and startling.

After a quick meal, she got out her journal and wrote down the name "Yuma Blackstone" and stared at it for a long moment. Who was he? An acquaintance of her mother's?

A change of clothes put her in an excellent frame of mind. Grabbing her notebook, she set off for the paper. Pemberton was out, but Ned Cross was at his desk.

He glanced up at her knock. "Come in."

"Do you have a minute, Mr. Cross?"

"Make it short."

Where had the friendlier man gone? This version of him intimidated her.

"Are you still intent on investigating Brannock?" he asked.

Was she? The image of him kissing her that morning popped into her head. Where exactly did she stand on that subject? She didn't know what she thought about him, to be frank. She'd witnessed a side of him she'd never seen, and it hadn't been for her benefit. He hadn't faked that tenderness and sincerity with Leah.

"I'm not sure, but I'm here on another matter, something of a personal nature, and I want to pick your brain." She went inside and took a seat in the only chair that wasn't piled high with papers and files. "I have a question. Have you ever heard of Yuma Blackstone?"

"The killer that struck fear in the hearts of everyone in the state?"

Grace's mouth dried. A killer? Good Lord! "Yes, that must be him."

Had he tried taking her mother's life? The scar marring her face suggested as much.

"The tally I saw numbered just shy of two dozen white, Mexican, and Native American victims. What does this have to do with you, Miss Sam?"

Hearing him address her that way took her off guard. Sometimes she heard it so seldom, she forgot the newspaper name she'd taken.

"A piece of memory has come to haunt me, Mr. Cross. I want to see what I can find in our files here."

Ned Cross propped his elbows on his desk. "Mind if I ask what kind of memory?"

"Something that happened to me when I was ten that won't let me rest." Grace smoothed her skirt, wondering if coming was a good idea. Everyone involved was dead, so maybe it was best to leave it alone; still, her commitment to the truth wouldn't let her.

Something said this was important to her personally. She inhaled sharply and told Ned Cross about her abduction. "Before the robber died, he yelled out, 'Tell her about Yuma Blackstone and what he did to her mother!' Then he said that I deserved to hear the truth. Only I don't know what that meant, and I hope to find out."

Cross was silent for a long moment, then he leaned his chair back and folded his hands across his stomach. "The man liked to carve his victims up—the face, arms, body. Does your mother bear any scars?"

Grace nodded. "She has a scar running the length of one side of her face. My grandpa said it used to be frightening. Over the years of keeping the skin moist, it's a thin, white line now."

"Have you asked her about it?"

"Yes, only to have her change the subject. That's why I'm trying to dig it up on my own."

"I see." Cross sat up. "You'll find some things in the files, but probably not as much as you need. Do you ever have nightmares about being abducted?"

"I used to, but not much anymore."

"That made national news. I didn't realize you were the lost child." He scribbled some dates on a scrap of paper. "You can begin when Blackstone hung out here for a time. The outlaw was always in trouble. Then, you might check the year of his death, when he finally met his end."

She took the list Cross handed her and stood. "Thank you for all your help." Grace went out, anxious to get started.

"Miss Sam?" Cross's face was solemn, his mouth in a tight line.

"Yes, sir?"

"Expect nightmares when you read about Blackstone. Not for the faint of heart."

Grace nodded, hurrying down the hall to the archives room, but paused at the door. Maybe she should leave it alone. Would finding out the truth change her life? The answer was no. Nothing would change the fact that she was a Legend, that her legacy was safe, and that Houston and Lara were most definitely her parents.

Even so, she couldn't turn away.

She'd always been curious about her mother's scar, and this was a chance to perhaps learn what had happened and why her mother could never speak of it.

The first dates Cross had written down were some time before her father's marriage to her mother. Blackstone had fallen in with Fort Worth's sheriff Big Jim Courtright, and from the accounts, Blackstone had done his best to take over Hell's Half Acre. Some had thought the killer had done some nasty work for the sheriff, and chances were, he had.

Yuma had racked up at least ten deaths by his gun during that time and sliced up the faces of women all up and down Rusk Street. He was arrested numerous times, never charged, and was finally run out of town.

More articles after that had detailed much the same in nearby towns. Not one mentioned Grace's mother. The picture she got of the man was that he operated as he wished and was brought up on charges with little or no time served.

"Bully," Grace spat. "You should've gone to prison."

Her heart hurt to think of her sweet, beautiful mother attacked and left horribly disfigured. She couldn't prove that Blackstone had done it, just had a hunch, and given what the bank robber had said, a pretty solid one at that.

She moved on to the year of the man's death. A reporter in Dodge City had written it and quoted her father and some of the drovers. Houston told of killing Yuma after he kept attacking.

A stillness came over her. Her father had killed him? She'd never known.

Further reading had just one mention of her mother and saying she and her baby had been lucky to survive.

The date read September 11, 1877. She'd turned a year old in June that year.

The skin on her neck pricked. *Her parents married in May 1877.* Something wasn't adding up.

Workers began to drift by the door, and the clock chimed five. Grace jotted notes, put the files away, and left. Had Houston and Lara been acquainted before they married? But no, Stoker told her they'd never seen each other before the wedding. What had she deserved to know? The question haunted her. Was Houston her father?

Of course, he was! Maybe Stoker was wrong. After all, he was old. How good was his memory? Her father and mother had relations before the wedding. That was plain and simple.

She'd have to make a trip home to the Lone Star. For someone who hadn't wanted to go, she was now impatient to get back.

A slice of memory cut through Grace's head, and she sagged against the wall.

The robber Carl covered her with a thin blanket against the night breeze. "Don't be scared. I ain't gonna hurt you, and I ain't gonna let these others hurt you either. I've waited a long time to meet you."

Who was Carl? Was she supposed to know him? Why couldn't she remember all of it instead bits and pieces?

Inhaling a shuddering breath, she took a minute to clear her head, then pushed out the *Fort Worth Gazette's* doors. Deacon Brannock stood in the evening shadows.

He hurried to her. "I wanted to catch you."

Shock rippled through her. "What are you doing here?" No one knew about her newspaper job, not even her own brother. Darn it!

"I sort of followed you. You can be mad later. Leah is hurting bad and needs you."

Fourteen

"WHAT'S WRONG?" GRACE GRIPPED HIS ARM. "SPEAK."

"She's bleeding and in pain." Brannock stared at her through wild eyes. "I don't know what to do."

Why did he assume she had expertise in these matters, for God's sake?

She walked faster. "Did you send for the doctor?"

"Couldn't find one willing to come. Doctors tend to stay clear of my part of town. You're Leah's last hope. My last hope."

Defeat in his voice tugged at her. "Try not to worry. Sometimes this is normal."

As she tried to put a brave face on for him, her memory flew to one instance on the ranch that involved a new mother who'd bled to death. She'd always thought it extremely sad that the woman never got to hold her beautiful baby girl. And that the child never knew her mother. Childbirth was often plagued with problems, but she didn't voice any of those concerns to him.

They remained silent the rest of the way. Harry met them at the door and took her light jacket. "I'm glad you came, Miss Grace."

"Is there any change?" She glanced up the stairs from where loud moaning came.

Harry wrung his hands. "No, ma'am."

Leaving the men downstairs, Grace hurried up to the second floor. Leah was holding her stomach and lying in a blood-soaked mess. The baby lay in a crib, thank goodness. "Try not to worry, Leah. This might be nothing."

Leah grabbed her hand. "It hurts and then this blood…" Her voice trailed off.

"Let's get you cleaned up so I can see." She went out and hollered for Brannock to fetch water and cloths. While she waited, Grace found a clean gown and helped the young mother to a chair in which she'd put a thick blanket. "Rest here while I strip your bed."

In no time, Grace got the girl cleaned up and into the fresh gown. Brannock waited outside the room, ready to lend a hand should Grace require his help.

After an examination that told Grace very little, since she lacked expertise in such matters, she smiled confidently at Leah and said the only thing she could. "You're going to be all right. How is your pain?"

"It's subsiding. So you think I'm in no danger?"

"I'm fairly certain. Everything seems normal, and the blood flow is almost stopped."

"Thank God," Brannock murmured, suddenly beside the bed. He took Leah's hand.

Grace hadn't heard him and didn't know when he'd entered the room. He stood so close that his sleeve brushed against her, and she noticed the frayed cuff and a patch near his elbow. She'd assumed he made a lot of money selling whiskey, but if he did, he could afford better.

She gathered the sheets and other soiled items and headed toward the stairs.

Brannock stopped her. "I'll take those."

She shook her head. "I already have them. If you don't have anyone to wash them, I'll be happy to do it."

He stiffened and gave her a cold look. "We can manage to do our own laundry."

"I only want to help, but since it's not appreciated—" She thrust her load at him. "Don't bother finding me again if you have any other medical problems. You're welcome, by the way."

"I didn't mean it like that."

"You know, maybe me coming wasn't a good idea. Goodbye, Brannock." She hurried down the stairs.

"Wait!"

Grace kept marching toward the back door. Harry grinned from behind the long bar but made no move to stop her.

Brannock let out a shrill whistle that nearly burst her eardrums. "Stop." He grabbed her arm. "I can't let you leave mad."

Coming to a halt, she whirled to stare at the man who made her so crazy. "Why do we always keep doing this?"

"I don't know." He laid the soiled bedding aside and ran a hand through his dark hair. "Stupid pride, I guess. I don't want a woman taking care of things for me."

If not for the crooked grin that melted her heart, she would've smacked him good. She couldn't hold back a laugh. "You sound pitiful. I'm not about to rob you of your male pride."

"Forgive me? I promise to be good."

For probably about as long as a snowstorm in the Sahara.

"You're a maddening, two-bit scoundrel, cowboy." She became aware of how close he stood, his broad chest so near, and found herself struggling to take in air. Her racing pulse was even harder to control. Why did he have to make her furious one second and send this heat inching up her back the very next?

Harry shoved a tea tray between them. "Truce?"

Grace kissed the bartender's cheek. "Thanks, Harry. Just what I needed."

"I thought so." Harry's eyes twinkled. "If you want to tie into the boss, I'll hold him down."

"A great idea. Thanks." Grace took the tray and carried it into the small kitchen area. "Sit down, Brannock. We're going to talk."

"I take sugar with my tea." He pulled out a chair for her and sat in the other.

She added two cubes to his and handed it to him. "Just because

I offer to do certain things, it's not because I want to take over your life. It's only an offer. Got that?"

"Yes, ma'am."

"Secondly, I am not a doctor. I suggest you find a good one, since you seem to need a man of medicine frequently."

He nodded, rubbing his arm as though it pained him. "Anything else?"

Grace studied his rugged, dark features over the rim of her teacup. "Forget you saw me at the newspaper."

His leg brushed hers under the table, much too lazily for it to be accidental. "Now, princess, how can I do that when it clearly happened?" He glanced down at the table, then back up. "Do I get to ask why?"

"It's personal."

"I see." His voice tightened, the slow drawl gone. "You appear to be calling all the shots here—in *my* place of business, I might add."

She let out a long exhale and knew she had to give him something. "It could hurt people I love if they find out. I don't intend to let that happen."

"Because they think you're behaving yourself, and your articles are about them, right?"

Hell and damnation! He'd hit the nail on the head. Heat rose to her face. She had to change the subject. "I think I hear Leah. Maybe she's hungry."

"Nice try. I read the articles about the Lone Star Ranch and your family. I'm guessing you're"—he hesitated, lifting an eyebrow—"Sam Valentine?"

Damn him. Now what? Confessing didn't hold much appeal. The silence dragged. Brannock hadn't touched his tea, which had probably turned cold.

Finally, Harry poked his head in the door, saving her from answering. The bartender grinned. "It's gotten awfully quiet in here, but I don't see any blood."

Grace got to her feet. "You're a dear man, Harry. I have to be running along."

"I'll walk you to the streetlights." Brannock spoke low to Harry, then turned stiffly to her. "That is nonnegotiable, princess."

"Fine." She moved to the back door and stepped out into the growing darkness. Frankly, she was glad he'd insisted. Besides, fighting or not, there was something about being with Brannock, surrounded by the night that tucked around them. It was like they were alone in their own private universe for just a little while. She slid her arm through his elbow, and they walked along.

"Why do we always fight?" She glanced up at his stony profile shaded by the brim of his hat. "No matter how things go, we seem to end up mad at each other before we part ways."

"I could point out that you always expect to be right and always expect me to give in to you." When she opened her mouth to argue, he quickly added, "But that would only start another argument, and I'm much too tired."

Grace laughed. "Is that right? Know what I think? We're like oil and water."

"I suspect you're right."

She noticed how he kept scanning the darkness for trouble. For Leah's husband? Did Deacon Brannock ever really relax?

Maybe he had things in his past equally as bad—or worse—than hers. Grandpa Stoker was fond of saying that you never really know someone until you drive cattle together and spend time on the ground under the stars. Brannock might have good reason to be the way he was and choose to live in the roughest part of Fort Worth with the town's filth.

Her thoughts went to the newspaper and her mother. "Brannock, did you ever know a man called Yuma Blackstone?"

His steps slowed. She thought he must've not heard her until he muttered, "Might've."

Hearing the hated name sent Deacon back to one of the dingy, airless rooms in Miss Sally's house of ill repute. He'd been six years old, and his mother made him hide under the bed as she did each time a customer knocked. But this one night, he'd peeked out at a large man with yellow hair, wearing a thin mustache.

When the customer bent down to take off his boots, he saw Deacon. Growling like some crazed animal, the man hauled his scrawny body out by the neck. Deacon still remembered the fear that paralyzed him.

His mother, Iris Reno, called him Yuma Blackstone and begged him not to hurt her boy. Yuma backhanded Iris and sent her tumbling across the room, then the man took out a knife and turned his attention on Deacon.

"Don't hurt him! He's just a boy!" his mother had screamed. "I'll take him somewhere."

"Fine. Lock him outside," Yuma had ordered.

Deacon closed his eyes, remembering the long, frigid night in the dead of winter, no coat, no shoes, no blanket, while his mother entertained the yellow-haired devil who liked to flash his knife. Iris hadn't fared any better than Deacon. Miss Sally had kicked them out because Iris had been in such rough shape and unable to work. It'd taken a month or more for her to heal.

And that was the first time he'd hated anyone bad enough to kill.

"What's wrong, Brannock?" Grace gently rubbed his back and jerked him from the nightmare.

His eyes flew open, and he blinked hard. "Nothing."

"Stop. You were shaking and in the grip of something. Just be honest for once."

He released a long breath, wishing she'd drop it. "Only a memory. Let's get you to the safer part of town."

They resumed their walk.

"Why did you ask about Blackstone?" Had Grace encountered him also?

She told him about her abduction and what little she knew of Yuma Blackstone. "I had forgotten the words that abductor yelled at my father until they stormed back from the blue recently. Now, I can't seem to think of anything else. I have to find out what he meant and why he said I deserve to know what Yuma did to my mother. I can't let it rest. There's something... I feel this is important. Am I wrong to want to know?"

"No. It might affect your life."

"That makes me feel better." She gave a tense laugh. "Maybe I'm not too crazy."

"Were you terrified when those bank robbers took you?"

Grace glanced up. "Not at first. I thought I could demand they release me, and they would." She laughed. "Up to then, that's how it was on the ranch. Everyone spoiled me pretty bad."

"I'm shocked! Not you! No."

"Stop the mock horror." She playfully slapped his arm.

"What happened when the robbers didn't bow to your demands?" For all his teasing, he knew she must've had a rude awakening. At ten years old, she'd still been a kid.

A frightened one.

"I overheard them discussing ways to kill me and knew I was in the deepest trouble of my life. Two of them were mean and hit me, especially when they discovered I'd been leaving scraps of my dress along the trail. That's when I knew my father had best get there fast."

The scene played out in Deacon's mind. He saw the little girl Grace had been. The robbers' hands on her. Tears running down her face. Dirty after days of riding.

Yeah, Houston would've known red-hot rage.

"I assume he made it." Deacon already knew how the rancher's size pretty well put the fear of God in everyone, so he could imagine the robbers' panic to see him coming at them. Then getting an eyeful of Grace's condition must've multiplied the kind of anger running rampant inside Houston.

Oh yeah. That much was sure.

Grace half turned. "I'm going to have to leave for a few days. My father is insisting I come home for a short stay and now, when I get there, I need to ask around for more information on Blackstone. That's where I'll find answers to my questions."

"You'll find no answers here," he agreed.

A part of Deacon hated the thought of her leaving. The days would be empty. But he had to look out after Leah and Izzy. If Grace were here, she'd want—no, *insist* would be more accurate—on helping, and he didn't want her to spend more time in this dangerous part of town.

"How long will you be gone?"

"A week, maybe less. Will you miss me, cowboy?" she teased.

Careful or you'll reveal too much.

He laughed. "You mean like sleeping later without you ladies banging outside my window? And actually opening for business without fear of vandalism?"

"Oh, please," she said dryly, rolling her eyes.

They walked along in silence for a good block.

Deacon was the first to talk. His tone was serious. "I have a favor to ask. If you can't or don't want to, say the word, and I'll drop it."

"What is it? If I can help, I want to."

"Leah and the baby are not safe here. Pickford will find them eventually." Deacon stopped walking and rubbed his face. "Would it be too much to ask to take them to the Lone Star? Leah doesn't shirk from work, and she's smart. She won't make any trouble. All she wants is a chance to love and raise her child in peace."

Grace touched his arm. "Say no more. Of course, they can come. Mama will love taking Leah under her wing."

"Thank you."

Deacon put an arm around her waist and drew her closer, wishing he could tell her everything he held back. But the moment he did, he'd lose her friendship or whatever the hell this was. Maybe it was just finding a way to not be enemies, but for the first time in his life, he knew real hope.

Grace looked up at him with those shimmering blue eyes and leaned in, her head tilted. He lowered his mouth and devoured her moist lips. The depth of passion shook him. And for long moments, they seemed locked in a world that blotted out space and time.

He explored the recesses of her sweet mouth, his tongue thrusting, dancing with hers.

One hand drifted along the curves of her body, learning what drew whimpers for more. The kiss ended only when they ran out of air.

Deacon released her, studying her face. "I hadn't planned to do that. Sorry."

"I wasn't objecting." She took a half step back, a hand on her throat. "I will say you're full of surprises, saloon keep."

This woman who made him mad enough to fight a grizzly had more passion, more strength, more courage than any woman he knew. He stood watching the gentle sway of her hips as she walked toward her residence.

Yes, Grace Legend had all that and more.

❧

That night, he rode out to Will Bonner's. The moonlight shining on Diablo's black coat turned it a color Deacon had never seen before. The mustang stood in the center of the round pen, staring at him.

A screen door slammed, and a few moments later came Will's

voice. "I thought I heard someone ride up." Will ambled to the pen, took his place beside Deacon, and propped a foot on the rail. "What do you suppose that horse is thinking?"

Deacon chuckled. "Probably that he'd like to stomp my guts out and sling them all over this ranch."

They stood in silence for a several heartbeats.

"Why don't you turn him out, Will? Let him go back to his herd. He probably has a pretty little filly or two waiting for him."

"And beat you out of that money for taming him?"

"Money isn't everything, Will," Deacon answered quietly. "I won't miss what I never had."

Will turned to face him. "So you're giving up?"

"The choice is yours. I'll do whatever you want."

"Let's try a little longer. I gave up on Frances. Should've tried to put the will to live in her, but her illness exhausted me. In the end, it was a relief not to face her pain-filled eyes every day. I don't want to give up on Diablo too." Will glanced up at the sky. "Sure are a lot of stars out. Gets a man to thinking about things. Deacon, do you ever wonder about your dad? What kind of man he was?"

"That's a place I don't want to go. Best leave that alone."

"Guess you're right. Your mama and sister are gone." Will let out a long exhale. "See what I mean about the stars?"

"I wonder if banging my head against a stone wall, trying to make something from nothing is worth it. I'd kinda like to get on a horse and just take off riding and see where I wind up." But then he'd get to missing Grace and come right back. He was a hopeless case.

"I think every man has those yearnings one time or another." Will slapped at a mosquito. "You should come out, and we'll catch us a mess of catfish. Might be more satisfying than riding horseback across the country."

"Suppose you're right. A man can always find a measure of peace in dropping a hook in the water."

"How's the saloon business?" Will took cigarette makings from his pocket.

"I'm seeing a little more profit." He told his friend about Leah and her tamales. "I think she has something there, but she's leaving in a few days. I don't know who'll make 'em then."

"Can't you hire someone?"

"Can't afford it. Things are a little tight."

Diablo finally lowered his head and turned around to show Deacon his butt. He chuckled. The horse had a sense of humor. Nope, it wasn't time to quit yet.

The horse—and Deacon's life—had possibility.

Fifteen

GRACE KNEW SHE WAS PACKING TOO MUCH FOR HER TRIP. She'd only be gone for a week. Unable to help herself, she grabbed another dress and stuck it in. It was her grandfather's favorite.

Drawn by the bright morning sunlight, she went downstairs and out the back door. An old rusted wagon of her little sister's drew her. At the beginning of spring, Grace had turned the wagon into a flower bed, and now a mass of pink, purple, and yellow petunias spilled over the sides. The sight brought a smile and thoughts of Izzy.

She hadn't seen him since the day those big boys fought with him and stole his wagon. The kid's heartbreak of missing his mother had deeply touched her. If only he'd agreed to come live with her. Even for a while.

Except now, he seemed to be missing. Needing a walk, she went in for her derringer and took the street that led to the Acre. She'd look one last time before she left for the ranch.

The Three Deuces was silent, and the doors shut. It was early, though.

If ever there was a good time to come to this part of town, it was now. Most people in these establishments slept until noon at least. The exception seemed to be Deacon Brannock, and that was most unusual. Maybe he'd once worked as a cowboy and still kept the hours? Such things were ingrained in a true man of the land. It took no imagination to see him riding horseback across the range.

"Lady, would you like to buy one of my flowers?"

The question jarred her from the mysterious saloon owner.

She glanced down at a little boy about eight or so and a little girl even younger, both barefoot. They looked like siblings and probably were. The boy grasped a handful of limp crepe paper flowers. He looked at Grace with such hopeful eyes.

She offered a bright smile. "How pretty. How much are they?"

"Five cents each."

"My goodness, that's certainly a steal." Her attention swept to the little girl whose stomach growled. Who knows when they'd last eaten? Tears suddenly lurked behind her eyes and she had to look away for a moment and clear her throat. "I think I'll take them all."

She dug in her handbag for a dollar, far more than the flowers sold for, but any less wouldn't sit well. The boy stuffed the money in his pocket and gave her the flowers. "Who made these? Your mother?"

"Our big sister. She says no asking for a handout. We gotta give folks something."

"You know, my mother says the same thing. It's good business. Your mother must be very proud of you."

"Her died," the little girl mumbled.

The boy glanced up at Grace through his long hair. "Sissie takes care of us, and we help."

A girl that must've been around fifteen whistled from the corner and waved to the siblings. "We gotta go." The boy smiled, the first time since they'd approached Grace. "Thank you for buying our flowers."

"You've made me very happy." She watched them go as a sob built. It wasn't right. Not their situation and not Izzy's.

She wiped her eyes, determined to find him. Up the street and down she went, with no results. The red wagon was missing from the boardwalk where he stayed, so maybe he was delivering something or drumming up more business. She was about to give up when she spied him scurrying along, head down.

"Izzy?" she called. Her voice seemed to startle him. "Wait."

He hurried toward her, looking left and right. "Miss Grace, you ought not to be here."

"What's wrong? Are those boys bothering you again?"

"No, ma'am."

"Then who? I can see you're scared."

He led her behind some barrels against a building. "There's something bad going on down here."

"What? You can tell me."

"Kids are disappearin' and I don't know where they're going. Promise you'll stay away." He slid his arms around her waist, worry lining the small, freckled face looking up at her.

She caressed his hair and shoulders, yearning to take him home with her. To keep him safe. "I can't promise that. I go where I'm needed. Do you still have the paper with my address on it?"

Izzy nodded. "But I gotta lay low. Bye, Miss Grace."

She pulled him into a hug, dying a little inside at his thin body. "Be safe. I love you, Izzy."

The boy sniffed. "I love you, too, Miss Grace."

Before she could say more, he was gone, pulling his red wagon. Was someone really taking the kids off the street, or was it his overactive imagination?

Why hadn't she paid attention to this homeless problem before? Had she been too self-centered or just hadn't noticed? Maybe Brannock was right about her.

✎

Deacon went to Will's water barrel for a dipperful to quench his thirst. He'd arrived at the ranch before dawn and ate breakfast with the rancher, then started to work with Diablo.

The horse still tried to kill him when he entered the round pen, but this time Deacon was ready and clung to the top rail. Diablo didn't come as close as before, either because the last time had hurt him too, or maybe he'd taken a liking for Deacon. Now that was hilarious.

Diablo stood in the center of the pen, watching his every move. Eerie, the way he stared.

Deacon went to the little garden that was nearby and pulled up a carrot. He dangled it over the rail of the pen. "Want something tasty?"

The horse moved slowly, eyeing him suspiciously. Any sudden movement would send him running, so Deacon stayed still, praying the horse would begin to trust him. At last, Diablo stood close enough to get the treat, but instead of taking it, he just stared at Deacon.

"Come on, boy."

Ears pricked straight up, Diablo finally took the carrot in his mouth and retreated to eat it.

"See, that wasn't so bad, was it? I'm not the devil."

They seemed to be making progress. Encouraged, Deacon got back in the pen and stood still, watching the mustang's body language. The swishing tail indicated he was probably irritated. His raised back leg seemed a subtle threat. Deacon moved toward him, tempting Diablo with another carrot. The horse clearly wanted it, yet he wouldn't come to claim it. Finally, after a good ten minutes of caution, he came in and took the carrot from Deacon's hand.

"That's impressive" came Will's voice.

Deacon could see Will Bonner from his periphery. It didn't pay to take his eyes off Diablo though. "I can do a song-and-dance routine too if you'd like."

Will laughed. "Now that I'd pay some serious money to see."

Deacon climbed out. "Need something or just curious?"

"You hungry? It's almost noon."

"I can drink some coffee if you have it. But I have to get back for the lunch crowd. It's picking up, and Harry might need help." He gave the rancher a half smile. "Sorry."

"To be honest, I look for ways to keep you here longer." Will's quiet confession settled over Deacon. The man must be lonely. Too bad he didn't have sons.

"When are we gonna do some fishing?" Will asked as they walked to the house.

"You know, I was thinking about that. What if I come back out after lunch? We'd have two or three hours." Spending time with Will might help get rid of the demons for a little while. The rancher had his own brand of medicine for cleansing a soul.

Day after tomorrow, Leah and the baby would leave with Grace, and he wasn't sure how he'd deal with the emptiness she'd leave. Maybe he'd spend more time out here.

He held the door for Will and entered the kitchen where they'd had breakfast that morning. The explosion of dirty dishes was still as they'd left them. Mrs. Bonner would be clucking her tongue something fierce.

Will lit the stove. "Nothing's the same anymore. I guess that's why I try to hogtie you when you come out." He lifted the battered coffeepot and set it on the flame.

"You have the other ranch hands." Deacon wondered why they let Will get so lonely.

"I'm not close with any of them like I am with you." Will rubbed his bristly jaw. "Damn if I didn't remember to shave this morning."

Dark circles under Will's eyes said he wasn't sleeping either.

"Have a seat, son." Will's voice seemed strange, like it was far off.

When Deacon turned around, Will clutched his chest, all bent over. He rushed to get the rancher into a chair. Will's gray face scared him. "What's wrong? What can I do?"

Will groaned and seemed unable to focus his eyes. Deacon grabbed a glass and went to the kitchen pump. He held the water to Will's mouth. "Take a sip. Come on. Just a sip."

At last, he got some water into his friend, then he put an arm around him under his armpits and half-carried him to his bed. Deacon sat down to keep watch. Maybe he should get one of the ranch hands to go after the doc. Then it dawned on him that they were riding fence.

He started to get up when Will opened his eyes. "Glad you're still here."

"What happened? I want the truth."

"This ticker of mine goes haywire sometimes. Sorry." Will raised an arm and weakly brought it to his face.

"I'm glad I was here, or you'd be lying on the floor about now. I'm going for the doctor."

"Over my dead body."

"You need some medicine. Or something," Deacon insisted.

Will's eyes flashed and he managed to sit up. "I got a whole dad-blamed cabinet full of pills and such. Don't need any more to just sit there."

"You're supposed to be taking them, you stubborn fool."

"Ain't nothing in those pills that can cure a man of a mess of regret and a broken heart."

There was the crux of the problem, plain and simple. Deacon helped him up and back to the kitchen where nothing would do for Will but to have that cup of coffee.

Deacon left a little while later. As he went out the door, he glanced back at the man with a broken heart who'd given him the best gift of all—friendship. He was scared to leave. Who knew if Will would be alive when he came back?

Sometimes maybe all a man had to live for was another person, and when that was gone, there was nothing. Will Bonner was only half a man without Frances.

Deacon pondered that a moment and realized an empty life held no appeal. He wanted no part of that loneliness again. He had to have someone to live for. Leah and little Johnny for sure. Possibly Grace one day?

Grace was waiting when he returned to the saloon. "Where do you disappear to these days, Brannock? Harry wouldn't tell me a thing. He's good at keeping your secrets."

Irritation crossed his eyes. "No secret. I've been helping a friend."

"I don't mean to pry. Sorry. You just seem different somehow." Her gaze went to his boots and what was stuck to the soles. "Is that manure?"

"Can't a man have some privacy? Have you ever thought I don't want you to know everything?" He went behind the bar to wash his hands. "Why are you here?"

"I saw Izzy this morning. Brannock, he said kids are disappearing off the streets and he was terrified. He clung to me, crying. I don't know how to help him, and I hate to leave town with him like this." She put her hands to her mouth and tried to still her shaking.

"What else did he say?"

"That he had to lay low for a while and told me to stay away from this part of the city."

"Good advice. You should listen." He spoke to Harry as he came from the back room, then turned his attention back to her. "Don't worry. I'll find the boy and put him somewhere safe."

Grace ran around the counter and kissed his cheek. "Thank you."

"Don't mention it. Anyone that messes with the boy messes with me. I'll handle it."

She wouldn't want to ever cross Deacon Brannock. The encounter would be brutal.

Harry opened the doors and people streamed inside. Her fears calmed, Grace paused for a moment, her gaze on the man who filled her dreams. If only she didn't have to leave.

Sixteen

TWO DAYS LATER, A LITTLE PAST THE NOON HOUR, GRACE stepped off the train into a cold rain in Medicine Springs, Texas. She took a deep breath of the damp air, pulled her jacket close, and buttoned it against the spring chill. Crockett followed, helping Leah.

Glancing around, things hadn't changed that much. The depot had gotten a little bigger, and they'd added a new saloon—the Red Boot—but the sleepy town still moved at the pace of a one-legged cur.

Crockett turned the collar of his coat up around his ears and stood ready to help Leah navigate the steps. Instead, she handed her bundled son to Crockett and made her own way. Watching her brother hold the tiny baby in his big arms brought a lump to Grace's throat.

He'd grown up when she wasn't looking. He was probably just being helpful, but what if there was an attraction between him and Leah? Except Leah was still bound by marriage.

At least for now, until they could do something about that.

"Good, Tompkins is here," Crockett announced, handing the baby back to his mother.

Grace waved to their foreman. She took Leah's arm and they stepped over a puddle to the surrey.

Tommy Tompkins hopped down and came around. The long-time foreman still had a full head of brown hair that brushed his shoulders and, although his age was hard to gauge, she figured him to be around her father's age. "It's a mighty fine day indeed when you come home, Miss Grace. Yes, it is."

"We brought a houseguest. Leah and little Johnny will be staying here for a while."

Tommy removed his hat. "Welcome to the Lone Star, ma'am."

Leah shook his hand. "Thank you, Mr. Tompkins. The baby and I are grateful for the hospitality. I've never been this far west, and it's very beautiful."

"We like it." While Crockett and Tompkins collected the bags, Grace shared a few things about the ranch. "Sam Houston gave part of this land to my grandfather Stoker Legend as payment for fighting in the Texas War for Independence. As my grandpa was able, he bought more to add to it, and it's now one of the largest spreads in the state."

Leah laughed. "Deacon didn't tell me you were from a rich family. I'm impressed."

"Rich in land, that's all. We still work for a living." Crockett climbed into the surrey, taking the seat next to Leah. He tucked the blanket around the squirming, fussy baby.

Grace found a lump filling her throat. When had her little brother become a man possessed of such gentleness? The sight startled her a bit. He'd always been a kid to her.

"How was your trip, Miss Grace?" Tommy asked.

"Uneventful." She groaned. "It seems like something interesting could've happened to break up the monotony."

Crockett laughed. "Train robbing has seen a bit of a decline. What a pity. Life can be downright boring."

"Ain't that the truth?" Tommy set the surrey in motion, and the black fringe hanging from around the top swayed to the rhythm of the clip-clop of the horses. "Miss Grace, nothing is ever boring with you around. I have to say Stoker will be happy to see you."

She leaned forward, concern and worry switching places as they rode toward the ranch. "Is he feeling all right? Still riding every day? Still keeping up with Ransom? Eating good?"

"Hey, take a breath before you bust a gasket." Tommy half turned on the seat. "Stoker kicks my rear on a daily basis."

Crockett chuckled. "Then he's not near ready for the boneyard."

"Stop it." Grace whacked his arm. "Don't even joke about a thing like that."

"Grandpa is too cantankerous and mean to die."

Leah put little Johnny on her shoulder and patted his bottom until he quieted.

Grace huddled in her jacket. She dearly loved her grandpa, and even the remote possibility that he could die set her heart pounding. She had a special bond with him and couldn't picture life without her Stoker.

She leaned to speak to the foreman. "I want to stop at headquarters before going on to our house."

The first year of their marriage, her parents had built a home a mile from headquarters and Stoker's residence. Her mother had been drawn to the solitude and the magnificent view of the Red River, and Houston would've given her the moon. Still would.

"Figured as much. Your parents might very well be there." Tompkins flicked the reins at the team of matched black horses.

Grace watched the passing countryside of the land she loved— the low rolling hills and deep ravines, the mesquite and small cedar trees, the air so crisp and fresh she took it all the way down to her toes. She liked the city, but this? This was sheer heaven.

A flash crossed her vision, and suddenly she was ten years old and with the bank-robbing kidnappers.

"I say we just cut the brat's throat and leave her body for the almighty Houston Legend," said the robber named Slim. "Don't know why we brought her to start with."

"Because I said." Carl released a string of curses, and Gracie clapped her hands over her ears. "We're collecting on a payment. If you don't like it, you can part ways."

"You brought us this way on purpose. This is far off the trail.

Dammit, Carl, what's going on?" asked a third man. She didn't like the way he looked at her, didn't like what was in his eyes. When she started to cry, he drew back a fist and knocked her sideways, then jerked her up by the hair.

Blows rained. Blood, so much blood.

Shaking, Grace stuffed her fist in her mouth, hoping Crockett or Leah hadn't heard her strangled sound. She sat in silence for a good while before she was able to stop shaking.

Crockett, Leah, and Tommy talked about the land. Finally, Grace regained her composure and occasionally threw in some tidbit.

Anticipation began to grow for the first glimpse of the tall Texas flag waving proudly at headquarters. True as always, her breath caught in the back of her throat when she spotted the symbol of sacrifice and courage. It had flown in the same spot ever since she could remember. Memories grew thick of how she'd sat on Grandpa Stoker's lap and listened to him tell about the Texas heroes who'd fought and died for freedom. Still today, she could list them and quote chapter and verse about their exploits. Whenever they'd had guests, her grandpa had let her entertain and astound them with her knowledge of the state and its people.

The sun broke through the clouds as Tommy brought the surrey to a stop in front of the huge, two-story, white stone building that served as Stoker's residence and ranch office. The small town across from it with a telegraph, mercantile, doctor, and school looked the same. She didn't spot any new businesses.

With the ranch so far from the nearest town in the beginning, Stoker had seen the need to make things easier for his family and employees, and thus had created the vital services. He was one of the most caring men she'd known.

Grace took Tompkins's hand and stepped down. For a long moment, she stared up at the majestic flag and inhaled. Then her gaze shifted to the foot of the flagpole and the huge bronze star that hung suspended between two large poles. An old legend persisted that a person would determine their true worth if they slept beneath the star.

She blinked hard, the fragrant land wrapping its arms around her.

"This is the most thrilling sight I've ever seen," Leah murmured beside her. "I have goose bumps."

"You know, it doesn't matter how many times we see the flag flying, it always takes our breath." Crockett nudged Grace. "Are you finally going to sleep beneath the star while you're here?"

"I don't know." She just might. As much as she doubted it possible, to get answers about Yuma Blackstone would be worth the discomfort of the ground. As for her true worth...that one really had her stumped. She was so unsettled, unsure about her life.

Crockett explained the legend to Leah, who said she might try it sometime.

Their eleven-year-old sister, Hannah, raced from headquarters, her long, brown braids flying. "You're back! You're back!"

"Yes, we are." Grace hugged her for several long heartbeats. "I've missed you."

"You've been gone forever." Freckles marching across Hannah's pert nose gave her an impish look, which was exactly her sister's personality. "I got a new horse."

"What kind?"

"A buckskin. I named him Mister Pete." Hannah slid her arm around Grace's waist. "He's a yearling and faster than all get out. You should see him run."

"I'm sure I will." The door opened, and their parents emerged arm in arm. Houston said something, and Lara stared up at him with love on her face. Grace had never seen anything so beautiful. She gave them both a hug. "It's good to be home."

She drew Leah and the baby forward and made the introductions. "I hope you don't mind if they stay a little while."

"Of course not. You know better than that." Lara asked to hold the baby and cuddled the tiny bundle to her bosom. Houston touched the small cheek with a finger.

"How's the big city?" The thin, white scar that must've been so painful was visible on the right side of Lara's face. A few gray strands had snuck into her mother's auburn hair since Grace last saw her, but she remained such a beautiful woman.

"Fort Worth is still there. Lots going on with the temperance movement." Grace's gaze flew to Crockett, standing with their father and Hannah. Tompkins had driven the surrey back around to the shed. "God, I missed this."

"I'd hoped so," Lara said, smiling.

Grace glanced around. "Where's Grandpa?"

Her father laughed. "He rode out with Ransom early this morning, saying the two of them were going to chase down strays up in the wash. I expect they'll be back in a bit."

"Should he be doing that?"

Houston snorted. "Good luck trying to tell him he can't!"

"I see your point." At the sound of galloping horses, Grace whirled around in time to see dirt flying, and her grandpa neck and neck with Ransom in a race to see who got there first. Stoker was acting like a kid in knee britches.

The duo reined up and dismounted. Both were covered with dirt.

Stoker beat his hat against his clothes and created a dust storm around himself. "My Gracie! Come here, girl."

Grace hurried to give him a big hug. "That was some fancy riding." She leaned back and sucked in a breath. When had he become so wrinkled? For the first time, she noticed he'd gotten old.

"I knew I could beat this whippersnapper." Stoker draped an arm around her seventeen-year-old brother's shoulders.

Ransom had gotten taller while Grace had been gone. The

top of his head measured at their grandpa's nose. He took more after their mother's family—blond and fair-skinned. In all else he favored their dad, especially the love of the land.

Grace introduced Leah to the two men, then Ransom gave Grace a big bear hug. "Sis, I want to hear all about the city."

"I'll describe it in a word—noisy. A lot of people are driving those newfangled automobiles."

"Oh, man! I'd really like to see those. How fast do they go?"

Crockett came over, grinning. "Some can do a whole thirty miles per hour when they're running wide-open."

Ransom whistled. "I'd like to see that someday."

"You will," Grace assured him.

"I predict everyone will own one before too much longer," Crockett said.

"Except us." Ransom groaned. "We'll still be stuck with horses until the second coming."

Houston laughed. "Automobiles cost a pretty penny. Save your money and buy one yourself, son."

Stoker suggested they go inside. Except for Crockett and Ransom, continuing their conversation about horseless carriages, they all moved into the interior of the huge residence and ranch office. Lara handed the baby back to his mother, and the two women went on into the kitchen. Most likely little Johnny needed feeding. Grace plunked down next to her grandpa.

He squinted hard at her. "Heard you've taken up with those infernal temperance folk tearing up the country, trying to make us men toe the line and strip us of our comfort. I said it has to be some mistake. No granddaughter of mine would join up with such a rabble-rousing bunch."

Here it came. The moment she'd dreaded.

With a deep breath to bolster her, Grace gave the old dear a smile. "It's true sure enough. I joined them because I'm tired of others trampling on my freedom. I want to exercise a right to vote and take charge of my life like Crockett. Shoot, even Ransom, five years younger, gets to live as he pleases, own property, and decide his own fate. But not me."

"Dammit, Gracie!" Stoker slammed his hand down on his knee, sounding like a rifle shot. He accepted a glass of amber liquid from her father and shook his finger. "I just have one thing to say. You women have always ruled the roost, little girl."

Anger rose. Why couldn't people see her side? "Then why can't I buy property unless a man says I can?" Grace went to the window and stared out over the vast ranch.

"What do you want to buy? I'll help you, and so will your father."

"That's not the point, Grandpa. What if you or my father aren't around? How would I buy it then?"

"Your brothers."

Grace threw up her hands. "Sorry, Grandpa, that's not the world I want to live in."

Her father got to his feet. "We've all had some upsetting times lately, and we're about ready to go in to Fort Worth and whip that editor Pemberton at the paper."

"Horace Pemberton at the *Fort Worth Gazette*?" She prayed her voice wasn't as squeaky as it sounded. Heat built and sweat trickled down her back.

"The one and only. Would you know anything about him, Gracie?"

She shot a desperate glance toward the door.

Grandpa Stoker picked up a folded newspaper and jabbed a finger on an article. "This is a bunch of horse dung!" he thundered. "According to this, I'm fighting with everybody in Texas. And how the hell on God's green earth did they find out what I sold my yearlings for? That's my damn business."

"You do disagree with quite a few people," Grace quietly pointed out. "When did you start taking the *Fort Worth Gazette*?" They weren't supposed to ever read those. Shoot!

"It was your mother's and Ransom's idea," her father said. "You can imagine the upheaval those articles caused."

"I'd like to know just who Sam Valentine is!" Stoker again slammed his hand down on his knee. "Maybe I'll take the train in and find out."

"Grandpa, you're working yourself into a heart attack." Grace worried her lip.

"That sounds like you're taking sides." Grandpa pierced her with his eyes.

"No, of course not." Grace could think of nothing that would diffuse the situation.

"I hope to never see that from you. There's such a thing as family loyalty, young lady." Stoker mumbled something under his breath and looked ready to write her from his will.

If she couldn't diffuse a bomb, it seemed prudent to leave. Grace jumped to her feet. "Excuse me, I need to speak to Mama, then take my things on over to our house."

Stoker captured her hand. "Don't go far."

"I won't," she promised, kissing his cheek, her frustration tamped down. "We have a chess game to play."

"Don't think I've lost my touch, young lady."

Her heart was relieved that he hadn't lost his trademark booming voice.

She laughed. "No chance." She strode to the door and paused. When she turned back, she found him already in deep conversation with Houston, again struck by how much he'd aged.

Glad to be away from the discord, Grace hurried to the kitchen. They weren't supposed to ever get the paper, ever read those articles. Hopefully, it would all die down. But how could it when Pemberton was holding several of those articles to run later? Good Lord!

She might not be able to outrun this but she could try. Grace hurried to the kitchen. But her father's warning about keeping the family out of her activities sounded in her head. Why hadn't she listened? She groaned aloud.

Hannah came up behind her. "What's wrong, Gracie?"

"I have a problem I don't know how to fix."

"Can I help?"

"You know what? Let me see what I can do first. Then, I'll sure pick your brain." Grace put an arm around her little sister.

Hannah chattered up a storm as they walked along. All of a sudden, a certain gray-eyed cowboy saloon owner crossed her mind and her stomach quickened. Their late-night walks, his warm touch, his deep voice swept past her homecoming.

It used to always puzzle her how random thoughts could flash from the blue in the midst of a joyous family gathering. So when Deacon Brannock popped into her head with his piercing gaze and almost-perpetual frown on his full lips, she found it an odd but welcome distraction. As she went to help her mother in the kitchen, memories of his kisses—and the slice of heaven she'd found in his arms—burned inside her.

Yet she knew how quickly things could sour.

True, he'd worn no frown when he'd kissed her. Instead, strange desire had smoldered in his eyes like a banked fire. But...

What was he doing now? She wondered if he even thought about her at all, although there was no reason whatsoever why he should. A few innocent kisses meant nothing to a man like him. The thought of other things that would likely mean a lot more than kissing brought rising heat to her face.

Seventeen

His thoughts on Will Bonner, Deacon scoured the streets in the lower east end after dark, hoping to catch sight of Izzy. Deacon didn't know if someone was taking orphans off the street, but he didn't like the feeling rolling around in his gut.

Something wasn't right and he needed to find out the truth one way or another.

If anything happened to that boy, it would put him in a bad place. Izzy was more than an orphan. The kid had become almost like family. Deacon had promised Grace he'd find him, and she was counting on that.

But dammit, as much as he'd like, he couldn't take in everyone to raise, and he had Will to see about as well. He'd ridden out early that morning to check on the rancher and found him as prickly as all get out, complaining about the weather, the lack of rain, the price of cattle, and pretty much everything else.

Diablo had seemed fractious as well, stamping the ground and sending angry signals, so Deacon had ended up leaving.

He brought his attention back to his search. Up ahead, the lights of the Silver Nugget splashed into the street. Three men stood outside, arguing. There was something about one that looked familiar. He moved closer. It was him. Seth Pickford. The little he could overhear had something to do with money.

"I know you took it!" Pickford grabbed the man's shirt and threw a punch to his face.

They traded blows until a beefy man ran out. "Break it up. Move out of the door. Go somewhere else."

The trio went on, disappearing into the night.

Though Deacon missed Leah and the baby, he was glad they were far away.

Shaking his head, Deacon dodged drunks, horses, and scantily clad ladies of the night. Finally, he ran across the same youngster he'd spoken with before. "How's it going, Simon?"

"Ain't seen nothing, Mr. Brannock. Not even any haints." The kid looked skinnier and dirtier than the first time. He dragged a sleeve across his nose that had a scab on the end. "They's some people trying to round all of us up. Said they'll give us a home. But I ain't buying it. No, sir."

"Really?" Deacon wondered if it was true. "Who told you about this?"

"One of the bigger kids. I think he was tryin' to scare me, though. He don't believe in haints."

"Not everyone does." Deacon refrained from asking him if he'd seen any and laid an arm across the boy's skinny shoulders. "What's wrong with having a home and people to care about you?"

"Aw, they just say that to make folks think they're good people. But as soon as no one watches, they drag out the razor strop. They put me in one of those homes after I lost my fam'ly. I don't trust 'em. Don't trust anyone." Simon squirmed out from under Deacon's arm and spat on the ground.

"It sounds like you're speaking from experience."

"Yep." Simon glanced up at Deacon. "I rode the orphan train here, and a husband and wife picked me out. They hollered amen at the drop of a hat and hallelujahed me plumb to death. They fooled the preacher good." Simon wagged his head. "My bed was a box in the corner and food was a cold biscuit. Made me work in the fields, they did. I ran away."

The story wasn't new. Deacon had heard it before. "When did you last eat?"

The kid scrunched up his face and chewed a dirty fingernail. "Ain't sure."

Deacon handed him enough money to last several days. "Go get you something, and if you're looking for work, come by the Three Deuces."

"Thanks, Mr. Brannock." The boy took off so fast, he lost one of his shoes and had to come back for it.

The sight hurt Deacon's heart. He wished he could take them all off the street and give them a good home with plenty of food. There was so much want in the world, and Fort Worth's was just a drop in the bucket.

He wandered back to the saloon, which was packed to the rafters. They were doing a booming business these days and putting money in Deacon's pocket again. He might go buy another vest to replace the one Pickford ruined. But first was a looming problem. Now that Leah had left, who was going to keep making the tamales?

Harry and him? How hard could it be?

For the next three hours, he helped Harry serve drinks, keeping an eye out to make sure no one got too drunk. It was funny, but most of the men just wanted to eat. He could hear Grace suggesting he turn the saloon into a café.

For no reason at all, he tipped back his head and hooted.

Harry gave him a strange look that suggested Deacon had lost what good sense he had. "What's so funny, Boss?"

"I just thought of Grace."

"I see." Harry shrugged. "I don't know why that makes you laugh, but I'm glad to see something other than a frown on your face."

"I—forget it. You won't understand." Deacon didn't rightly either, so how could he explain to someone else?

The woman made him mad enough to sling a buffalo through a church steeple, but he missed her. She was growing on him, and he couldn't wait for her to get back. He was saving up a few topics to spar with her over.

He hoped she was getting the answers she yearned for at the ranch. A body needed to understand certain things about themselves.

And take it from him, sometimes past mistakes exacted a high price.

❧

Deacon started at eight o'clock that morning and had worked to make tamales using the recipe Leah had jotted down. He tried to remember everything she'd rattled off. But no matter how careful he was, they ended up either looking like cigars or something you found in an outhouse.

"Harry, come here!"

The bartender appeared at his elbow and roared with laughter. Finally, he wiped his eyes. "Sorry, Boss, but we might get arrested if we serve those."

Deacon glared. "Do you think you can do better?"

Harry backed up, hands raised. "Don't make me do this. Please. I can't."

"Dammit!" Deacon threw the large spoon he held. "I'm ordering you to try your hand."

"This is against protest." Harry wiped his hands and stepped to the pan of tamale mixture, then reached for a corn husk. He put a spoonful of filling into the husk and rolled. When he turned loose, the innards fell out. "See?"

Deacon drew his eyebrows together and sighed. "You have to tie them, don't you?"

"Maybe. I can't recall, but we don't have any string, Boss."

"Okay, what can we use?" Deacon glanced around and grabbed some toothpicks, jabbing them through the corn husk. The whole mess fell apart and plopped on the floor. "Argh! Dammit!" He whirled away, putting his hands on his hips.

"Hey, I have some fishing line. Do you think that'll work?" Harry asked.

"Well, it sure can't hurt. Go get it, and we'll cut some lengths." Hope rose. Deacon waited while Harry went for his fishing box, then they cut the line up into five-inch sections.

"It's sure getting hot in here." Sweat trickled down Harry's face.

Deacon stuffed a corn husk so full he couldn't roll it. He cussed a blue streak. "Harry, hold this shut for me while I tie it."

Between them, they managed—then it, too, dropped to the floor. Deacon swore like a sailor and looked at Harry, then picked it up and blew the dirt off. Or at least he hoped it did. Shrugging, he placed it in the pile with the others. Dirt would only add a little extra crunch. He tried two more with a little better result, but not enough to brag about. They were ugly.

"Jesus, I'm about to burn up! Prop the back door open, Harry."

His bartender looked relieved to have something to do. When he came back, his shirt was unbuttoned and hanging open. "Boss, we got a line outside halfway down the block."

"No joke?"

"I'm serious."

Deacon glanced at the six dozen they'd already steamed. "Go let them in while I make a few more."

A minute later, it sounded like a herd of elephants tromping in. Deacon quickly used the last of the dough and masa, then eased those into the pan to steam. When they were on to cook, he collapsed at the table, fanning himself. This was harder work than digging ditches.

Harry stuck his head in. "I need help out here."

"Coming." It took all Deacon's strength to pull himself to his feet. He glanced at his soiled apron and waded into the crowd.

For the next two hours, he worked nonstop. He plunked a plate down in front of a beefy-looking man at the bar.

The patron glared. "What's this?"

"Six tamales. Just what you ordered."

"They sure don't look like the ones I got a few days ago."

"Well, they are. They just look funny. The woman who used to make them left."

"Get her back, Brannock, or I'm going somewhere else. Forget it, just bring me a beer."

Complaints circled the room. Deacon would have to find a cook and fast. He wondered if he could entice one or two of the working girls on the street. Or teach some of the street urchins. They could stand on chairs.

Whatever he did, he had no time to waste, or else he'd have to give up on the food idea and go back to serving only liquor. A knot rose in his stomach. That would put him at odds with Grace again, and he rather liked the taste of her kissable lips, her wild heartbeat. God help him.

Even though he stood in danger of her discovering his secret and learning his real identity, he could no more send her away than speak Cherokee, Chinese, or pig Latin.

Eighteen

GRACE MADE LEAH AND LITTLE JOHNNY MADRID COMFORT-able in their quarters after lunch before she opened the door of her old room. Instant warmth wrapped around her. The same quilt still covered the bed, and the same books lay on the desk with a sharpened pencil near. She'd spent hours and hours pretending to be a reporter, unearthing murderers' dastardly deeds and skillfully questioning the accused that Crockett always played, catching him in lie after lie until he confessed in a squeaky voice.

How different life was from pretend. She loved her job as a reporter, but it was nothing like what she'd thought. Writing inter-esting, thought-provoking articles was hard. Darn hard.

Her mother tapped on the half-open door and came in. "You don't know how happy I am that you're home."

"It's really nice. I miss this place when I'm not here."

"Thank you for bringing Leah and the baby. What's his name?"

Grace laughed. "Johnny Madrid. I didn't want to tell her that sounds like an outlaw name."

"It sorta does." A gentle smile curved Lara's mouth. "It's nice having a baby around. I've been pining for one again. I miss that sweet smell and kissing those little feet."

"This way you can have that without giving birth."

"Exactly."

"I delivered him, Mama." Grace told her about that night and trying to remember everything. "I was scared out of my mind, afraid I'd do something that would lead to their deaths."

"But you didn't." Lara hugged her. "I'm proud of you."

Grace wandered to the desk in the corner and ran her finger across it. "I remember the game Crockett and I played when we were young. Even back then, I wanted to go out and save the world." Grace put an arm around her mother. "I know you and Pa worry about me, but please, just let me have some room. I haven't forgotten your teachings, lessons, and advice. It's all still in my head and I won't do anything foolish."

The sudden memory of jail crossed her mind. "Well, I'm trying my best anyway."

"Come and sit, Gracie." Her mother went to a small settee in the room, and Grace followed. "You were such a beautiful baby. Your large blue eyes and golden curls drew people like bees to honey. But you'd shake your finger at them and jabber like you were scolding. You were a bossy little thing, even back then."

Grace laughed, thinking of Brannock. "Some would say I haven't changed much."

Lara had worry lines around her eyes, and the white scar seemed to rise from her otherwise flawless complexion. "Your pa told me about jail and these temperance women. Be careful."

"I'm trying to follow my conscience and duty and stay within the law."

"Sometimes bad things can happen without us doing anything to draw them. That's what frightens your father and me, and it's something we can't warn our children enough about."

"What are you saying, Mama?" Grace searched her mother's dark-green gaze. Despite the years, Lara Legend was stunning with her auburn hair and smooth features.

"Evil exists in places where you least expect it. You have to stay aware."

Grace gently traced her mother's scar. "What happened here, Mama? You never talk about it."

"That would serve no purpose except to dredge up old, painful memories that are best forgotten."

What were they? Grace wanted to yell.

Instead, she took her mother's hand and chose a different path. "Sometimes we have to face the truth even though it drives a dagger in us. Fragments of memory have been coming back from the time I was abducted. The hitting, their filthy language— the names they called me." Grace struggled to still her quivering lip, and though she worked to keep her voice even, she lost the battle. The words came out bruised and angry. "How powerless they made me feel. Like I was some toy to do with whatever they wished."

Lara tore away from her and jerked to her feet. Raw, naked emotion filled her voice, something Grace had never heard. "Forget what they did. Don't let them inside your head. Never let them in, or they'll steal a part of you."

Grace kept her voice gentle. "Is that what happened to you, Mama? Is that what the person who scarred you did?" She enveloped her mother in a hug. "Who is Yuma Blackstone?"

Lara jerked back in horror. "Never speak that name to me." She ran from the room.

"I'm sorry, Mama." Grace stared after her. What to do? Follow or leave her mother be? More questions than ever filled her head.

"What was that all about?" Houston asked from the doorway.

"I think I hit a raw nerve." Grace picked up a small, embroidered pillow and clutched it to her stomach. "I was asking about the scar, and she became upset. I shouldn't have mentioned Yuma Blackstone."

"You didn't know." Houston folded his arms around her. "Let her be. Just don't bring it up again. Some things are best left buried."

"Even if they affect another person?" She glanced up. "My abductor yelled that I deserved to know. Why won't anyone tell me?"

Pain crossed his brown eyes. "Honey, he didn't know what he was talking about. Yuma was one of the most wretched, depraved men that ever walked the face of the earth, but he's dead now, and you don't need to be concerned with things of that nature."

"I saw an old article recently that said you killed him when you went on that big cattle drive to Dodge City. What happened? Please."

"Yuma Blackstone and his gang dogged us almost the entire way. Eventually, they began killing a drover a day, trying to force me to turn the herd over to him. I saw we stood no chance of outrunning them, so we holed up and fought back. He ended up dead." Houston placed his hands on her shoulders. "Let it lie. It's over."

"Thank you." Grace knew that wasn't all to the story, but it was enough for now.

He kissed the top of her head. "It's good to have you home. Take a nap, then put on a pretty dress and let's enjoy the time we have."

"All right, Pa." It was clear she'd reached a dead end anyway.

"Think of some funny stories to put a smile on your mama's face."

"Sure." Grace followed the tall figure of the man she'd loved all her life. She couldn't imagine having a better father.

But she had a burr under her saddle. If her mother and father wouldn't tell her the rest, she had Stoker and her other grandfather—Till Boone. And if they refused, she'd go to her uncles on her mother's side—Virgil and Quaid Boone.

Somehow or another, she'd unravel this mystery that was eating her alive.

❧

After the saloon closed for the night, Deacon bolted the doors and climbed the stairs with a glass of bourbon. Optimism that he'd not felt in a while lightened his step. The till was full, and he hadn't seen hide nor hair of Seth Pickford. If he could just figure out where Izzy was, things would be a lot better than they'd been in a long while. But although he'd scouted the area, he'd found nothing.

Had the boy encountered a drunk and been killed? His chest tightened. For Izzy to die with no one to hold his hand would be unimaginable.

The door to Leah's room stood open. Emptiness stared back. Deacon closed his eyes and his conversation with Leah the previous day filled his head.

She'd stopped him as he went past her room and wanted to talk. His arm had gone numb, and he lost his grip on a glass of bourbon, barely catching it before it crashed to the floor.

"When did you last see a doctor about that, Deacon?" she'd asked.

"Leave it be." He hated his tone, but sometimes life was what it was. No use trying to sugarcoat things. "I think I'll go to bed. I'm glad you're going with Grace to the Lone Star."

She jiggled the baby. "It's only temporary, Deacon. As soon as it's safe, I'll be back." Uneasiness filled her eyes. "I'm worried about you. Who will make the tamales?"

"It's my problem." He pulled to his feet and turned to give her a smile that hopefully softened his gruff words. She'd looked like someone had kicked her dog. "Look, you got a raw deal when you threw in with me, honey. I'm sorry. You deserve better."

That was the last real conversation he'd had with her.

"Dammit to hell!" Unable to bear the empty room, Deacon went to his own quarters. He stared out the window, sipping on his bourbon, massaging a bit of life back into his arm and hand. He might as well take a room next to Harry for all the sleep he got these days.

He rubbed his face, listing all his shortcomings. Weary, he dropped onto the bed, laid his gun next to him, and stared at the ceiling through bleary eyes.

A huge crash downstairs was followed by yells. Deacon grabbed his Colt and jumped to his feet, hitting the stairs running. With the saloon lit by only one low lamp, he couldn't see a whole lot. Harry came from his room in his long johns.

"Who's there? Come out now or I'll shoot," Deacon ordered.

The figure of a man stumbled toward the alley, flailing his arms. "Get this thing off me!"

"Halt!" Deacon fired two shots.

The man launched himself through a window, screaming bloody murder. Just as Harry made it to the lamp and raised the wick, their attack cat, Sarge, leaped onto the long bar, looking quite pleased with himself.

Deacon raced into the alley, but the intruder had disappeared. After searching the length of the dark passage, he went back inside. "He got away."

"Not all of him." Harry motioned to Sarge. The cat had a good deal of blood and human hair on him. "I think we're gonna have to give him a raise, Boss."

After the laughter died, Deacon agreed. "He's mighty protective of his home."

"Who do you figure that was?"

"Not sure. Maybe Pickford. Lord only knows. It could've been someone thinking of robbing us. We've raked in the money the last week." Deacon picked up a large, broken pickle jar.

"Do you think you hit him?"

"Not sure. Maybe." Deacon got the broom, hoping he had put a hole in the trespasser, while Harry picked up the feline and went to wash off the blood in the sink.

They cleaned up the plank floor as best they could and put away the broom and mop.

Harry laughed. "Too bad we don't have Grace here to help. Where is she, by the way?"

"Left town to visit her folks on the Lone Star." Deacon poured a drink for him and Harry. "But I don't think she'll be hanging around here a lot. She has a job."

"You don't say? I'll miss her." Harry downed the amber liquid in one gulp.

That made two of them, but Deacon was careful not to voice that. The moment a man spoke his thoughts was how sure they'd turn to nothing.

"Best to not get attached to anyone, I guess," Harry muttered, his tone gloomy.

"Yeah, that's what I decided a long time ago." Deacon finished his drink, setting the glass on the bar. "Come daylight, I'll search the alley for anything the intruder might've dropped that could provide a clue."

Harry picked up Sarge. "Will you report this break-in to the sheriff, Boss?"

"No. We'll handle it ourselves."

And if the man broke in again, he'd find a bullet waiting.

⟡

Grace spent the week making nice with her family, in addition to going to visit her Boone grandfather, Till, and her uncles. As expected, everyone refused to tell her a thing about how her mother received the scar and Yuma Blackstone's role.

Had the attack happened while on that cattle drive? If so, that would've driven Houston over the edge. But if that's when it occurred, it didn't explain what the kidnappers had yelled.

Disappointed in her mission, she was sitting on the porch at headquarters late one afternoon with Hannah, watching how the dying light played across the land she loved, when her mother rode up on a beautiful brown gelding.

Lara grinned. "Looks like you're enjoying the fresh air. I thought I'd find you with your grandfather." She dismounted and unhooked a basket from her pommel.

"He took off with the boys. I think I wore him out talking." Grace laughed. "Well, actually, we were arguing fit to beat all, like usual. He gets a kick out of challenging me." She put an arm around her little sister. "Hannah and I were discussing what she wants to be when she grows up."

"I want to be like Grace," Hannah declared. "I'm going off to see the world and find a handsome man to marry."

"Hey, that's not what I'm doing, you little imp." Grace tickled her sister until she begged for mercy.

When the laughter died, Grace found her mother staring. "What?"

"I'm proud of you, Grace. You find such worthy causes to fight for. I think you probably find deep satisfaction."

"I do, Mama."

"For once, I'd like to make a difference in the world too. Women need a voice."

"Yes, they do." Grace wondered where her mother was going with this. Lara seemed restless.

Hannah got up and wandered off.

"It's been a long day." Lara sat next to her, seeming to enjoy the quiet. A comfortable silence stretched. "You know, I used to envy the closeness you shared with Stoker."

Grace raised her head. "I never knew that. I'm sorry, Mama. I don't love you less."

"I know. Don't apologize. You have some kind of deep connection with Stoker that you never had with anyone else, and I think you need that kind of relationship and vice versa. He's really perked up since you've been here."

"Has he been sick?"

"Just the normal aging stuff. Nothing to worry about."

"When I got here, I saw his age for the first time, and it shook me."

"He'll be eighty-two on his next birthday." Lara stared off into the setting sun. She seemed to have something on her mind. Grace waited, and finally her mother spoke. "Your father told me about a saloon owner you've met. How well do you know him?"

What could she say? That his kisses made her knees weak and her heart pound?

This line of fishing made Grace nervous. She coughed. "I've only seen him a few times, so I know very little about him. His name is Deacon Brannock."

"That's a strong Irish name."

It would be if it were really his name.

Suddenly, she wanted to confide in her mother, so she told her about Leah, the baby, and Deacon. "I like him, Mama. He's gotten protective of me and walks me back to where the streetlights are. When he touches my arm, I get all quivery inside and my knees go weak."

"Be careful, Grace." Her mother smiled. "See, I remembered your new name."

"I noticed. Thank you."

"I'm working on your father and brothers."

"I appreciate that."

"This may be considered prying, but I'm going to ask anyway. Has Mr. Brannock kissed you?"

"Yes, he has." And she took the memories out at night and relived the feel of his lips, but she kept quiet about that. "Mama, I enjoy his company, and when I'm with him, he makes me warm all over. But this isn't love."

"What do you think love is like?" Lara asked softly.

Grace thought for a moment. "Love is when you want to look at someone all the time and you feel like dying when he's not there. You start to have the same thoughts and you can't stand it when you don't touch. Like you and Pa. I look at you two and see love in your faces and in the way you try to be near each other."

Lara laughed, and her scar puckered a little with the motion. "That's pretty much it."

"Mama, can I tell you something?" Grace bit her bottom lip.

"Anything." Lara tucked a tendril of blond hair behind Grace's ear, and the tender touch created a warmth inside that she'd missed.

"I don't think Brannock had a very happy life. Sometimes sadness drips off him like cold rain. And sometimes the ice in his voice frightens me."

Lara sat up straighter, concerned. "Do you think he'd ever hurt you?"

"No, absolutely not. Never." Grace laughed, thinking about their first encounter and her whopping him with that sign. "He's certainly had plenty of chances if he were the mean sort."

Lara studied her a long moment. "You're too old to forbid seeing him, but if you ever feel threatened or that your life is in danger, run as far and as fast as you can. I mean that. I'm speaking from experience."

"Are you talking about Yuma Blackstone?" Grace asked softly.

Her mother gripped Grace's hands hard. "Daughter, you have a strong backbone but never think evil can't find you, and that's all I'm saying." Lara rose, grabbed her basket, and went inside.

Deep sadness washed over Grace as she watched her go. Oh God, she knew her mother's secret! Or as close as she'd probably ever come.

The thought of a man doing despicable things to such a kind, gentle woman made her physically ill. No wonder everyone had kept silent. They were protecting her.

And so would Grace. The truth be damned. She was dropping this.

Never think evil can't find you.

A shiver raced up her spine. Evil had found Lara Boone Legend. Evil had cut her face.

Branded her.

Grace sat there, thinking about her life and the man she couldn't seem to forget.

Brannock wasn't Yuma. She was positive that no matter how mad she made him, he'd never harm one hair on her head. Yet that appeared immaterial. She had no feelings for him no matter how hot and achy his kisses made her. Now to convince her heart of that.

Nineteen

HER LAST NIGHT AT THE LONE STAR FOUND GRACE IN A strange mood. She wandered out to stare up at the sky. There must've been ten million stars dotting the expanse and the view took her breath. Her gaze shifted to the base of the flagpole and the enormous bronze star suspended between two vertical pieces of steel. She noticed a lacy pattern on the ground where pale moonlight shone through the points that had been cut out.

She'd seen it many times but not in a while. Inhaling a wondrous breath of the fragrant air, she aimed her feet to the sight and sat beneath it.

If anyone had asked what she was worth in terms of how she'd helped make the world a better place, she'd have shrugged. Did anyone ever know for sure the impact they had on places or people?

"I think I've made a difference in some areas. I really do," she murmured.

But did she know her worth as a woman? She exercised fairness with everyone, loved dogs and horses, and tried to be kind.

She drove people crazy with her headstrong ways. She was trying to change. She truly was.

Journalism could be a key. If she could write good, measured, and fair articles that promoted change in people or circumstances, she'd be content. That was her goal.

Grace lay down in the cool grass and gazed up at the beautiful, mysterious heavens. A gust of wind set the bronze star swinging back and forth. Back and forth. Her eyes grew heavy and her breath became shallow and even.

The soft, fragrant grass made a comfortable bed, and she soon dozed.

The face of an elderly gentleman with a long, white beard appeared in a dream. She recognized her great-grandfather Legend from the large portrait Stoker had hung in the living room.

"Grace, you are both blessed and cursed with a strong curiosity for things you don't understand. You must learn to temper your anger and impulsive urges with patience and understanding, my dear."

"Can you tell me how? I can use help."

"Slow down. Don't be in such a rush. Dig deep inside, and you will find wisdom and strength far beyond what you think you may possess."

A wisp of smoke drifted across her vision. "I have many unanswered questions about Yuma Blackstone and my mother. The robber said I deserve to know whatever it is, but no one will tell me."

Great-grandfather shook his finger. "Some things are not ours to know."

"Even if it concerns me?"

He sighed. "Even then."

"I appreciate the advice. My impulsiveness sometimes gets me in a lot of trouble."

"I've seen that. Each time you feel it coming on, remember your time in jail."

"That was horrible. Were you there?"

"I am always with you, Grace."

"I just want to know one thing—will I marry a gray-eyed man?"

A sudden flash shot across her eyes and her great-grandfather vanished just as quickly as he'd appeared. Cranky man. Grace guessed he didn't deal in telling fortunes or romance.

She fell into a dreamless sleep and didn't wake until daylight. Someone had covered her with a warm blanket and Hannah rested beside her, asleep.

What a crazy dream. Great-grandfather had looked so lifelike, and a sudden wish that she could've met him came over her. She ran a hand over her eyes, trying to make sense of it before pulling Hannah next to her. "Hi there, honey. Did you sleep here all night?"

Hannah opened tear-stained eyes. "I don't want you leave, Grace."

"I know. But I'll be back soon."

"Do you promise?"

Grace kissed her sister's soft cheek. "Cross my heart."

"I love you, Grace. Will you ride horses with me?"

"Let's go now before I have to pack."

Excitement to return to Fort Worth and her work wound through her. Seeing family was nice, but she had things to do. Lots of things.

∾

Saturday morning, Deacon rose at dawn, rubbing his bleary eyes. He hadn't gone to bed until around 2:00 a.m., so it'd been a short night. But he'd dreamed of Diablo, and a strong feeling was pushing him toward the Bonner place. He got dressed and collected his horse that he stabled at the livery.

The house was quiet. That worried him a bit, but he figured Will could be asleep.

Deacon saw no sign of any of the ranch hands, but often they went into town to kick up their heels on the weekend. Diablo stood against the rails of the round pen, dark eyes staring.

"Okay, you got me out here. What do you want?" Deacon climbed to the top rail and sat. "What are we doing? Tell me."

The mustang pricked his ears and took a step, then another and another. Deacon sat motionless, waiting. A yard away, the horse stopped, his flanks jerking. Still Deacon didn't move for the longest. When he did, it was to reach into his pocket to pull out a sugar cube. He held out his hand. "Got something for you."

Diablo came close enough at last and took the bite of sugar. Instead of retreating as he had each time before, he stayed and ate a second one that Deacon gave him.

"Pretty good, huh?" Deacon climbed into the pen, and the horse moved to the opposite side. It was like a dance they were doing. Deacon moved to the center, and Diablo came back. "Looking for more sugar? You have to give me something first." He began walking slowly toward the horse, his hands at his sides. "I won't hurt you. Don't be afraid."

When he finally stood at the horse's side, he laid his hands on the beautiful coat. "You're a handsome fellow. Maybe we can be friends."

A strange feeling, some unexplained energy, passed through his hands. Deacon laid his face where his hands had been. Tears filled Deacon's eyes. Someone had hurt this horse. He'd suffered as Deacon had. The knowledge was profound and shook him to his core.

They stood in the quiet, the early sunlight on them. As far as who offered comfort to whom, Deacon didn't know. Such peace washed over him, and he hoped Diablo felt it too.

Finally, Deacon raised his head and reached for a rope he'd placed under his light coat, and bit by bit, he slipped it over Diablo's head. The horse snorted and skittered back but Deacon kept a firm hand on the rope. "I won't hurt you. We're just going to exercise."

He slapped his end of the rope lightly against his trousers, and Diablo began to run around the pen. He ran the horse for ten minutes one way and switched directions. Each time Diablo slowed, Deacon started him running again.

After twenty minutes, he let him stop and stood with his back to Diablo, trusting, praying the horse wouldn't run him over. He heard nothing for what seemed like an eternity.

Just as he was about to give up, the horse gave a soft snort and nudged Deacon's shoulder.

Overcome with emotion, he turned to face the animal everyone had labeled a killer. Though Diablo appeared ready to bolt any second, he let Deacon touch his face.

He slowly placed his hand on the small area below Diablo's ears on his forehead and gently rubbed. "That feel good?" The mustang released a soft snuffle.

From now on, Deacon needed to come out daily, but he didn't know how he'd manage that. A little more pampering, and he called it a good day, pleased with the progress. Next would come harder stuff—getting Diablo accustomed to the horse blanket, bit and bridle, then the saddle. Once they'd jumped those hurdles, Deacon would have to ride him.

Thinking about the chore of getting on Diablo's back, he turned his attention to the still-silent ranch house. Concern crawled up the back of his neck as he walked to the kitchen door.

Inside, the house was as quiet as a tomb. "Will? It's Deacon." He moved past the dirty dishes. "Where are you, Will?"

He moved on into the parlor where he'd played many a game of checkers with Will. Then he saw him.

Will sat silent and motionless next to the window. An eerie feeling washed over Deacon.

Dead?

Although his boots made plenty of noise, Will didn't stir. His eyes were open.

"Will? What're you doing?" Deacon moved across the room and rested a hand on the rancher's shoulder.

At last Will glanced up. "Didn't hear you come in."

"What's going on? Were you deep in thought?"

"Hell, Deacon, who knows?" Will stood, wiping his eyes. "How long you been here?"

"Since dawn. Wanted to work with the horse. We reached an

understanding today." Deacon glanced around and spied a half dozen pictures of Frances lying on a table. They hadn't been there the last time.

"That's good. I'm glad you didn't give up. Want some coffee?"

"I can always use a cup, you know that." Deacon knew he couldn't leave anytime soon with Will like this. He waited for Will, and they ambled toward the kitchen together. "How about we go fishing this afternoon? How does that sound?"

"You can be gone from the saloon that long?"

"I'm the boss. I can do whatever I want, and I'd like to spend the day with you."

A happy gleam came into Will's eyes. "It'll be like old times."

They talked about the good days over a pot of coffee, ate, then grabbed the fishing poles. Although Deacon had a lot of things to do, he put everything aside for an old friend and rowed out to the center of the pond. Will seemed more like his normal self as they settled in for a peaceful time under the wide expanse of blue Texas sky.

Deacon enjoyed the day, talking and laughing and catching fish. As dusk approached, they rowed in with a nice stringer of catfish that they cleaned and cooked over an open fire.

"Will, come into town with me and spend a few days."

The rancher snorted. "Hell! I ain't up for wild living in Hell's Half Acre."

"I could put you to work making tamales."

Will laughed. "And who would run this place?"

"You got people. By the way, where are they? I haven't seen hide nor hair of them."

"Went into town for some fun. They'll come draggin' in tomorrow, hungover and broke."

"I remember." The fire crackled softly as darkness set in. "How about it?"

"Naw, I ain't up to that." Will was quiet a moment. "Or much of anything else."

Deacon gave him a side glance and tried to act casual. "More problems with your heart?"

Will swung around and barked, "You my doctor now?"

His chest aching for the man, Deacon laid a hand on his knee. "Just a friend," he said softly. "Someone who cares."

In the following silence, Will picked up a stick and tossed it in the fire. "Had another spell the other morning, and I've been thinking a lot about Frances."

Deacon thought about that later as he rode back to town. Will Bonner was losing his reason for living, and there was nothing Deacon could do. He couldn't make someone live if they didn't want to.

Quite possibly seeing Diablo gentled enough to ride was all Will was hanging around for.

Twenty

On Sunday, Grace found herself again in Fort Worth. She left the Lone Star disappointed that her quest for the identity of Yuma Blackstone had ended in failure. All she knew was that Lara had suffered evil so horrific, she couldn't talk about it—and Yuma was at the center.

She had to let it go and not mention it again. For her mother's sake.

Her thoughts went to the crazy dream, and the jury was still out on how much she believed. Still, it was a comfort to know her great-grandfather was watching over her.

The day before she'd left, she received a telegram from Mr. Pemberton at the paper telling her to catch the next train. He had an important assignment for her.

To say the least, the unusual request kept her in suspense all the way home, and she was pacing back and forth in front of the doors when the *Fort Worth Gazette* opened.

She went straight to Pemberton's office, and his rumpled appearance told her he hadn't gone home for a wink of sleep.

He waved her in and got right to the point. "As you know, we've become much maligned in newspapers all over the country. They call us all sorts of names such as Panther City, Fort Crunk, Cowtown, Queen City of the Prairie. Okay, some aren't bad. But this town has sadly become known as the wildest, most dangerous place to live in all of Texas."

"I agree, but I'm not seeing your point, sir."

"There's been developments around town, Sam, and I want you

to write some human interest articles." He lifted a cigar from his ashtray and gave it a puff. "You're probably wondering why I chose you." A knock came at the door. Pemberton opened it and spoke low to a reporter. He finished and turned. "No one in this office has the tenacity, the stubborn-mule approach when it comes to chomping down on something and not letting go."

Grace frowned, not sure that was a compliment. Others certainly hadn't thought so. "I see. I'll do my very best to bring this to a successful conclusion. What's happened?"

The short editor placed his cigar in the corner of his mouth and began to pace. "Groups are cleaning up the city, and they started their campaign doing something about the street children."

Grace froze. Force wasn't always the best policy, even if the motives were good.

"What exactly are they doing, sir?" Grace joined him in walking the length of his office and back, her thoughts on the poor, unfortunate kids with no homes, no food, no families.

Pemberton continued. "They're going to find those kids a home. Short of that, they'll put them on an orphan train and send them West to families who'll take them. If New York can do that, so can Texas. I think if you'll appeal to the citizens, they'll have no need to ship any out of here."

Grace flipped open her notebook. "Understandable, sir. Who's spearheading this?"

"A group of churches have banded together. Start with Garvin Moore at the Presbyterian church on Franklin Street." Pemberton stopped, and Grace nearly plowed into him.

This was the biggest job she'd ever had, and to fail would ruin her in the newspaper world.

"You can count on me. I think this is a great project and has been needed for quite some time." To find kids like Izzy a home would be wonderful. They could go to school and thrive.

"One more thing. A boy named Simon came in here with

Deacon Brannock to report his friend Izzy missing. The boy was quite distraught, and I ended up promising him we would do our best to find Izzy. Give that your best shot, Sam, so I can say we tried. I don't want to let the boy down."

Her heart froze. Izzy had vanished. Her thoughts went back to her last conversation with the poor, sweet kid doing his utmost to survive. It wasn't fair. Nothing about this whole rotten thing was fair. She remembered how he'd clung to her and cried his heart out. He'd been so scared. Why hadn't she done something?

"Yes, sir. Thank you for having faith in me."

At his dismissive nod, she left and made her way to the notorious Hell's Half Acre. After asking everyone she encountered if they'd seen Simon and getting a no, she rapped on the back door of the Three Deuces.

Harry answered. "Miss Grace, how nice to see you. I'm glad you're back."

"I arrived this morning. Is your boss around?"

"I thought I heard someone." Brannock lounged in the kitchen doorway, his face half hidden by the shadows.

Grace took a deep breath to tamp down her anger before speaking. "My boss told me you took a boy down to the paper to report Izzy missing."

He stiffened. "Are you accusing me of something? Because it sure as hell feels like it."

"Don't be ridiculous." Grace looked away from his steely-gray eyes and inhaled another sharp breath to still her shaking. "I told you about talking to him and how scared he was. I thought you were going to find him and put him someplace safe." She put a weary hand to her eyes, telling herself not to cry. "We've wasted precious time. Izzy could be…" Her lip quivered and left her unable to complete the thought.

His gray eyes flashed. "I've wasted no time. I've been out searching for the kid every spare minute."

Now he was mad. Darn it! The urge to fly into his arms and let him hold her was powerful, but his stern, forbidding features stopped her.

She twisted her hands. "I'm sorry. I'm just so worried. He's important to me, Brannock."

"Tell me again what Izzy said to you."

Her chin quivered, recalling his fear. "He told me there was some bad stuff happening on the streets. He was terrified and crying, said he'd been staying in hiding. He wouldn't tell me anything else. Do you think someone has hurt him?"

"They'd better not." He whirled, dismissing her.

Grace hurried, catching him at the bottom of the stairs. "Wait. Why did you go to the newspaper and not the sheriff to report Izzy missing?"

"The sheriff and I have…a history and not an especially good one. He wouldn't have listened. Izzy is unimportant. He can't vote or donate money. He's—" Deacon's voice broke.

"He's just a sweet little boy with no family to his name," she finished softly. "Can we start over and pretend I've just entered?"

He hesitated, hurt and disappointment lining each crevice of his face.

"Please, Brannock. Let's not fight. I didn't mean to accuse you of anything."

Perhaps it was the heartache and panic in her voice that made him turn and bow from the waist—though he still frowned. "My name is Deacon Brannock and I'm pleased to meet you, Miss Grace."

"Thank you, kind sir." She smiled and curtsied low. "You have a lovely establishment."

"It's not much, but it's mine." He stood even with her again. "Would you care to talk?"

Grateful tears filled her eyes as she nodded. They found a private table in the corner, and he held her chair.

For the next half hour, he filled her in on what he knew about the boy, Simon, he'd befriended. Grace watched the man across from her, his deep voice filling the quiet and touching places inside her as few had. He wore his sleeves rolled, revealing thick, blue veins under the surface of his arm and powerful muscles that quivered with each movement. Only an imbecile would accuse Deacon Brannock of being soft. Hardness showed in his eyes. Whatever he'd suffered in life had sculpted him into something close to a chunk of unyielding granite.

Except during certain times when he allowed her to see his soft heart.

She held her tongue until he'd finished. "Pemberton asked me to do some looking around. Whatever this Simon said to him, he touched my boss's heart and got him to promise to try to find Izzy, and now it's my job. This could be simple. My boss said the churches have gotten together and are rounding up these street kids and finding them homes in an effort to clean up the city. Maybe they collected Izzy."

When he glanced up, his eyes of smoke and steel under dark, slashing brows met hers, and Grace found the effect quite unsettling. He held her gaze for what seemed a full minute before she was finally able to look away. If anyone could find Izzy, it would be him.

"It's possible."

Desperate to cover the effect he had on her, Grace opened her notebook and took a pencil from her handbag. "I think the first thing would be to talk to Reverend Garvin Moore. We should find him at the Presbyterian church. Maybe he'll have a list of kids they've scooped up."

"I hope so."

Her voice trembled, and tears stung the backs of her eyes. "I think of Izzy being frightened and alone, and I can barely stand it. The poor kid has been trying to survive his entire life." She bit her quivering lip. "When will someone give him a chance to grow up?"

He folded his large palms around her hand. "Try to focus on us finding him."

"What if all we find is his broken body?"

"We won't. And when we locate him, I'm bringing him to live with me here."

"He'll love that." A ray of sunshine broke through and gave Grace hope. "Thanks for the encouragement."

"I only give that to the best people." He kissed the sensitive flesh of her palm.

Grace loved the teasing warmth. "Then I'm doubly lucky. If we pool our resources, we'll find him quicker. What do you say, partner?"

"Try to get rid of me. I have a vested interest in finding Izzy." He winked. "Say, what happened to your temperance ladies? I kinda miss your efforts to shut me down."

She tipped her head to the side and rolled her eyes. "Miss us like the plague, you mean. We sort of parted ways with Carrie Nation and her advocating violence. I believe the pen is mightier than the sword and have switched my efforts to the more peaceful kind."

He leaned in to place his mouth at her ear, sending goose bumps over her. "I do miss seeing your pert behind marching in front of my door."

Grace raised an eyebrow. "My pert behind?" She laughed. "I doubt you paid me one bit of mind."

He moved back in his chair. A strange light smoldered in his gray eyes, and Grace grew warm.

His voice came barely louder than a whisper. "I noticed."

What was he doing? She had no idea how to reply and was saved having to when Harry brought tea for her and coffee for Deacon. So flustered was she that she reached for the sugar cubes, forgetting she took tea without sweetener.

"Thank you, Harry. You are a godsend." Grace watched the ponytailed bartender return to the kitchen.

Whatever had gotten into Deacon seemed to have been temporary because he dropped the flirty conversation and returned to the man she knew.

"How is Leah? Did she like the ranch?" He lifted his cup. "I don't want her unhappy."

"Then stop worrying. Leah loves my parents and my crotchety grandpa Stoker. My little sister, Hannah, has attached herself to Leah and the baby and is making herself a nuisance, I fear." Grace laughed. "I never would've taken you for a mother hen."

"My apron is invisible. How did your quest about Yuma Blackstone go?"

"Not well at all." She told him that beyond her father's short recounting of the cattle drive and the stand he and his drovers had made, no one would discuss Yuma. "He attacked my mother, or my name isn't Grace Legend."

"You're probably right, knowing the man. Sometimes things are too painful to talk about. Will you drop it?"

"This ended when I left the Lone Star. I'm done. I have to respect my mother's right to keep it buried." Now, she had to focus on solving the case of the missing children. "Besides, I need to devote myself to talking to Reverend Moore, writing articles for the paper, and finding Izzy."

"I have some free time before business cranks up here. But since the break-in, I've been staying close."

The danger of this lower part of town never went away, reminding her how tenuous life was for some. Heaviness sat on her chest. "Did they take anything?"

"Didn't have time. The attack cat foiled whatever plans he had."

She laughed. "That cat is certainly worth his bowl of milk."

Brannock pulled a bronze token from his pocket. "I found this in the alley. I think the intruder dropped it."

She looked at the round disc that gave the bearer one free night at Miss Pearl's Boardinghouse, the familiar term for a house of ill repute.

"Any thoughts on who it might've been?"

"None I can voice. I'm just grateful Leah and the baby weren't here." Brannock pinched the bridge of his nose and let out a long exhale. "I'm glad you're back."

"Me too."

They finished their tea and coffee, and Brannock put on his worn Stetson. "Ready to go sleuthing?"

"I am, Sherlock." But the lighthearted banter died on her lips.

Izzy was out there in the city somewhere, afraid and probably hungry, and she meant to bring him and his little red wagon home where he was safe and loved.

Twenty-one

THEY WERE ABOUT TO BEGIN THEIR SEARCH FOR IZZY WHEN a knock sounded on the back door of the saloon. Deacon opened it to find an old, thin-hipped woman with silver hair done up in a topknot. A traveling case sat at her feet. "Can I help you, ma'am?"

The tall stranger gripped a black shawl around her. She was so skinny, she had to stand twice to make a shadow. "Excuse me. I'm looking for Harry Jones."

"Yes, ma'am, he's here. Come in." He picked up her case and hollered for Harry.

The bartender came from the kitchen. "Aunt Martha. What brings you to Fort Worth?"

She sighed. "Harry, I hate to trouble you, but I wonder if I could have a place to sleep for the night. I'll go somewhere tomorrow."

Harry hugged her. "Aunt Martha, of course you can spend the night." He introduced Deacon and Grace. "What happened to Uncle Clyde?" he asked her.

"That old coot! I left him. He went to town all spruced up, tipping his hat left and right, and had the gall to wink at Essie Sowers."

"How many times have you left him? Fifteen? Twenty? It seems a monthly fight."

Aunt Martha drew herself up. "I ain't gonna put up with his sashaying around, and Clyde knows that." She folded her hands over her bony chest. "I deserve a loving, faithful man."

Deacon almost lost the struggle to keep a straight face. "Are you hungry, ma'am?"

The tall woman craned her neck, maybe looking for the

kitchen. "I'd be obliged for a little something. Whatever you can spare."

Harry yanked Deacon into the kitchen. "We can't get involved in their spats."

"Why not?"

"Their fights never end, just move from one subject to another." Harry's eyes widened and his tongue worked to get the words out. "Then before you can turn around, they both move in, lock, stock, and barrel. She's crazy," Harry whispered. "And he's crazier."

Wasn't everyone? The wheels in Deacon's head whirled. "Can she cook?"

"Yes, but—"

"She can make tamales, Harry." Deacon said it real slow so Harry couldn't miss the meaning.

"Yes, but—"

"If she can make tamales, maybe she can make empanadas and other things."

"She can, but—"

"What's your problem, Harry? Spit it out."

"Clyde. Clyde is the problem. Him and his pet monkey that shits everywhere, the little devil. And the pissy varmint steals food." Harry took a deep breath. "The last time I visited them and spent the night, it got in the room where I slept and took all my clothes and hid 'em. I ended up having to wear one of Aunt Martha's dresses until we found 'em. I ain't ever gonna forget that." He shuddered.

Deacon could hear Grace and Aunt Martha in the other room and knew he had to make a decision. He glanced at the pitiful pile of tamales they'd been unable to sell, and dirty pans and dishes everywhere. Looked like a tornado had passed through. "Yeah, but she can cook. I'll live with a monkey for that. I'll kiss the damn monkey for that. Maybe Clyde won't find out where she is."

And even if he did, no other saloon in Fort Worth had a pet

monkey. Folks would flock to see that if the food failed to draw them. A monkey.

"He will. Clyde always does. Go ahead and do what you think is best. I warned you."

They went to join the ladies. Deacon cleared his throat. "Martha, I have a position open for someone who can make tamales and I'll give you room and board if you can."

"I've never had any complaints about my cooking, Mr. Brannock. I had a big family, and then Clyde and me moved in with my sister and her bunch until she passed. I reckon cooking for a bunch of men ain't much different."

Deacon's gaze flicked to Grace, who nodded, then back to Martha. "You're hired, and if you can start tonight, I'll throw in five silver dollars."

Harry tried to work up enthusiasm. He truly seemed to. "I hope you say yes, Aunt Martha. We need the help."

Grace laughed, taking the woman's arm. "Ma'am, I hope you don't hesitate too long, or these men might tie you to a chair. They're pretty desperate."

"Then the answer is yes. I think we might be a good fit for each other until Clyde comes crawling to me." Martha's long face was replaced by a smile. "But this time, I'm not taking him back. No, siree." She glanced around. "Well, I'd best get busy. There's no time to waste."

Harry carried her suitcase upstairs, and Deacon and Grace showed her to the kitchen. "I'm sorry about the dirty dishes," Deacon said. "I didn't get around to washing them. You don't know how much I appreciate this, ma'am."

"You just want tamales made? Is that all? I can make other things."

A flash of excitement rushed through Deacon. "Such as?"

"Red beans and rice, fried pies, biscuits and sausage."

"Empanadas?"

"Meat or fruit?" she asked.

"Meat."

"Yep, I sure can."

"I could kiss you, ma'am." Deacon started toward her, and she threw up hands.

"Not ma'am. Call me Aunt Martha and we'll all get along."

Grace kissed her cheek. "I think you're going to fit in fine."

For the first time since Leah left, Deacon felt the weight lift. This woman was going to save the saloon, and he and Harry their sanity.

He said a prayer that Clyde took his time making up. Part of him grieved that the monkey wouldn't be coming, though. It was a damn good money-making idea.

"Look the kitchen larder over and make a list of what you'll need. I'll bring everything back with me when I return." He put his arm around her shoulders. "Thank you for coming, Aunt Martha. This is your new home."

The old woman's eyes sparkled. "Bless you, sonny."

Harry returned. "I'll help you, Aunt Martha. We'll whip these dishes out in no time."

"It was a pleasure to meet you." Grace gave her a hug. "I think you'll be happy here."

"You sure are a pretty thing, Miss Legend." Aunt Martha's eyes twinkled. "I have a feeling I'll see quite a bit of you, unless I miss my guess."

Deacon's mind churned. "Don't tell me you're in the business of telling fortunes too." That would be too lucky.

"Rest easy, Mr. Brannock. I gave that up years ago."

It sounded like there was a story there, but he didn't ask. He'd learned that when you meddled in someone else's pot, you ended up with burns. A few minutes later, he and Grace left, armed with a list of items that he'd bring back.

They first went to the big Presbyterian church and met with Reverend Garvin Moore.

The man ran a hand across his weary face. He clearly wasn't sleeping much. "We knew when we started this that it would be a large, slow undertaking, but we didn't know just how big a task it would be. We have so many, and it's barely a drop in the bucket. If you can give me a minute, I'll look at the list in my office to see if Izzy...uh Israel Anthony is here."

"Thank you." Deacon led Grace to a bench and sat to wait.

"I hope we find him." Grace patted his arm. "Are you serious about offering him a home?"

"Dead serious. In fact, I've been thinking of a way I might help the reverend. With us expanding the food we serve, we'll have a kitchen full of dirty dishes. Until the kids get adopted, they can wash dishes, clean tables, and do all kinds of other things. But I'll also send them to school. They need an education."

Her blue eyes sparkled. "Yes, they do. You have a great plan, but the number of jobs you can offer is limited."

He released a troubled sigh. "That's the sad part. I want to help all the kids."

"You know the church congregations will raise holy hell about the kids working and living in a saloon."

She had a point.

"I know. There's always a fly to spoil the ointment." He sent her a suspicious glance. "Are you still hoping I'll close the saloon?"

"Me?" She feigned shock. "Do you think I'd do that?"

"Faster than you can bat those pretty eyes. I'm a saloon owner, and I'll probably always be a saloon owner. Get used to it, princess."

His work with Diablo crossed his mind, but he didn't want to tell Grace yet in case it fell through. Success seemed iffy. Will could up and die, or the horse, and leave him with nothing to show. Best not to tell her. He'd do anything to keep her from seeing him as a failure.

They lapsed into silence for several moments, and somewhere deep within the church came children's laughter. It sounded like they were playing.

"Brannock, what if we never find Izzy? What if we never learn what happened to him? Can you live with that?"

"I'll have no choice, but the kid will always stick in my mind." He told her how clever Izzy had been in finagling the red wagon. He chuckled. "That boy knew he had me wrapped around his finger."

"You left the wagon there under that boardwalk? What were you thinking?"

"That he'd want it when he came back and expect it to be there."

"We need to take it to the Three Deuces for safekeeping."

"I guess you're right, Grace. We can pick it up on the way back."

Reverend Moore came down the hall. "I'm sorry. The boy isn't here."

So much for hoping. "Could he be at another church?" Deacon asked.

"I'm afraid not. This is where they're bringing them. Folks who want to adopt are already coming here."

Grace introduced herself as a reporter from the *Gazette*. "I'm curious, Reverend. How much interest has there been?"

"We've already placed ten children with good families, so we're hopeful the project will see all of them soon living healthy, happy lives."

"Can I quote you on that?" she asked, taking a notebook from her bag.

"Of course."

"I do pray you're right. This is such a wonderful thing you're doing." Grace quickly wrote down what the man had said.

"Thank you for your help, Reverend." Deacon shook his hand. "If Izzy does happen to show up here, please send word to the Three Deuces. I'm very concerned about his welfare."

"I understand, and you can be assured I'll do my best to help find him." Moore glanced toward the door as a well-dressed couple entered. "If you'll excuse me."

With nothing else to do, Deacon ushered Grace out. He turned to her on the sidewalk. "Where else, Miss Sam?"

"To the general store I suppose, then back to the Acre. We can stop and collect Izzy's wagon on the way." Grace took his elbow. "Then I must go home and write my first article for Pemberton about the churches looking to place the street children in homes. I'm not sure what to write for those that follow. Any suggestions?"

"Why don't you talk to a few of the kids Moore already has and get their perspective?"

"That's an excellent idea." She was silent a moment as they walked. "Brannock, where else can we look for Izzy?"

"I've scoured every inch of the Acre and talked to all the other business owners. I have no other suggestions. I'm tired of finding nothing." He wondered if Grace found his obsession with Izzy a bit odd, but he didn't see it that way at all. His own upbringing took the blame, he supposed. As a boy, he'd had little companionship and certainly no playmates other than his little sister, Cass. They were expected to keep out of sight and speak in low whispers. To disobey would've gotten their mother booted out on her rear.

Yes, he had a soft spot for the kids in Hell's Half Acre. No place to belong, no one to care. No hope.

Deacon knew quite a bit about all that.

Twenty-two

Back on Rusk Street with noon approaching, Deacon collected Izzy's red wagon and belongings, surprised but glad they were still there. He and Grace had turned toward the saloon when he saw a boy running into an old shack. "Did you see that?"

"Yes. Do you think it's Izzy?" Grace squinted. "I can't tell."

"I don't know, but we'll find out." They reached the leaning building with its rotting boards and Deacon was afraid to hope. "Izzy, is that you? Come out, son."

"You don't have to be afraid," Grace called. "We won't hurt you."

A shadowed face appeared at the opening. Two scared eyes came into focus. "It's me, Simon."

The poor kid's voice shook. It must seem like the end of the world to him. Who knew the last time he'd slept or eaten? Deacon reached into the sack of things from the general store for some jerky. "Here, Simon. You look hungry."

The boy snatched the food and fell back into the shadows of the old dilapidated building.

"What happened to the money I gave you?" Deacon asked. "It was enough to buy you a little food."

"A big kid slugged me and stole it. I'm sorry, Mr. Brannock."

"It's okay. Some things happen beyond our control." Deacon pressed against the side. "I can protect you, give you a place to stay where no one will find you." He'd seen so many like Simon and Izzy over the years. If he could help just one, he'd feel less of a failure.

Grace leaned forward. "Take him up on that offer, Simon. You're all alone out here."

"They's some men tryin' to get me." Simon's voice was low and frightened.

"They're going to find you a home, son. They mean no harm." Deacon hoped to quell the terror in the boy's eyes.

"No, these are bad, bad mean ones. They took my friend, and I hid."

That didn't sound like Reverend Moore.

"Come out and let's talk." Deacon moved back a little, and Grace followed to ease the pressure. "You can trust me."

"Promise to keep me safe?" Simon's whisper barely reached Deacon.

"I do. I'll make sure no one finds you."

Silence ensued. Deacon listened to the boy chomping on the jerky. If worst came to worst, they could grab him and force him to come along, but that would be the last option. Trying to force their will on Simon wouldn't sit well, even though it might be for his own good.

Simon's face appeared in the slight opening. He chewed. "Okay. I'll try your place, Mr. Brannock. But I ain't saying I'll stay long. Walls make me jittery. Cain't run."

Grace gave a low cry and covered her mouth. Tears filled her eyes.

"I know, Simon," Deacon said softly. "But it's best for now. No one will get you."

A heavy sigh sounded. "I guess."

He and Grace helped Simon from his narrow hiding place and hurried him to the Three Deuces, where the nervous boy glanced around. They seated him at the kitchen table, and Harry gave him a glass of cold milk.

Aunt Martha had taken the purchases and disappeared into the kitchen. Izzy's red wagon was safe upstairs.

"Simon, these people taking kids off the street aren't mean." Grace leaned forward and took the boy's hand that was covered with scabs and scars. "They want to find homes for everyone where you can be fed and cared for."

"I'm doing jus' fine. I don't need 'em. Why don't they leave us alone?"

"Son, they can't. Folks are wanting the streets and the town cleaned up." Deacon leaned against the wall. "They have to do what the people want. Wouldn't you like a home, a bed to sleep in, food to eat?"

"It's been so long, I don't remember what it's like." Anguish filled Simon's low voice. "Sometimes I don't remember my fam'ly."

Grace rose and brushed a kiss to the top of his head. "All the more reason to let Reverend Moore find you all of the comforts."

Simon waved his arm to brush her away and spilled his milk. His eyes grew large. "I'm sorry."

"That's all right. I'm going to leave you alone." Grace moved to Deacon as Harry and Aunt Martha arrived with a wet rag and a fresh glass of milk. She laid her head on Brannock's shoulder.

Deacon gave her a sideways glance, admiring the way her golden hair curled down her back. When she lifted her face and caught him staring, he shifted but didn't lower his gaze. "You tried your best, Grace. It's hard for them to give up everything that's familiar, even when it's not working. The streets are all any of these kids know."

"I just realized that. It's so sad." She wiped her eyes.

A noise sounded behind the bar, and Simon jumped out of his chair, his eyes darting wildly.

"It's all right, Simon. It was only Harry. You're safe."

"Why don't you listen to me, Mr. Brannock? They's some mean people. They took Izzy. Now they grabbed my friend Davey. Went off in a black ice wagon, and I don't know where."

Deacon pulled the trembling boy to him. "Okay, we'll start looking tomorrow. We'll try to find Davey and all the others."

Simon settled a bit, then spying Sarge, he went to pet the persnickety cat.

"I think we'd best work on finding that ice wagon." Deacon's arms folded around Grace, relishing the feel of her body. "Would you take supper with me?"

"Where? Here?"

"Yes. I don't want to leave Simon alone. We can eat in the kitchen, away from the noise in the saloon." He lifted her wrist and kissed the underside. "Say yes."

"All right."

"Do you need to let your brother know?"

She shook her head. "He went to Weatherford this morning on business."

"I guess you're in the clear, then."

Grace worked in the small kitchen washing Aunt Martha's pans, then when the old aunt finished, Grace and Deacon made supper preparations while Simon took a nap upstairs. The kid was tuckered out and had probably been up all night keeping watch against the well-meaning saints.

There wasn't a lot of elbow room, and with Brannock's large body taking up most of the space, Grace kept running into him. It took some time to figure out a system, but once they did, everything smoothed out. She kept noticing him rubbing his arm and flexing his hand. Then as they were carrying everything to the small table in the kitchen, he dropped a bowl of mashed potatoes, barely catching it before it hit the floor.

Grace took the bowl from him and put it on the table. She pulled him aside. "What's wrong, Brannock?"

"Nothing. Just clumsy." He wouldn't look at her.

"No, it's more than that. You've been rubbing your arm and hand for the last half hour. For once, just tell me straight-out."

"Just something I struggle with." He walked away, but Grace followed.

"I see that much. Do you lose feeling in your arm? I want to help."

He blew out a loud whoosh of air. "You can't. No one can help."

"Will you admit you lose the ability to feel?" she pressed.

"Look, it's nothing to fret about."

"Will you stop being such a stoic man? How long has it been this way?"

"A few years. It's *my* arm so don't worry about it."

She stretched to kiss his cheek. "Someone has to. Guess it's my job. I take it you know why you lose strength in it."

"Drop the subject." He whirled around her and went to get Simon before the crowd in the saloon got too rowdy.

While he was gone, she set out the corn, fried chicken, and gravy. A few minutes later, everyone took a seat.

"Wow, I ain't never seen so much food!" Simon's eyes widened. "Are you rich, Mr. Brannock?"

"Not hardly, son."

The conversation was lively, with lots of laughter for Simon's benefit. No long faces to put a damper on the meal. Brannock had gotten over his bad mood and teased Simon until he got a smile. They weren't much different from the Legend household, Grace found.

When they finished doing the dishes, Brannock hung the dishtowel. "I'll walk you out."

Grace took his arm, and they moved into the fragrant night air. She was instantly aware of his closeness, his height. The top of her head barely came to his chin. Her short stature was one thing she'd always regretted about herself and would change in a heartbeat if she could.

"I wonder what Leah's doing, and if she likes the ranch." She glanced up at him and found his stare a bit unsettling. "I don't think Seth will find her there."

"I'm not worried. It's a relief to have her safe."

"Why did you take Leah in, Brannock?" Grace asked softly.

"She reminded me of my kid sister who lost her life when she was a little older than Izzy. Cass never saw her twelfth birthday."

The heavy sorrow in his voice touched Grace. "If she looked like Leah, Cass was a pretty girl. What happened to her, if you don't mind me asking?"

His face closed. "Rather not talk about it."

"Okay."

They walked past a rowdy saloon from which loud music and voices spilled. Suddenly, a man staggered out the batwing doors and into Grace. She let out a yell and fell against Brannock.

He grabbed the drunk and slung him roughly aside. "Are you okay?"

Half-dazed, she glanced down in dismay at the long rip in her dress.

"Hell! I'm sorry." He put an arm around her and hurried her past the joint.

"It wasn't your fault. I'll see if it can be repaired."

"Let me know how much, and if it's beyond fixing, I'll buy you a new one."

"That's not necessary, Brannock."

"Oh, but it is." He drew closer and put an arm around her. "This is why it's not safe for you to come to this part of town alone."

"I know. I'm glad you were here."

Against her objections, he ended up walking her all the way home, and when they arrived, he stood in silence, his hands at his sides. His dark mood created a wall between them. "I'm no good for you, Grace."

She laid a light hand on his arm, afraid of what he was saying. "I'll be the judge of that."

"Your world and mine can never meet. The gap is too wide."

"You're just tired and missing Leah, the baby, and Izzy. Can we talk tomorrow?" She swallowed the lump in her throat and blinked hard. "Please," she begged.

What could she say? What could she do to keep from losing him?

"Maybe. Good night, Grace."

He strode away, leaving her standing at her door staring after him. She didn't get a kiss, not even a peck on the cheek. "The stupid drunk ruined everything," she said to herself.

Then asking about his sister had spooked him. Whatever had happened must've left severe scars. And she had no way of finding out more unless Brannock relented and talked.

Or she learned his real name.

"Slim chance of that," she whispered into the night.

Grace released a sigh and turned, glad for something to do at the moment that didn't require thought. With Izzy's disappearance, Brannock's mysterious past, the temperance movement, her job at the newspaper, and Yuma Blackstone, her head was about to burst.

≪∽≫

About ten minutes later, a knock sounded on the front door. Grace hurried. Brannock must've come back for some reason. Her heart raced. "Coming."

She unlocked the door and threw it open wide. "I'm glad you—"

Only it wasn't Deacon. She didn't recognize the man dressed in shabby clothes, a sneer on his lips, a scar on his neck that looked new. What she saw in his glittering eyes sent panic racing through her. She'd seen similar at ten years old.

Without a word or scream, she reached to slam the door. He stuck his foot between it and the doorframe, stopping it from closing. Shaking, she pushed with all her might, but she was no match for him. He shoved the door open and grabbed her arm.

A second man crowded behind him. "Hey, Pickford, I thought we were only going to scare her."

Seth Pickford.

"Change of plans," Pickford barked. "She's coming with us."

Grace grabbed on to the doorframe and clung, but the two men yanked her hard out into the night. She screamed at the top of her voice, hoping someone would hear her. They pulled her down the walk toward a wagon.

Her gun. She had to get to the gun in her pocket.

Pickford shifted and forced her back against him, his forearm lodged across her windpipe. She could barely breathe. If she didn't free herself before they reached the street, she wouldn't give two cents for her life.

Two lavender rhododendron bushes well over six feet tall stood on either side of the walk. One of the men would have to release her to pass through. Sure enough, Pickford's partner turned her loose and stepped back.

Grace yanked the gun from her pocket, twisted her arm, and pressed it into Pickford's gut.

Before she could fire, the partner saw it and wrenched the gun away, sending it flying somewhere in the darkness.

She tried to remain calm. Gathering her courage, she spoke in a loud, firm voice. "What do you want? Turn me loose."

"Where's my wife? I know you brought her here. Get Leah for me," Pickford growled, his foul breath gagging her.

Grace worked her tongue and finally managed to speak. "She's not here. Leah is far away."

"You lie!"

"It's true. Your wife left town."

A pair of garden shears lying next to the bush gave her hope. If she could get to them, she could defend herself. In a sudden move, she twisted in his grasp and broke his hold. Letting out a cry, she grabbed the shears and swung.

The blades caught Pickford's stomach, but his clothing snagged the weapon, wrenching the shears from her hand. The second man tackled her, grabbing her hair, yanking her head back.

Pickford came at her, gripping his stomach. His face was the stuff of nightmares. "You little bitch. I'm gonna kill you."

Gasping for air, Grace stared at the rage on his face. Oh God! She couldn't run, couldn't hide, couldn't defend herself.

There was nowhere to go. "Leave me alone and get on your way. I won't report this."

The second man laughed, pulling out a knife. "Did you hear that, Pickford? She won't say anything if we're real nice."

Empty-handed, Grace worked her tongue in her parched mouth. No sound came out. She had to do something or she'd die. She opened her mouth and yelled the name Pickford knew very well. "Brannock! Help, Brannock!"

To her surprise, running footsteps sounded, then a familiar figure emerged from the darkness. He raised a gun and fired. The bullet hit the second attacker. The man let out a yell and ran into the night. The rescuer grabbed Pickford and wrenched his arms behind his back.

"Are you all right, Grace?"

Then she saw Brannock's face, and her knees tried to buckle. "I'm fine. Did I conjure you up?"

"I was coming back to apologize for leaving like I did when I heard you yell my name." His mouth quirked into a half smile.

Pickford growled, trying to break free. Brannock hit him on the head with the butt of his pistol and knocked the man out cold.

"Thank God for your guilty conscience." Grace's heart soared. "I'm glad you came back."

He took her in his arms and gave her a kiss she would remember to her grave. Eyes closed, her heart hammering wildly, she clutched his vest with both hands and parted her mouth ever so slightly. He slipped his tongue through the opening and danced with hers.

A groan from Pickford broke the kiss.

"Go into the house and lock the door, Grace. I'll dispose of the trash where he won't bother you again."

"Good." Aware of his eyes following her, she went into the house and bolted the door, then slid to the floor in a puddle, her legs too weak to carry her upstairs.

Twenty-three

A CRASH JARRED DEACON AWAKE. HE JUMPED TO HIS FEET, yanking his gun from the holster. The place was dark, and for a moment he didn't know where he was. A burning candle, tables, the long wooden bar finally jogged his memory. Ah, the Three Deuces. He put his Colt away.

His boots crunched on glass. Glancing down, he made out the shape of a broken whiskey bottle. Must've fallen off the table.

Deacon swayed and sat, head in his hands. Dammit! What had he done?

Images lurked at the edges of his memory. A gurgle. A man's face. Grace. The burning need to keep her safe yet knowing he wasn't good enough for her.

One by one, the events of the previous evening came back. Why had Grace had to ask about Cass? Unbeknownst to her, she'd stirred a boiling pot and poured it into his gaping wound. It drove home all the reasons why he would never be the right man for Grace.

But dammit, he didn't have the strength to push her away. He couldn't.

Every bone ached, and his pounding head felt like a mule had stomped on it. Maybe if he rested his eyes for a minute, he'd be able to think.

Slowly, light began to drift through the cracks in the boards. People began to stir beyond his doors, horses pulling wagons, new-fangled automobiles backfiring, the drivers making liberal use of the horn. Damn it to hell! For two cents, he'd pump them full of lead.

Harry came from the kitchen. "I see your demons came calling. Coffee, Boss? Or hair of the dog?"

Deacon pondered the choice for a long heartbeat. "Coffee." He had to keep his wits about him. He rubbed his stubble. "What time is it?"

"Eight o'clock."

He scowled at the blood on his white shirt. How? Whose? He'd have to shave and get presentable in case Grace did happen to drop by for that talk after delivering her article to the paper. "Can you bring my coffee upstairs?"

With Harry's nod, he went up to his bedroom, albeit a bit slow. Wouldn't do to wear a soiled shirt, looking like a ghost who haunted creaky old mansions and cemeteries. By the time he'd washed and was searching for a clean shirt, Harry brought coffee.

"Want breakfast?" Harry asked. "Aunt Martha is whipping up a feast."

"I don't think so." Deacon spied a shirt lying in the corner. He picked it up and sniffed it. It'd do, he guessed. "We need to take some clothes to the laundry. Will you take care of it?"

"I can do that. Besides, Aunt Martha might need me to run some errands."

"I'm glad she's here. We needed her." Deacon slipped into the shirt and worked at the buttons.

"You said a mouthful." Harry nodded but didn't leave. "Did you sleep any at all?"

"Never went to bed." Deacon took several swallows of coffee and went to the washstand to shave. "Too much to think about."

"Watch out, or you'll start looking like me."

"Heaven forbid." Deacon lathered his face. "I went to check on Simon about midnight. The kid's gone."

"That's too bad. He was awfully skittish being here, so I half-way expected him to fly the coop." Harry turned away. "I hope he stays safe. Poor kid."

By nine o'clock, Deacon was downstairs and answered the knock on the wooden doors.

Grace looked rested and radiant despite Pickford assaulting her. "Good morning, Brannock. Am I early? Looks like you might've just gotten up."

"Nope. This is my normal me." He pushed aside the batwings for her, not about to tell her any different. "After last night, I wouldn't expect to see you this cheerful." Other than a bruise or two on the delicate curve of her throat, she showed no ill effects from Pickford.

"I'm alive, and that's reason enough to be happy. Has something else happened?"

Harry came down the stairs with the laundry. "No sleep, Miss Grace. And Simon's gone," Harry said.

Worry darkened her eyes. "I wish he'd have felt safe enough here."

"The trouble is he don't think there's anywhere safe," Harry mumbled.

And that truth sat in Deacon's stomach like a wide boulder. These walls kept Simon from running when he needed to escape.

"Maybe we'll see him while we're out." Grace looked at Deacon curiously. "You don't look good, Brannock. Are you sure you're up to searching for Izzy?"

"I'm sure. Harry, on second thought, I'll take the laundry."

They left, and Deacon dropped the soiled clothing off at Sweet Sue's two blocks up on the corner. The day was nice, but there weren't many people out.

Grace chewed her lip as they walked, bothered by something. "Thank you for coming to my rescue last night. I do think Pickford would've killed me. Either him or the friend he brought with him. Did you recognize that one?"

"It was dark, and I didn't really get a good look at him."

"Deacon, what happened to Pickford? Where did you take him?"

Of course, she would be curious. Any normal person would, but this seemed more than that.

"You're safe. I brought him back to the Three Deuces and locked him in a shed in the alley. Why?"

"No reason, I just wondered."

"You won't have to worry about him. I don't think he'll bother you again." Pickford had screamed and yelled all the way back, but few drunks had paid him any mind, since that was a regular occurrence in the Acre.

"That'll be a relief. He frightened me bad. I wonder about the man you shot." She gave him a worried look. "Although he took off running, he could turn up dead."

"Might. But he brought it on himself by attacking you. He deserves what he got."

"Let's put that out of our minds. I thought we might go back to the church to see if Izzy's there, and anyplace else we can think of."

"Good idea." He helped her across a street. "What's the verdict on your ruined dress?"

"I left it at a dress shop to see what they can do. I'll let you know. I haven't forgotten."

"Good. I meant what I said about buying you a new dress if that one isn't repairable. How did Pemberton like your article?"

A wide grin covered her face. "He's running it today and will run another tomorrow. He asked me to write more."

"Smart man. Pemberton likes your work." He shot her a glance. The chilling thought hit him that if he'd been five minutes later last night, she'd be dead, and they wouldn't be having this conversation.

Grace looked especially lovely. Her golden hair curled around her oval face and spilled down her back, and pink cheeks colored her delicate skin a beautiful, healthy shade.

He liked that she'd dressed conservatively—a white blouse and dark skirt. Where they were going, it paid to try to blend in. Flaunting your station in life tended to meet with catastrophe and people itching to take you down a peg. That was the reason for the gun he wore. He noticed the absence of jewelry on her. Smart.

They stopped by the Presbyterian church and spoke with a woman who told them they still had no Izzy. "I hope whoever has the boy is treating him right." Grace sounded forlorn.

"Me too. We need to find that black ice wagon."

"Want to check on some ice houses around here?"

"I was thinking we should." Deacon took her arm, and they aimed for the two nearest ones. "Harry suggested that we check the orphanages around here. Maybe someone in the Acre took him there." He didn't have the heart to add that morgues were also possibilities. Those he'd check himself.

Hope filled Grace's eyes. "Good idea."

He didn't want to tell her that if anyone had gotten Izzy onto an orphan train, they'd never find him. No telling where the boy would land. Or with what kind of people. A sudden urge to haul off and hit something took hold. Life wasn't fair to little boys—or grown men.

"Will you try to look for Simon?" she asked.

"Won't do a lick of good. Even if I bring him back, he won't stay."

"I suppose not, but his paralyzing fear breaks my heart."

It did his too, but there was nothing to be done about it.

They struck out at the two ice houses. No one had ever seen a black ice wagon on the streets of Fort Worth. Deacon hadn't either. Only white. They went on to call on the two orphanages with no better results. The people they spoke with were very sympathetic and told them they just sent a group of older children to the train depot to head West.

"If you hurry, you might catch them," the woman said.

Praying they'd make it, Deacon and Grace arrived at the Texas and Pacific Railway Station just as they were loading the kids. He scanned the face of each child, his heart breaking at their sobs and hurt, angry eyes. Grace knelt beside several and wiped their tears, giving them a hug. But although Deacon had come with hope of locating Izzy, they reached the end of the line without finding the red-haired, freckled boy with bright blue eyes.

Deacon led a distraught Grace onto the platform, where she broke down and buried her face against his chest, clinging to him.

"I'm sorry. I shouldn't have brought you." He rubbed her back up and down, his heart aching for her and the children. "It's not fair. None of it."

At last she raised her head and took the handkerchief he offered. "I don't understand why things have to be this way. They're so sweet and scared to death. All they want is for someone to love them."

"I know." He pulled out his pocket watch and checked the time, discovering it was the noon hour. "There's a little café on the corner. Let's eat."

Soon they were sitting at a table. Grace ordered a bowl of soup, and Deacon got chili.

"Brannock, I have to report in at the newspaper when I leave here. I don't think I'll have time to do anything else today."

"Me either. I have to get the saloon open."

They talked about the kids getting on the orphan train, and Deacon prayed they'd find happy homes.

"Life is hard on little ones." The sadness in Grace's voice touched Deacon. He reached for her hand and gave it a squeeze.

"I'm glad you're here, Grace. I enjoy your company."

"When we're not fighting, you mean?"

Deacon laughed. "Even then."

"You're awfully kind."

"I try. Ready?"

Grace nodded. A patron jostled into her as she tried to get up from the table and pushed her back into her chair. "Oh, dear. I apologize, mister."

Head down, the stranger went on without a word.

"What was that?" Deacon started to go after the rude man.

"I don't know." She glanced down, and next to her bowl lay a folded square piece of paper. She picked it up and opened it, letting out a little cry.

"What?"

Grace's face had turned ashen. She handed him the paper.

The note read: *You are not who you think you are.*

Deacon scanned the small café's few patrons but saw no sign of the man. Hell!

"What does this mean?" he asked Grace.

"I don't know. This is crazy." She was shaking, and he had to help her up. "Maybe he was just trying to scare me." Fear clouded her blue gaze and she gave a weak laugh. "It worked."

"Did you get a good look at him?"

She pushed back her hair with trembling fingers. "No. He walked by as I was trying to stand and shoved me back into my seat. I thought I'd pushed the chair into his path. He was gone by the time I gathered my wits. Once he left the note, he must've run out the back. Did you see him?"

"I confess I wasn't paying a lot of attention. I saw him enter the café out of the corner of my eye but dismissed him. My thoughts were on...other things." He released a long sigh. "If you're not Grace Legend, who do you think you might be?"

"This is ridiculous! I am Grace Legend. My father is Houston and my mother's Lara. I can belong to no other."

"Of course." Only sometimes what you thought you knew was quite different from reality. Deacon had experience in those matters.

The waitress, an older woman, hurried over. "Is anything wrong? You look upset."

"Do you perhaps know the man who was just in here?" Grace asked.

"No, ma'am. I never saw him before."

Deacon thanked the woman then took Grace's arm. "Let's get out of here."

Outside, he put his hand to the small of her back. "I'll walk you to the newspaper."

"Thank you. That makes me feel better in case the man follows me."

But as it ended up, they caught the mule-drawn streetcar, just to lose anyone who might be trailing. They got off at Throckmorton and Sixth Streets and walked half a block to the *Fort Worth Gazette* building.

Deacon was relieved to see some of Grace's color return. He took her hand. "Will you be all right? Can you get someone to see you home?"

"Sure. In any event, I will leave way before dark. Don't worry about me."

"I do." He scanned the area but saw no one loitering nearby. "I'd stay if I could."

"No, I won't hear of it." Her voice sounded stronger. "You have things to do, and I don't need a babysitter. I'm a big girl."

"Strange things are happening in this city. It's not safe for a woman to be out alone."

"Be that as it may, I won't stay locked in my home. I carry a weapon in my pocket, and I'm not afraid to use it."

"That's the spirit." He yearned to kiss her lips but settled for her cheek and ran a fingertip across her jaw. "Stay safe, princess."

"You too, Brannock."

He stood watching until she was inside. All the way back to Hell's Half Acre, he pondered the meaning of the note, then went back to Grace telling him about the robbers who'd kidnapped her and what they'd yelled.

Could the man's yelling have concerned the identity of her father?

No, absolutely not. Deacon shook his head. Houston Legend was her father.

Still…

Was it possible he wasn't? Deacon puzzled over it as he went to check several nearby morgues for Izzy. Relief swept through him to find they had no little boys.

❧

Grace didn't feel as exposed inside the newspaper. She took the note from her pocket and read it again. A thought struck her. Maybe the man had been talking about her reporter name of Sam Valentine.

The dark cloud lifted. She wasn't really Sam Valentine. No one was. Someone had evidently discovered her work at the paper.

Moments later at the desk where she worked in the office, Grace wrote about the sobbing orphans who'd gotten on the train while it was still fresh in her mind. She spoke about the injustice of a society that couldn't take care of the children, begging Fort Worth citizens to open their hearts and purses.

The way she saw it, the temperance movement, suffrage, social reform, and all the rest were tied together. People cried for change. They wanted a safer world. Wives wanted sober, kind husbands. Kids needed parents to love them. She poured it all out and took the article to Pemberton.

A glint of admiration shone in his eyes. "Good work, Valentine."

She made it to the door before he called her name. "Yes, sir?"

"Don't go to Hell's Acre alone. It's far too dangerous. There was another murder this morning—a man by the name of Pickford."

"Seth Pickford?"

"That's it. Someone found him about dawn two blocks from the Three Deuces. He was shot between the eyes."

Pinpricks crawled up Grace's spine. Brannock said he'd locked the man in a shed in the alley.

What was it he'd said? Oh, yes: *I don't think he'll bother you again.*

For a moment, she thought she'd be physically ill. She raced from Pemberton's office to the water closet. Splashing water on her face and taking deep breaths, she got her stomach to settle.

Men fought all the time. Houston had killed Yuma Blackstone to save his drovers. It was justified. Her uncles and Grandpa as well had all put bad outlaws in the ground.

Had Brannock killed the despicable man? He certainly had motive. There was lots of bad blood between them. Had he grabbed the opportunity and ended their dispute? There was a difference in shooting an attacker and the coldblooded murder of an unarmed man.

Not only that, many believed he was the one years earlier who'd killed and nailed that man to the outhouse door.

Dear God! She was going to be sick.

Had she been totally wrong about him?

She already knew Deacon Brannock was living under a false name and was a dangerous man. Plus, he disappeared sometimes and no one knew where he went. Was it any big stretch to think one reason for that might be because he was a murderer?

Twenty-four

Her thoughts on Deacon, Grace left the *Fort Worth Gazette* while the sun was still shining, as she'd promised, and went home. She hadn't been there long when Crockett arrived.

"You're early, little Brother." Grace was going to tell him the news about Pickford but didn't get a chance.

"We're having company tonight, Gracie. Uncle Virgil and Uncle Henry are in town."

"Good." Grace always loved seeing her mother's brothers. "On business?"

"Yep. Cattle buying. Uncle Virgil bought five hundred acres next to his spread and is chomping at the bit to add to his herd."

"Did he bring Susan along?" Grace thought of Virgil's wife as a sister and liked her sweet personality. Henry had never married. He'd been born with a learning problem, what most people called slow, and had never lived on his own.

"Nope, it's just the men. It's a hurried trip."

"I guess I'd best get supper started then." Grace went over their pantry list and soon had a hearty stew bubbling.

She took the strange note to Crockett in the parlor. "What do you make of this?"

He read it, anger darkening his face. "Where did you get it?"

She told him about the café and the rude stranger. "He was gone by the time Brannock looked for him. Should I be worried?"

"It does sound rather disturbing. Not really threatening, but ominous."

"I know."

"Be careful and always be aware of your surroundings." Crockett handed the note back. "I'd suggest you stay home for a few days, but I don't need a crystal ball to figure how that'd turn out."

She would rebel quicker than little brother could spit. "I always keep a derringer in my pocket."

"You're a better shot than I am," her brother admitted. "I wish you'd stay away from the lower part of town."

"That's not fair, Crockett. I was here, safe in our home, when Pickford and his buddy tried to kill me. I didn't go looking for them."

"I'm sorry, sis. I know you didn't invite them over here."

Grace clenched her hands tight. "There's been a development. Seth Pickford was found shot to death this morning in the Acre, and I don't like my suspicions." She told Crockett what Brannock had claimed. "Of course, someone else could've killed the despicable man. I doubt he had many friends. But what if Brannock did it? He hated the man."

Crockett released a low whistle. "Pickford's death sure solves a lot of problems for Leah. Others too."

More than even Crockett knew, but Grace kept silent.

"Stay away from the Acre." Crockett gave her a pointed stare. "It's a good place to end up dead."

"I have my work. Are you forgetting?"

Surprise rippled across his face. "I thought you gave up marching with those temperance women."

"I have for the most part." Trying to keep her secret work at the newspaper from Crockett was becoming hard. "I, uh…I'm finding other ways to help without much participation. I give motivational talks and so forth when I'm needed."

"Good. As for the note, use common sense and be on guard."

"I will." Grace breathed a sigh of relief that he'd dropped it. Maybe she should tell him. The articles she was presently writing posed no problems for her family, and she was proud of them. But he left the room before she could confess. It wouldn't hurt to wait a little longer.

Two hours later, a knock sounded, and the house was filled with deep voices and kidding.

"Grace, you're looking as pretty as a speckled pup," Virgil said, hugging her.

"Why thank you, Uncle. I'm glad you and Henry finally came for a visit."

"City living seems to agree with you and Crockett, though why is beyond me." Virgil wagged his head. "Nothing but scalawags and no-accounts here. The Lone Star has everything you could want."

"Except for a few things. How's Uncle Quaid? Has he managed to rope a wife?"

"Nope. My twin seems contented to stay a bachelor."

Grace laughed and moved on to Henry. "We have lots of talking to do, Uncle Henry."

Henry grinned. "I have a secret, but I can't tell you what it is."

"Not even if I tickle you?"

"Nope. Pa said to seal my tongue."

"Don't you mean seal your lips?" Grace asked with a smile. She loved Henry's way of simple talk. Despite his learning problem, he always got to the heart of a matter.

"Maybe. I ain't supposed to tell something." Henry ducked his head.

"We all keep a few things to ourselves. It's okay, Uncle Henry."

"I like Leah. She's nice. She had to get a baby—" He clapped a hand over his mouth.

Grace wondered what he'd been about to say. "What do you think of little Johnny?"

"He cries. I hold him. Sometimes he wets on me and pukes. I don't like that."

Before Grace could reply, Henry asked a dozen questions about the stockyards.

Later, when they moved to the table, she had trouble keeping her attention on the conversation. Surrounded by her uncles' voices, she remembered something Izzy had said. *Ain't got no ma. No pa either. Got no fam'ly. Jus' me.*

⇛

As was his habit of late, Deacon got the saloon past the busiest part of the night and slipped out the back door. Sarge stood guard and gave him an angry cat-cussing up one side and down the other. "I don't know why you're so all fired mad at me, but you better watch it, or you might end up in the tamales."

The threat had barely left Deacon's mouth before Sarge presented his butt, leaped to a spindly tree, and disappeared into the darkness. "Good riddance."

Having won his argument with the sour-faced tomcat, Deacon moved down the street, keeping to the sides of the shadowy buildings. The night air was alive with music, voices, yelling, and occasional gunplay, and he was glad he'd worn his freshly cleaned Colt. He swung by the porch Izzy had claimed just for curiosity's sake. The quilt, blanket, a burlap sack containing a few clothes, and scant other belongings were still there.

Dammit!

Tears welled in his eyes. Deacon could've been Izzy very easily. The boy had asked for so little and worked hard for what he got.

"I swear on my life, I will find out what happened to you, and if possible, bring you home," Deacon muttered thickly.

"Who you talking to, mister?" The voice belonged to a woman of the evening, leaning against the side of the Painted Pony. Someone had apparently worked her over.

He moved closer and saw even more bruises. He handed her a handkerchief, and she wiped her tears. "I can see things aren't going well for you tonight," he said softly.

"Ain't any of your concern."

"No, it isn't. Pardon me; I'll be moving on. I got troubles of my own." She tried to hand him back the handkerchief. "Keep it. You might need it again."

The young woman looked up at him and touched her split lip. "What trouble would you have?"

He told her about Izzy. "I'm worried for the boy's safety."

"I overheard a man a few nights ago, and it didn't make any sense until now." She dabbed at her bloody lip. "He wore a fancy suit with a gold watch fob hanging from his pocket. A big ring on his right hand. Looked like some kind of sleazy politician. He laughed and said they were cleaning up the city just like folks wanted."

Excitement burned inside him. "Do you know what he meant?"

"Yep. He said drowning them in the Trinity would fix everything."

Deacon's blood turned to ice. "Did he actually say *he* was drowning them?"

"Not exactly."

"Anything else?"

"Fancy man had a gold tooth flashing in front and a million-dollar smile, but he was all black coal inside." The lady moved closer. "Aren't you Deacon Brannock of the Three Deuces?"

"That's me. Do you have a name?"

"Jane."

"Nice meeting you, Jane." He gently touched her arm. "You can get out of this life if you want to. It'll only lead you to a grave."

Her words were soft. "It's too late for me, Brannock. I'm all used up. I'd welcome a grave if it would bring some peace."

"I understand that."

"I've done a lot of bad things, though."

"Me too." The words had slipped from his mouth before he realized it. "Maybe we're in hell right now."

"I know I am." She tried to smile but it fell short. "Take care, Brannock."

"If you overhear anything else, I'd be obliged if you'd send a message over at my place."

"Sure." She opened the door and went inside.

"Good luck, Jane," he said quietly. Deacon mulled everything over.

He walked up and down the street and found it eerie. Normally, he'd see a dozen kids or more, but tonight he saw zero. That explained why no one had taken Izzy's things.

Thoughts whirled like the colors on a roulette wheel and stopped on another child who hadn't gotten to grow up—Cass, sweet little sister Cass.

A painful lump formed in his throat, blocking his airway. Over the years, so much had happened that had been beyond Deacon's control, but he remembered every second of Cass's last day.

The sky had been a robin's-egg blue, with not a cloud dotting it, and the cool breeze had held a hint of fall. Cass always had a happy disposition, but that day laughter bubbled up like seltzer. Deacon was playing cribbage with her under an apple tree outside his window where it was cool.

Then McCreedy had shown up drunk and spoiling for a fight. McCreedy with a gloating smile and an evil heart. Cass dead. So much blood. Her body limp. Mouth frozen wide-open in a scream.

"Dammit, let me go! Let me forget!" Deacon curled his fists, closing his eyes to block the images that haunted him even after eleven long years.

When would he stop reliving that?

Chest aching, he continued his lonely walk. Moving over one street, he neared the corner of the next block when he heard yelling.

He ran to where he could see, and the hair on his neck rose.

Two men held a boy about eight or nine, and the kid was yelling his lungs out.

"Hey! Let him go!" Deacon pulled his Colt and, running, shot above the men's heads.

They dropped the kid and took off. Deacon gave chase, trying his best to catch the scum. But in the end, he lost them in the pitch-black. Hooves struck the street as the horses raced away. Was it a black wagon? He had no way of confirming.

By the time he returned, the boy was sitting up. "Take it slow and easy."

"Thanks, mister." The boy sniffed and dragged his sleeve across his nose.

"What's your name, son?"

"Joel."

"That's a fine name. I'm Deacon. Where do you call home?"

"Don't got one."

That's what Deacon figured. "Would you like to come to my place? I'll give you a room and food." When the kid hesitated, Deacon added, "You'll be safe there."

"You have food?"

"I do. Bet you haven't eaten much lately."

"No, sir."

"What do you say?"

The boy hesitated. "I don't know. You ain't gonna lock me in?"

"Nope." Deacon stood and gave him a hand. "What'll it be, Joel?"

More hesitation and looking him up and down. "Okay. I guess I can stay for a day or two."

In a short time, Deacon opened the back door of the saloon as Harry was getting ready to lock up. The saloon was empty, with no sign of Aunt Martha. "We have us a guest." Deacon introduced them. "Joel is going to stay for a few days until he gets sick of us."

Harry nodded, smiling. "I'll try not to make you sick, young man. Do you like eggs?"

"Yes, sir." Joel was slowly inspecting the room, and Deacon

knew beyond a doubt he was marking the exits and places to hide. Now that he was in the light, he could see the boy was probably about ten or eleven. Joel's shaggy, blond hair and clothes he'd outgrown said he'd been on the streets for quite a few years. Who knew the last time he'd bathed?

If he stuck around, Deacon vowed all that was going to change.

He poured himself some coffee and peeked into the kitchen that was spic and span. "Where's Aunt Martha?"

"Bed. She was so tired, I thought I'd have to carry her up the stairs."

"She does work hard. I'll take some eggs, too, Harry, if you don't mind. With plenty of bacon." He took a seat next to Joel and leaned forward into the lamplight so the kid could see his face. He filled the silence with talk about the weather, the cat, animals in general, and anything else he could think of that might put the boy at ease. "I had a dog growing up, but I'm liking cats now. Sarge thinks he's a guard cat and keeps burglars away."

"I had a cat once a long time ago."

Joel's voice came so unexpected, Deacon thought he'd imagined it. But the kid's tears spoke of some distant, painful memory.

"That so?" He pretended not to see the tears. "What did you name it?"

"Missy. She was a girl and slept in my bed. I miss her." Joel paused a moment and wiped his eyes.

"You must've loved her very much."

"Yep." Joel let out a long sigh that seemed to carry the weight of the world.

"I hope Harry will be out with the food soon. I'm starving." A million questions ran through Deacon's head to ask, but he knew he had to go slow.

Harry moved about the kitchen, whistling softly. Joel kept shooting Harry curious glances.

"I don't have any folks left anymore, but I can still remember how my mother used to rub my back sometimes. Man, that felt good." Deacon watched the boy draw little circles on the table with a fingernail. "And we had this swimming hole that we used to go to in the summer to cool off. But things always change." He would stop his reminiscing there—before his life had turned blacker than rotting flesh.

Joel nodded but said nothing.

Harry brought two plates of food over. "Hope you're ready to eat."

Deacon winked at the boy. "Joel and I tried to gnaw the table leg off if that tells you anything."

Joel gave a small laugh. It wasn't much, but it was an improvement.

"You should find these eggs and bacon a lot easier to chew." Harry set the plates in front of them, then pulled silverware and cloth napkins from a pocket. "Would you like some milk, young man?"

"Yes, sir."

Harry went back to the stove and returned with a plate of food for himself and glass of milk for Joel. The three wasted no time in filling their stomachs, then Deacon took Joel upstairs to Leah's room.

Deacon opened the door and lit the lamp. "This is your bed. If you like it and want to stay, we'll go get your belongings tomorrow."

Joel walked slowly around the room. "Where's the cat?"

"Sarge is either outside or in Harry's room. He doesn't have much to do with me."

"Do you think he can sleep in my bed? Just like I used to do with Missy?" Joel's words came so halting and slow, it took a minute for the question to register.

"Maybe we might arrange that. Give me a second." Deacon went downstairs to Harry. "Is Sarge in your room?"

"He was the last time I looked."

Deacon shared what little Joel had revealed, and the bartender swallowed hard. "I'll go get Sarge. I hope the cat can bring him some comfort."

"Thanks, Harry." Deacon went back upstairs and found Joel sitting on the bed with his shoes neatly on the rug. "Good news. Harry's bringing Sarge."

Joel flew off the bed and threw his arms around Deacon. "Thank you."

The frail body pressing against him brought a lump filling his throat, and for a long moment, Deacon couldn't speak. Finally, he managed a few words. "You're doing us a favor, keeping that contrary cat in here."

That night Deacon slept a dreamless sleep, the first he'd had in months while sober.

⌒⌒

Grace rose before dawn, got dressed, and slipped out, leaving their guests asleep. She had an idea for an article, one that would hopefully arouse more sympathy for the orphans. While she ate breakfast in a small café, she wrote about life on the street and the spirit that fought tooth and nail to survive.

"More coffee, miss?" The waitress waved a pot.

"Yes, please." She went back over what she'd written and was happy with the emotional angle that might appeal to their readers.

By the time the newspaper opened, she stood by the doors, feeling hopeful.

Pemberton was at his desk, sipping on a cup of coffee. "Valentine, I didn't expect to see you again so soon. You were just here."

"I have another article I wanted to ask you to run." She pulled a paper from her leather satchel and handed it to him.

He read it silently, then sat back. "Excellent."

"What I was hoping you'd say, sir. I'll keep writing them." This was more encouraging than she'd hoped.

"You may just turn into a regular reporter one day. Whatever you need, just let me know."

She left the *Fort Worth Gazette* with a spring in her step and stopped back at the house. The men had left, and Crockett's note said their uncles would have to spend another night.

Grace pushed her hair back, her mind in a whirl. Questions she wanted to ask Brannock were burning her tongue, and she fervently prayed the answers he gave would clear him. She knocked on the back door of the Three Deuces a little over a half hour later. Harry let her in.

"Morning, Miss Grace. You're up and about early."

"I had to take care of some things." She glanced around. The place was a lot cleaner since Aunt Martha arrived. It was beginning to look more like a café than a place to buy whiskey. "I like the changes. Business is good, then?"

Harry grinned. "Booming. The place is packed around lunch and suppertime."

Brannock came from the kitchen, wearing a blue shirt with the sleeves rolled up. It looked new. She'd gotten so used to seeing him in worn clothing, that it took her aback. The vest appeared to be leather, again a surprise. He hadn't bothered to button it. From her vantage spot, the thick muscles of his forearms were plainly visible. His full mouth curved in a smile, and he carried a cup of coffee. For once, he looked rested.

Was it because Pickford was dead? He had to have heard.

He crooked an eyebrow. "What? Haven't you ever seen a man drink coffee?"

"I've never seen you in new clothes before."

Harry excused himself. Maybe to give them privacy.

Her gaze followed Harry to his room, then she turned back to Brannock. "You didn't have time to shop for clothes yesterday, mister."

"Business is good, so I asked Harry to pick these up for me."

"I like his taste." A noise above drew her gaze to the ceiling.

"That's Joel. I rescued him last night from two men trying to abduct him. He looks a little older than Izzy. Been on his own for quite a while."

"Poor kid. I don't know what this world is coming to. Thank God you stopped those men. Did you get a good look?"

"No, they ran when they saw me coming." Brannock sighed. "The poor boy was so traumatized it took me a while to talk him into coming here for the night. I hope he stays, but I won't take any bets."

"What time was that?"

"About midnight. I walk the streets most nights once we close or business dies down." He finished his coffee.

Grace filed that tidbit away. He even went all the way over to her house.

"I guess you heard about Seth Pickford." She watched his eyes for changes but he met her gaze, never blinking.

"The news is on everyone's tongue up and down the street." Brannock pinched the bridge of his nose. "The list of suspects is a mile long. Pickford wasn't the kind for friends."

"I've gone over that night in my head and some things bother me." She couldn't forget his state yesterday morning and the fact he'd clearly been drinking and smelled of whiskey. Trying to erase a guilty conscience? "You said you locked him up in a shed in the alley."

"That's right." A frown deepened the crease in his forehead. "Where are you going with this?"

"Was Pickford alive?" She hated pressing, but she needed to know, to believe in him.

"He was."

"Can you prove it?"

His eyes hardened to gray flint. "Do I have to?"

"I'm just trying to help you in case—in case they come after you. You could be in serious trouble." She touched his arm. "Did you kill Pickford?"

"No. But if I'd wanted to, I'd have drowned him in the Trinity and weighted his body down with rocks. No one ever would've found him."

"Could be you were too far away from the river."

"Look, he was alive when I put him in that shed. Can I prove it? No." His angry grays pierced her. "I swear on my mother's grave, I did not kill the man. That's going to have to be good enough."

Twenty-five

THE SILENCE INSIDE THE THREE DEUCES WAS THICK. GRACE'S unspoken accusations sparked anger he didn't want to feel.

When was it ever going to stop? Being under a cloud of suspicion wore thin. Even now, he could see that Grace halfway believed he'd taken Pickford's life. Deacon could see she didn't want to. But she couldn't help it. Deacon had a mysterious past. He lived in the shadows, hiding things.

"He was alive," Deacon repeated. "I didn't kill him."

"One more question, and I'll drop it."

"Ask away. I have nothing to hide."

"Why did you tell me that Pickford would never bother me again? Do you have a crystal ball that reads the future?"

He hesitated a moment, trying to think of what to say. "Of course not! I promised that because I was going to make sure you'd have nothing to fear from him anymore." Frustrated, he ran his fingers through his hair. "I didn't know how I was going to accomplish that. One idea was to put him on a freight train bound for the West Coast." He reached for her hands. "I was going to do whatever it took to keep you safe. And yes, as a last resort, even putting a bullet in his sorry brain. But I didn't."

Grace was silent, studying him, seeming to wrestle with what to believe. She finally gave him a shaky smile and reached for his hand. "I trust you. If you say you didn't do it, you didn't."

"Thank you for that." The tension began to leave his body. He didn't care one iota what others thought about him. But Grace— Grace's thoughts and opinions meant everything to him.

"You could be in real trouble with the law though. If we make up a good story—"

"Stop. The truth is all I need. The truth will either stand or fall."

"I agree." She glanced to the second story. "Now, tell me about the kid upstairs."

Deacon led her to a table and got coffee for them both. He told her about the two men who were preying on the boy. "I'm not sure what they had in mind to do with him, but you can bet it wasn't to offer him a home."

"That's despicable. And sick." The more she stayed in the Acre, the dirtier, uglier, and deadlier the area became. The streets truly were no place for kids.

"Earlier in the evening, I met a woman named Jane, and she might prove helpful. She's a working girl down at the Painted Pony, and someone knocked her around good." Brannock spoke in a quiet tone. Probably didn't want Joel to overhear.

Grace tried to figure out how that involved her. "Helpful with what?"

He moved closer. "I'm not sure yet. Maybe finding Izzy. She overheard a conversation, and the man talked about drowning kids."

Grace's eyes grew large. "You think he might've done something to Izzy?"

"Don't know yet." He sat back. "I'm not ruling anything out."

"We can't afford to. What was this Jane like?"

"Sad. Jaded. Tired of the life. I honestly think she'd get out of the business if she had any other alternative. I felt sorry for her."

"I want to help women like that, show them there's an easier way. Maybe after we find Izzy, I can turn my attention to that."

"You never seem to be satisfied. The wheels in that pretty head are always turning." He kissed her fingers.

There was so much need everywhere he turned. Deacon thought about his goal of owning a piece of land. If he had that, he could start a place where kids would be safe and cared for. The fresh air, taking care of animals, lots of room to run and play would do wonders.

But that was far from happening. At times it seemed ages away. He'd come close over the years and something always snatched it from his grasp. That's why he couldn't tell Grace.

He wanted that land so bad he could taste it.

That brought him to Will and Diablo. He needed to go out there soon. The itch was strong to plant his feet on that good soil and fill his lungs with fresh air.

"What if you could have anything in the world and price was no object? What would you choose, Grace?"

∽

His raspy voice, his lips on her fingers, prickled the skin on Grace's arms.

"I declare, where is this coming from so early in the morning, Brannock?" She became acutely aware of his nearness, and a thin sheen of perspiration covered her skin. A droplet formed and trickled ever so slowly between her breasts. To make matters worse, she'd worn a light pink dress, which would allow every bit of moisture to show.

"It's a simple question. What is the one thing you'd choose?"

"I don't know. Maybe sail to Paris or go up in a balloon." What did she want? She'd never really thought about more than her journalism. "I think I might buy my own newspaper. Or write a book."

"With those fanciful aspirations, my dear Miss Grace, you must've hung around with the wrong kind of people." He nibbled on her fingers.

"Cows, Mr. Brannock. I hung around with cows."

"More's the pity." He straightened.

"What do you want more than anything in the whole wide world?" she asked.

"My own land free and clear."

He stated that in a firm voice, no hesitation at all. Yes, she could see him being a rancher. "I hope you get it, Brannock. I really hope you do."

"I've never heard you call me Deacon. Why is that?"

She shrugged. "Some men are first-name kind of people and others—" Grace wet her lips, wondering why she was so breathless. "There are certain others whose last names fit them better. You're a last-name kind of person." She took a tremulous breath, feeling the weight of what she was about to do. "That is if Brannock is indeed your last name."

He placed his mouth at her ear. His breath fluttered a tendril of hair. "I'll never tell."

"Come on, give me something, or else I'll walk out and go talk to Jane at the Painted Pony by myself. Did she perhaps give you more than just a little information?" She patted the side of his face. "What's the going rate these days for an hour?"

Brannock grinned. "Jealous?"

Grace gave an unladylike snort. "In your dreams. I'll see you later."

"Hey, people in the Acre rarely get up before noon."

Grace smiled sweetly and pushed back her chair. "Not all are in the Acre, Mr. Brannock."

He grabbed his Stetson, covered the space in two strides, and held the door. "After you."

Once they were away from the Three Deuces, all teasing stopped, and he became pure business, much to her relief. She didn't know how to take the flirty side of him, didn't know if he was doing nothing more than gauging her reaction to him. The best thing to do was try to keep her attraction to the handsome saloon owner tamped down.

He could break her heart. What was it her mother had said? If she ever felt threatened or that her life was in danger, to run as far and as fast as she could.

Brannock made her feel just the opposite. She wanted to run to him.

Grace pushed those thoughts away. She had to concentrate on her job and make good use of the time they had.

"Where are we going?" Brannock asked.

"The hospital. Maybe Izzy got hurt and has been in the hospital all this time."

"That's a good idea. Why didn't I think of that?"

"Maybe because you're such a loner." She stopped and faced him. "If you were to get seriously hurt, you'd drag yourself upstairs and lick your wounds until you healed. Regular people use doctors and hospitals."

He frowned. "I have to say, you missed something. I would surround myself with plenty of whiskey to dull the pain."

Grace rolled her eyes. "That part was a given."

They visited several hospitals, asking around about a boy named Izzy or an unknown boy who'd come in. Nothing.

Dejected, Grace turned back toward the Acre and marched to the Painted Pony.

Brannock pulled her to a halt before she made it inside. "Hold it right there. I'll go in and ask about Jane. You wait here." He started to push through the door and paused. "I mean it."

"Okay, okay. Go get her. We're wasting time. Shoo!" She waited for what seemed like an hour, then went to peer over the batwing doors. She could see no one in the dim saloon. Grace waited a little longer, and just as she started to push inside, Deacon appeared with a red-haired woman sporting bruises. She wore a torn, skimpy dress that came to her knees.

Deacon made the introductions. "Grace wants to ask you a few questions."

Her heart went out to the woman who bore the scars of her hard life. "Thank you for agreeing to talk to me, Jane. It's about the customer ranting about drowning kids."

"Little boys," Jane corrected. "Only little boys."

"I wonder why. You said he was well dressed?"

"Yeah, that's why he stuck out. Those kind steer clear of this neighborhood unless they need…other services." She released a tired sigh as though the weight of the world were on her shoulders. "I found something after Brannock left last night." Jane pulled out a scrap of paper and handed it to him. "The man left this with Francine, hoping she'd come to his room."

Grace jostled his elbow to see. The paper said Jim Quarrels, Room 106, the Palace Hotel.

"Oh, Jane, thank you!" Grace felt like hugging the woman. "You don't know how long we've searched for a place to begin. Maybe this will lead somewhere."

"I'm glad to help."

A burly man poked his head out the door. "Get back inside, Jane."

She jumped and lowered her head, then without a word, disappeared into the dim business that smelled of stale beer, smoke, and vomit.

Anger and sadness fought for Grace's attention. "For two cents, I'd go in there and give that man a piece of my mind."

She took a step when Brannock grabbed her. "No you don't. That's no place for you."

"But you saw the way that man treated her."

"I did, and there's nothing we can do about it. Jane has made her choice."

His calm voice irritated her. "You don't always have to be right, you know."

Deacon lightly took her arm. "Aren't you forgetting we have someplace to be?"

"Not one bit. I can't believe our good fortune." Grace glanced up at him. "Where is the Palace Hotel, and what kind of place is it?"

"It's a couple of streets over and not as run-down as these." He took her arm and helped her down the steps. "Don't get your hopes too high. He said nothing that tied him to Izzy. Besides, he's probably checked out as long ago as it's been."

"I know." Still, it was something, and that was big when you counted all the days Izzy had been gone with zero to show in finding him.

They located the hotel. Grace scowled at the number of men sitting outside the doors, some on benches and others on the bare ground. Warning bells went off in her head, and she moved closer to Brannock.

"Stay close," he murmured, putting an arm around her.

They walked up to the desk. No one was around. Deacon rang a bell sitting on the counter. A middle-aged man came from the back. "Can I help you?"

"I hope so." Deacon took the paper from his pocket. "We're looking for Jim Quarrels. I believe he stayed in room 106 a few days ago."

"I'll have to check our records."

While the clerk checked the register, Grace glanced around. The lobby was clean and empty, in stark contrast to the outside. Why were all the men loitering by the door?

A few minutes later, the question was answered when a large wagon pulled by draft horses arrived. All the men climbed aboard. Aha! They must work in the fields. With the men gone, she could relax.

"Here it is." The clerk glanced up. "Mr. Quarrels stayed two nights and checked out."

Grace smiled. "Thank you for being so helpful. Can you tell us where he was from? I met him over supper, and I want to send him birthday greetings. We laughed about us both having the same birthday next week. He was such a nice gentleman."

Brannock cut his eyes her way and gave his head a warning shake.

"Mr. Quarrels was from Joshua, Texas, ma'am." The clerk closed the register and didn't appear in the mood for other questions.

"I do thank you, kind sir." She let out a sigh. "I wish there were more men like you."

The clerk stood straighter and pulled his vest together. "I like to do what I can."

Brannock took her arm and propelled her toward the door. "Thank you," he called over his shoulder.

"I do hope you get the birthday greetings sent to Mr. Quarrels, ma'am."

"Oh, I most certainly will, sir." Outside, Grace jerked away. "What's gotten into you?"

"I could ask the same. What was that ridiculous story about birthdays?"

"Really, Brannock? I was being a reporter and getting information. How else were we going to get the town he was from?"

"By asking?"

"I was finessing."

"You were lying."

"Just a little white one. Those don't count." Grace slipped her hand through his elbow. "How soon do you want to go to Joshua?"

"I'm leaving in a few hours. You're staying here."

"I hardly think so, Mr. Brannock. We go together. It's my story."

They walked in silence for a whole block before he finally spoke. "You're too stubborn for your own good."

She shrugged. "I guess I'm far too old to grow out of it."

Agreeing to meet at the livery on Madison Street to rent horses, she went home. Crockett and her uncles arrived right behind her. She told them her plans. "Joshua isn't that far, and I should be back by nightfall."

Crockett had a conniption. "No, Gracie. That's crazy. You don't know Quarrels. For that matter, you don't know Brannock. Izzy isn't your responsibility. I know you want to find him, but he's no kin."

"I have to go. Don't you see? I have to find him, and this is our best shot to date."

Virgil glanced from one to the other. "She's old enough to make her own decisions, Crockett. I've met few women as smart as Gracie. Or as good a shot with a firearm."

"Gracie's tough," Henry said. "And you're not the boss of her."

That struck her as funny. She started laughing, and soon they all joined in. In the end, Crockett had to give in.

She went upstairs to pack a few things just in case something kept them from returning by nightfall. It paid to be on the safe side.

Henry knocked on the open door. "I wish I was going. I'd help you find the boy."

"I bet you could. Between us, we'd get answers."

"Will you have to get a baby?" Henry picked at a fingernail, his face dark.

Grace jerked around. "What did you ask?"

"If you'd have to get a baby. Lara had to get you. She cried a lot, and Yuma cut her bad."

Stunned, Grace sat slowly on the side of the bed. "Henry, are you sure?" Sometimes he got mixed up about things and they came out backward.

"I was there, and I saw everything." Tears filled Henry's eyes. "I didn't want Lara to die. So much blood. The doctor came and got a needle. Papa got the gun and ran for his horse."

The secret Henry wasn't supposed to tell came spilling out, and he couldn't seem to stop. He rocked back and forth, in the grip of the nightmarish event. Tears spilled down his face. "Yuma put a baby in Lara's stomach. She didn't want him to, but he did anyway."

"Oh, Henry. You don't have to say anything else." Grace rose and put her arms around him. "Stop."

But he didn't seem able. "You grew in Lara's belly, and when you came out, I held you. I love you, Gracie."

"I love you, too, Henry."

"And when Houston took us on the cattle drive, Lara killed Yuma, and I was glad."

"Don't you mean Houston killed him?" Was Henry confused again?

"Nope." Henry wiped his eyes. "Lara shot him. I threw rocks at him, and Lara shot him dead with his own gun."

Shaking, Grace dropped back to the bed, digesting the startling information. *No! No! No!* This couldn't be. A noise at the doorway drew her attention.

Virgil was standing there, rubbing his jaw, sorrow filling her uncle's eyes. "It's true, Grace. All of it. Yuma Blackstone fathered you."

Twenty-six

THE NAME GRACE HAD LEARNED TO HATE HUNG IN THE STILL room. "It can't be," she whispered. She couldn't have the blood of a killer running through her veins.

Ice coated her heart. She shivered and sank to the floor. "There has to be some horrible mistake."

"I know it's a shock after believing a certain way all these years." Virgil put an arm around Henry. "You were never supposed to know, Grace."

Henry rocked back and forth. "I'm sorry, Virgil. I didn't mean to tell. I'm sorry. Oh!"

Crockett filled the doorway. "It's all right, Henry. Secrets are hard to keep. Sometimes they have to come out. Gracie, I'm sorry you had to learn about the secret this way," he said quietly.

She raised her face and glared at her brother. "Did you know too?"

"No. This is the first I heard," Crockett assured her.

It was odd thinking of him as her half brother. One spoken word had changed everything. She wasn't Grace Legend. Stoker wasn't really her grandpa.

A killer, one of the most despicable men to once walk the earth, was her father.

Dear God! He'd sliced her mother's face, one of several horrible, violent acts. How could she live with this? How could she walk amongst people and not be ashamed?

Crockett went to her and lifted her up, staring into her eyes. "This changes nothing. You're my sister, just the way it's always been."

"How can you say that? How can you look at me? I'm repulsed, so why aren't you?"

"Stop that kind of talk." Crockett kissed her cheek. "Words can't change how I feel about you."

"I'm sorry," Henry cried. "I'm a bad, bad man."

All of this was making her young uncle crazy. She went to him. "Uncle Henry, you're not bad, and no one is mad at you. Please, it's going to be fine."

"No, it won't. I'm sorry, sorry, sorry."

Grace wished she knew how things would ever be fine again. Her life was in shambles. Somehow, someway, she would get through this. Maybe someone could tell her how.

"Let's go downstairs and make coffee," she suggested wearily. "I have questions."

Virgil put an arm around Henry. "Just for a bit. We've decided to head back to the ranch earlier than we planned."

A short while later, they sat at the table with steaming coffee.

Grace patted Henry's hand to reassure him. "Uncle Virgil, start at the beginning and tell me everything."

"Only what I can. Some isn't my story to tell." Virgil cradled his coffee cup. "Please don't run to Lara with this. She's worked hard to put her nightmare behind her, and Houston would skin me alive if I rip the scab off."

Virgil told how Yuma had ridden onto the ranch and caught Lara by herself in the barn. "I knew right away he was trouble. He wore evil like a suit of clothes. Afterward, Lara crawled from the barn on her hands and knees, all broken and bleeding, her face in a godawful mess. I rode for the doctor, then Pa, me, and Quaid went out looking for Yuma. We didn't find him that night or any of the hundred after. Lara had you nine months later. Houston married her to give you a name."

"Houston is my brother, and he's a good man," Henry said matter-of-factly.

Giving her a name was truly noble of Houston. "Then what?" Grace asked.

"Houston put together a cattle drive a month or so after the wedding, and he let Quaid, me, and Henry go along."

"Yuma showed up," Henry blurted. "He was bad, bad! I hated him."

"He followed us and started killing one drover a day." Virgil rubbed his face, his voice weary. "Houston and lead drover Clay Colby spent a lot of time hunting him, but they couldn't find him. Finally, we dug in, determined not to lose any more men, and there was a huge gun battle."

Grace set her coffee down. "Every account I read stated Houston killed him, but Henry said Mama pulled the trigger."

"That's correct. He caught her while Houston and the men fought off the attackers. She kept filling Yuma with lead until she emptied the gun. Houston took the credit to protect her."

Grace's chin quivered. "He's not really my—" She took a moment to compose herself. "He's not my father…but I wish… I love him like one."

Virgil wrapped her in a hug. "Keep loving him. Houston raised and protected you. To him, you are his daughter and you always will be. He's never looked at you any differently than he does the other kids."

Why couldn't someone noble and honest and good have created her? She felt drained. "I have one other thing. I've been having flashes of memory of the robbers who kidnapped me when I was ten. I remember one, Carl was his name, saying taking me was payback, and then another time he told me he was taking me to my kin. I never knew what he meant."

Virgil nodded. "He was Yuma's younger brother. He wasn't just riding through. He came for you."

"I have one question left. Does Grandpa Stoker know about all this?"

"Yes. It was his and dad's idea. They collaborated and got Houston to agree to the marriage. The funny part is—Houston and Lara never met before the wedding. The first time they saw each other was in front of the preacher."

"And Houston agreed to that?" Grace couldn't imagine such a thing.

Virgil grinned. "Yep."

Houston's character went up even higher. Grace had a lot to think about.

Not long after, Virgil and Henry gathered their things and left for the ranch.

Grace froze. She was supposed to meet Brannock. She didn't feel much like going. If she wasn't, she still had to go talk to him. What could she possibly say? *Oh, by the way, my father is a murderer and rapist, and I probably have all those despicable tendencies in my blood, so watch out.*

Crockett put his arms around her. "I don't know how you feel, so I won't say that. I will say that it makes no difference to me who your father is. It doesn't change anything. You're still my sister."

"Thank you, little brother. I suppose a few words can't change a lifetime of believing certain things."

"No, they can't." He smiled. "Go meet Deacon Brannock. The best thing you can do to prove to yourself who you are is to find that boy."

Grace kissed his cheek. "Thank you, Crockett. I'm sure he thinks I've met with trouble."

"The ride to Joshua will do you good."

"Maybe." She paused at the door. "If we don't make it back, I'll stay in a hotel. Don't worry about me."

"You're the most resourceful person I know, Grace." He grinned. "See? I remembered your name."

"Just don't forget it."

If only she could forget what she now knew about herself. She rubbed her palms, wishing she could remove the tainted blood inside her.

～～

Deacon leaned against the side of the livery, wondering what had happened to Grace. She was usually prompt and she'd been excited to go to Joshua. Had she met with an accident? He paced back and forth. Maybe he should go to her house. He took out his pocket watch and flipped it open. Two o'clock. She should've been here two hours ago.

That was about when the sheriff had cornered him, asking questions about his relationship with Seth Pickford. The sheriff's pissy attitude had made Deacon angry enough to bite a mangy bull, but he'd answered truthfully and told how Pickford had assaulted Grace.

Dammit, why wouldn't anyone believe him?

Pickford was two rungs below Satan, and Deacon would say good riddance. Deacon wouldn't waste a single thought on the man. It was odd that the sheriff had found a token coin in Pickford's pocket identical to the one Deacon had found in the alley after the break-in. That settled in his mind the question of the identity of the criminal.

A newfangled automobile passed by, backfiring and belching smoke. Coughing, he waved his hand to clear the air, cussing the driver. Why anyone would want a contraption like that was beyond him.

A mule-drawn streetcar approached and stopped, letting a woman off. He narrowed his gaze, relieved to see Grace in a riding skirt and leather jacket.

He strode to her and took a light bag. "I was beginning to wonder about you."

Her somber expression wasn't like her, and it appeared she'd been crying.

"What happened? Are you all right?"

"I will be in time. Sorry I'm late."

Deacon pulled his hat lower. "Have a fight with Crockett?"

"I'd rather not talk about it right now. Did you get the horses?"

"Yeah. I rented you an old mare that's ready for the glue factory."

"That's good."

Huh? Any other time she'd be raising cain. Now it barely got a murmur. Something was definitely wrong. They climbed in the saddles and navigated through town and out into the lush countryside. Grace didn't utter a word. Whatever was eating at her had to be bad.

When they stopped at a little stream to water the horses, Deacon glanced at her. "Dammit, Grace, what's wrong? This silence isn't like you."

She raised her head. "I got the answers to all my questions today. Can we just ride?"

"Sure." What questions? Then it dawned on him, and his breath froze. *Her Yuma Blackstone questions.* That could certainly account for the silence. "Who told you?"

"My uncle Henry." She walked down the stream and stood, staring off.

Shit! This was bad and could only mean something like Yuma was her father. Yep, that would do it. He didn't pry, and pretty soon they rode on. He'd have to wait and let her talk in her own time.

Dark clouds began to gather. He hoped the rain held off, at least until they made it to Joshua.

They rode in silence mere feet apart. An occasional glance at her revealed deep hurt and anger. Normal feelings when someone destroyed your world, but he'd give anything to have the funny Grace of this morning and the ridiculous story she'd made up about dining with Jim Quarrels and sharing his birthday. Deacon released a soft snort.

Her zest for life and passion for causes was one of the things he liked most about her. She didn't hesitate jumping into trouble with both feet and worrying about how to get out later.

They arrived at Joshua and rode down the only street, passing a small hotel, two saloons, a telegraph office, a café, and a jail the size of a water closet. The town didn't have much to recommend it.

He reined up at the hitching post in front of the hotel and dismounted. "We'll go in and ask around. If you'd rather not come, I'll do it myself."

"I'll come." She threw her leg over the saddle, and together they entered the no-name building that was identified only by a small, swinging sign with the word "hotel" in block letters.

Deacon removed his hat and led Grace to the desk where a woman sat puffing on a cigar. "Pardon me, ma'am, I wonder if you could help us."

"You need a room?"

He glanced at Grace and found the idea of running his hand across her tempting curves appealing. She scowled, seeming to read his thoughts. "No, ma'am. No room."

"If you didn't need a room, why did you bother me?"

"I'd wanted to inquire about a man named Jim Quarrels. He's supposed to live hereabouts."

Grace fished in her pocket and pulled out a dollar. "We'll make it worth your while," she said sweetly, pushing it across the counter.

The clerk took the cigar from her mouth, picked up the dollar, and held it to the light. "Who was that again?"

"Jim Quarrels." Deacon added a smile this time.

"You kin?"

"Not exactly. We're trying to find a boy named Izzy, and we thought maybe he could help us."

The woman gave him a toothless grin. "Mr. Quarrels is just like his name. He's a mite quarrelsome. He'd as soon take a shotgun to you as not. Yep, he's quarrelsome all right." She wagged her head. "That's about all I know. Never been to his house, so cain't rightly tell you where it is. The missus and a boy used to come to town once in a blue moon, but I ain't seen 'em in a long while." She leaned closer. "I heard he keeps her locked up on account of he says she's gone crazy, and he probably killed the boy, drowned him in the river like he threatened a dozen times. None of us asks. Ain't good for our health."

Jim Quarrels sounded like a man to steer clear of. If the boy was Izzy, no wonder he'd left. Poor kid.

Deacon put his hat on. "I appreciate your kindness, ma'am."

Just then a clap of thunder shook the hotel. Things were going to get ugly.

"I hope you brought a rain slicker," the woman called as they walked to the door. "Come back if you need a room. Ask for Sally."

Outside, shielded from the rain by the overhang, Deacon stared at the deluge, wishing he'd thrown in slickers. The light from the little café drew his attention. "Grace, it's almost five o'clock. Let's go eat and try to wait out the storm. Maybe it'll be a quick one."

"Good idea."

Moments later, they entered the café, looking like two drowned rats. Deacon restrained his impulse to shake like a dog. They took a seat and glanced around at the other patrons eyeing them suspiciously.

"Have I grown horns, Brannock?"

"I think we both have."

They ordered, then talked about Sally and her information. "I halfway thought she was pulling our leg. Do you think she made all that up to warn us off?" Grace asked.

"I could be wrong, but I don't think so. You loosened her up with the dollar."

"We still don't know where he lives, and it's raining. We can't even get home now."

"Don't worry." He slid his hand on top of hers. "If worst comes to worst, I'll get you a room at the hotel, and I'll sleep in the livery."

Her gaze met his. "I refuse to sleep in a bed while you spend the night with the horses." She pulled her hand out from under his and drew a design on his skin. "Besides, this town, the people are a bit creepy. Not sure if I'll close my eyes. I might not anyway with everything."

"Tell me what Henry said."

Tears bubbled in her blue eyes. "Turns out, Yuma is my—" She swallowed. "Yuma fathered me in a sadistic, unimaginable way." A tear crawled down her cheek. She pulled away her fingers that were drawing on his hand. "I'm the daughter of a monster," she whispered.

"I'm sorry, Grace. I don't know what to say." He wished he could whisk her away to a mountaintop where she could forget it all. But he knew there would be no forgetting this.

Some things stayed with a person forever. This was one.

For him, it was the day some bigger kids told him he was a bastard child. One dared to call his mother a name, and although the kid was lots bigger, Deacon knocked out two front teeth.

He brushed the tear from her jaw with a knuckle. "Sometimes it helps to talk about it."

"Will it, or is that just what everyone says because they don't know any other words?"

"I care, Grace. More than I have for anyone." His words were soft, and he'd never meant anything more. Grace had battered through his walls and charged into his heart like a soldier on a gallant steed.

He hadn't been the same since.

The waitress brought their food. Between mouthfuls, Grace told him everything, and he hated the monster with every fiber of his being. Thank God he was dead, or Deacon would hunt him down and one of them would die. If ever a devil had walked the earth, it was Yuma Blackstone.

Deacon wiped his mouth and laid down his napkin. "I wish I

had something helpful to say that would ease your pain. A very wise man once told me that it doesn't matter the color of your blood, your name, or your money. What matters in the end is how you've lived your life and the kindness you've shown. Everything else is immaterial."

The other customers got up and left, leaving the place to Deacon and Grace.

"Good advice, I suppose." She ran a finger slowly around the rim of her teacup. "But what will having his blood do to me? It has to come out in some form."

Would she become eaten up with hate and evil? Would she find joy in making people miserable? Maybe it was all lying dormant, waiting for something to trigger it.

Was she doomed to become Yuma Blackstone?

Twenty-seven

"STOP. YOU'RE WRONG, GRACE. JUST BECAUSE YUMA WAS A monster doesn't mean you will be. No more than a father who likes cornbread passes it down to his son." Deacon gave her hand a squeeze. "It doesn't work that way. You have a good head on your shoulders and make sound decisions. Besides, you have half of your mother's blood, and that dilutes his."

Grace sighed. "I know you're trying to help, and I appreciate it."

The anguish still dulled her eyes. Maybe no one could say anything to make it better.

"Dear God! No one has offered a description. Do I look like him, Brannock?"

He caressed her face, cupped her strong jaw. Yuma's shaved head, strange, silvery eyes, thin mustache above his sneer, the evil carved into each line of the man's face popped into mind. "No. Not even one iota. I would never, ever have guessed."

"That's a blessed relief. I wouldn't want to look like him."

"I imagine you got your mother's looks."

The rain was coming down harder than ever instead of letting up. "We'll talk more, but right now we should decide what we're going to do. We don't know where Jim Quarrels lives, and it'll be dark early with the rain. I think we're stuck here."

"Crockett knows I may not get home tonight. I think it's the hotel."

"Me too. I just wanted to make sure you're okay with it."

"It's the only thing that makes sense."

The words came out dull and toneless. Deacon wished he could say something to put her back the way she was.

"All right. I'll take you back to the hotel to wait while I get the horses out of the rain. Will you be okay there until I get back?"

Grace picked at the cloth napkin. "I'll be fine. We have to take care of the horses first."

Deacon helped her from her chair and took her to the hotel. They saw no sign of the cigar-smoking woman.

She plucked his sleeve. "I'll wait here in the lobby until you get back. Besides, Sally is probably eating supper."

"I'll hurry." He kissed her cheek and went to collect the horses.

The livery wasn't far, and he soon had them in a stall with feed. Deacon threw the saddlebags over his shoulders and slipped and slid back to the hotel in the soupy mess.

Grace rose from a sofa, looking relieved to see him. He caught her putting a small derringer in her pocket.

"Miss me?" He put an arm around her narrow waist.

"What are you fishing for, Brannock? I'm fresh out of compliments."

Now that was more like the Grace he knew. Not all the way, mind you, but coming back.

The toothless clerk came through a door. Deacon's spurs clinked on the wooden floor as he went to the desk. "Miss Sally, we're going to need a room after all."

"For you and the missus?"

No, for the horses. And Grace wasn't his missus. Deacon ground his back teeth, feeling no need to explain. "Just one for my...her."

Grace shook her head. "No, we're together, Sally."

The woman pulled out the register. "You're in luck. I have one room left."

That was funny because he neither saw nor heard anyone else in the building. "When did you fill them?" he asked.

Sally looked at him like he'd given her a cussing. "For your information, I had a run while you were at the café." She pursed her lips in anticipation of his next question. "I saw you go there through the window."

The woman probably pressed her nose to the glass, spying on them.

Deacon leaned against the counter and stuck a matchstick in his mouth. "That so? I'm curious. How many rooms do you have altogether?"

"Three. Sign the register, and I'll take you back. The missus looks mighty tired. Your room is right next to the kitchen."

"Why didn't I know that?" Deacon murmured to Grace, removing the matchstick.

"It's fine. Anything is fine. Be grateful," she whispered.

"I am. It's just that nothing is working out. I'm tired, I'm drenched, and I'm irritable." On the other hand, he was in a hotel with the woman of his dreams, and they had nowhere to go until tomorrow. He brightened.

Sally unlocked the door and lit the lamp. The room left a lot to be desired, both in cleanliness and amenities, but a screen with a mountain scene stood in one corner, and a small fireplace occupied the other. A bug ran across the floor, and the woman stomped it and grinned up at him. "You might have a little company. The sheets are used. I only wash 'em once a week on Mondays." She scratched under her arm. "I think I might've skipped this last one. Cain't remember."

"Would you have an extra blanket, Miss Sally?" he asked in his best voice, hoping that helped. Grace would have to sleep on top of the covers which would require a blanket. He still planned on making do with the livery.

"I reckon I can spare one," Sally said. "It'll be extra."

Deacon glanced at Grace, who was dead on her feet. "How much, ma'am?"

"Two bits."

"Fine." He moved to close the door behind her.

Sally stuck her head back in. "Breakfast will be one dollar apiece. It's at eight sharp."

Grace sat on the bed. "Thank you, ma'am."

Once the door closed and Deacon heard Sally's footsteps fade, he sat next to Grace. "You must've had your reasons why you told Sally we were together, but I can't see it. I'm trying to protect your reputation. I'll wait until she brings the blanket, then I'll go to the livery."

She faced him, her face haggard. "It doesn't matter what they think. We'll never see these people again. I can't sleep alone." Her eyes filled with tears. "Everything I thought I knew about myself turned out to be false. I'm a killer's daughter, and I can't stand the idea of being alone in the dark. You're all that stands between me and Yuma Blackstone. He'll come for me as soon as I close my eyes. I know he will."

He put an arm around her, and she laid her head on his shoulder. "Okay, whatever you need, princess. I'll try to give you some peace to the best of my ability."

A knock sounded, and he took not one, but two blankets from Sally and thanked her.

Deacon thought of the extra clothes they'd brought in his saddlebag and her carpetbag—soaked through. The contents were doing them little good now.

Locking the door, he went to the bed and put the blankets down. "I don't know if or when these were ever washed, but you need to get out of those wet clothes and wrap a blanket around you." When she didn't move, he shook her, repeating it. Finally, she stood and moved to the screen.

Deacon hung the blanket over the side. "Take your time. I'm right here."

"I'm sorry I'm not—" Her voice broke.

"Hey, you're fine. No apologies." He lit the fire, then glanced around the room for a place to sleep but saw nothing. The room had no furniture except for the bed. Looked like a long night on the hard floor. With the bugs. He eyed another one crawling toward him and smashed it.

"Brannock, you're wet too," Grace called. "Undress and use the other blanket."

"All right." Dry would feel good even if it was only a blanket.

A glance toward the screen found Grace's riding skirt draped over the top. Something white and filmy followed. Her underthings. Deacon swallowed hard. Heaven help him.

If he survived this night with his sanity, it would be a miracle.

❧

Grace wrapped the blanket securely around her and moved from behind the screen into a warm glow. "That fire looks divine. It's already warming up the room." And crawling up her neck.

Brannock could've stepped from her fantasy. Thanks to the wind and rain, his tousled, long hair, black and glistening in the firelight, seemed to beg for her touch. The rakish slash of dark brows and piercing gray eyes…mmmm. Desire swept over her. She yearned to know how his skin felt under her fingers. He'd secured the blanket around his waist, leaving his upper body bare.

He raised a hand to the dark growth along his jaw. "You all right? Don't tell me Sally has a ghost too."

Grace shook herself. "I sure hope not. The bugs are more than enough."

"I killed another while you were undressing."

"Ugh! I wish you hadn't told me. How will I get any sleep?" She laid her clothes next to the fire with his. She'd have to remember to shake them out come morning.

"Sorry. Didn't mean to add to your misery."

Grace sat on the bed and he perched next to her. "You aren't. I'm thankful to be out of that storm. I'm sorry for being such a ninny, but I just couldn't be by myself tonight."

He put an arm around her. "Quit apologizing. I'm glad I could be here."

She rested her head on his shoulder. "I'm so tired. It feels like I've lived a dozen lifetimes since my uncle Henry told me Yuma was my father. I was born from such horrible violence. My poor mother. I wish I could talk to her."

Houston deserved thanks for giving her a name and a home. He loved her and he'd shown it countless ways.

"Violence often gives birth to beauty," Brannock said softly. "A raging fire gives way to green growth and tree rebirth. From a volcano and earthquakes come mountains, streams, and valleys. Expect no less for you. No telling how much good can come from Yuma's darkness."

What a nice comparison. Brannock surprised her.

She raised her head and turned to face him. "I don't feel very pretty."

"Oh, but you are. I wish you could see you as I do." He lifted a strand of hair, rolling it between a thumb and forefinger. "Your hair looks like spun gold."

He gently placed his lips on hers. The kiss fanned sleeping embers, and flames leaped to life. A moan slipped from her throat. She slid an arm around his neck and a hand into his hair. Brannock pulled her closer, a large hand behind her ear to anchor.

Grace knew this night would change her in ways she least expected. She leaned back and searched his eyes. "I want you, Brannock. I want you in every way."

"Are you sure that's not hurt talking? You've been through hell today."

"I'm positive. Do you not want what I'm giving?"

He tucked her hair back and let his fingers drift down the column of her throat. "Princess, I want you more than anything on earth. I've yearned to lay you down under me ever since we first met." He took a deep breath. "I just want to make certain you're doing this for the right reasons. I have no wish to be used or made a fool of."

"I promise I will never do that. Sparks flew between us the first day I marched in front of the Three Deuces and I know I didn't imagine that." Her lips twitched. "I'll never forget our initial meeting. And our war of words." She grew warm under his intense stare.

Brannock laughed. "You have so much passion and you live life to the fullest." The pad of his finger drifted down her throat and across her collarbones. "I feel like I've grabbed the tail end of a lightning bolt. You've turned me upside down until I barely know my own name."

"That was the plan, my dear saloon keep." She leaned forward and kissed his throat.

His eyes pierced her, seeing all the things she tried to hide. "Grace, if we do this, it will be for real, not some wild fling. Do you view me—this—as a mere flash in the night? If you do, we stop here."

His sense of honor, and maybe a good deal of self-preservation, came as a shock. She'd never seen this side of him, and it shook her to the depths of her soul.

"I'm not interested in something quick and temporary." Her voice became raspy. "Lay back, Brannock."

When he did as she asked, she curled against his side. "I want to run my hands over every inch of you."

"Do it to your heart's content," he whispered hoarsely.

Given free rein, Grace ran her palms across his broad chest, feeling each muscle, tendon, and bone. She paused at a scar. "What happened here?"

"I was stabbed."

She continued until she encountered the puckered skin of another scar. "And here?"

"Shot."

"Deacon, that's horrible! You seem so calm." She realized in her shock she'd used his first name.

"How else would I feel? They happened years ago on my way to fighting for my place in the world."

She scrutinized every inch of his chest, stopping at his brown nipples. She'd seen her shirtless brothers' chests a lot. But Brannock's fascinated her. Everything about the hardened steel beneath muscle and bone of this man captivated her. She ran her fingers slowly across the hard nubs. They were so sensitive, puckering when she blew on them, and when she rolled them between a thumb and forefinger, they became distended and hard.

The blanket covering his privates rose to a point. While she hadn't seen a man's erection, she'd seen plenty of horses' and how they'd raced along the corral or fence lines in a frenzy, trying to get to the mares. A shiver danced through her as moisture collected between her thighs.

"That feels good, princess."

Grace bent and licked his nipples, and he sucked in air between his teeth. In a swift move, he rolled, putting her beneath him. He stared down. "My turn."

Goose bumps prickled her skin. Promises of things to come filled his eyes. *Oh my!*

Deacon nuzzled behind her ears and kissed the column of her throat, pressing a kiss to the hollow where her heartbeat throbbed.

"Don't stop," she said breathlessly. "I'm in heaven."

His mouth was doing amazing things to her. He reached the edge of the blanket and paused. Feeling wild and daring, she moved the obstruction aside, and he buried his face in her naked breasts.

Grace closed her eyes and soaked up each sensation as he lavished attention on her sensitive nipples and breasts. He tweaked. Brushed. Sucked.

She thrust her hands into his hair. "Please! Don't stop."

If she had known the depth of pleasure he'd awakened, she'd never have sent her paramours running. Then she shook her head. No, this kind of thrill could only have come with Deacon. The act was just a small part of the equation.

It took the right man at the right time in her life.

As he'd done from the start, he aroused such deep feelings that seemed to come from her bones. He knew how hard to touch, where to stroke, the whisper of his breath across her skin. She had no doubt he was aware of the pleasure his caresses gave her. Knew the fire raging inside her.

Deacon lifted her arms above her head and anchored them lightly on the bed, piercing her with those beautiful gray eyes, his hair falling around his face. "Tell me what you want, Grace."

She licked her lips, a smile forming. "You. I want you."

"To do what?" His voice was soft, teasing.

"I want you to drive me wild with desire until I can scarcely stand the thought of anything else. Wipe out every sad thought."

"I'll do my best, my heart."

While he lavished attention on her flat stomach, legs, and breasts, she ran her palms over every part of him she could reach.

Dear God! Her body seemed on fire and trembled with a strange, consuming need. Waves of something wonderful and new washed over her, leaving her shaken.

He lifted his head. With a tug, he removed the rest of the blanket and rested a hand on the entrance to her body. When she'd gotten accustomed to the feel of his hand, his fingers began to move—softly, tenderly, seeking her wet warmth.

Although this was her first time with a man, she knew how things went from growing up on the ranch, so she wasn't afraid. She wanted to become a woman, and she wanted it with Deacon Brannock.

His fingers were pure magic, and the higher he took her, the more rapid her breathing until she could hardly bear the unbelievable pleasure.

Greedy, she reached for more of whatever it was just beyond her grasp. Suddenly, she tumbled onto wave after wave of the most delicious sensations she'd ever felt in her life.

Tears welled in her eyes. This man who'd suffered and still suffered with his hand and arm had more to give than the richest man in Fort Worth. He had such a soft heart for the street kids, Leah, and little Johnny Madrid.

Deacon lifted himself on top of her and pushed his length inside. Soon, she was climbing again, aching for the sweet, engulfing waves of release.

"Take it, darlin'. It's there," he whispered. "All for you."

Her body shuddered and seemed to fly apart into some unknown place where orbs of beautiful color tumbled around her.

Delicious spams gripped her of unimaginable proportion. Deacon stiffened and clasped her to him, his lips sealed on hers. They grabbed for the last of the elixir that might bring them every happiness.

Twenty-eight

DEACON AWOKE A LITTLE LATER TO THE SOFT CRACKLING FIRE and Grace's gentle breathing. She lay with her head on his shoulder and a shapely arm thrown across his belly. His heart swelled.

If he were granted one wish, he'd tuck her inside and shield her from every problem and hurt. Frustration ran through him that he could do nothing to help soothe her misery now. He'd lived with the pain of being called a bastard his whole life but couldn't tell her how to fight back.

A deep sigh escaped him as he gently brushed her cheek with a light knuckle.

The long lashes feathering against her skin held traces of tears. She had strength though, and when she got her feet under her again, Lord help them all.

He'd never claimed to be a saint, and he'd done a lot of bad things, so he didn't know why providence, fate, the powers that be had put her in his life. Grace had never been afraid of him, and that right there was a miracle. In fact, she'd seemed to delight in going toe to toe with him from the first.

Thickness filled his throat. Something was happening that he couldn't control. The lock around his heart had fallen away.

Love wasn't possible for someone like him. No one could love the hard man he'd become. But whatever this was, it seemed to be unfurling like a beautiful flower, and he felt like running and jumping and screaming his happiness to the world.

He wished he knew what to do about the things he kept from her.

Would it hurt if she never knew his secrets? Maybe not, but he didn't want anything between them. Still, he took a huge gamble in opening up.

He touched her sleeping face, caressed her strong jaw.

"Thank you," he whispered. Strange, but he didn't even know what he thanked her for.

Taking pity on him?

Marching in front of the saloon?

Giving him her body?

His thanks extended to a great many things. All those empty nights he'd spent alone with nothing but the sound of his own heartbeat melted away.

This was for real, and so was Grace.

He covered them with the blankets. His eyelids grew heavy. "Sweet dreams, darlin'. You're safe."

❧

Deacon woke before dawn to clanging and banging in the kitchen next to them.

Grace opened her eyes. "What's that? Sounds like we're in the middle of temperance marchers."

"Only Sally, I suppose, making breakfast." The fire had gone out in the small chimney. He eyed the few pieces of wood of various sizes stacked beside it. "Want to draw to see who gets the fire going?"

"Not really." She propped her chin on his chest and drew lazy circles on his bare skin. "I'm hungering for you something awful."

"Let me light the fire, and I'll see what I can do about that." He hurried bare-assed across the floor, completed the job, and wasted no time crawling back under the blankets and snuggling against her enticing curves. "That better?"

"Much." She kissed his chest, his lips, her hand slipping between their bodies. "I found something I like."

"So did I." His hand followed the shape of her body, and soon they were breathing hard again, on their way to sweet surrender.

❧

A rich, quiet glow filled every empty space inside her. Grace had never been so contented, so complete. She kept wanting to hug herself and embrace this joy.

Once she recovered and got some strength in her shaky legs, she dressed and looked out the window. "The rain's stopped."

"Good." Deacon strapped on his gun belt. "If I have to stay here all day, you'll kill me."

"You poor, poor darling."

Deacon stood in front of her, his eyes smoldering. He slid a hand into her hair and pulled her close. "I meant what I said. This is not a joke or anything I take lightly. You're the one for me, Grace."

His gaze made her warm all over. She twisted a button on his shirt, wondering what he meant. Was he wanting to marry her? Court her? What?

Finally, she trusted her voice to speak. "So what are we going to do? What exactly are you wanting?"

"I'd like to marry you whenever things become more stable. How do you feel about being my wife?"

Excited prickles raced up her spine. Marry? Having a strong man like Brannock for a husband would be a challenge, but she found the idea most appealing. The thought of living with him, sleeping next to him, being a wife would fulfill her daydreams.

"Would you still operate the saloon? You know how I feel about plying liquor."

"Sit down. Let's talk." When they were seated, he took her hand. "I understand all your reasons for being against spirits. Honestly, I do. You certainly have a right to speak up against establishments that serve it." He squeezed her fingers. "Can we compromise? Can you accept that I have a right to keep the Three Deuces open for a bit longer?"

"Yes, I can. After all, you probably sell more food now than drink. I have a feeling the saloon is only the means to you reaching your dream." Her voice was soft as she searched for the right words. "Can you admit that it has to do with owning your own land?"

There was the manure on his boots, his disappearances, their sharing of dreams. That had to be it.

He brushed her cheek with his lips. "You've found me out."

For the next half hour, he told her about his plan of making enough money to hopefully buy some land. "I've also been helping out a friend on his ranch, and that may or may not lead to a good stake. Not sure yet, so don't get your hopes up. It could come to naught."

"Oh, Deacon, please don't keep these secrets from me. Why didn't you tell me?"

"Because nothing is sure. This is all subject to falling through."

"But you could've told me."

"I'm not made that way. It's too iffy to mention."

"Still, I want to know so I can offer support." Seeing his insecurity about the future was an eye-opener. He really wanted his own land, and if she could help him get it, she would.

This trip had changed the course of her life, and she welcomed the fresh direction.

She started to say she had to talk to her mother and father about marrying Deacon but...she didn't have a father. She owed Houston for taking her in and raising her, and she did love him, she really did, except they had a lot of air that needed clearing, and she didn't exactly know where their relationship stood.

All she knew was that she loved the warm tingles racing around under her skin.

If only she could talk to her mother and figure this out. Or her great-grandfather. Where was he when she needed him?

Grace brushed her lips softly across Deacon's cheek. "Marrying suits me fine—after a period of time."

Deacon frowned. "How much time?"

"Maybe a month or two."

"Are you even serious about us?"

"I'm scared, Deacon. So much is happening. I feel like I'm inside a raging hurricane."

He took her hands. "I'm sorry. Of course you're scared. Your whole life has been wiped away in one fell swoop."

"What name do I use? Boone? Legend? Blackstone? What name?"

"Darlin', use the one that feels comfortable. Houston gave you the Legend name. Do you really want to give it back?"

"No." She was just miserable and confused.

"Then keep it. Are you mad because Houston didn't tell you?"

"Not mad. Hurt maybe. I understand why he kept the secret though. It's not an easy thing to tell."

Deacon folded his arms around her and rested his chin on the top of her head. "You need to hash this out with him at the first opportunity. You won't find any peace until you do."

Grace nodded, pushing from his arms. "I agree. Let's eat some breakfast and try to find out something about Izzy."

"We don't have a lot of time. That storm ruined our plans." His gaze met hers, saying volumes. "But you'll never hear me complain."

"I wouldn't have missed this, Deacon. Not one second."

They ate a hearty meal of fried eggs, bacon, flapjacks, and fried apples. Sally definitely turned out to be a better cook than she was a hotel owner. Odd that there was no sign of any of the other guests.

Sally lit up a cigar as they went out. "You and the missus try over at the general store or the saloon. Someone will know how to find Quarrels."

Deacon put his hat on. "Yes, ma'am. You have a good day."

The saloons weren't open yet, so they went to Marshall's General Store. A man greeted them. "Can I help you?"

Deacon pushed his hat back with a forefinger. "We're looking for someone—Jim Quarrels. Would you know him?"

Grace glanced around the store and found it clean and well stocked. Kinda unusual for a small town like Joshua. She turned her attention back to the clerk.

"He comes in about once a week. Can't say I like him. If you have dealings with him, I'd tread softly, mister."

"Why's that?"

Foreboding went through Grace. Everyone they'd met that knew him had nothing good to say. But then Quarrels had shot his mouth off about drowning kids. Maybe he'd drowned Izzy.

"He leads a group of misfits and ruffians. Our sheriff died six months ago, and since then, they got even worse, riding up to folks' houses and issuing warnings to either pay them money or pack up and leave. I hope we find a new sheriff soon."

Grace couldn't imagine living here with Quarrels and his group on the loose. The nice clothes and money he flashed in Hell's Half Acre must've been some of the ill-gotten spoils.

"Sounds like a bad bunch." Deacon shot her a glance as though to make sure she was close. "Actually, we're searching for a young kid named Israel Anthony, but we know him as Izzy. He disappeared, and we're concerned about his welfare. Quarrels showed up in Fort Worth mouthing off, so we wanted to talk to him and see what he knows about Izzy."

The clerk's demeanor changed from polite to concerned. "Poor kid. I wondered where he went. A sad situation, but I haven't seen him in a while."

Grace stepped to Deacon's side. "Mister, whatever you can tell us about him will be greatly appreciated."

"The Anthonys lived outside of town. Izzy's pa was killed in an accident, and his mother married again. Phillip Vinson had a son a few years older and as mean as a snake. Vinson hated Izzy with a passion, always looked for reasons to whip the boy. Izzy came home from school one day to find Vinson on the porch. The bastard handed him his clothes and told him he was no longer welcome, to find another home."

Anger washed over Grace. "How old was Izzy then?"

The clerk studied the counter for a long moment. "Seems I recall he was seven or eight. Not near old enough to make his own way."

"He's been living on the streets in Fort Worth for a while, and we've been helping him. Like I said, he disappeared well over a week ago, and we want to make sure he's all right." Deacon released a worried breath. "Jim Quarrels was overheard boasting about drowning kids and that's why we came. We haven't had anything else to go on. If you'll direct us to Vinson, we'll be on our way."

"Wish I could. Vinson, the missus, and his boy packed up and moved away. Don't know where. All I know is good riddance." The clerk wagged his head. "I sure feel sorry for Anna, though. She was a saint. Never gave anyone a speck of grief."

Grace's heart ached for Anna and Izzy. She'd heard similar stories but never when she'd known any of the people. It sounded like Anna wasn't a strong woman, or she wouldn't have stood for Vinson kicking her son out into the cold. Grace wished she could give Phillip Vinson a piece of her mind, and she wouldn't stop until she sent him back to wherever he came from.

Her hopes had been so high that they'd find Izzy here in Joshua. But she did find something else. She cast Brannock a smile, and a frisson of happiness curled along her spine.

He wanted to marry her, make her his wife.

Grace's stomach flipped upside down. He was unlike any man she'd ever known, and being with him gave her such a thrill. She'd noticed how women turned to look at him. That she was the lucky one released a flood of hot tingles through her.

He turned and caught her staring. Warmth rushed over her.

Deacon thanked the clerk and turned to leave, offering his elbow. She slipped her hand around it, glad he couldn't read her thoughts and know how he made her feel.

Outside, he paused on the only street. "I think we might as well go back home. But I'm not giving up on finding him."

"Me either." Grace glanced up at him. "I'm glad we came."

Just then, half a dozen riders thundered into town and blocked them. Grace boldly stared at the men, most in ordinary, everyday clothes. One, however, stood out in a blue military coat, gloves, and a blue hat with a thick yellow cord as a band. Arrogance was in his bearing and expression.

"State your business," the man barked.

Deacon snorted. "Are you the law now?"

"The only one here. What are you doing in our town?"

"Looking for someone. Is that a crime?"

Fear set Grace's heart racing. Deacon would challenge this group and then what? Would she have to take him back draped over a horse?

She plucked his sleeve and spoke quietly. "Let's just go."

"They're not going to let us." Deacon shifted, taking a wider stance, the muscles in his jaw clenching. His eyes drew her attention. They'd turned to hard ice.

Three of the riders dismounted and formed a circle around them.

Deacon rested a hand on the butt of his Colt. "Do you really want to do this?"

One of the three stepped back.

"If you're sure you want to start something, I'm more than ready to oblige." Deacon's deep voice echoed in the suddenly empty street. "You might not like the finish."

"Quarrels?" one of the riders asked. He looked nervous.

So this was Jim Quarrels. Grace didn't think much of a man going around playing general and scaring everyone.

The man dismounted and stood in front of Deacon. His gold front tooth glinted. "Your name?"

"That's none of your business. You have no authority here," Deacon answered.

"Parker, take charge of the woman," Quarrels ordered.

Deacon didn't move a muscle although his jaw tensed. "Touch my wife and die!"

Grace hadn't seen such thick tension since she was ten years old and Houston made the robbers turn her loose by sheer intimidation. Her breath seemed frozen inside.

The two men next to her stepped back.

Brannock seemed as cool as winter snow, but inside, she imagined he was full of nerves as he took a step forward, nose to nose with Quarrels. "Now, here's what's going to happen, Quarrels. You're getting back on your horses and riding out. We're going to get our horses from the livery and leave your town." He paused. "Either that, or I can put a bunch of you face down in the street. Now, I can do whatever you choose. But make no mistake, my wife and I are riding away, breathing and healthy."

Quarrels flicked a gaze between his men and Deacon, then stepped away. "I'll let you go this time with a warning. Come back and I *will* lock you up for whatever reason I can find."

Grace released her pent-up breath and watched the men climb back onto their horses. In less than sixty seconds, they were gone as fast as they'd appeared. "That was scary."

"I've seen worse. He's nothing but a little man trying to play soldier and not having a clue how."

She placed her hands on her hips, sarcasm and anger spewing. "And to think I was going to wish him a happy birthday. He can kiss my foot!"

"I don't want him kissing any part of you. Not even your foot." Deacon swung away, rubbing his arm and hand, clearly trying to get feeling back. Oh no! Fear of how the outcome could've gone gripped her. Of all times to leave him vulnerable.

She moved around his broad shoulders. "Was your arm numb the whole time you faced off against them?"

He didn't answer, just kept staring ahead, massaging some life back into his limb.

"How did you manage to look so calm?" She took his hand and stroked each long finger, his palm, and across his wrist, then up his arm.

"I had to." His stricken eyes found her. "I can make my hand do whatever I need it to."

But what would happen if one time he couldn't? Willpower only went so far. Grace didn't point out the obvious. She could see he already feared that.

"You're a strong man, Deacon Brannock. I can't imagine being here with anyone else." She brushed a kiss to his cheek. "You called me your wife."

"I hope you didn't mind."

"It's strange, but I feel like I am already married. That was so sweet."

He was ready to kill a man to protect her, and it made her heart swell that he thought her worthy. Like priceless china.

No doubt he would've killed Pickford if it had come to that. The unwritten law of the West laid out that a man was justified in protecting a life in whatever way he had to. The Legends had lived by this code ever since Grace could remember. That's just how it was.

Brannock glanced down, his gaze tangling with hers. He put an arm around her waist, drawing her closer. "I meant what I said last night. That was forever. As far as I'm concerned, we're as married now as we'll ever be. A preacher is just a formality for others."

"I feel that way too."

They got their horses and rode toward Fort Worth. Grace's head was full of heated touches, passionate kisses, and lovemaking with Deacon—and what to do about his daring proposal. Some people married for money. Some for protection. Some for convenience. Others for love. What reason fit her? Deacon wasn't rich, and she didn't know if she loved him or not. That left protection and convenience. Both pointed to her. Deacon wanted to keep her safe and shield her from any repercussions.

A thought froze her. What if she found herself with child? The babe would need a name.

The scenario hit too close to home. *Her mother married Houston to give Grace a name.*

Would she be forced to ask the same of Brannock?

She glanced at Deacon's strong profile, remembered the way he'd stood up to Quarrels back there. He'd make a fine father, and he loved children.

Grace knew his feelings about one thing for certain. He wouldn't stand for anyone talking about her or pointing fingers. Warmth rushed over her. No matter what name he used, he was a good man.

The false name issue was one more thing they'd have to get out in the open if they wanted a life together.

They had almost reached Fort Worth when Deacon pulled up at a pretty little stream. "Let's stop here for a few minutes."

"Good idea." She dismounted. "I've been doing a lot of thinking since leaving Joshua. Why did you call me your wife when those men threatened us?"

"I knew that carried a lot more weight, and I needed some power. Are you upset?"

"No." Truth was, she rather liked the thought. A warm feeling whirled in her stomach.

There were a lot worse things than pretending to be hitched to Deacon Brannock. She couldn't help but see the way his muscles moved across his broad shoulders when he walked and how his tight denims outlined his perfectly formed butt.

Her cowboy. If she had her way, he'd be on a ranch herding cattle, instead of in a saloon wrangling drunks. Maybe soon.

Yes, there were a whole bunch of worse things than playing wife to a cowboy living the wrong life.

Twenty-nine

"I've had a lot on my mind, too, since we left." Deacon led the horses to the water, then found a flat rock for them to sit on under the branches of a cottonwood. Once they'd settled, he sank into the depths of her vivid blue eyes, not wanting to be anywhere else. "I don't want any secrets between us, Grace. That's never helped anyone start a new life together."

The only problem was, he didn't know where to start. So much of his life was lived in shadows.

"I don't know anything about you, Deacon. Do you have any family?"

"No. Not anymore. What I have to tell you is the hardest thing I've ever done." He put an arm around her and let the faint scent of apples from breakfast bolster him. They blended with nearby sage, bluebonnets, and Indian blanket until the air seemed alive.

"I don't judge, Deacon," she said gently. "You can tell me anything. I've sensed something very dark inside you."

"That's pretty accurate." He took a deep breath and prayed Grace wouldn't walk away. "My mother, Iris, was a soiled dove, but she loved me and my little sister, Cass, with all her heart and fought to keep us together. She was a beauty, with long, black hair and blue eyes. Iris was always a favorite. Cass and I had to stay hidden, or Mama would've gotten kicked out. I never knew..." Deacon stared up at a robin busily making a nest in the tree and swallowed the thickness lodged in his throat. "I never knew my father." He barked a laugh. "He was probably the lowest piece of scum on the earth."

"Oh, Deacon. Don't think that." Grace threaded her fingers through his. "He might be a really nice man who would've loved you."

"Doesn't matter now. I tried not to let it bother me then because Cass needed reassurance more than I did. Neither of us knew who fathered us."

"Take it from me, knowing doesn't make it any easier. I'd rather not know than to have mine."

"True. I'll tell you my experience with Yuma later, but first let me finish." Deacon picked up a piece of grass. "I was six years older than Cass and on my own at seventeen, working on cattle and horse ranches, when everything changed. She was eleven, and we were playing cribbage under an apple tree next to a small room where I lived. Cass was so innocent.

"A fellow named McCreedy came by. He was older than me by a few years, and I could tell he'd been drinking. We'd had trouble before. He started calling Cass vulgar names I won't repeat, saying it was about time she went into the family business. Cass started crying. I shoved McCreedy, telling him to leave. He laughed. I hated him, and that's a fact."

"I wouldn't have liked him either. He sounds like a bully."

"He followed Cass that afternoon and dragged her into the woods. I found her later." Deacon tried to speak but nothing came out. He bit down on his knuckles. Grace put an arm around him. He was trembling so. "Someone had strangled Cass."

"I'm so sorry, Deacon."

He didn't seem to hear her, so locked in the horror was he. "I went looking for McCreedy. Found him with his friends. He bragged about ridding the world of one less whore. He pulled out his gun, and I went for mine and put a bullet through his black heart."

Grace strangled a cry. She saw it all play out in her head. Deacon was like these street kids. He'd never had a normal home.

And poor Cass. She never got to grow up and fall in love. Never kissed a boy or known stability. She'd never had much of a chance, and if she'd have lived, she probably would've followed her mother into that kind of life.

Tears welled in Grace's eyes as she rubbed Deacon's back.

"They put me on trial. Houston was there as a witness, and if it hadn't been for him, they would've hung me. As it was, I got six years in prison due to my age and Houston saying he'd seen McCreedy pull his gun first and heard him bragging about what he'd done."

"I hope he rots in hell."

Deacon pulled her closer, seeking her warmth. "Some people would say that about me."

"Dumb people who don't know you. Since Houston was there, did this happen near the ranch?"

"Close. Medicine Springs."

"My family does quite a bit of business there. It's amazing that you met my...Houston...so long ago and just when you needed his voice."

"I'll always be grateful. I thought he might recognize me when he came into the Three Deuces, but I guess I've changed too much."

"Well, you're older now and I'm sure changed a lot physically. What about Iris?" she asked gently.

"She passed away in her sleep a year after Cass. I think she died of a broken heart."

A bird in the cottonwood chirped happily. A far cry from Grace's and Deacon's black moods.

"You said you'd tell me about your experience with Yuma," she prodded.

"We lived in the Texas Panhandle, and I was six when he paid to spend the night with my mother." Deacon told her about Yuma pulling him from under the bed, spending the freezing night outside, and how horribly his mother had been beaten. "He didn't cut her like he did your mother, but that was only because the man overseeing the girls took the knife away. She got lucky."

Grace turned sideways on the rock and laid a hand on his jaw. "I'm glad you told me all this, Deacon. I wish you'd trusted me sooner."

He kissed her open palm. "I never wanted you to know the sordid details of my life. I didn't want any of this to touch you. Some people would use it against you."

"Like my past is as white as the driven snow. We can't help who we're born to."

"Heed your own words, darlin'."

"I'll try. Learning the truth has brought about so many changes."

They'd finally opened up to each other and talked about so many things. Deacon was freed of secrets. Grace kissed him and sent heat into his core. Oh, for a bed. He yearned to make her say his name in that husky little tone she used when she was aroused.

Her lips reminded him of strawberries—plump and juicy.

She sent him a look of admiration. "You worked as a cowboy?"

"I developed an aptitude for working with cattle, but my real love is horses. I found a way to gentle them without the cruelty of breaking them. When I got released, I went back to it for a time, but my arm won't let me do a whole lot. Then I won the saloon in a poker game."

She grinned. "Let me guess. Three deuces?"

"Yep."

Grace chuckled. "The other guy must've had a horrible hand."

"A pair of fours."

"Good Lord!"

That reminded him. He'd yet to give her his birth name. Maybe he'd wait. But no, he'd vowed to come clean. All the way. Deacon cleared his throat. "I have one more confession. I don't want anything left between us."

With the exception of his work with the wild mustang. Why speak of something that might not turn out? There would be no point.

"What's else is there?" Grace asked.

"The name I was born with—it's Blade Reno. Reno was my mother's maiden name."

Grace's smile touched the darkness inside him, making everything light. As horrible as his past was, he'd gladly go through everything again if she would march in front of his saloon and throttle him with her sign.

"I like Blade Reno, but it doesn't sound like you. Deacon Brannock suits you best."

Deacon worked with the piece of grass he'd picked up when he first began his story. "When we marry, I suppose you just picked your name, future Mrs. Brannock." Holding her gaze, he slipped the ring of grass he'd made onto her finger. "I will always remember this day and how special you made me feel. I'm the luckiest man in the world."

"I'm truly the luckiest woman," Grace whispered, tears welling up. She touched the flimsy grass ring with reverence.

❧

They rode on, talking about where Phillip Vinson might've taken Izzy's mother. "There's no way of knowing." Grace maneuvered her horse until her leg touched Deacon's. "The trail is a dead end."

Deacon tugged his hat lower onto his forehead, his long hair brushing his shoulders. "Even if we find out where Vinson lives, it doesn't mean Izzy is there."

True enough, but why did he have to be so practical? That was okay, though. Everyone had to have a few faults.

"Is there anything we can do?" She'd be willing to lasso the moon if it would help.

"We can still look for him in town. Someone could be holding him. And you can write your articles and keep his name in front of people. Maybe one of the paper's subscribers will spy him and come forward."

"I can certainly do that. Pemberton seems to like my articles."

"So do I." Deacon moved his horse as close as he could and kissed her.

She was going to hate being in town and unable to make love to him. What would happen with the closeness that had developed between them? Sometimes things faded, and there was nothing a person could do to stop it. Grace made a silent vow to see him as much as possible and take advantage of every opportunity.

A glance at the fragile ring on her finger created a thickness in her throat. Such a small thing that came straight from Deacon's heart. He hadn't said as much, but each action revealed deep caring.

Everything he'd told her came back. She thought of his mother and sister and what growing up in a place like that must've been like for a boy. So much had been out of his control. Six years in a prison was a long time to be locked up and would definitely change a person. Now so much made sense—the fake name, his anger at constantly being targeted for crimes, his dream of owning his own land. His protective tendencies.

His warning sounded in her head. *Touch my wife and die.*

Grace knew he would've shot that man of Quarrels's this morning if he'd grabbed her. Deacon didn't make threats lightly. And back when she'd first met him, he'd held off the gang of men attacking Grace and her ladies with paint and manure. What he said, he meant. There was something honorable in that.

The idea for an article came to her. "Deacon, do you mind getting my pad and pencil from the saddlebag? I want to jot something down."

He grinned. "I envy that you can work anywhere." He reached inside and handed them to her.

"It is a good thing. I love what I do, Deacon. I don't plan to give it up."

"If you mean when we marry, you won't have to. I want you to do whatever makes you happy."

"Many husbands would put their foot down. I'm glad you see it differently."

"Writing is a part of you. I will never take that away." He kept silent while she wrote.

When she'd finished, she passed it to him. "See what you think."

He read it and glanced up. "This is excellent. Bringing Phillip Vinson's name out into the open might help us find him at least. I have a feeling he's still in the area."

"And there's a chance that someone who knows him or Izzy's mother or Izzy himself will read this and contact me at the paper. I feel very hopeful, Deacon."

"I think it's the right way to go." He sighed. "I just wish I had some money, so I could put up a reward for information."

"There's no use wishing for things we don't have. I could get some from Grandpa Stoker, but I don't want to ask unless it's absolutely necessary."

"I'm happy that you still consider the Legends family. That's good."

The bonds were too deep for her to cast Houston and Grandpa Stoker aside. "I have to. They're a part of me."

He slid a hand under her hair and brought her close, claiming her lips. She met his kiss, gripping his vest, loving the solidness of his large body and how special he made her feel.

Breaking the kiss, Deacon studied her. "I agree. Just hold off a while on asking for money."

Grace and Deacon returned the horses to the livery and parted ways—Grace to the *Gazette* office and Deacon back to the saloon.

She reprinted the article, making it neater, and turned it in. Pemberton agreed to run it in the morning paper. Satisfied and hopeful, she turned for home with a smile on her face.

Business at the saloon was brisk to say the least. Deacon waded through the line of people and made it inside. The place was a bedlam with hollering, banging on the tables, Sarge screeching, and Joel dropping an armful of glasses, shattering them.

Relief lined Harry's face. Only one hunk of hair remained in the leather strip tying his ponytail. He waved Deacon over. "Help! This is insane."

"What's going on?" Deacon shouted over the din.

"Aunt Martha's new additions!"

Little Joel walked by with a broom. "Hi, Mr. Brannock. Sorry about the glasses."

"It's fine, son. Thank you for pitching in." Deacon tied an apron around his waist and stared dumbfounded at the crowd. "Where do I start, Harry?"

The man threw up his hands. "Pick a spot."

Deacon worked nonstop until they closed at midnight, then collapsed at a table. Harry joined him. Joel and Aunt Martha had gone to bed an hour earlier. Deacon glanced at his bartender. "What was that, Harry? What was that madness?"

"Aunt Martha tried something new yesterday. She called it a sandwich. It's meat, cheese, and onions inside this big biscuit. Word spread, and you saw what happened."

"All I know is that I've never been as tired or the till so full. I may have to threaten that woman with death if she leaves." Deacon rubbed his weary eyes. "I may sleep a week."

"Did you find Izzy in Joshua?"

"No."

"Then the trip must've been wasted."

"I wouldn't say that at all." Deacon needed to pinch himself. Grace amazed him with her openness to lovemaking. He smiled.

Harry lifted the corner of a brow. "I see. I'm happy for whatever transpired."

"Me too." But Deacon knew not to put too much stock in his good fortune.

Life would sooner kick him in the teeth as not.

❧

Grace opened the door to her and Crockett's house to find Houston and her mother. She set her bag down and fumbled for something to say. Finally, she kissed her mother's cheek. "I didn't know you were coming."

Houston looked twice as uncomfortable. He stood, his stance wide, and gripped his hat in both hands. "Virgil told us what happened after he and Henry got home. Then Crockett sent a telegraph." He sighed. "Honey, I'm sorry you had to find out that way. I always intended to tell you the facts, but the years passed and it became too easy to put off."

"Let's sit in the parlor," Crockett urged. "It's more relaxing."

Looking haggard, Houston dragged his intense gaze from Grace. "Yes, of course."

They all took a seat except Houston. Grim, he planted himself behind her mother.

"My head is still reeling from the shock. I hardly know what to say." Grace clasped her hands tightly together in her lap and kept her eyes glued to her mother. "You suffered such an immense tragedy. I'm so sorry for what Yuma did to you. I understand why you didn't want to talk about it."

Lara held a lace-edged handkerchief to her mouth. Her beautiful eyes held sorrow. "The past is best forgotten. But for you— now, you won't be able. You did deserve to know. I just couldn't bear to break your heart."

"Maybe if you know the circumstances, it'll help." Houston laid a kiss on the top of Lara's head. "Pa and Till Boone got together and connived to get Lara and me married. Pa hatched this story that he'd gambled away the ranch to Till but said I could get it back for us. All I'd have to do was marry Lara. I didn't know her. We'd never laid eyes on each other. Of course, I was furious. It seemed in those days he was always drinking too much and losing big hands at cards, then expecting me to clean up his mess."

"That sounds like Grandpa," Crockett said.

"I was furious and told Pa where he could put his plan. But then—" Houston coughed and his voice softened. "Then I heard about you, Grace, and your need for a name." He came around the sofa and took Grace's hands. "I couldn't refuse. You were such a beautiful child, and when you closed a little fist around my finger, I knew I'd done the right thing." He wiped a tear from his eyes. "Your tiny touch won me over and I was sunk."

Grace's eyes filled as well, and her lip quivered. She loved this big man with a soft heart.

Houston went on. "In that moment, you became my daughter as surely as if I'd fathered you, and over the years, you kept that spot. I've never been sorry one single minute." He held out his hands, and Grace let him pull her to her feet and against his chest. "Being a father means so much more than donating to the baby's creation. In fact, that's the smallest part. I hope you can forgive me for not telling you."

Grace looked up at the man who'd raised her. "I love you, Pa. I'll never stop loving you."

Houston kissed her cheek. "I've watched you grow into a beautiful woman, always proud of your curious nature and kind heart. You're everything I ever wanted in a daughter, and you've brought me unbelievable happiness."

She dropped to the floor at Lara's feet, and Grace laid her head in her mother's lap. "I'm sorry for trying to make you relive the horror."

Lara smoothed Grace's hair. "You gave me a reason to keep living when I wanted to curl up and die. You are so loved by us all."

Houston put a hand on her shoulder. The nights when he'd held her when she was sick or scared of the storms came to mind. And the time when she'd sat by his side through a long winter night, helping a mare go through a difficult birth.

There hadn't been a moment he'd not been there for her. She lifted her face to him. "Thank you for giving me a name. You might like to know...I'm keeping it."

Until she took Brannock's.

Thirty

"I'm glad you came for a visit. It's nice." Grace wished she could talk to her parents about her feelings for Deacon, but that wouldn't be fair to him. They needed to be together when they spoke of their plans to marry. "How long will you stay?"

"Two days," her mother answered.

Houston took a glass of bourbon from Crockett. "I'm going to have a meeting with Horace Pemberton at the *Gazette* and find out who this Sam Valentine is and why he's writing articles about our family. Pemberton owes us an apology at the very least."

Grace choked, her heart racing. "I don't think that's needed."

"Why the hell not? Tell that to your grandpa. He hasn't simmered down yet and probably won't until the second coming." Houston snorted. "That Valentine doesn't even know us, yet he hangs all our dirty laundry out for the world to see, printing all our disagreements and business dealings, which are a daily occurrence with Stoker for a father. And don't get me started on what we're selling cattle—and land—for. Hell, it isn't anyone's damn business. We've always kept such things quiet. We aren't gonna be made a laughingstock either. Someone's gonna hear about this."

Grace's thoughts whirled. "Sam Valentine is a shadowy character, and he may even have left the paper." She stuttered. "He, uh… he—" Got shot and died? Left town? Went into hiding?

Houston leaned forward. "What, Grace? You sound like you know the man."

She forced her racing heart to slow. "No. I simply read that

Pemberton sent him to Austin to cover a trial." Yes, that sounded good and would keep him out of town.

"Grace, you looked flushed," her mother noted. "Are you feeling all right?"

"I'm perfectly fine, Mama."

The stern warning her father gave her when she came to Fort Worth to live sounded in her head. *Whatever you do, keep the family name out of your activities. I mean it. Don't sully our name, our reputation, that we've worked hard to protect.*

Grace tried to breathe past the lump in her throat.

"Regardless of where Valentine is, I'm still having a meeting with Pemberton, and you can count on that." Houston rose and went up the stairs with his drink in hand.

Hell and damnation! She had no choice but to tell them what she'd done.

Her parents were going to be furious. Not to mention Grandpa Stoker.

She tossed and turned all night, then finally rose at dawn and dressed. Her mother and father were already in the kitchen and had breakfast on. Her father and Crockett sat at the table with coffee.

Grace put the teakettle on to heat. "I have a confession."

Houston narrowed his eyes. "What have you done, Grace?"

"It's a long story." She avoided his gaze and took a seat.

Lara turned from her task at the stove. "I think we have time, dear."

"It's about the *Gazette* and—" She raised her eyes. "I'm Sam Valentine. I wrote those articles."

"You?" Houston's voice thundered like Grandpa's. She winced at the explosion.

"I wrote them. I wanted to be a reporter at the paper, but Pemberton said I had to prove myself. He knew my real name, so he told me if I'd write some interesting articles about life on the

Lone Star and did a good job, he'd move me up and give me meat-ier assignments. I could be a real reporter." She lifted her chin. "I'm good at what I do, Pa, and I never gave away anything that would ruin us. Folks liked reading about us."

"Well, I'll be!" Crockett looked proud of her. "I never guessed."

"Grace, I loved those articles." Her mother came to give her a hug. "I thought they were clever and humorous. I found myself laughing aloud at times. Especially when that bull got loose and tore through town, then started chasing Stoker, and him having to jump into a rain barrel to escape the beast."

"Thank you, Mama. That was a favorite of readers."

Houston stayed silent so long, Grace wondered if he'd gotten so mad, he'd lost his voice. Finally, he spoke. "You have a lot of talent, honey. You never wrote about anything too awfully embar-rassing, I guess. You know how obsessive the family is about our privacy." His gaze pierced her. "You broke our agreement."

"Yes, I did, and I'm truly sorry. I shouldn't have used the Legend name that way."

He shook a butter knife at her. "Furthermore, you tried to hide it by using a fake name."

"I can't deny that."

"Have you learned anything?"

Grace gave him a wry smile. "Not to try to fool you and always tell the truth?"

"If I had a bit of sense, I'd drag you back home." He put down his cup and stood. "And if I'm being honest, I'm so proud of you, honey, I could bust." He pulled her up. "You came here not know-ing anyone, finagled your way into a job with a big newspaper without a lick of experience. I may need you to give me some les-sons on a few things."

Grace found herself engulfed in his arms. This was what being a real father was. She'd never been prouder of the name he'd given her so long ago.

✄

Deacon rode out to Bonner's place early that morning. The crisp air was just what he needed to clear his head that was still buzzing from his and Grace's big night. He dismounted at the back door of the ranch house and went inside. Dirty dishes still covered every bit of counter space.

Will glanced up from the stove. "Want some eggs?"

"Sounds good." Deacon got a cup and poured coffee. Will looked better than he'd seen him in a while. Maybe that day of fishing had gotten him back on track.

"Glad you came out. You look…happy." Will chuckled. "Of course, your happy face is the same as all the others with your frown only half covering."

"Go ahead and make fun." Deacon took a sip of coffee. "I have some news."

"Which kind? Sad, happy, in between?"

"Depends, I guess. Grace Legend and I are getting married."

"Ho!" Will turned, waving the egg turner. "That's cause for celebration." He reached above the stove for a bottle of whiskey and poured some in his and Deacon's coffee.

"Whoa, Will! I have to be on my best behavior. I'm meeting Grace's parents tonight. She sent word they're in town."

"You nervous?"

"Does a porcupine have quills? Of course, I'm nervous. What if they don't like me?"

"Who wouldn't love that pretty face?"

"A father with a shotgun?"

When the eggs were cooked, they sat at the table and Will told him about asking for Frances's hand. "My knees were knocking together so hard, I just knew her father heard them. But I proved to him that we had true love." Will pushed his plate back. "When you meet Houston Legend tonight, you look him square in the eye and let him know that you're as good as any man that ever walked. Then prove to him how much you love his daughter." He paused. "You do love her, don't you?"

Deacon wished he knew what love was. He knew plenty what it wasn't, but he'd never seen it in action. Fair to say his mother had probably never seen it either—only a man's fists and curses. He knew he felt differently about Grace than any other woman. He loved spending time with her and kissing her. That had to be love.

"Of course I do. Grace does funny things to my stomach."

Will laughed. "I think you're going to be all right."

"I hope so." Deacon appreciated the talk. There were days he really wished he had a father to talk to about such things. It was difficult going alone, trying to figure stuff out as he went.

After they ate, Deacon washed all those dishes and cleaned up the kitchen. Will dried, doling out more advice—some good, some not so much. Then he went out to work with Diablo.

The horse lifted his tail and came right up to him, seeming glad to see him. Deacon took him out of the round pen and put him into the larger one. The blanket frightened Diablo, and he took off in a panic, the whites of his eyes showing. But after Deacon used soothing words and gentle hands, Diablo stood with trembling legs and let Deacon lay the blanket on his back.

He took the blanket on and off repeatedly until Diablo saw there was nothing to fear.

Then he introduced the saddle, the weight completely foreign to the horse. Diablo bucked and twisted, and the saddle ended up in Deacon's arms. No amount of words or touches worked this time, so he called it a day.

Saying goodbye to Will, Deacon went back to the saloon, worried thoughts turning him inside and out. The possibility existed that Houston would forbid him to marry Grace.

And if that happened, he'd sink in deep despair.

That night, Deacon arrived at Grace's house at the appointed hour. By the time he rapped on the door, his nerves were strung tighter than a piano wire. He ran a finger inside his shirt collar. The blasted thing was choking him. Most of his shirts were collarless and thin from repeated washings. He'd be happy to get this behind him.

Grace opened the door, looking radiant in a blue, flowing dress, a rebel as always, leaving off the volumes of petticoats. He made a silent bet that she'd address him by his last name, even though she'd begun to use his given name more and more these days.

"Brannock, I'm so happy you came." Her voice sounded a bit breathless. "Come in."

Strange how she could make him forget his tight collar and her disapproving parents. He forgot everything except the vibrant, exciting woman holding his hand.

"How could I refuse you, princess?" Indeed, only a blind man would be able to manage that, and he was anything but blind. He kissed her cheek, aware of the faint scent of…apple spice? The smell took him back to the small hotel in Joshua, and the memories drew a big smile.

"I made you a pie," she whispered. "Apple."

"Thought I smelled one. Will you bring me a piece or two after Houston throws me out?"

"He'd better not, or I'll run after you." She leaned in to place her lips on his for a bare second. "I keep a bag packed and a ladder at my window for such an emergency."

Deacon's chest tightened. What in the world did she see in a penniless saloon owner in the worst part of Fort Worth, his hopes pinned on a wild stallion that may never gentle enough to ride? He wished he knew. "Sounds like a desperate plan."

Grace slid an arm around his waist, leaning close. "I wish we could run off to Joshua and check in to Sally's hotel. Make love until we're famished, then eat in the little café. I need to feel your body. It's not the same as dreaming."

Memories whirled around him, piling up. "I have a powerful hunger for you, Grace."

"I'm glad." Her sparkling blue eyes and the low neckline of her dress that allowed him a certain view kept him grinning like some dull-witted moron. "We know how to make beautiful music together, and I'm happy you haven't forgotten me."

"Forgotten you? Pretty lady, you must've hit your head and lost your mind."

"Well, a girl never knows." She put her arm through his. "I'd love to talk more but we have to join the others, and tonight we let our intentions be known. It'll be fine."

"I hope you're right." He reached for her hand and noticed she wore the little grass ring he'd made for her. "You still have my ring."

"Of course I do. It's important to me. I cherish it as much as if it were gold."

"I'll get you a real one as soon as I'm able."

"No rush, this does fine. I'm very careful with it."

"You put it in Crockett's safe, do you?"

"Absolutely." She took his arm.

They followed the voices to the parlor. Houston came toward Deacon with hand outstretched. "It's good to see you again, Brannock." The smile on the man's face helped relieve some anxiety. "I don't suppose you brought any of those tamales."

"Not tonight. If you'll come by tomorrow, I'll give you all you want." At least the man liked his food if nothing else.

"Stop it, Houston," Lara scolded, edging around him to shake Deacon's hand. "I apologize, Mr. Brannock. My husband is barely civilized. I've heard a lot about you, and I can't wait to hear more. Thank you for being a good friend to our daughter."

"It's a pleasure to meet you, Mrs. Legend. I see where Grace gets her beauty."

Lara's eyes twinkled. "Thank you. I like a man who says what he thinks." The sea-green dress accented her eyes and set off her rich auburn hair. Lara Legend was a stunning woman despite the scar running down her face. Small wonder she captured Houston's heart.

"How are Leah and the baby?"

"Such a delight." Lara clasped her hands to her chest. "Leah's like having another daughter. I love that girl, and I could hold the baby all day. My heart is full."

"I'm happy to hear that." It sounded like Leah had fit in fine. Deacon glanced around, his gaze catching on Grace, so pretty in her vibrant-blue dress. She saw him and smiled, and he had trouble remembering he was talking to her mother.

After more small talk and a glass of bourbon that did little to ease the knot in Deacon's stomach, they went to the table. He couldn't have said what he ate, but it must've tasted good. The conversation was light with much laughter. Houston, Lara, and Crockett were easy to be with. They put on no pretentious airs, just seeming like normal people.

Once everyone had a slice of apple pie in front of them, Houston leaned over. "Are you sure we've never met? There's something about you that tries to spark my memory."

Deacon froze. If their connection became known, and his prison sentence, hell would freeze over before Houston would let Grace marry him. Deacon forced himself to swallow. "I don't think so, sir."

"I can't get past how familiar you seem." Houston shoveled in a forkful of apple pie.

While the two women washed dishes, the men enjoyed a cigar. Houston and Crockett talked of cattle prices, ranch business, and asked Deacon about the saloon.

Then they settled in the parlor where Grace took Deacon's hand. Her fingers were icy. Her shimmering eyes locked on his and at that moment he knew he'd follow her to the ends of the earth.

"We have an announcement. Of sorts." She dragged a tremulous breath into her lungs. "Deacon and I plan to be married."

Thirty-one

DEACON COULD'VE HEARD A PIN DROP. THE ENSUING SILENCE was deafening. *Here it comes.*

Ever since he'd arrived, he'd glanced around the house and couldn't help but notice the disparity between it and the Three Deuces. No way would he ever be able to give Grace the kind of life she was accustomed to. And he was sure Crockett's home didn't even come close to how fancy Houston and Lara's must be. Like he'd told Grace, their worlds were too different.

"You're what?" Red streaks crept up Houston's neck.

Lara gave a sharp cry, and Crockett got to his feet.

Grace looked about ready to bolt, except she didn't need her ladder—just the front door.

"We seem to have gone about this backward, sir." Deacon put a protective arm about her and drew her close against him. "I'm asking for her hand in marriage. True, I'm a poor man, but everything I possess I'll give to her. I have hopes that one day I can meet your approval."

"When did this happen? Isn't it a bit sudden?"

Deacon stood his ground. "Over the weeks since we met, then recent days of searching for a young boy who's missing, we've come to care for each other. I want to make her my wife." He wanted to add he'd do it with or without Houston's blessing, but he swallowed the words that would only make the situation worse.

Crockett didn't say anything but watched it all intently.

Houston rubbed the back of his neck. "From what I've seen, Brannock, you can little afford a wife."

"As I said, I'm a poor man but I have plans. I won't always be a saloonkeeper."

Lara moved to Houston's side, concern seeming to darken her scar. "Where will you live? A dirty saloon in a crime-ridden part of town?"

"Mama, that's not fair! We haven't even discussed that yet." Grace glanced up at Deacon, anguish in her eyes. "We have a lot of things to work out, which we can do in the coming months. It's not like we're going to run out and get married tonight. Deacon *is* the man I want. I didn't plan to fall in love, but I have. I'm utterly and deeply in love with him."

The avowal caught Deacon a little off guard. Neither had mentioned the word love to each other, and to hear her say it right out like that gave his heart a jolt. But he believed she meant it, and his chest swelled.

Growing up in a whorehouse, then living in Hell's Half Acre, he'd seen the dregs of society, people who spoke of love to fit whatever their needs were at the time. He didn't intend to be one of them. If love was some real, tangible thing, he was positive that what he felt for her would measure up against anyone's definition.

Crockett, quiet until now, spoke. "I've seen how Brannock protects her, and I've also seen how Gracie looks at him, and there's no question he'll make her happy if it's humanly possible."

The offhanded compliment drew Grace's laugh. "Thank you for that—I think."

"All we're asking for is a chance." Deacon's voice was quiet. "Grace is an amazing woman, and her happiness is the most important thing to me. I'd be proud to be her husband."

Grace loved her mother and Houston, and he wouldn't separate her from her family. That never boded well.

"Can you provide for my daughter?" Houston's question was blunt by any standards.

"I can't believe you, Pa." Grace threw up her hands. "You've never let a man's station in life determine his worth, so why are you now? His place is making twice as much money as any other on Rusk Street except for the bordellos. You should see the money he's making since he added food. He's a hard worker, and I make money too, from the newspaper."

Deacon met Houston's gaze unflinchingly. He wanted to tell the man about his work gentling horses, only it wasn't steady income. "I have a broad back, and I'll work my fingers to the bone doing whatever I need to do in order to provide for her. You can be assured of that, sir."

"You're rushing into this. What's wrong with taking a little time, making sure?" Houston glanced at Lara and ran his fingers through his hair. "This is a big step."

"We're going slower than you and Mama did," Grace said quietly.

"That's not fair, little girl." Houston's eyes flashed.

"I just want you to listen to us. We know what we're doing," Grace argued.

"They're just wanting to see to your welfare." Deacon put an arm around her. "It's a parent's job to keep you from making a mistake," he said quietly.

"I see I'm fighting a losing battle." Houston studied Deacon hard. "In that case—" He moved to shake Deacon's hand. "I trust you to take care of my little girl."

"I will." He'd protect and love her until the world stopped turning. Deacon glanced down into her pretty face, silently vowing that Grace would only get the best part, the unsullied part of him.

❦

Somewhere near, the steady *drip, drip, drip* of water sounded. Izzy huddled in the cold dampness, quivering. Blood still seeped from his nose, and he ran his tongue over a loose tooth. The hound that had crawled inside a week ago curled up next to him, and the matted, thick fur brought a little warmth to Izzy's bones. He moved his leg, and the chain rattled in the dark, smelly mine.

He sniffled, remembering his friends. Deacon who'd always given him some coins when he could afford to. His best friend, Simon, and the fun they'd had pretending they were brothers. And Grace, so pretty and soft and smelling like his mother. She'd been nice to him and kind. He still remembered her laugh that made him feel warm and cared for. Maybe he'd see her again one day when he got free.

Izzy missed his red wagon and working up and down the Acre. If only he could go back.

"I miss them, Shep," he whispered to the dog. "I'm gonna get out of here, and when I do, I'll take you with me."

"I'm scared, Izzy." The voice came from next to him—a kid named Abe. "I don't want to die in here."

"You won't. Be strong, Abe. I'm gonna get us out of here." Izzy didn't know why everyone in the group looked to him to figure a way out. Some were older than him, and all they could do was complain about their empty bellies and cold hands. "Can I tell you a secret, Abe?"

"Sure."

"I play a little game when my hunger gets too bad. I pretend I have a table loaded with food and can eat all I want. I start with the bread, then the meat. It's juicy and smells like my mama's kitchen. I work my way to the cakes and pies, and I eat and eat. By the time I finish, my belly seems full. Why don't you try it?"

"Okay."

Some of the others in their crew of two dozen murmured around him. Izzy drew the dog closer. Come daylight, he'd work on loosening the chain some more. His ankle throbbed where the metal cut into it. Probably bleeding too. But nothing felt broken. Long as he could walk, he'd be fine.

Shep whined and licked his face. Dogs knew things. Shep didn't trust too many people, and those he did could count themselves a true friend. Izzy loved him. "Thank you for being my friend," Izzy whispered. "I'm gonna take care of you."

What about the rest of the kids? Izzy wasn't sure what he could do there. He might have to leave and come back when he could bring Deacon. No one would beat up Deacon. He was stronger than anyone in the whole world, and he had a gun.

The only way to get them away from here was to kill Renick.

Yep, kill him dead.

Although pain shot through him, Izzy smiled and, using all his strength, made a fist.

Tomorrow.

⌘

The following day, Grace went back to the Presbyterian church and still left empty-handed. The same for the black ice wagon. The paper had come out with her latest article in it, so maybe she and Deacon would see some results from that. She was growing tired of trying so hard with nothing to show.

Where was Izzy?

Despair rode on her shoulders. Memories of how he'd clung to her haunted her mind. If only she'd insisted he come with her. If only she'd saved him. There were too many if onlys.

On the bright side, Joel had made himself at home at the Three Deuces, and so far, no one had raised a holy ruckus. Maybe people would leave him be. He was such a sweet little kid, and he'd wiggled his way into her heart.

With some time on her hands, she went back to the Painted Pony, where Jane worked, but once she got to the boisterous place, she didn't know what to do. Yells, angry voices, laughter, and more spilled from the doors. She didn't dare go in alone. Every warning she'd heard sounded in her head. Brannock was close. Maybe she should…

Noise at the end of the street drew her attention. Two dozen women marching toward her, banging drums, rattling tambourines and singing could only belong to the temperance movement. She relaxed and waited, not believing her luck.

The marchers stopped at each saloon but didn't go inside. The saloons with prior warning slammed and bolted their doors. The Painted Pony evidently hadn't heard. As the group approached, Grace slipped into the back. They stopped and gave the chant Carrie Nation had worked up for her followers.

"Let's go inside!" the woman next to Grace hollered, raising a fist.

As a man started to slam the doors, the women pushed their way inside. Grace found herself swept along. Once inside, a nasty brawl ensued between the male patrons and the women.

Grace glanced around the dim room, hit with the smell of smoke, unwashed bodies, and perhaps vomit. Two men had passed out on the dirty plank floor. She stepped over them and dodged a broom-wielding bartender. Then she spied several saloon girls in skimpy clothing on the stairs leading above and made her way toward them.

She recognized one. "Jane?"

"Get out of here. This is no place for you." The woman sported fresh bruises and a split lip.

"Please, I only want to talk." Grace held her long skirts in one hand and slowly climbed step by step. "Let me help. This is no place for you either. Or anyone."

Jane turned and hurried toward a row of doors with Grace following, shutting the door behind them.

"Why don't you leave me alone? I don't need you." Jane gave a sarcastic snort. "I don't remember your name, but I know you're one of the do-gooders. You come in here with your fine clothes and new shoes, pretending you care." Jane waved an arm around the room. "You don't care about me. This." Tears created a painted river down her face. She lifted her chin, her eyes blazing. "So take your fancy clothes, Bible verses, and pretty words and go back where you belong." Jane collapsed on the bed, a sad wind-up toy that had run down.

Grace didn't say a word. Noticing a water bowl on a washstand, she found a semi-clean cloth and wet it. Sitting beside Jane, she began to gently wash the woman's face, cleaning away the blood and tears. Grace stayed silent, waiting for Jane's anger, disgust, and shame to fade.

Finally, with Jane's face cleaned, Grace removed her shawl and put it around the woman's shoulders. They sat side by side, listening to the ruckus below drifting up the stairs.

Grace began quietly, her voice barely louder than a whisper. "I would imagine it's easy for a girl to lose her humanity in a place like this. You're a woman, Jane. A very pretty woman with a lot left to give to people who deserve it. The men running this place and these drunks aren't worthy to wipe your shoes on."

Jane gripped the shawl, covering herself. "I used to paint pretty pictures of happy people, families in love with life. Folks said I was good. I had a few paintings in museums." Jane licked her lips. "I had nothing but stars in my eyes. I had no idea of the way the world worked. I let a man sweet-talk me. I fancied myself in love with him. Before I knew it, I found myself here, doing things I never thought I would."

"Let me take you out of here." Grace glanced around for some decent clothes but saw only short dance-hall skirts hanging on a nail.

"Where? Who would have the likes of me?"

"I will. You can live with me and paint again." Grace smoothed back her hair, desperate to help Jane break free of this. "We can sell your paintings for enough to live on. I know we can."

Jane glanced up with hope beginning to sparkle in her deep-sunk eyes.

"All you have to do is take my hand and trust me. I can lead you back." Grace stood and opened a trunk at the foot of the bed. A normal dress lay on top of several petticoats. "I found you something to wear." She stretched out her hand to Jane, happy when she clasped it.

With Grace's help, Jane changed clothes. As she drew on each one, she seemed to put on another layer of respectability. Finally, with her hair combed and shoes on, Grace opened the door to find several of the working girls.

"What are you doing? Where are you taking Jane?" a young girl asked.

"I'm leaving." Jane's smile was beautiful to see. "I've gotten a better offer. Come with me, Goldy."

The girl snickered. "Not me. I ain't crazy. I don't have to lift a finger here. In a year, I'll be rich while you break your back doing laundry, cleaning, and wiping snotty noses."

"I ain't lost my mind either," said another, laughing.

The temperance women had moved on, leaving a mess behind. Several men sweeping up broken glass glanced up. One blocked their path, his beefy arms raised. "Where do you think you're going, Jane?"

"I'm leaving with my friend. You ain't gonna hit me anymore, Frederick."

A growl rumbled low in his throat, his hand curling in a fist, eyes threatening.

"Please, step aside." Grace eyed the group. None looked willing to give an inch; instead, they moved closer to surround them. She took her little gun from her pocket and pointed it at the one who'd spoken. "It seems every one to a man is hard of hearing. I don't mind shooting you if that is the language you prefer."

"Lady, you cain't shoot us all." Frederick's glare would probably cause Grace nightmares.

"True. But once I get rid of you, who'll step up?" The men began to back away, their hands raised. "Your friends are smart."

At last, he seemed to see the writing on the wall. "Jane ain't nothing to get shot for," Frederick snarled while backing up.

Once at the door, Grace turned. "It's been a real pleasure, gentlemen. I do hope the temperance ladies return to put you out of business."

"I'd watch my back!" Frederick yelled.

Grace entwined her arm around Jane's. "We'd best hurry."

She didn't breathe easier until they left Hell's Half Acre and didn't slow until reaching the street where she and Crockett lived. Maybe she should've stopped in the Three Deuces, but she hadn't wanted to worry Deacon. Once inside the house, she shut and bolted the door.

"This is it, Jane."

The saloon girl glanced around, open-mouthed. "This is so lovely."

"It's comfortable." Grace took the pins from her hair and shook it out. "What is your real name?" She knew women in Jane's profession kept themselves separated from their former lives.

"Meg Thorp." The woman let out a long, happy sigh. "God, it's been so long since I used that. Do you mind if I sit? My legs are shaking."

"Make yourself at home, Meg. I can get you something to drink if you'd like."

"No, thank you. I just want to sit for a bit and ponder my freedom."

Understandable when a person has started a new life. "Take your time. I'll get your room ready upstairs."

∽

Sniffing back tears, Izzy sat against the side wall of the mine, gripping his pick, the low ceiling overhead. He had to be smart about this, because he'd probably only have one chance to save himself and the others. He couldn't afford to show weakness or, even worse, mess up.

The backbreaking work of digging the coal from the walls exhausted them all. Then with little food on top of that, they were all weak from hunger. It seemed clear to Izzy that Julius Renick was going to work them to death and then bury them where no one would ever find their bodies. Izzy had heard them talking about the graveyard and how full it was getting. He'd also overheard them say there was an abundance of orphans, so if they lost some, they could always get as many as they wanted. He remembered the sound of their laughter.

One of the guards moved toward him, all hunched over due to the low ceiling. He was the meanest one next to Julius, always flicking the whip he carried, grinning when he hit them. "What'cha sitting around for? Get to work!"

"I don't feel so good," said a scrawny kid a little ways down from Izzy.

"You think I care?" Bull struck him with the handle end of the whip. The kid began to twitch real bad.

"Stop it!" Izzy cried, hurrying to the boy and laying on top to shield him. "You're gonna kill him. He's sick!"

"So? You think that exempts him from working? You're all snot-nosed brats that just whimper and snivel." He struck Izzy with his fist, then picked him up and slung him, the heavy chain rattling. "Back to work!"

Shep lunged, teeth bared. Pain burned through Izzy and took his breath. He blinked hard, bringing into focus the scared faces of those cringing against the wall.

The guard made a rumbling sound in his throat. "Keep that dog away from me or I'll bash its brains in and make you eat 'em."

Izzy kept his lip buttoned. Saying anything would only add fuel to the fire. He was worried about the kid—Davey was his name,

Izzy thought. Davey might not make it, and there seemed little he could do at the moment.

This situation was worse than at any point of his life.

Izzy closed his eyes and dreamed of happier times when his father was alive and they were a family.

Izzy waited until their tormenter wandered off, then sat up and reached for his pick. Davey roused and groaned. He leaned over the kid. "Just try to stay out of the light and lay here. Me and the others will form a circle around you. Rest."

Thirty-two

DEACON MISSED GRACE LIKE MAD. HE SPENT NIGHTS remembering their time together and how she'd felt in his arms. The whisper of her soft skin. The taste of her lips. It had been a week since the supper with her parents, and the days since had been a whirlwind with her spending time with Houston and Lara while they were in town and busy getting Jane set up. Grace and Lara had taken the woman shopping for new clothes and whatever else she needed.

One thing he was learning about Grace was to expect these surprises. He often wished he could see inside her brain, look at the spinning wheels and constant ideas.

In addition to everything else, Grace was working hard on a series of new articles for the paper. Although she'd come by a few times when she could, he missed the days they'd spent together.

Houston had come to get tamales before they left for home and didn't seem as friendly as before, but maybe Deacon had only imagined it.

Didn't matter. He wasn't marrying her father. Grace was the only one that counted in that respect. Deacon wondered what it would be like to wake up next to her each morning and go to bed next to her each night. His stomach did that funny little jump thinking about that.

A new routine developed quickly for him. Deacon spent his mornings at the Bonner ranch, working with Diablo and looking out for Will as best as the man would let him. Will had given him a wide grin when Deacon told him that Houston gave his blessing to marry Grace.

"Harry will be my best man, but I want you to stand up there with me too. You're the closest to a father that I have."

"Just try keeping me away," Will had said.

The horse seemed to be coming along better than the kind rancher. Some days Will just sat and stared into the distance.

There were bright spots with Diablo. He'd finally accepted the saddle, and though he threw a hissy at the bit and bridle, he'd adapted. Never in Deacon's wildest dreams had he thought he'd ever get this far with the horse.

Still, in spite of the leaps, Diablo wouldn't let Deacon ride him. Each time he tried, the stallion bucked him off.

That five hundred dollars waved from far in the distance, teasing Deacon. Thank goodness he hadn't said anything to Grace. She'd never know if he failed.

The long days at the Three Deuces bled one into another, with folks flocking in for Aunt Martha's cooking. Deacon desperately needed to hire extra help, and as miraculous as it seemed, he could now afford it.

Harry rose every morning full of gloom and doom. "Clyde's coming. I can feel it in my bones."

But so far, knock on wood, the man hadn't shown up to ruin things, although Deacon still thought having a monkey would put them on the map.

Izzy occupied most of Deacon's thoughts. He had a bad feeling in his gut about the kid's circumstances, hoping the premonition was nothing more than his imagination.

If he only knew where to go, he'd saddle a horse.

He cleaned a table off and wiped it down for the next customer. The noon hour was over, and already he had to get in gear for supper. He glanced through the open door at the bright sunshine spilling in. With families patronizing the place, it had seemed prudent to remove the batwing doors to make it appear more welcoming. Deacon was becoming used to them calling the Three Deuces a café. He just shrugged and let it roll off his back.

A long shadow fell across the floor. "Deacon Brannock?"

He glanced up to see two sour-faced deputies. "Can I help you?"

"Come along with us."

"Can I ask why? I've done nothing wrong."

"The sheriff wants to question you further about Seth Pickford's murder."

Harry watched from behind the long bar. Aunt Martha came from the kitchen with Joel.

"I've told him everything I know."

Of course, Grace chose that moment to step through the doors. Her blue gaze homed in on the lawmen, bringing a frown. "What's this about, Brannock?"

"Seth Pickford. They want to question me again."

"There's been new developments," said the deputy with a good deal of brown, wavy hair.

Grace hurried to Deacon's side. "Gentlemen, I'm the woman Pickford assaulted and intended to kill. Why haven't you questioned me?"

The other lawman, a slim gentleman, answered, "The sheriff knows your grandfather. Secondly, a woman of your standing would never kill. And third, Brannock was suspected years ago of killing and nailing his customer to the outhouse door."

Deacon watched the steam rise from the top of her pretty head. She was about to erupt.

Grace pursed her lips. "The fact that Mr. Brannock has no family like mine or standing, it has to mean he murdered that rotten-to-the-core Pickford? Have you questioned anyone else?"

"Yes, ma'am." The wavy-haired deputy scowled at Deacon.

Dammit! Deacon gripped the rag he'd wiped the table with. "What are these new developments you mentioned?"

"An eyewitness who swears he saw you put the bullet in Pickford's skull."

Grace reeled from the deputy's statement. For half a second, she wondered if she'd been wrong about Deacon.

No. She pushed her slimmest of doubts aside. Not possible.

With a low oath and eyes blazing, he swung to her. "I did not kill Pickford, no matter what anyone says. No one saw me put a gun to Pickford's head because I wasn't there. I locked him in the shed and went to bed just like I told you. For the last time, I didn't kill him."

The truth sat in his gray eyes. Lips could lie but not the eyes.

She slid her hand inside his. "I believe you." She turned to the older deputy with a kind face. "I'm coming with him."

"I'm afraid not, ma'am. Let's go, Brannock." The wavy-haired deputy took hold of Deacon's upper arm.

"Hold on a minute." Grace planted herself in front of the deputy, hands on her hips. "I'm a reporter for the *Gazette* and intend to see that no one railroads him. This will all be handled nice and proper according to the rule of law."

The two deputies looked at each other and shrugged. Grace marched behind them to the jail. They wouldn't get away with this. She'd make sure of it. Pickford was a no-good drunk who deserved what he'd gotten. If need be, she'd bring Leah from the ranch. Surely that would show what kind of man Pickford was.

The sheriff was none too happy to see Grace but soon learned there was little he could do about her presence after she threatened to get Stoker to call the governor.

She sat across the room, her notebook on her lap and pencil in hand. She prayed they wouldn't discover Deacon's prison record or that would be the end of his freedom.

Tears filled her eyes. He'd never gotten a fair shake. From the time he was born, the cards were stacked against him, and as he aged, the stack got higher and higher. The same seemed to be true of Izzy from what little she knew. Maybe that's why Deacon and Izzy had become fast friends. Why Deacon had a soft spot in his heart for little homeless boys.

The sheriff questioned Deacon for over two hours, asking him to account for every second of his time that night and the next morning.

"We have a witness swearing he saw you shoot Pickford in the wee hours that morning."

His face rock hard, Deacon shook his head. "It wasn't me."

"Did anyone see you before dawn to vouch for you?"

"No. My bartender, Harry Jones, and I keep late hours. Until I met Miss Legend, I slept 'til noon. We've been searching for a little homeless boy together."

The sheriff didn't look her way for verification. In fact, he treated her as though she were invisible. Not wanting to make things rougher for Deacon, she kept quiet but was ready to respond in case they asked her something.

Finally, Deacon asked the question she'd been dying to. "Why are you making such a big to-do over Pickford? He was worthless, nothing but a lowlife preying on others. He beat his young wife who was in the family way and might've killed her if I hadn't stepped in and hid her. He never did one bit of good that I could see." Deacon took a deep breath. "Sure, everyone knows I had no love for the man, and if that's a crime, then I'm as guilty as sin. But so are a good many others in the Acre. Throw a dart and you'll hit some."

Every so often the wavy-haired deputy stood behind Grace and looked to see what she wrote down.

The sheriff leaned back in his chair and laced his hands behind his head. "Brannock, it seems to me that you make a habit of ending the lives of those you deem worthless. Do you consider yourself judge, jury, and executioner?"

Anger cut slashes around Deacon's mouth and eyes. "No. But

I do intervene when a woman's life is at stake, and I *will not* apologize for that."

Growing up in houses of ill repute with his mother, he must've seen so much. His sister, Cass, died at the hands of a man equally as bad as Pickford. Grace's heart cried out for the little boy Deacon had been and the grown man he now was, still fighting the same battles.

Seldom winning.

At last, the sheriff let them leave. Grace couldn't help noticing how Deacon rubbed his arm and hand. They must've gone numb again. How she wished a doctor could fix him.

She didn't speak until they reached Rusk Street. "I'm sorry, Deacon. I can only imagine how tired you get of being questioned over things."

"They're looking for someone to blame." His voice was dull, his eyes tired.

"I know." She let out a frustrated breath. "I wish they'd leave you alone, though." She changed the subject, telling him about Jane. "You'll never guess her real name is Meg Thorp. Isn't that pretty?"

"Yes, it is. Thank you for saving her. She deserves a better life than that. Is her living with you temporary?"

"I have a feeling she can't wait to get her own living space. She's such a talented painter. I'll try to find buyers for her landscapes and portraits when she has enough. It makes my heart happy that I could help her. That life was slowly killing her. She just didn't know how to get out."

Deacon sent her an admiring glance. "You're good at getting people to see their worth."

"That's sweet, but I don't know how true it is." They were silent for several heartbeats. "Deacon, I'm disappointed that my article asking for information about Phillip Vinson hasn't gotten any results. I'd had such high hopes."

"I'm sorry, darlin'. Waiting is the hardest thing. I had to learn a lot of patience when I was behind bars. It seemed time dragged."

"I'm not completely losing hope, though." Grace had faith that someone would come through.

When they drew closer to the Three Deuces, Grace marveled at the line forming. "I'll stay and help. After that grueling session, I doubt you feel up to working."

"It'll help take my mind off things. I need to hire another person, though. This is killing Harry and Aunt Martha. Would Jane…Meg want to work for me for a little while? I'd pay her a decent wage."

"That's a great idea. I'll ask her, and I'm sure she'll jump at the chance to make money for her new life."

Grace loved every minute of her time with Deacon. Little by little, he was letting her see inside his heart that he'd kept walled up for so long. He cared about those close to him. Yet he still couldn't use the word love, and she wasn't sure he ever would. She tried to be patient and hope that one day he might say what she longed to hear. She knew how he felt about her, and that was enough for now.

When they touched accidentally as they worked, she got a jolt similar to electricity. It was very odd. A rush of heat built inside until she could barely stand it. If it hadn't been for the crowd and endless tables to wait on, she'd have dragged Deacon upstairs to his room and torn his clothes to shreds to get at what she wanted.

Grace laughed, imagining the calm, unruffled man's face. But then, smoldering fire in his eyes would've sparked and they'd have burst into flames.

Truth was, it had been far too long since the trip to Joshua. She wished she could whisk him back there to their little, cozy room and make love until daylight. Just him, her, and their bed.

Delicious wetness formed on the inside of her thighs just thinking about his naked body and the heaven she'd found in his arms.

Memories of making love—the passion, the kisses, the waves

of pleasure—continued to linger in her mind. If she couldn't have the man when these yearnings overpowered her, she'd take the memories and hold them close in her heart.

After closing the saloon, she hurried home to talk to Meg as promised.

"Oh, Grace, that's the answer to a prayer. I'd love to work for Brannock." Worry crossed Meg's face. "I'm not sure about working in the Acre, though. Frederick could find out."

"Honey, I doubt very seriously if he'd recognize you. You've changed so much." Grace loved the care that Meg took with her hair and fixed it in such graceful arrangements. New clothes helped a lot too. Looking at Meg now, no one would ever guess her former profession. "Deacon won't let anything happen to you."

"I know. Yes, I'll do it."

Grace hugged her. "I'm so proud of you."

The next afternoon, Meg went to work with a smile on her face that still showed faint bruises. She didn't seem to mind them. "At least no one will hit me if I object to a customer's treatment," she'd said.

Meg never talked about her job at the Painted Pony, but Grace suspected it had been pure hell and her boss had tried his best to destroy her spirit. Thank goodness Meg had been strong and determined. Crockett had welcomed her into their home and seemed to understand, as much any man could. Women didn't have easy lives, and sometimes their bodies were not even their own.

There was so much wrong in the world. Grace shook away her sadness and sat to write her article for the paper, her thoughts on Izzy and Simon's friend, Davey.

Who had taken them? And for what purpose?

❧

The evening was going well according to the new normal. Deacon was getting accustomed to racing around between the tables, setting down food and drink. Meg was a godsend, and her ability to catch on fast took some of the pressure off the others. Deacon liked her as Jane and even better as Meg. He kept a sharp eye out for her. Anyone who didn't show her the utmost respect would be kicked out the door.

Joel hustled around the room, collecting all the dirty glassware and dishes. The boy seemed made for this, and he thanked Deacon at the close of each night before he climbed the stairs with Sarge. Joel and the disagreeable cat had become unlikely buddies. Strange.

Thankfully, Deacon hadn't had any recent visits by lawmen concerning Seth Pickford's murder. Maybe they'd arrested someone else or at least turned their focus away from him.

The other killing they'd tried to pin on him crossed his mind. He knew a lot of people still continued to believe he'd done that. Truth was, he'd been looking for the man responsible for the shooting in the Three Deuces then hours later wound up on the door of the outhouse. It had been a matter of looking for money missing from Deacon's pocket.

Thank God no one knew about that or he'd be on trial for sure.

Why did these situations keep dogging him? He'd not killed anyone except the man he'd gone to prison for.

He let out a long exhale and put the nagging thoughts out of his head.

Reaching for the silver fob, he pulled his pocket watch out to check the time. They'd close in an hour, and he had plans, plans that involved the horse and wagon in the alley. Wanting for her pooled in his stomach. Tonight, he'd deliver Meg home and take Grace somewhere private. He'd drive until he found the perfect spot away from the city, where they'd be undisturbed. It had only been a week since he'd asked Houston for Grace's hand. And yet it seemed a year. He wasn't good at waiting.

Not when it involved velvety skin, a mouth that tasted like honey, and a supple body that drove him insane.

Thirty-three

THE MOON WAS FULL AND SPOKE OF SECRETS. THE WAGON SAT nearby with their clothes in the bed, the horses dozing. Deacon lay back on the blanket and drew Grace against him. He was already hard. One glimpse of her body bathed by the moonlight and he'd risen to attention.

"I've missed you, princess," he murmured against her scented hair. "I was about ready to kidnap you."

"I felt the same way." She rose on an elbow. "Does that make me a bad person?"

"The hell if I know. I'm the biggest sinner there is, but maybe your sweetness will offset my impure thoughts. The things I plan to do to you, lady."

Grace drew lazy circles on his chest and flicked her tongue over each nipple, her voice the lazy drawl he loved. "Tell me, cowboy, what plans might you have?"

"Come closer," he teased with grin.

She raised up, and he placed his mouth at her ear and whispered what he intended to do.

"Oh my!" Her heart hammered wildly against him. She slid her hand between their bodies, closing her fingers around him, and it took all Deacon's willpower to hold back the hunger.

"Uh, Grace…let's take this slower. It'll last longer."

She licked along the seam of his mouth, her hands moving, massaging every inch she could reach. Her beautiful blue eyes looked into his soul. Her kiss shattered the calm inside, the depth of feeling singeing his lips. His whole body was on fire, and he had no sane thought left in his head.

On the best of days, he had trouble maintaining his thoughts when she was around anyway. Tonight, it became impossible. The urge to hold her, to show her all she meant to him, and to fill her full of his love washed over him.

Breaking the kiss, she told him to roll over.

When he did, she straddled his hips, kneading, rubbing, and pressing kisses to his back and buttocks. "Damn, lady! You sure know how to wind a man around your finger."

Deacon loved the attention she lavished on him, but he hungered to make her cry his name and beg him not to stop. He flipped over, then rolled her beneath him, kissing her until he ran out of air.

Breaking the kiss, he trailed caresses down her throat, across her shoulders, then moved to her breasts. He sucked and molded and flicked the nipples of each. Grace arched her back, baring herself to him. With a cry, he buried his face in all that beautiful flesh.

This woman gave herself to him unselfishly and absolutely. That she did so humbled him.

She knew about the murder, prison, and his darkest secrets and loved him in spite of it. The woman he'd thought born of privilege, so far above him, loved the man he was, faults and all. The thought made him tremble.

He'd never known anyone like Grace. He pushed the hair back from her eyes, shaken by the depths of his feelings. "Darlin', you're something. I told you from the start that this is for keeps. I mean that more than ever now."

"For keeps," she whispered, staring up at him with that blue gaze that could see a forever.

"I love you, pretty lady." He nuzzled below her jaw. "I did from the first time I saw you with fire in your eyes. I have no idea what you see in me, but whatever it is, I'm thankful. I'm going to spend every second of my life loving you."

Tears bubbled in her eyes. "I wasn't sure you'd ever say the words. You're the sunrise in the morning, the sunset at night, my joy through the day. You're all I ever dreamed of finding."

Deacon leaned back a little. "I warn you married life won't always be roses. We'll have our fights."

"We'll have fun making up." She pressed a kiss to his chest.

"I'll have my moody days."

"Then I'll throw something at you, and we'll laugh."

"I'll have my whiskey on occasion." His warning turned out more of a growl.

"I've learned to accept that it's fine for some in moderation. Not all men are alike. I know you won't beat me."

"Never."

She pulled him down. "Love me as if the world is about to end, cowboy."

"Yes, ma'am."

Humbled by the gift she'd handed him, he knelt at her feet, kissing each little toe. Her feet were so small and dainty. He caressed her legs, her flat stomach. The touches, the kisses warmed Grace to what appeared a heated fever. She tried in vain to pull him up as was her nature and the way she plowed through life at breakneck speed. He would endeavor to teach her patience and that a slow pace had its advantages.

At last, he hovered over her, his erection poised at her wet entrance, and pushed inside. Her muscles quivered, then clenched around him, holding him fast.

Grace released a moan, gripping his back, pulling him in deeper. "Yes!"

He began the dance of their bodies, drawing out to just the tip, then thrusting hard. He kept repeating that, the friction of their bodies creating a bonfire of huge proportion. The urge to take his pleasure was powerful, but he resisted until he felt the cresting waves, and her body shuddered beneath him.

"Oh, Deacon! Yes!"

Honored that she'd chosen him out of all the men in the world, Deacon poured every ounce of the love he had into her.

Gasping, he rode the wave and fell over the edge, shattering in a million pieces as he clutched her to him. He held her until the last of their spasms died, then lay down beside her.

He stared up at the star-dotted heavens, tears filling his eyes. What he'd felt had been so profound, so beautiful, that words failed him. He was in love with his princess.

∽

Noon the following day, Deacon was rushing around the room when he spied a man barely five feet tall come through the door with a monkey dressed in cowboy gear, complete with a holster, perched on his shoulder.

"Martha, where are you? I've come for you!" he yelled.

Aunt Martha stuck her head out the kitchen door. "Clyde?"

Harry circled around to Deacon. "See? I told you so."

But Deacon's gaze was riveted on the monkey.

"Come here, sugar plum," Clyde crooned. "Come to Daddy."

Martha drew up short, her voice cold. "Are you giving up your philandering ways, you coot?"

"I only have eyes for you, sugar plum. I've missed you, sweetling."

"Oh, Clyde. Come to mama." Aunt Martha hurried to hug him, which looked a sight, since she stood a foot taller, and he had a full head of nutmeg hair to her gray. The monkey leaped down, evidently disturbed by the kissing and hugging.

"Just curious. How old is Clyde?" Deacon asked Harry.

"Don't know for sure, but I'd guess at least fifteen years younger than Aunt Martha." Harry muttered something that sounded like, "That little shit," and hurried to get the monkey away from a customer's plate where it was cramming food into its little mouth. "JESSE JAMES!"

Clearly no love lost between them, the monkey chattered, shaking a finger at Harry. As the skinny bartender grew closer, Jesse James yanked a little pistol from his holster, and shot, all the while chattering and shrieking fit to wake the dead. The miniature gun gave a little pop and discharged smoke. The customers were laughing hysterically. Harry never cracked a smile.

Deacon watched, entranced. This could have money pouring in. People would flock from all over to watch the hairy, little outlaw with the perfect name.

Land. He saw his piece of land. He saw his and Grace's future. And respectability.

Joel stood next to Deacon, his mouth hanging open in wonder. "He shot Harry, Mr. Brannock." Joel doubled over with laughter.

"I saw that." Deacon was glad to see the boy laughing.

Just as Harry closed in to capture the monkey, Jesse James leaped from table to table, then the long bar. As he reached for a full bottle of whiskey, Clyde clapped sharply, and the monkey clambered down and back onto the man's shoulder.

Deacon went to introduce himself to Clyde. Harry followed. "Welcome to the Three Deuces. I hope you'll make yourself at home."

"Planning to stay long, Uncle Clyde?" Harry scowled at the monkey that promptly stuck out his tongue.

The short-statured man scratched the back of his head. "Not sure, Harry. I hope you let bygones be bygones. Jesse James is real sorry he stole your clothes like that."

"I can tell," Harry said sourly. "Yes, he's so riddled with remorse he can't stand it."

The monkey chattered and pinched Aunt Martha's chest. She boxed his ears. "Clyde, he's getting on my bad side. Better give him a talking to, or I will."

"Sugarplum, he's just showing how much he missed you. I taught him a new trick." Clyde pulled a short piece of rope from his pocket and set Jesse James on an empty table. "I need something for him to rope."

Deacon glanced around, seeing nothing. Joel raced to the kitchen and came back with a milk jug. Clyde set it on the table, built a loop, and gave the monkey the rope. "Show them how it's done, Jesse."

Customers got up to watch and formed a circle two deep.

The hairy outlaw grinned, revealing a row of sharp teeth. He whirled the rope over his small head and released it. The loop settled over the milk jug, and the monkey did a somersault and clapped, plainly the consummate showman. Everyone pressed close to shake his hand, handing Clyde money for the show.

When they went back to their seats, Deacon pulled Clyde aside. "I have a proposition. Let Jesse James perform one show at lunchtime and two shows at supper, and we'll split the profits. What do you say?"

"Since I'm furnishing Jesse, I oughta get sixty and you forty percent."

Deacon thought a moment. Clyde did own the monkey. "Seems fair enough. Deal." They shook on it. "Do you have a hat to go with the cowboy outfit?"

"I packed it, but I'll get it out."

"Perfect." Deacon could see it now. He went to make some signs, and he and Joel tacked them the length of the street.

Grace was waiting outside the saloon on their return. She spoke to Joel, and he told her all about the monkey.

"He's real smart. I wish I could have one."

The boy's wistful words made her laugh, and Deacon didn't think he'd heard anything so sweet.

She laid a hand on the boy's shoulder. "I heard they were a lot of work. I doubt you'd want to clean up after one. But he sounds like a lot of fun."

They talked a little more, and when the boy went inside, she turned to Deacon. "I have an answer to the newspaper ad for information about Izzy's mother and stepfather. And guess what?"

"I haven't a clue."

"They live right here in Fort Worth."

"Let me tell Harry, and we'll head over." This should be interesting. Deacon had yearned for a chance to speak to the man who'd turned Izzy out to make his own way.

They soon found the house that needed paint, a new porch, and who knew what else. The man must be lazy. "I hope he tries to start something," Deacon muttered.

Grace grabbed his arm. "Promise me you'll keep your temper under control."

"I'll try, and that's all I can say. If Vinson goes for a weapon, I'll answer in kind." They went up the rickety steps, and Deacon knocked.

A surly boy of about fourteen or so answered the door. "Whatcha want?"

"I'd like to speak to Phillip Vinson or his wife." Deacon could hear two voices from inside. Sounded like arguing.

"They're busy."

Deacon wasn't going to let an ill-natured kid decide the outcome of their visit. "This is important. Can you get them? We'll wait."

Without a word, the boy shut the door.

A minute passed. Grace chewed her bottom lip. "Do you think he intends to come back?"

"Who knows? But I'm not leaving."

Another minute went by. Deacon pounded on the door. "Vinson, I want to talk to you."

The door jerked open. "Get away from here or I'll use this gun." The man, Phillip Vinson, Deacon presumed, held a gun across his stomach. His shirtsleeves were rolled up, and he wore a dark vest. His hair and goatee were light colored.

Deacon snorted. "I have a gun also. Want to compare? Come out, and we'll face off."

"Who are you?"

"Brannock of Hell's Half Acre. I want to ask you about your wife's boy, Izzy."

"I kicked that little snot-nosed brat out, and he's not coming back to my house. Ever."

A woman softly cried behind Vinson.

"Shut up, sniveling woman." He turned with fist drawn.

Deacon's voice came hard and cold as ice. "Hit her, and it'll be the last thing you ever do."

Vinson stared. "Telling me what I can do in my own house?"

"Let me spell it out. You're welcome to do whatever you like—except hit that woman." The man blinked very rapidly, a sign he abhorred being confronted. "If you do, Vinson, I *will* drag you out of there and beat the living hell out of you. I get plenty of practice in the Acre. So think about that."

Grace had backed away when it appeared there might be gunplay. Now she stepped to Deacon's side. "I wish to speak to the missus, please."

Vinson shook his head. "Nope, ain't gonna happen."

"I will stand here until I do." She lifted her chin. "I have lots of time, Mr. Vinson."

Brannock smiled at the soft words that held steel underneath. "Dynamite comes in small packages. I'd beware."

"Hell!" The surly man barked, "Anna, get your ignorant, no-good self out here!"

The woman came around Vinson. She was probably once a pretty woman with auburn hair but now it was stringy and unkept. Her dull, hopeless eyes were downcast, and she had a red mark along her cheek.

Grace put an arm around her. "Anna, we want to know if Izzy has been here. He's missing, and we're concerned."

Anna shook her head, eyes staring down. "Haven't seen him."

"We care about him. He's such a sweet boy."

"I hope he's all right. I can't—" She took a step closer and lowered her voice to a whisper. "Tell him I still love him."

"What are you whispering about?" Vinson yelled.

Deacon blocked the man from coming out. "The ladies are talking. It's none of your business."

Grace squeezed her hands. "I'll tell him. If he's alive, I'll bring him to see you. Would you like that?"

"Yes." Anna cast a frightened look behind at her husband. "I won't always live like this."

Grace gave her a smile. "I understand. Stay strong, and if you need help, come to the Three Deuces. You'll have friends there."

Anna nodded and stepped back behind her husband.

Deacon watched his expression and each movement, no matter how slight. Vinson's anger had built to a fine boil. "I'll be back later. If anything's happened to your wife, if she's stubbed a toe or gotten a sniffle, I'll yank you out of this house by your hair."

Rage reddened the man's face. Without a word, he slammed the door so hard, a windowpane fell out on the ground.

"I think that went well, dear." Grace tucked her hand around his elbow. "What time is the show? I don't want to miss Jesse James."

"You won't believe this monkey." Deacon tucked her close to his side. He knew she was strong and stubborn and full of life, but he couldn't believe how she'd stood up to Phillip Vinson's rudeness and insisted on speaking to his wife.

Grace made his life worth living, and the chance of seeing her smile, hear her laughter, brought happiness he'd never known.

❧

Deacon rode out to tell Will all his wonderful news and found the rancher hand-feeding Diablo carrots. The sight warmed his heart.

"I see you've made friends." He dismounted and clapped Will on the back.

"Seems so. I knew if anyone could fix him, it would be you."

"Well, the fixing went both ways." Deacon patted Diablo's long neck. "I finally told Grace I loved her, and she said she already knew it."

"We're not blind, Deacon! I don't know how you could not see it." Will laughed and patted Diablo's side.

"I've done so many bad things, I didn't see how anyone could even stand me. I didn't like myself much. It was Diablo here that opened my eyes and made me see I was worthy of being loved. Now if I could ever find Izzy and the rest of the missing boys, my life would be perfect."

Will pushed back his hat. "You will. Just a matter of time. A break will come."

"I hope so." Deacon watched some of the ranch hands ride up, dirty after a day's work. "And you won't believe my next piece of news. I have a monkey named Jesse James at the saloon."

"A monkey?" Will cackled. "I'll have to see this."

"Anytime. He wears cowboy clothes, complete with a holster and gun. Puts on quite a show. The crowds are going wild." Deacon propped his hands on the rail. "We're making money so fast, we can hardly take it all in. I think I can finally buy that piece of land I want for Grace and me."

"Grace. A monkey. Land. What more can a man want?" Will jostled his shoulder.

"Aside from finding Izzy, not a damn thing." Deacon's heart was the fullest it had ever been. He prayed nothing happened to ruin his happiness.

Thirty-four

THAT NIGHT, CROWDS POURED THROUGH THE THREE DEUCES doors, everyone anxious to see the little monkey, Grace among them. She stood near the long, oak bar, her focus on the man of her dreams. She'd never seen a wider smile or heard a deeper laugh as he navigated the tables and the crush of people standing.

Aunt Martha had made her signature sandwiches, along with the usual tamales. Deacon and Meg took orders while Harry served drinks. Joel stood ready to clean tables. The place buzzed with excitement, and money was flowing. They'd have a full till by night's end.

A mist filled her eyes. Deacon had struggled so hard to see the saloon turn a profit. The hairy, little outlaw, Jesse James, was the final piece to a large picture.

Her chest burst with love for Deacon and pride for what he'd accomplished. If this kept up, they could afford to buy a house soon, and that would solve where they were going to live.

If only they could locate Izzy and bring him home. Thank goodness he'd gotten away from that despicable Phillip Vinson. What a nightmare. Grace felt in her heart she'd see Anna again. The woman had to get a little stronger to break away.

Deacon joined her, giving her a kiss. "I never in a million years expected to see this."

"You did it. *You.*"

He draped an arm casually around her shoulders. She didn't think his gray eyes had ever been so clear. He cleared his throat. "I had help. The biggest was your belief in me."

Love for him spilled over. "No, Deacon. You finally believed in yourself."

"I don't know about that." His eyes twinkled. "If you hadn't come down here wiggling those fine hips, showing me the error of my ways, I'd have still been trying to eke out a living."

Grace laughed, loving this teasing. "I love you, Brannock. I truly and utterly do."

"Thank you for taking pity on me." He lowered his mouth to hers and sent heat through her.

A customer raised his voice at Meg, interrupting them. Grace stepped back and hurried to intercept the young woman while Deacon grabbed the unruly fellow, twisted his arms around his back and hustled him out the door.

One look at Meg's face, and Grace wanted to rush out and stomp the piece of manure. "I'm so sorry, Meg. Don't let him bother you. There will always be hateful, overbearing people."

Meg released a shaky sigh. "I know. I'd just thought I was through with all that."

"If you want to go on home, I'll fill in for you. You're as good as anybody."

"That's very kind, but no, I'll stay." Meg lifted her chin high and pulled her shoulders back. "I won't do that to you and Brannock."

Uncle Clyde emerged from the kitchen with Jesse James, and a stir went around the room.

"Guess I'd best get the show started." Deacon stood on a chair and raised his arms to silence the throng. "Folks, it gives me great pleasure to introduce Little Jesse James. He's here to delight and entertain you. Men, he might even steal your watch, ladies, your handbag, if he gets the slightest chance, so I'd keep them out of reach."

Clyde lowered him on the table they'd set aside for the show and took out a harmonica. The monkey grinned real wide and began to do a stiff dance with unexpected somersaults thrown in for good measure.

The little scamp appeared to enjoy being in the spotlight, and everyone loved watching.

Grace laughed at his mannerisms. But when she caught the look on Deacon's face, she got a lump in her throat for the little boy with nothing. She lifted a hand and subconsciously fingered a gold filigree necklace she'd worn just for Deacon.

He met her gaze and moved to her side. "Just wait for his cowboy routine."

Sarge glared from a high shelf. All of a sudden, he leaped into the show with Jesse, hissing and slapping, his back raised. Chattering fit to beat all, Jesse dodged the blows, his teeth glistening in a strange grin. He whipped out the tiny gun from his holster and aimed it at the irritable cat, shooting. The crowd roared with laughter.

The harmonica music of Clyde's got faster and faster until it sounded like a galloping horse.

A customer sat nearby, his gun hanging at his side. Jesse spied it and made a dive, pulling the deadly weapon from the holster, pointing it. Everybody scattered with some ducking under the table.

"Oh, hell!" Deacon ran forward. Grace watched, her heart in her throat, praying no one got shot.

Clyde dropped his mouth harp and held out a hand. "Jesse, bring that to me. Be a nice monkey and bring it here."

Jesse raised the gun and fired. The bullet penetrated the tin ceiling. Sarge still seemed intent on getting some slaps in on the usurper and stalked closer. Jesse took aim.

Just as he pulled the trigger, Deacon grabbed the weapon. He flipped open the cylinder and removed the bullets before handing it back to the owner. "You might leave that at home next time."

"Sorry." The man stuck it back in his holster. "I've never been around monkeys before."

"This one is a sly little devil." Deacon pocketed the bullets, and Grace noticed that Harry scooped Sarge up and put him outside.

The customers either took their seats or stood, but not one left.

She turned her attention back to Jesse James, who took a small length of rope from Clyde and proceeded to rope various items, as entranced as all the others. Deacon was right. Jesse James would put the Three Deuces on the map.

In the second show, Jesse grabbed a woman's handbag before anyone could move and scampered up to the rafters. It took some doing to get him down.

After the last customer left, Grace helped Deacon count the money, astounded at his cut of sixty-eight dollars and a few cents. "I can't believe this." She threw her arms around his neck and kissed him.

Deacon held her tight for several seconds. "I should've gotten a monkey years ago."

The door opened, and Deacon swung around. "We're closed, mister."

The man, dressed in clothing that had seen better days, removed his hat and crushed it to his chest. "I'm not here to drink. Looking for Brannock."

Deacon rose. "I'm Deacon Brannock. How can I help you?"

Grace clung to his arm. If this was trouble, she'd meet it by his side, her rightful place.

The stranger wore a holster and gun but made no move for it. She took in his high boots and suspenders, the type muleskinners favored. He walked to Deacon. "I heard you were looking for some little boys."

Shock raced through Grace, followed by excitement.

"That's right. Who are you?"

"Slim Wade. I deliver supplies from Fort Worth to the company store over at Thurber, and I overheard some men talking about a boy named Izzy and how much trouble he was making. They said they might have to—" He glanced down. "Might have to kill him."

They couldn't let anyone kill that sweet boy.

Thurber? Grace's thoughts whirled. They had a coal mining operation she seemed to remember. There was something about the ceilings being so low men had to lay on their backs or work on their knees to dig the coal out of the walls. Young boys would have little trouble. Yes, it all seemed to fit.

"There's some strange doin's over at Thurber," Wade said. "Secret stuff. The company owns everything in the town, all the businesses, hospital, doctor, everything. They put a high fence around it with guards."

"Sounds like a bad place." Deep concern filled Deacon's voice. "You're sure the kid's name was Izzy?"

Wade nodded. "Can't forget anything that different. Another thing: the men I overheard said some of the kids are sick, but the boss won't let the doctor in to see them. They don't appear to care if any die. Said they'll just throw them in a grave and find more. Their lives aren't worth two cents."

This was getting worse by the minute. If they were sick, they couldn't run.

"To be clear. They're keeping the boys inside the mine? Why?" Her mouth went dry.

"Izzy seems to be organizing the group and constantly tries to break out, so they've chained them in the bowels of the mine." Wade stood. "Well, that's all I came for. Hope you free them. I'll let you folks be."

"Wait. Are you hungry?" Deacon asked.

"I missed supper. Living alone don't allow many creature comforts."

"Harry!" Deacon called.

The ponytailed bartender came from the kitchen. "Yes, Boss?"

"Will you get this man some of those sandwiches? He may know where Izzy is."

"I hope your search is over. I'll get the food." Harry disappeared into the kitchen.

In no time, Wade was eating and washing the sandwiches down with beer while he drew a map of Thurber and the nearby mine that had fifteen shafts. "Two trains take the workers to the mines each morning and pick them up at night. They chain the boys up inside the tunnels. They never see sunlight or get to wash the coal dust off."

"How horrible!" Grace could only imagine what Izzy and the other boys were going through.

But not for long. Hope thundered inside her. They had to go get him.

Before it was too late.

Full at last, Slim Wade stood. "That was mighty fine. Thank you." He turned to Grace. "Ma'am, I hope you have a nice evening. I don't know who Sam Valentine is at the newspaper, but if not for his articles, the name Izzy wouldn't have meant anything. I hope you bring the boy home."

"Thank you, Mr. Wade." Grace clasped his hand. "You've been a tremendous help."

"I can't agree more." Deacon saw him to the door. "You're welcome here anytime."

As soon as the door closed, Grace folded the map of Thurber. "Ready to go?"

"I do this alone." He reached for his hat and put it on, then checked his Colt.

"Don't even think about leaving me, buster."

"I'm not going to argue about this. It's too dangerous for you."

She planted her hands on her hips. "We wouldn't know where he is if it hadn't been for my articles."

"True. But no."

"Deacon Brannock, Izzy and those boys might need me. You heard Mr. Wade say some are sick. I can take some medicines and things." She paused, pursing her mouth. "I'll just follow after you leave."

He let out a frustrated sigh. "All right. Only if you do what I say and don't take risks."

Grace kissed his cheek and ran for the door before he left her. She'd worked too hard to bring these kids home to miss the rescue.

But she knew this wouldn't go smoothly. Things always went wrong. She reached for Deacon's hand. A ripple of fear went through her as they hurried to catch the train for Thurber.

❧

The train seemed to inch along. Deacon wanted to get out and push it.

"We'll get there." Grace sat in the seat beside him and reached for his hand. "We'll make it and bring Izzy back home. Hopefully, to his mother."

But what if they didn't find him? Wade could be wrong. Izzy might not be there.

Or he could be dead.

Deacon leaned his head against the back of the seat. "I'm glad you came. You're always the voice of reason."

"Surely you're talking about someone else. I'm certainly not very wise or calm."

Her dress of dark blue was lovely and quite unsuitable for this late-night journey. So was the gold filigree necklace shining around her throat. One day, he meant to drape her in jewelry and fine things. She wouldn't suffer for marrying him if he had any say in the matter.

"I mean you and no other."

"Even when me and those women broke into the saloon with hatchets and busted your liquor?"

"I stand corrected. But although you broke in with them, you held back and didn't destroy anything," he pointed out. "A momentary lapse of judgment. And you came back and cleaned up the mess."

"Only because my father made me." She made a wry face. "I was afraid of you and would've given anything to escape that punishment."

"Ha! You, afraid? Of me?" He laughed. "I don't think you've ever been scared of anything."

"You'd be surprised. In my defense, it was all those stories I'd heard about you. The men you'd hurt, killed, nailed to the outhouse door." She ran a fingertip up his arm. "You looked savage the day I appeared to clean the spilled whiskey. You barely contained burning anger."

"All I could see was what I'd lost that I couldn't recoup. Gone was my goal, my hard work of saving for a piece of land. Luckily, your father fixed everything with the liquor."

Grace sighed. "I was really perturbed with him. He undid everything in our fight against the sale of alcohol."

"You seem to have reconciled yourself." Deacon lifted her fingers to his mouth and kissed them.

"It was the food. As much as you deny it, you're much more a café than a saloon now." Her laugh was low and throaty. "And I've given up my Don Quixote lance. It's time to stop tilting at windmills."

He thought about that a moment. "Princess, don't ever stop. The world needs your fire." He glanced out the window at the darkness. "But damn if you're not right about one thing. I guess I'll have to rename the Three Deuces."

For the next half hour, they bounced around ideas for new names. Deacon couldn't take his eyes off her. The beautiful, sassy lady utterly bedazzled him.

The train pulled to a stop, and the conductor hollered that they'd arrived at Thurber.

Deacon became all business. No one had to remind him of the purpose of coming. The weight of the Colt on his hip reassured him that he would give as good as he got or better. He gathered two rifles, put an arm around Grace's waist, and they left the train.

Not a breath of air stirred in the night, and a heavy pall hung over the town awash in moonlight. No one else got off, and the Texas and Pacific train hurried on as though it didn't want to get caught in the evil that lived here.

The pale moon painted the buildings a sickly shade of ash.

Grace shivered beside him. "Oh God, I hate this place."

Thirty-five

DEACON STOOD FOR A MOMENT, GETTING THE LAYOUT. THE fenced-in town had hundreds of little one-room houses surrounding it, where the miners and their families lived. Two small trains sat parked on tracks that led toward the mines. Wade hadn't known how far away the mines were. That would've been helpful.

A guard shack stood at the fence opening. A man came out. "Whatcha doing here?"

"Isn't this…? Oh, man, I think we got off at the wrong town. My wife and I were going to Strawn to visit her folks." Deacon threw up his hands and paced the length of the platform. "I feel foolish. What are we going to do now?"

"Mister, why are you carrying two rifles plus your handgun?" the guard asked.

"These?" Deacon chuckled. "They belong to my father-in-law. I was taking them to him. He lives in—"

"Strawn," the guard finished. "I heard the first time."

"Right. I hope you didn't think we were going to shoot up the town."

"I never met you before, so how would I know?"

Grace patted Deacon's chest. "I assure you, sir, that we have nothing of that sort in mind. My father would kill him. He doesn't stand for using rifles for anything but hunting game. He doesn't like my husband very much to start with. He demanded we get the marriage annulled, but when he found out about our"—she lowered her voice to a loud whisper—"numerous indiscretions, he thought we'd best stay married."

The guard chuckled. "Come on in. There's a hotel in town where you can stay until the train passes back through."

A hotel. That couldn't be more perfect. "Come on, honey." Deacon helped her down the platform steps. The guard let them into the town, warning them not to get too curious and stay on the main street.

Thank goodness he didn't offer to take them to the hotel. This worked out better than Deacon had hoped. He kept Grace moving toward the tall hotel towering above the rest of the buildings until they were out of sight of the guard.

"Let's cut across this lot to the train tracks and follow them to the mine. Be best to make as little noise as possible, although most people are asleep."

"We don't need to arouse anyone's suspicions. Deacon, my blood is running cold. I have a horrible feeling."

"It's just nerves."

Outside of town, they encountered pastureland and could move faster. They had to be finished by dawn or they'd walk into a firestorm. They trod down the tracks in silence. Deacon thought of everything that could go wrong. Who knew what kept Grace from talking? She'd seen bad things before, and he had a feeling this was about the worst anyone could face. Guards, a fence surrounding the town—once they got past those hurdles was an unknown train schedule. He didn't know when it would arrive again.

Then another uncertainty was his ammunition. He'd brought enough for a small fight. Nothing larger.

"Deacon, I'm scared. So many doubts are circling in my head."

"Mine too. You wouldn't be human if you weren't afraid."

Her face seemed drained of color, but maybe it was the silvery wash of moonlight. "I've left so many things unsaid, and maybe I won't get a chance to say them. Can we stop for a minute?"

Deacon stopped and laid down the rifles. He gave her a kiss and pulled her against him. "I'm no good at talking about feelings,

Grace. I do know my life changed when I met you. The world was a dismal and lonely place, and you pulled back a curtain and let the sunlight in. When we get out of this, some things are going to be different. I promise you."

Grace lifted her face and gazed into his eyes. "I never thought I'd love anyone like I love you, Deacon Brannock. I don't care if you're a saloon owner, a lawman, or an undertaker. I want to spend the rest of my life in your arms, but if this is all we have, I'm proud to say that you make me the happiest woman alive. You're all I've ever wanted. I'll go to my grave knowing that I've loved the best."

"I hate to let you go, darlin', but we should get moving. I have no idea how much farther it is."

She stepped out of his arms. "Wait." She unclasped the gold necklace she wore and placed it in his palm. "To remember me by."

Unable to speak for the emotion clogging his throat, he put the necklace into his pocket and picked up the rifles. They walked a good distance and finally came to the end of the tracks. A sign above the entrance read THE TEXAS AND PACIFIC COAL COMPANY. An owl perched on the sign hooted, then all was quiet.

"Grace, I want you stay out here and hide with one of these rifles. You can be my lookout. If anyone comes, fire into the air." He brushed back strands of golden hair. "If anyone threatens, shoot to kill. I've heard of your skill and know you're an expert."

"Believe me, I won't hesitate."

"Good. Wade said there are fourteen tunnels. It might take a while to find the boys."

"Just get them out alive."

"I'll do my best." He pulled her in for a kiss, then walked through the opening, reaching for a lantern hanging against the side and lighting it. He took her necklace from his pocket, pressed his lips to the dainty metal, then returned it for safekeeping.

Deacon didn't turn around but kept looking forward. He wanted the last picture of Grace to be her eyes shining, full of love, her lips slightly parted for his kiss. That was the way he wanted to remember her if they would never have another chance at happiness. He dragged a lungful of air in and got about the business of finding the boys.

The mine was as silent as a tomb, the ceiling so low, he had to bend over.

A short way inside, three tunnels converged. Which to take? The one straight ahead probably descended deeper into the ground. For some reason, he didn't think they'd take the boys miles underneath the surface. They'd have to be bringing food to them and wouldn't want to have to walk too far. The other two were probably about the equal depth, but which one?

Sweat popped out on his forehead. A wrong turn would waste precious time.

He'd once heard that right-handed people tended to prefer right directions over left. Since three-fourths of the population was right-handed, maybe the culprits who'd stolen the boys took the right tunnel. Feeling somewhat confident, he fished paper and pencil from his pocket and drew the three tunnels, marking the right one. Returning them to his pocket, he proceeded.

A short distance, and he encountered two more. He stood in indecision. Left this time. Again, he marked it on his paper where, hopefully, he could backtrack and not get lost.

The mine seemed a living thing, groaning and belching amid the constant drip of water. At times, his lantern flickered. Air was coming in from someplace.

But where?

Deacon seemed to be inside the belly of an ugly beast. His back ached from being constantly bent. If only to be able to stand upright or to sit for a few minutes, but each time he was tempted to sit, he thought of the boys and, out of sheer will, kept moving.

The endless maze of tunnels and decisions exhausted him.

Sometimes he reached a dead end and had to retrace his steps and take a different direction.

He kept attuned for sounds, stopping to listen every so often. Constant doubt that he'd find the youngsters lingered in the back of his mind.

An hour or two had to have passed since he'd left Grace. He was dead on his feet but couldn't afford to rest or even slow. Where were they?

Would they make it out alive?

❧

Grace huddled in some brush, her eyes glued on the mine entrance, praying to soon see Deacon leading the boys.

Night sounds pressed close, and each noise startled her and gave her jumpy nerves a jolt that sent her heart careening like a runaway train. The sky turned a lighter gray. Dawn was near.

Her breath caught. *Miners and bosses would arrive for work very soon.*

Where was Deacon? She pressed a hand to her mouth.

Suddenly she spied a group of riders approaching at a trot. She readied the rifle with shaking fingers. The guard must've checked at the hotel and found she and Deacon hadn't checked in. A hue and cry probably went up.

She waited until they pulled up at the mine entrance and counted five men. Putting one in her sights, she pulled the trigger. The bullet struck him, but where or how bad she didn't know.

They scattered like a covey of quail, taking cover behind some metal ore cars loaded with coal.

A quick rachet of the lever put another round in the chamber. When a shooter raised his head to look, she fired again, this time missing. Sweat formed above her lip. Deacon wouldn't be able to hear inside the mine, and if he and the children came out now, they'd be caught in the crossfire.

Thank God for the darkness. She knew they hadn't pinpointed her position yet, which gave her an advantage.

"Who's that shooting?" one of the riders called.

She stayed silent and searched for another target. No one was moving.

"Whoever you are, you're trespassing!"

It sounded like they were getting desperate. She had no intention of answering back, of letting them know a woman held them at bay.

"Mr. Renick, the boss man, will be here soon. He ain't gonna be happy about this. Let us come out, and you can go on your merry way!"

"Yeah right," she muttered, raising the rifle. Aiming, she fired at the top of the coal car, the bullet pinging off the metal.

The sky slowly lightened to shell pink, and still the minutes passed. Had the men left their cover and snuck around behind her? She turned to scan the brush and scrub oak, dotted with mesquite. In the distance came the sound of a train.

The miners were coming to work.

Arms suddenly grabbed her from behind, and someone yanked her rifle away. She faced five angry faces.

"A stinking woman," one spat.

She lifted her chin. "A stinking woman kept you pinned down, and I see two of you are bleeding. You probably need to get that seen to. It looks painful."

One had a wound to his shoulder and another to his ribs.

"Lady, you don't want to know what I wish I could do to you," snarled the guard they'd passed coming in at midnight. He put her rifle over his shoulder. "I thought this belonged to your father."

"He let me borrow it." She gave him a frosty glare. "He also taught me to shoot."

"What're we gonna do with her?" The speaker clearly wasn't a miner, in jeans, vest, and battered Stetson. "Boss hired us to keep nosey trespassers from sniffing around."

Hired guns—all except for possibly the two guards.

The five of them stared at each other, shrugging. They didn't know what to do with a female. "You could let me go, and I'll get back on the train." Her voice held a hopeful note.

The same guard shook his head. "No chance, lady. Where's your partner? Inside the mine?"

"We got lost on the way to the hotel. He went in search of a cup of coffee."

The lights of the train shone in the distance, and the rumble of the large engine shook the ground. She recalled Slim Wade saying the miners rode out in two trains. She glanced again and made out a second train trailing the first.

Doom settled over her. Even if Deacon brought the boys out, they'd only fall prey again to their captors.

There would be no way out of this.

No miracle.

No second chance. For any of them.

∽

The sound of movement reached Deacon's ears. He stopped, trying to figure out which direction it came from. The mine was bad about echoes. The silence was broken by whispers. Young voices. To call out to them might bring trouble.

He crouched in indecision. Finally, he spoke softly. "Izzy? Izzy, it's Brannock."

Everything went quiet. He seemed to feel the fear.

"Izzy?"

This time a very young voice replied. "Mr. Brannock? That you?"

"Yes. Where are you? I need to get you out of here. Don't have much time."

"We haven't passed, so we're ahead of you. We'll keep coming."

"I'll meet you. Look for my lantern." Hope flared inside Deacon. Now, to meet up and hustle them out before the miners came to work.

Two curves in the shaft, then Izzy exclaimed, "I see your light."

"Good."

"Oh no, we're dropping Davey."

Deacon heard Izzy fuss someone out. According to Slim Wade, the kid had turned out be quite a leader. Deacon kept inching along, his back hunched and aching. He rounded another curve and stared in amazement.

A group of a dozen or so kids marched behind Izzy and a shaggy dog. They were all covered in black coal dust from head to toe. The whites of their eyes provided sharp contrast. Two boys carried another boy who must be Davey. Deacon didn't think he'd ever seen anything so beautiful. He hurried to take the sick kid, giving the lantern to one in the group, and Izzy, the rifle.

"You came! You found me. You found us."

"Where did you get the dog?" Deacon asked.

"He wandered into the mine, and I think he must've got lost." Izzy glanced up, determination on his dirty face, ready to fight. "I won't leave him."

"I wasn't going to suggest that. Does he have a name?"

"Shep."

"I like it." Now that they'd cleared that up, Deacon got them moving.

While they walked, Izzy told of how they'd managed to tackle a guard and get away. It took time for him to keep consulting his paper that would get them back to the main tunnel. The children were subdued, as if they worried about what faced them once they reached outside. Though he, too, worried, he maintained a cheerful front, keeping thoughts of freedom in their heads.

The idea of being free beat inside the hearts of everyone he knew. It meant everything to a man. To a boy too.

His thoughts were on Grace and what might've happened after he'd left. Both had known the risks and hadn't shied away from doing what they must. He guessed that's what he loved most about her. She dove in when something needed doing and didn't give up until the job was done. She was as tenacious in her zeal of fighting for women's rights and writing articles as she was in picking out her wardrobe.

If they survived this, he knew she'd plaster the newspaper with articles blasting Thurber and the man who owned the town and mine.

The piece of land he'd had his eye on crossed his mind. As soon as everything fell into place and he could buy it, he was giving up city life faster than he could aim and shoot. He'd return to the wide-open spaces where a man could breathe. Grace would love it, and he could picture her there. She'd spoken in wistful tones so often about the Lone Star. They both loved the land, the wide sky, breathing fresh air. Strangely, he felt it was what he'd been born to do. The saloon would give him the means to live that cowboy lifestyle he loved.

After Will paid him the money they'd agreed on, he could buy that land a lot quicker than he would have. His land. The thought sent his soul soaring. His dream come true.

As they neared the entrance, the rumble of train engines shook the mine, raining coal dust down on their heads. Maybe they still had time. "Hurry, boys. Just a little farther." He couldn't wait to be able to straighten his back.

They finally burst into the fresh air and straight into the barrels of a half dozen rifles.

Their luck had run out.

Thirty-six

"RAISE YOUR HANDS!" BARKED A DEEP VOICE.

The big spotlight on the lead train blinded Deacon. He finally stood upright and eased his crooked spine straight. With a forearm to shield his eyes, he counted five armed men. He might've considered taking them on if not for the glut of grim-faced miners behind them coming to work.

Where was Grace?

He scanned the faces.

"Brannock!" she yelled.

He finally saw her slight figure squeezed into the line of men with guns. One man was gripping her arm. Dammit! Thoughts whirled. How could he get them and the boys out of this? They were seriously outnumbered.

"I ordered you to raise your hands!" the same voice yelled.

"I'm holding a sick boy, dying for all I know." Heavy scorn dripped from Deacon's voice. "Sick because you brought him and these other kids here, chained them up down below for so long in the cold and damp, half-starving."

The miners with their pickaxes and shovels pressed closer.

"Take his gun and the rifle that boy's holding!" the spokesman shouted.

Someone rushed forward to comply.

"Everyone here follows orders, Brannock." One of the men with rifles took a step forward. "These kids are not our fault. If we don't do what the boss says, we get kicked out."

"How do you live with yourselves? How do you sleep at night?"

Deacon tightened his grip on Davey. They'd have to pry the boy out of his hands. He spared a glance down into the kid's face. His eyes were closed, his mouth hanging open, his breath coming in loud gasps. "We need a doctor here!"

Grace spoke in a loud voice. "I'm a reporter for the *Fort Worth Gazette*, and I can guarantee you that I'm going to plaster this place across the newspaper. Folks outside of here will find out what kind of town you have, and believe me, they'll arrive in force to turn it into kindling."

The armed men huddled together to talk, and one mounted up and galloped toward town. The spokesman's tone was as unbending as before. "No doctor. We've sent for the boss man."

"Fine," Deacon answered. "I'd like to talk to him anyway."

While they waited, a large German pushed his way to the front. "Das boss, he keep das children chained in mine?"

"Get back behind us!" one of armed men yelled.

The miner glared, standing his ground. "I want answer."

Like a flash, Deacon saw a way clear of the standoff. The miners' faces reflected deep concern and growing anger. "Yes, your boss did. He had them stolen from town and brought here to work. When they tried to escape, he had them chained. Not a pretty picture of the man you work for." He motioned to the armed men. "Unless I miss my guess, several of those men are hired guns to keep you miners in line, to do his dirty work."

A growl rose from the German's throat. He and his fellow workers advanced on the armed enforcers, subduing and disarming them. They herded them into the dark mine.

The German handed Deacon his handgun and rifle. "Get die kinder on der train," he told Deacon. "Hurry. I tell engineer."

The man spoke to the miners, and they all rushed to help the boys and Shep to the second locomotive. It would have to go in reverse all the way back to town, but that must be how they always returned, since he saw no way to turn around. Deacon carried sick little Davey, and Grace followed, her skirts cracked against her ankles like pieces of rawhide.

Her anger sliced through the space between them. "You just wait. When I get home, I'm going to write scathing articles about this place."

"I have no doubt you will, darlin', and maybe it'll make a difference."

Her chin quivered. "These poor people living here. It's like a prison."

"I know." He wanted to take her in his arms and reassure himself that she was unhurt. But the approach of galloping horses reached him. "Hurry, Grace."

The miners lifted child after child through the door as fast as they could. Deacon hollered over the babble of voices. "Kids, when you get inside, lay on the floor. Don't raise your heads."

If the mine boss couldn't see them, he'd think the train was empty and ride on by. Deacon didn't stop to give himself one thought. He turned to Grace. "You too. Go with the children. I'll try to give you time to get away. When you get to the Texas and Pacific depot, get them on board as quick as you can."

Her stricken gaze sliced through him. "I can't leave you behind, cowboy. I won't."

He handed Davey off to one of the miners to carry on board and his rifle to Izzy. He took Grace in his arms. "You can. You can do anything you set your mind to. They have no one else. I have to keep this from happening again and again. I'll join you. I promise."

With her wild heartbeat pounding against his chest, he lowered his head and drank of her lips, then pushed her away. "Get on and lay flat. Don't make a sound or let the boys."

She clutched his shirt with both hands, panic in her beautiful eyes. "Come with us."

The big iron wheels of the train began to turn. "I'll stay and buy you time. It's the only way to get the boys out." He picked her up and placed her on the moving steps. "Goodbye, princess."

"I wish there were another way." She blew him a kiss.

Deacon turned away, blinking hard. "I love you."

He hurried back to the group of miners guarding the entrance to the mine and told them his plan. "Do you have dynamite?"

"Ja." The big German waved to someone, who rushed over. A few guttural words, and the second man held out a bag filled with explosives.

As expected, the two riders flew right past the locomotive and came to a stop in front of Deacon. "I ought to have you shot for trespassing." The speaker dismounted, his deep, sunken eyes raking over Deacon. His manner, his bearing, his voice was arrogant. He wore a heavy pistol hanging from his hip. The mine owner. Deacon had no name for him. Yet.

He loathed arrogance over everything else about a man. He ground his back teeth, glad Grace and the boys were away from this place.

The second rider, a slight man with small hands, slid from the saddle. He was quite a bit younger than his boss. To Deacon, he looked like an accountant, someone who worked with numbers. Maybe he'd counted the boys when they brought them in.

"I suppose you might try to have me shot." Deacon narrowed his gaze. "But I wouldn't advise it."

The mine boss stalked to Deacon. "Why's that?"

"Look around you." He waved his arm over the miners. "Even with your money, your clout, that big gun in your holster, you're no match for them."

"They work for me. They do what I say, or I'll fire every last one."

"Are you sure they're loyal? You might take a closer look, Mr.—"

The arrogant bastard drew himself up and didn't seem to believe anyone existed who didn't know him by sight. "Julius Renick. And what name do I put on your tombstone?"

"Any name you want. Deacon Brannock, Blade Reno, or maybe Jesse James."

Irritation crossed Renick's eyes. "Whoever you are, you're a trespasser who has the unmitigated gall to come onto my land illegally. And to do what?"

"To stop you."

"Good luck. You either have to be blind or stupid." He looked around for his armed thugs. "Where are those men I hired?"

The German miner rested a palm on the gun stuck in his waistband. "We change job. You mine."

"You big dumb bastard!" He turned to his companion. "Take charge of this tinhorn."

The underling's eyes widened. "Me?" He stared at Brannock. "I—I—why not Felix?"

Deacon chuckled. "Having a little trouble, Renick? I'm a little bigger than the kids you stole from Fort Worth." He whirled toward the mine, clutching the explosives.

"Don't walk away from me!" Julius Renick bellowed. "Stop!"

A click sounded, and a bullet sped past Deacon. He froze. "If I turn around, you're going to die."

Thick silence in the gray dawn spoke for Renick's lack of courage.

Deacon hurried on. At the mine entrance, he told the miners to remove the armed men and hold them outside. When everyone was out, he dug for a match.

Behind him, he heard the miners take the boss's gun.

"Where are my boys? If you've stolen them—" Renick's threat died in his throat when Deacon whirled.

"Your boys? The child stealer is you, you sick bastard! I rescued them from that dark prison. They're children."

Renick's nose flared. "I was giving them a chance. None have family or homes, just living on the street. No one missed them, so what's the fuss?"

"I've heard enough." Deacon removed dynamite from the explosives burlap sack and struck the match. He held the flame to the bundle he gripped—looked to be six sticks. Not enough to destroy the mine, but they'd seal the opening and require months to clear the rubble. The miners would still have jobs.

The air smelled of rain, and the heavy clouds appeared to promise a downpour.

Deacon drew back his arm.

"No!" Renick struggled to free himself from the hands holding him. "No!"

"Too late." Deacon tossed the dynamite into the dark depths and ran, throwing himself onto the ground with everyone else.

The explosion was deafening, shaking the ground for miles. Fire, smoke, and black coal belched from the opening, triggering a second explosion caused by the volatile coal dust. Dangerous debris rained down on them. Thank goodness Grace and the boys had gone.

When the noise died, Deacon got to his feet and ran for the nearest horse, several hundred yards away. It and all the other animals had retreated a safe distance from the chaos.

"Damn you, Brannock!" Renick yelled, running after him. "That's my horse!"

Then the mount was probably high quality. It took a moment to calm the spooked animal, but when he did, Deacon threw himself into the saddle. Renick grabbed his leg and yanked.

Deacon kicked him away, only to have one of Renick's hired guns latch hold of the headstall. The horse's eyes rolled back in his head, and it tried to rear.

"Turn loose!" Deacon pulled his gun and aimed at the man's head. "I *will* shoot."

Glaring hate, the hired gun released his hold, and Deacon spurred the horse to a gallop. He rode across the prairie land and thundered down the streets of Thurber, not stopping until he reached the train platform.

Grace ran from cover and caught him in a dismount, tears running down her face. "I heard...felt...the explosion and..." She threw herself into his arms, her voice quivering. "I thought you'd gotten blown up."

"Just the mine. Where are the boys?"

"Underneath the platform."

"Good. A nest of hornets will be coming as soon as they can catch a horse, aiming to stop us from getting on the train." He hurried her down with the boys, their skin still blackened with coal.

"Mr. Brannock! I knew you'd come." Izzy hugged him. "Thank you for rescuing us."

"You're welcome, but you had already rescued yourselves. The only thing left was for me to carry Davey. How is he, Grace?"

"Sleeping." She took Deacon aside and spoke low. "I'm really worried. Davey is struggling to breathe, and he has a high fever. We've got to get him to a doctor."

Deacon glanced at the tracks that ran beside the platform, and the threatening clouds. A distant rumble of thunder reached him. "Did you see a schedule posted anywhere?"

"The next one is at 8:20 this morning."

He pulled out his pocket watch. An hour and ten minutes. Damn! "It won't take any time for the owner and his henchmen to figure out where we are. We have to get ready. Does anyone know what happened to the rifle I put on the train? Izzy?"

"Sure, Mr. Brannock." The ten-year-old they'd searched so long and hard for reached and handed him the rifle.

"Thanks, son." Deacon checked the chamber and found it full of cartridges. He scowled. This must be the one he'd carried into the mine when he searched for the boys. "Grace, do you know what happened to your rifle?"

"Those men took it from me."

To count, they had one rifle and his Smith & Wesson. That wouldn't be enough to hold off seven armed men. Then the possibility existed that Renick would stop and gather more from town. Who knew the size of his army before it was over and done? Deacon saw one plus—he still had the box of ammunition. The wheels in his head started moving. Barring a heavy downpour, maybe his plan would work. It was all he had.

"Deacon? What are you thinking?"

"Shock and chaos. Maybe. Hope so."

He poured out half of the rifle cartridges and handed the rest to Izzy. "I'm going to show you how to take these apart and dump the gunpowder into something. I'll need it done in a hurry. Do you think you and your friends can do that?"

Izzy shook back his long hair. "Yep, we can do it."

"Good." He took the other box of ammunition for his Smith & Wesson and did the same thing. A glance around for some kind of container to hold the gunpowder showed slim pickings.

Grace tapped his shoulder. "Here. Will this do?"

She handed him a lacy handkerchief and a discarded whiskey bottle. "Found the bottle under this platform."

"Excellent!" He took them and kissed her cheek. "Boys, I want some of you to find as many hefty pieces of wood that can serve as clubs."

They ran to search with Shep scampering beside them. Deacon turned to Izzy and five other boys. "Here's what I want you do." He showed them how to take the cartridges and other ammunition apart, and they set to work.

Deacon took Grace out of earshot. "I'm going to give you the rifle. When they come, fire into the lines of gunpowder that I'm going to pour. Once the gunpowder explodes, fire at the attackers. Make every shot count, and we might stand a chance. If not, we won't be alive to get on the train."

Grace closed her eyes for a moment and took a deep breath. "You don't have to tell me the odds. I already know how badly we'll be outnumbered."

"Try to stay out of the line of fire. We'll move the boys to the back under this platform and pray none get hit. I'll be getting as many as I can with my gun. And this." He pulled out two sticks of dynamite from inside his shirt. She gasped. "I saved these in case I needed them. Wish I had a whole case, but I can still do some damage if I get good throws."

"What can I do now?" Subdued and anxious, Grace glanced up at the clouds. He didn't have to ask what she was thinking.

"Help me make some trails in the brush for the gunpowder and keep checking on Davey. That kid has to pull through. I don't know what's wrong with him, but it's bad. Could be pneumonia or pleurisy. Make him comfortable and pray we get to Fort Worth in time."

"Deacon, I know our chances are slim of making it, but if I have to die, I'm glad I'm with you when it comes."

"Hey, pretty lady, we're not giving up." He brushed her cheek and cupped her mulish jaw. "I agree it looks a bit hopeless with only a rifle and my Smith and Wesson, but we've got a lot of fight left in us. Well-placed shots can turn the tide. Whatever happens, we end this here on Texas soil. A lot of good men have spilled blood fighting against people like Julius Renick. These boys are depending on us to save their lives, and that's what we're going to do."

Defeat vanished from her blue eyes. "Thanks, I needed to hear that. I had a weak moment." Determination crossed her face as she brushed her lips to his, then marched out to find something to use as a hoe. She came back with a piece of wide metal. "I don't know what this was used for, but I found it beside the depot door. Maybe they won't mind me borrowing it."

"Doesn't matter. We'll put it back." Deacon used the heel of his boot to make a shallow indention in the ground a yard away from the platform.

Light rain began to fall, and his heart plummeted to his stomach. Dammit! Take away the gunpowder, what could else could they fight with? He stared at the ground, his head in his hands.

If only they had one break. The bite of frustration twisted in his stomach.

But the thought of giving up wasn't in him. Then he had an idea.

The whiskey bottle Grace had discovered just might work. He scoured the area around the lonely depot and found one more empty one. Prying the depot door open, he collected two lanterns hanging on the wall and a gallon of kerosene inside a cabinet. He yanked the small curtain off the window, grabbed a can, and hurried out.

The clock in his head was ticking off the minutes as thunder and rain set the stage for the showdown.

He made quick work of emptying the gunpowder from the bottle into the can. Praying this would work, he and Grace filled both whiskey bottles with kerosene and made wicks from the curtain. "I feel a little better now."

Grace nodded. "Me too. We can throw the lanterns as well."

"Absolutely. We'll fight with everything we have. Renick never met anyone like us." The man had picked on the wrong people. The boys were itching to give the owner back a little of the grief he gave them.

"I think the rain's letting up some." Grace smiled. "Maybe this will go our way."

"Maybe." Deacon thought she was just trying to be optimistic and loved her for that.

The ground was a little wet but had no standing water. Since the gunpowder was of no use for anything else now, he decided to go ahead and pour it. He'd just started the remaining line when the earth under his feet began to tremble. Thundering hooves of at least fifteen horses were bringing their riders closer. This was it.

"They're coming!"

Thirty-seven

"TO YOUR PLACES!" DEACON HURRIED TO FINISH THE LINE AND tossed the can. He hoped the boys would stay where he'd put them. With a nod to Grace, who sheltered with the rifle behind a stack of crates on the platform, he slid the Smith & Wesson from his holster, in plain view of the riders.

Calm descended. The time had passed for worrying. Now came the doing.

Julius Renick raised his hand, signaling his riders to stop. "Deacon Brannock, my man is going to read a list of crimes against you."

Deacon recognized one of the five hired guns sitting to Renick's right. The man opened a sheet of paper. "Trespassing. Entering the town of Thurber unlawfully and with malicious intent. Trespassing into the mine. Removing working boys. Train theft. Threatening Julius Renick with death. Blowing up the mine entrance." The man refolded the paper and put it away.

"I believe you left out spitting on the sidewalk," Deacon answered calmly.

"This isn't a joking matter," Renick snapped.

"Since it's my neck, I'd say not."

"We're here to arrest you. Give yourself up. We'll let the woman go."

"I see. And the boys?"

"They belong to me."

"Then I suggest you jump off the nearest train trestle."

The hired gun raised his firearm. Deacon squeezed off a shot and sent a bullet into some part of his body. Everyone scattered, and the gun battle began, giving riders the advantage of racing around the platform.

Grace's rifle found a lot of targets. She barely finished firing before she had another man in her sights. Deacon lit a match and threw it onto the nearest line of gunpowder. It ignited and unseated three riders, the horses galloping off.

Renick's men descended into mass confusion. Deacon jumped off the platform and fought hand-to-hand.

Out of the corner of his eye, he saw the boys whack the attackers' knees and legs. In some cases, the boys dashed out to drag the downed men into the brush and proceeded to beat them.

Grace reloaded and lifted the rifle to her shoulder while Deacon grabbed a stick of dynamite and threw it into a clump of riders who'd ditched their horses and came at him. They lay groaning and wounded.

One by one, Deacon and Grace whittled Renick's men down to a handful, having ignited all the gunpowder, bottles, and the two sticks of dynamite. But she'd probably fired her last cartridge, and he'd put all the ammunition he had into his gun. Still, they could wield them as clubs if they had to. He'd use whatever he had at his disposal.

The boys made it bad news for any to be caught a foot near the platform, and the dog did his fair share too, biting and hanging on for dear life. They'd become fierce fighters. But then they had been all along, living on the street the way they had, then chained in the mine.

Renick retreated to watch. Grace took aim just as his horse turned, and the projectile struck the saddlebag. That was it. Renick took out a white flag and waved it.

"I'm out of cartridges," Grace called. "What about you?"

"None except what's in the cylinder of my pistol. I'm down to one or two shots."

"What do you think Renick wants?"

"Anyone's guess." Deacon climbed onto the platform and waited for Renick. The mine owner wore a somber face, his deep-set eyes angry. "It looks to me like you've been whipped, Renick. Give up while you still can. We have a lot more to throw at you if we need to." He didn't mean to fib, but a good gambler never let the enemy see his cards.

A noise rumbling in his throat, Renick stepped out of his saddle and onto the platform. "I have to say you put up a good fight. I'm still going to arrest you."

Deacon barked a laugh. "You and what army? You're beat. How does it feel to be whipped by a woman and bunch of kids?"

Julius Renick pointed below, and the spit dried in Deacon's mouth. A battered and bruised hired gunman had Izzy, his forearm around the boy's throat.

"Hurt him, and there's not a rock big enough for you to hide under."

Grace came from behind her cover, eyes flashing, hands on her hips. The useless Winchester lay on the platform, out of cartridges. She stalked to Deacon's side. "You're lower than a nest of scorpions. Turn the boy loose. This far south, you might not've heard of my family—Stoker Legend and his sons? They'd love to squash you under the heel of their boots just like the bugs you are."

A moment of unease crossed Renick's eyes before quickly fading. "I've heard of them, but unfortunately for you, lady, they aren't here." His cold smile spoke of evil. "I *will* have the boy killed. All I have to do is lift my hand."

"Do it, and you'll have every lawman in the country down on you." A layer of steel underscored Deacon's answer.

Grace narrowed her eyes. "You can be assured I'll detail every bit of this in the newspaper, and it'll spread across the country. What do you think will happen next?"

The jackass holding Izzy let out a howl, holding his crotch and doubling over, his face green. Izzy must've kicked or hit him. The remaining boys, except for Davey, lying near death, ran out and attacked the hired gun with their clubs. The man curled up in a ball, both arms protecting his head.

Seeing his chance, Deacon's fist connected with Renick's jaw and knocked him backward on his rear. The jolt sent tingling waves up his arm, and Deacon lost feeling in his hand.

Renick staggered to his feet. Wiping the blood from his mouth, he went for his gun. Deacon stared, sweat popping out on his forehead, his hand useless. He was looking death in the face.

Having positioned herself on his right side, Grace whipped out his Smith & Wesson and fired. Blood stained Renick's chest, and he fell face-first.

Deacon held his arm. "Take the gun and go see about the boys. I'm fine."

"You're not fine. Stop saying that!" Nerves seemed to have gotten the best of her as she hurried off.

Deacon kicked Renick's gun away and rolled him over. The mine owner groaned, looking up at him. "I almost got you."

"Haven't you heard? Almost only counts in horseshoes." Deacon glanced toward town, where men straggled through the gate. All were hobbling, holding a bloody wound, or somehow impaired. A buggy careened past them and out the entrance to Thurber. He thought he could see a black bag on the seat. "Doctor will be here soon."

Deacon picked up Renick's gun in his good hand and jumped off the platform. Boys sat on every square inch of Renick's hired man, and Grace held his head down with a foot. "Looks like you've fixed him good."

A boy named Finn looked up with a grin. "We knew you were tired, Mr. Brannock,"

"That I am." But when Deacon met Grace's gaze, the weariness melted away.

As though sensing his need to hold her, she moved to his side. "How's your arm?"

"Better." He pulled her close and buried his face in her golden hair. "You make a heck of a partner to have in a fight. I'd like to hold you like this all day."

The buggy he'd spied pulled to a stop, and the occupant grabbed a black bag.

"Unfortunately, I need to speak to the doctor. See if he'll look at Davey."

"Of course." She stepped back. "I'm not going anywhere."

The black-clothed man headed for the steps up to the platform. Deacon cut him off. "One moment, sir."

"My boss is lying up top with a gunshot."

"I know. I'm the one who put the bullet in him. But I need you to take a look at a very ill boy that I carried from the mine where Renick had him chained."

The doctor's head jerked around. "I didn't know anything about that. Yes, let me take a look."

After examining Davey, the doc stood. "He's in dire shape and needs a hospital."

"We're catching the train when it comes. Will he make it to Fort Worth?"

The doctor reached into his bag and pulled out some pills. "These may help the fever if he comes around and can swallow."

"Thanks. I appreciate you taking a look at him."

"Hey, Doc, get up here!" Renick shouted. "I'm paying you to take care of me."

"I'm being called. Good luck to you." The doctor shook Deacon's hand and hurried off.

Grace marched Renick's sullen employee up the steps to the platform, a gun at his back, after the doctor left and took his boss. He sat against the side of the depot building with Deacon guarding him. They'd take him into town and turn him over to the law.

As for Julius Renick, Deacon would have the stationmaster tele-graph the Texas Rangers, and a few of them would come to collect Renick in short order. Izzy and his little gang of cutthroats, their faces still black with coal dust, perched on the edge nearby with their legs hanging off. Shep lay down beside them and seemed to be grinning. Or so it looked like to Deacon. His teeth were white against the black dust on his fur.

A wagon rumbled up, and the dour-faced stationmaster got out. Grace went to speak to him about paying for the kerosene, curtain, and lanterns. "Name a figure, and I'll wire you the money we owe for using everything when I get to Fort Worth."

"No, ma'am." A smile transformed his face. "I'm glad to see Renick and his bunch get their just deserts. You get those boys back to town and give them a bath."

"I appreciate that."

Deacon grinned. Most people despised the fenced-in town of Thurber. Hopefully, a new mine owner would treat everyone better.

A train whistle sounded, and the Texas and Pacific pulled to a stop amid Izzy and his friends' cheering. Deacon wasn't sure if they were excited to go home and get a bath or to be rid of Thurber.

∾

Grace held Davey in her lap, praying they'd get to a hospital in time to save him. The boy had roused once and took some water. Thankfully, they'd gotten him to swallow one of the pills the doctor had given them for him, but that was all.

Her gaze went to Deacon, with the boys and dog two rows up, keeping them occupied. The stationmaster had shown them where to get water, and Deacon had washed their faces and hands at least. His affection for them was always apparent. He seemed to see himself in them.

She loved that man so much and couldn't wait to be married and spend the rest of her life with him. She had a picture in her mind of waking up next to him, his sexy smile as they made love in the early, rosy dawn. Her stomach quickened, yearning washing over her in waves. She didn't know how she'd wait until they could find time to be together.

He rose and came back to where she sat, taking the empty seat. "How is he?"

Davey's pale face, gasping for air, eyes closed, didn't offer much hope. "No change. How much farther?"

"I spoke with the conductor when he ambled by fifteen minutes ago, and he said a half hour." Deacon lifted Davey's limp hand. "Wish there was some miracle, but I fear we're fresh out. Poor kid. He didn't have much of a chance when he came into the world."

"Do you know what happened to his parents?"

"Izzy said they got separated two years ago when they arrived in Fort Worth. They couldn't speak English and were on their way West. Davey assumes they went on."

"How sad. If he dies, we'll be the only ones to mourn."

"His parents mourned when they lost him and probably still do." Deacon glanced out the window. "When we get to town, I'll hurry to find a wagon to transport Davey to the hospital. There may be a hackney at the depot we can hire and that would be a godsend."

Grace took a deep breath. "Every second that passes is one less for this sweet boy."

"The cold of that mine had to be the cause. Hopefully, the Texas Rangers will take care of Renick and put him away for a long time."

"Don't forget his thugs too. The sorry bottom-feeders." Grace shook with anger. "How soon were they going to Thurber?"

"A matter of hours. They should be there now."

"Good. I hope they get them all, put 'em behind bars, and never let them out. They shouldn't be allowed near decent people." Each time Grace thought about it, she got mad all over again.

"We'll be called on to testify at their trial." Deacon yawned.

They had gone thirty-six hours without sleep. He was exhausted. She was too worried and angry to be sleepy. "I'll gladly tell anyone who'll listen what Renick and his men did." Then she remembered Deacon being under suspicion for Pickford's death and another worry heaped on top of the others. The state could throw out the case against Renick all over something Deacon didn't do.

He put his mouth to her ear and whispered, "Quit worrying. It'll make you gray haired."

"Would you marry me if my hair turns?"

"Princess, I would marry you if you had purple, green, or orange hair." His eyes twinkled as she leaned for a kiss.

The moment his lips met hers sent her heart into double-time. And in that space of time, all problems melted away. If she lived to be a hundred, she'd never tire of kissing him.

A few minutes later, the train whistle blew. They'd arrived. From then on it was hectic, but Deacon talked a man with a wagon into taking them all to the hospital, where a sour-faced nurse took one look at the black coal dust on the boys' clothing and the dog and made them stay outside.

A doctor took one look at Davey. "Pneumonia." He hurried the boy down the hall to a room. Within a half hour, they had him in a bed with moist plasters on his chest, giving oxygen treatment, and injections of something they were told would bring down the fever.

Deacon caught the doctor by the arm. "Will he make it?"

"I'm hopeful, and you should be also. The boy's a fighter. Why don't you and your wife get some rest?" Without more, the doctor hurried off.

"It's funny how everyone assumes we're married. Let's make it so." Deacon's gray eyes twinkled.

"I'm all for doing it soon." He didn't know it, but Grace had already scuttled the notion of a prolonged wait a few weeks ago. If not for her parents, she'd say her "I do" today. She couldn't do that to them though, and she wanted them to be there.

"How about two weeks?" he suggested.

They should find out if Davey would make it by then. "Yes, I'll let my family know."

He pulled her close. "We're really going to do this."

A nurse came in, and they quickly broke apart, but their gazes locked, and Grace was the happiest she'd ever been.

∽

Outside the hospital, Deacon kissed Grace, and they parted. She hurried toward home to bathe and get a bit of rest. Deacon loaded the boys up and took them to the saloon. It took a while and a lot of threats to get them and Shep past the monkey and upstairs, where Aunt Martha took charge of bathing them and putting them in clean clothes that he'd picked up on the way over.

The noon crowd had come and gone, and all was quiet. Deacon sat drinking coffee with Harry and talking. He told Harry about the events in Thurber, Renick, and little Davey.

"Sounds like some tense times." Harry glanced at the monkey at the end of the bar where it was eating an orange. "Look at that mess he's making. For two cents, I'd open the door and shoo him out."

"Don't tell me you and Jesse James haven't kissed and made up."

The look Harry gave him could've melted bullets. "That monkey's going to be the death of me yet. He managed to get into my room. I think he knows how to pick locks. He got one of the spittoons and poured the contents on every clean shirt, then pissed on my bed. Sarge has hightailed it, and I don't where he's gone, but I'd like to be with him wherever it is."

It was no laughing matter but Deacon worked to keep a straight face. "Jesse's got it in for you."

"That's not all. Last night he got into the liquor and was one drunk monkey this morning."

"Wasn't Clyde taking care of him?"

"Him and Aunt Martha were busy upstairs fornicating." Harry rolled his eyes. "Sure hope they don't make more little monkeys."

Deacon threw back his head and laughed. "So business was good?"

"Best day so far. Seems word is spreading, and you've got yourself a gold mine." Harry was silent a moment. "I don't know if I can take this, Deacon. I warned you this would happen, but did you listen to me?"

"I'll have a talk with Clyde. Jesse shouldn't have the run of the place and I'll try to find Sarge."

Harry glanced away, silent.

"Jesse is fun entertainment, but I need you, Harry," Deacon said quietly. "You're like a brother."

"You are to me too." The man sighed. "Thank you, Deacon."

Everything Deacon had said was true. Harry meant so much more than just being his right-hand man. He was family. Deacon's gaze followed the despondent friend to the door of his room.

Where could Sarge have gone?

Izzy clomped down the stairs and rushed to throw his arms around Deacon. "You brought my red wagon here. Thank you! I thought I'd never see it again."

Deacon blinked hard. The boy's gratefulness for every kind act touched him. The words hung on the tip of his tongue that he and Grace went to see his mother, but he swallowed them. That would only make Izzy sadder, especially if Anna wound up staying with Phillip Vinson.

"I thought you'd want it, and I didn't want anyone to steal your things." Deacon got down on eye level. "You're not going back to the streets. You and Shep will live here or with Grace and me once we're married. I'm going to keep you safe from now on."

Izzy's eyes filled with tears, and his bottom lip quivered. "Do you mean it?"

"More than I've ever meant anything." Deacon put his arms around the boy, the words he wanted to say choking in his throat. "Welcome home."

"What about the others?"

"I'll find homes. Good homes, where I know the boys are wanted."

"They'll like that." Izzy glanced up through his long hair, freckles marching across his nose. "We're real tired. All of us. It was scary in that dark mine for so long. Shep helped us have hope." His lip quivered again. "I think the angels sent him. Don't you?"

"Without a doubt. Why don't you go lie down and rest?" Deacon watched him move toward the stairs and stop as Harry came from his room, arms full of laundry.

"Mr. Brannock, do you think Davey will be all right? He won't die, will he?"

The question caught Deacon off guard. An answer escaped him.

Harry came to the rescue. "Young man, God didn't send Brannock to get you all out of that mine to let one of you die. Davey's gonna be okay."

"Thanks, Mr. Harry." Satisfied, Izzy went on.

Sometimes they all needed to hang on to hope, and if a few words could bring that to a little boy, it didn't matter if you believed them yourself or not.

Thirty-eight

DEACON'S GAZE FOLLOWED IZZY UP THE STAIRS BEFORE turning again to his bartender. "Appreciate you stepping in, Harry." Deacon clapped him on the shoulder. "I was afraid to lie to the boy. He needs to have hope."

"Anytime, Boss." Harry grinned. "You'll never guess what I found hiding under these clothes."

"Jesse James?"

Harry snorted. "Nope, Sarge. I feel some better now. Do you think it was one of those God things?"

Stranger things had happened, and Deacon wasn't discounting anything. "Maybe so. I'm glad you're able to smile again."

"I still meant what I said about that damn monkey."

"I'm on my way to speak to Clyde now." Deacon headed in search of Jesse's owner. He found Clyde with binoculars trained on the half-naked women in the windows of the nearest whore-house. "Have time for a chat, Clyde?"

The little man jumped half out of his skin and thrust the bin-oculars behind his back. "Sure. You won't mention to Martha what you just saw, will you?"

"Depends."

"On what?"

"It depends on you being willing to curtail Jesse James's she-nanigans. He's about to run off my best friend and bartender." Deacon glanced down at the height-deprived man. "Here's the deal. Keep him on a chain, in a cage, or otherwise contained, or we'll have to part ways."

"Now, look here, that monkey goes wherever he pleases." Clyde looked for a box to stand on. Finding none, he got on a chair to look Deacon in the eye. "This is about Harry, ain't it? He hates Jesse."

"No, this is about keeping an orderly place. Jesse throws trash everywhere and doesn't mind peeing wherever he takes a notion. I'm tired of it." Deacon pinched the bridge of his nose. "Clyde, we're making good money, aren't we?"

"More than I've made anywhere. But—"

"And you like being in Martha's bed?"

"Yes, but—"

"Clyde, I'd hate for her to find out your little secret. I would feel just horrible about that. She has such a temper."

Clyde's face dropped as he laid down the binoculars. "All right. All right. I'll find something to do with Jesse."

"That's the spirit." Deacon helped him off the chair. "See? Was that so hard?"

"We've been working on something special, in case you care." Dejected, Clyde went off to find the cowboy monkey.

Mission accomplished. Deacon went to meet Grace at the hospital. Their lives, the wedding, were starting to come together. Grace arrived on his heels.

Deacon kissed her cheek. "You look as fresh as a peach tree in full bloom."

She laughed, glancing down at her peach-colored dress. "I do, don't I? I'm glad it doesn't reflect my mood. Meg contacted her family in Illinois and is leaving Fort Worth."

"I'm sorry to hear that, but I think she'll make a good life for herself now, thanks to you."

"I know. I've just become very fond of her."

He took her arm, and they went inside to Davey's room but found it empty and the bed made. Tears filled her eyes.

"Oh, Deacon! He died all alone." She buried her face in his chest.

He put his arms around her. Poor kid. Maybe they should've stayed, but they'd had so much to do and the other boys to see about. "Let me go ask about his body. The least we can do is give him a proper grave."

She took a handkerchief from a little purse and wiped her eyes. "I should've stayed with him. He was so sweet. Yes, please go ask."

He approached the desk. "Can you tell me how we can claim the little boy that was in room 119?"

The nurse looked up. "Davey?"

"Yes. I don't have a last name. We rescued him from a mine."

She flipped a paper over. "Oh, he's not dead. We moved him down the hall where we have better equipment. Room 124."

Relieved, Deacon hurried back and told Grace. She wiped her tears, and they went to find the new room. Davey was on an oxygen machine and awake.

"We're so happy you're better." Grace laid a light hand on his head.

Davey seemed confused. "Who are you?"

"We rescued you from the mine, along with Izzy and the others. You were really sick." Deacon found a chair and took it to Grace. He stood next to the bed. Davey looked so small and fragile. "As Grace said, thank goodness you're at least awake and able to talk."

Davey's smile was weak, but there all the same. "I don't remember much. Thank you for getting us out. Izzy's my friend."

"So we hear. Can we get you anything?" Grace asked.

The boy shook his head.

"Okay, get some rest and feel better. Grace and I will be back to check on you tomorrow." Deacon covered Davey's hand with his palm.

Feeling hope surging through his chest, Deacon told Grace he had one more thing to do. "I'll meet you tonight for Jesse James's evening show. Clyde said he's been working on something special."

"Excellent!" Grace kissed him and got on a trolley car.

Meg was waiting inside the house, two large bags at her feet. Grace hated the thought of her leaving.

"I hate goodbyes." Meg twisted a handkerchief, her chin quivering. "I can't believe my family still wants me."

Grace hugged her. "Well, they'd better is all I have to say."

"I'm not sure what to tell them when they ask where I've been."

"Honey, the West is an awful big place and no way to verify anything. Choose whatever you want to be and stick with it. I've found the closer to the truth it is, the less you'll get tripped up. I wish you could stick around for the wedding. Jesse James will be my ring bearer."

Meg laughed. "Good luck there. That monkey has a mind of his own."

"This wedding will be the talk of the town for sure." A wagon pulled to a stop out front. Grace pulled Meg close. "If something happens and you want to come back, you're always welcome here. Of course, I don't know where I'll be living, but Harry can tell you."

With a nod and thanks for everything, Meg opened the door and went to meet her future. Grace stood waving until the woman disappeared from sight. People came and went from someone's life. Some stayed a short while, others much longer. But all left a mark of some kind. Meg's would be lasting.

∝

A little while later, Deacon rode onto Bonner land. He needed to see Diablo. And Will, of course. The man had been on his mind.

Will stuck his head out. "Stop in for coffee when you're done."

"Thanks, I will."

At the sight of Deacon, Diablo pranced around the larger corral where they'd been keeping him. Ears pricked, he ran to the rails when Deacon dismounted, swishing his tail.

"Hello, friend." Deacon patted his sleek neck, then reached in his pocket for the sugar cubes he'd brought. Diablo didn't hesitate in taking them off his hand.

Locating the horse blanket, bridle, and saddle, Deacon returned. Diablo remembered the blanket but eyed the saddle suspiciously. He stood long enough for Deacon to touch the saddle to his back before running.

"I know this looks awful scary, but it won't hurt you. I promise."

Three other tries were unsuccessful as well. On the next one, Deacon was able to get the saddle buckled on before Diablo broke loose and galloped around the corral. When the horse settled down, Deacon introduced the bit. What he'd thought would be the hardest, turned out pretty easy. It took a dozen attempts to get in the saddle and on Diablo's back. But he made it.

The first two passes around the corral were in a half-buck, half-trot kind of ride, but Deacon hung on and managed to smooth Diablo out. Will waved from the window.

Pride swept through Deacon. He'd managed the impossible.

Three of the ranch hands stood and watched, shouting and hooting.

Deacon dismounted and remounted Diablo several times, and the once-wild horse seemed to want to please. They might have to rename the mustang now. He'd bring it up to Will over coffee.

At last he removed the saddle and bridle and let Diablo run inside the larger corral in front. He'd brush the horse down and give him some oats later.

Whistling, Deacon opened the kitchen door. Will sat at the table. "I have to say I'm a bit sorry that I won't see you as often after this."

Will didn't speak, didn't turn around. His heart lurching, Deacon moved closer and touched his cold shoulder, peering into the rancher's face. Will's sightless eyes were open.

No heartbeat. No life.

No! Deacon lowered his friend's eyes and dropped into a chair, his head in his hands. Will had seemed fine when Deacon arrived. And when he'd managed to stay on Diablo, Will had waved from the window. All had been normal.

Still, it only took a second for a heart to stop beating.

Deacon raised his head and took note of the paper and money in front of Will, his hand still holding the stubby pencil. Seeing his own name on the paper—a letter, it appeared—Deacon reached for it.

> Deacon,
>
> I wish I could've told you all this in person, meant to, but the good Lord has other plans. I see you out the window riding Diablo. You did it, son. Here's the money I owe you. Will Bonner never welshed on a deal. I've also slipped in a wedding present. You won't need to buy that land, though.
>
> I've thought long and hard about what I'm about to tell you. I paid a visit to your pretty mama twenty-nine years ago, and I'm fairly certain you're the product of that chance encounter. Can't prove it, but you have a strong family resemblance. That was the only time I ever cheated on Frances. We'd had a spat the night I left on a trip to Medicine Springs. I confessed my transgression, and she forgave me. A year or so ago, I talked to her about deeding this ranch over to you and she liked the idea.
>
> You'll find the papers all fixed up proper-like on my desk in the parlor. I want you and Grace to be happy living here. All those little boys too.
>
> I've watched you over the years and seen the fine man you've turned into. I'm proud to call you my boy. Thanks for the memories, son.
>
> By the way, Frances says hello.

Deacon wiped his eyes. "Well, I'll be." He patted Will's hand. "You could've spoke up sooner...Pop."

All the times when Will questioned him about his father crossed his mind. Come to think of it, Deacon did resemble him in looks. Maybe in a few actions too.

His heart heavy, he went out to get the ranch hands to help him wrap Will in a blanket and put him in the wagon for his last trip to town. The men were somber and respectful, speaking of their deep loss. Before heading out, Deacon sat on the wagon seat and stared at the catfish pond, remembering their last time out there together. He broke down in sobs as he took Will Bonner by for one last look.

Diablo stood unmoving in the corral. As they passed, the horse dipped his head as though in a salute. Will probably had a tear in his eye for the wild mustang he never gave up on.

By the time he got back to the saloon, Grace was there, anxious to see little Jesse James perform. But first, she needed to hear the news.

"We have to talk. I have something to tell you." He took her hand and led her upstairs to his bedroom and closed the door. They sat in the chairs he kept there. "I've kept a secret from you. Not that I was afraid of what you'd say, but because I couldn't bear to see your disappointment when I failed."

She gently touched his face. "I would never feel anything but love for you, don't you know that? You're in my heart to stay. Now what's on your mind?"

"I'm a cowboy."

Grace laughed. "If you think that's some big secret, I'm here to tell you different. I knew that from the first moment I saw you. It was in the hat and the way you stood."

"No, that's not really the secret. What I'm trying to tell you is that I've been going out to Will Bonner's ranch and trying to gentle a wild mustang his men caught." Deacon told her about the deal they'd struck.

"This is incredible." Her glistening blue eyes said how proud she was.

Deacon held back the grief closing in and pulled the letter from inside his vest. "I finished with the horse this morning. I rode him for quite a while. When I went inside the house, I found Will dead at the table. He'd written this letter to me and had the money laid out."

She took the letter he handed her and silently read it. Then she looked up, tears bubbling in her eyes. "Oh, Deacon. I'm so sorry about Will. He must've been a fine man. This is something you've wondered for so long. Do you think he was your father?"

"I have no way of knowing, but I'd like to think so. He was always very easy to be around, and we shared many a fire. It's definitely possible. I sort of resemble him I think."

Her eyes met his and she threw her arms around him. "You have your land! We own the Bonner ranch! Now we have a place to live and where we can put all these boys."

She kissed him soundly, and Deacon didn't think he'd ever had a day quite like this one.

Thoughts tumbled over and over in his head, the happy mixed with the sad. He had a funeral to arrange and a marriage to plan. Plus, a million things in between. Life was a strange circle of love and loss, happiness and sorrow. A new door opening when one closed.

When she pulled back for air, she wore a mischievous smile. "Can the monkey live out there with us?"

"No. The monkey has to stay with Clyde. Get that out of your head now."

"Can we think about it?"

Deacon pulled her to her feet and turned her toward the door. "No. The monkey belongs to Clyde, end of story. We'll have a dog. Shep is all we'll need."

"But—"

He kissed the objections right out of her. A lesson he was learning.

ॐ

They went to check on Davey and found the boy continuing to slowly improve. He perked up when Grace told him he'd be living on a ranch.

"With horses?"

Deacon laughed. "With horses and cows and the dog Shep."

"It's like a dream."

"That it is." Grace smoothed back his hair and kissed his cheek. She left the hospital with Deacon, a happy glow in her heart. "I want to see Will Bonner."

His gaze tangled with hers. "Are you sure? I don't know the mortician's policy, but I guess we can find out."

The mortician seemed a bit surprised. "This is a little irregular, but I'll allow it."

He led them into a back room where Will lay on a table, still in his clothes, hands folded across his chest. "Can we have a moment?" Deacon asked.

The mortician silently stepped out.

Grace moved closer, gripping a lacy handkerchief. "Deacon, he looks so kind. Yes, there is definitely a resemblance. The hair and the angles of his face."

"If you say so. Maybe you're just wanting to see what's not there."

"No, that's not it at all." She covered Will's crossed hands with hers and spoke to the man. "I'm sorry I never got to meet you, but I want you to know the difference you made in our lives. Thank you for taking Deacon in and being the father he never had. You don't know what that meant. He needed you to guide him, and it sounds like you did. I can't wait to move to the ranch and raise all these boys. They needed a home so desperately." Her voice cracked and she wiped her eyes. "And I need them to take all the love I'm longing to give."

"Are you ready to go?" Deacon put an arm around her.

"Did you speak to the mortician about a service?"

"Not yet. He said we'd do it when I came back today. Now is probably a good time."

"Where is Will's wife buried?" Grace asked.

"On the ranch. We'll lay him beside her."

They found the mortician and made all the arrangements to bury Will on the land he loved next to Frances. The afternoon sun had started its slow slide beneath the horizon by the time they arrived at the Three Deuces.

Jesse James put on quite a show, chattering, shooting his little gun, and grinning, keeping the crowd in stitches, especially when Sarge decided to grab his share of the spotlight. Of all the spitting and slapping. Grace had never laughed so hard. Then came the moment she'd waited for—the surprise.

Clyde pulled Jesse into the kitchen. Grace waited with bated breath. Deacon moved to her side. "I hope this is good." He nuzzled the back of her neck.

The kitchen door opened, and someone clapped three times. Out ran Shep with Jesse standing on his back, balancing, clinging to a small set of reins. The monkey's grin was hilarious. And then he stood on his head with his feet in the air.

"This is amazing," Grace hollered over the laughter. "Are you sure we can't take Jesse with us? He could learn to ride Diablo."

"Not on your life. I'd never get any food. You'd always be watching him."

"You're just jealous."

"Damn right."

Grace leaned back against the man she loved, her heart bursting.

Thirty-nine

A KNOCK CAME ON DEACON'S DOOR EARLY THE NEXT morning. Harry announced there was someone downstairs wanting to talk to him.

"She wouldn't give a name," Harry added, handing him a pair of trousers.

Feeling as if he'd been stomped on by Diablo, Deacon dressed and went down. A woman stood with her back to the stairs. "Ma'am? Can I help you?"

She turned, and he recognized Izzy's mother, Anna. "I'd like a word about my boy."

"Can I offer you something to drink? Tea or coffee?" The saloon wasn't so dim to where he could miss her fresh bruises.

"Thank you but no."

"Then have a seat." Deacon pulled out a chair for her and they sat. "Grace and I rescued Izzy from a mine in Thurber where he'd been taken after being kidnapped. The owner chained him and some other boys up and forced them to work, digging out coal."

Anna gasped, putting a hand over her mouth. "Is he hurt?"

"No, ma'am. In fact, he's upstairs sleeping." Deacon narrowed his eyes. "Can I ask what your intentions are? If you've just come to see him and will leave, I don't know if that's wise. You'll only break his heart all over again."

"I appreciate your concern, Mr. Brannock, but it's not needed." Anna lifted her chin. "I've left Phillip and will never go back. I finally had enough, and no one will make me give up my son again."

"I'm glad to hear that. It took courage." Deacon was happy to see some backbone.

Nervous, Anna clasped her hands together. "I have no place to live, Mr. Brannock, but I intend to find one and a job. When I do, I'll be back for Izzy."

A beat of silence filled the air between them.

"If you don't mind helping out here and waiting tables, I'll hire you on the spot. Business is booming, and I'm about to be married. This place is more a café than a saloon."

"Then I'll accept. Thank you for the offer."

Izzy stood at the top of the stairs. "Mama? That you?"

With a cry, she ran toward him, arms outstretched. "I missed you so much."

Deacon yawned and stretched, watching the happy reunion. Harry brought a cup of coffee. "Did you ever think to see that, Harry?"

"Nope. I guess life turns out all right in spite of all we do to help it along."

"Let's find her a place to sleep." Deacon stood. "I guess she can have my room."

Jesse chattered up a storm, scolding Harry from the corner that had been sealed off with chicken wire to make him a home, complete with his own saloon. He stuck out his tongue at Harry, who returned the salutation. Deacon laughed and went back to his bed.

❧

Not a cloud was in the sky that afternoon for Will's private funeral. Only Deacon, Grace, and the ranch hands were in attendance, and a minister spoke a few words that made Grace cry.

When they lowered Will into the ground next to Frances, Deacon shed tears as well, remembering the man who'd been a good father and treated him like a son. He hoped Will was happy being with the love of his life. Together, Will and Frances made an exceptional team, but apart, they were miserable.

If Grace and Deacon had that kind of relationship, they could whip the world. He glanced at her and reached for her hand. He'd spend his life trying to be good enough for her and put a smile on her face.

Once the ceremony was over, Deacon pointed out where he would build a large bunkhouse for the boys. "They'll start Monday. I've asked Anna if she'd like to live here and ramrod them. She said she'd love to."

"I'm so glad." Grace slid an arm around his waist. "Everything is falling into place."

"That it is." He aimed her toward the house, to the food they'd brought the ranch hands and preacher.

Everyone was subdued but ate like horses. After everyone left, Deacon stuck a note with the word "Busy" on it to the outside of the door and took her upstairs with the pretense of looking at the furnishings.

"I want you to look at everything and see what else we need," Deacon told her. "We have money now."

"Cowboy, there couldn't possibly be anything lacking. This house is complete."

"Humor me." He took her hand and led her up the stairs to the larger of the bedrooms.

Grace stopped at the door, staring. "This is lovely. I thought it would be full of Will's belongings and his bed, and I was a bit leery of sleeping where he and his wife had."

"I know. Wanted to surprise you. I bought some new things and stored all of Will's out in the barn until I can go through them. You like it?"

"I'm speechless. When did you have time to do all this?" She moved into the room and ran her fingers across the lavender-and-pink coverlet on the large four-poster bed, taking in the soft rug and little table with chairs in a corner. Then she opened the drawers of the chifforobe and chest.

"I think you'll have plenty of room for your things. If you need to use them all, I'll find something else for mine."

"Don't be silly. There's room for everything." She grabbed his vest and pulled him to her. "Kiss me like you mean it, cowboy."

Deacon obliged, giving her a kiss that singed his lips. He ran his hands down her luscious body, cupping her heavy breasts, love for her spilling over.

Their mouths still locked in the kiss, he went to work on the buttons of her dress. "We have to break this bed in," he mumbled against her lips.

She broke the kiss. "It's daylight. What will the men think?"

"That the boss has good taste." He finished the row of buttons and slid the dress off her shoulders.

"But Will's not cold in the ground yet. What about him?"

"Hush, princess, or I'll think you don't want me." He nuzzled her neck, taking the pins from her hair and letting it spill over his hands. "Pop is too busy where he is, making love to the missus. He'd be the first to say this house needs our love to bless it. I'm not a smart man, but I do know how my father thought. He wouldn't want us all sad and weepy. He'd tell us to grab every moment and wear the springs out."

"Then let me help you out of those boots and stuffy, new clothes, dear."

A few minutes later, they fell breathless onto the bed, legs tangling. Deacon's lips found Grace's and he crushed her against his chest, taking, giving, savoring all that was in his grasp.

Breaking apart, he whispered against her face. "I love you so much, Grace. You don't know how happy you've made me. I'll never take you for granted, and if I ever do, I want you to get a gun and shoot me."

Her blue eyes sparkled. "With Jesse James's little pistol or your big one?"

"You know the one I mean." A growl rumbled in his throat, teasing.

Grace grew serious. "I could never hurt you." She gently touched his face and traced his lips with a fingertip. "Thank you for letting me love you. I wasn't sure you would. Our love is an eternal flame for all to see. You're mine, Deacon Brannock."

He saw love in her eyes and smoothed her hair with trembling fingers. "You're the light of my life. My hope, my future. And I can't imagine living one day without you."

Emotion spilled over. "Will Bonner, hide your eyes," she whispered brokenly.

Sunlight spilled through the window, bathing them in glorious splendor. They took their time, gently caressing and loving each other. Then Deacon lowered himself atop her.

Her tight wetness around him, they started the climb that led to that beautiful, glimmering paradise. Primed and ready, it didn't take long. Deacon lay gasping, immersed in the waves of pleasure.

A few moments later, Grace glanced at him. "You got a bed with sturdy springs."

Deacon chuckled. "So it appears."

She rolled toward him and kissed the crow's-feet at the corners of each eye. "You are my legend, my love, the one safekeeping my heart."

"I see." He brought her fingers to his lips. "You're like a warrior. You go around saving everyone. Even me. Thank you."

He was sure Will was smiling. He lifted his hand to his forehead in a salute to the man, the father he'd always wanted, the man with a heart of gold.

❧

"It's so good to be back!" Clutching little Johnny Madrid, Leah hurried from the train platform to Grace and Deacon. "I've missed you."

Grace hugged her close. "Our wedding wouldn't be the same without you." Grace leaned back to look at the glowing young woman so full of confidence. Her forest-green dress, hair arranged artfully high on the crown was a far cry from the frightened young girl who'd left. "Fresh air of the Lone Star agreed with you. You're lovely, my dear."

"Let me have the boy," Deacon growled, reaching for little Johnny. "We have man things to discuss."

"Don't pay him any mind, Leah. He's practicing in hopes of being a papa." Grace linked her arm around the woman's. "We have many, many things to talk about. And I want to introduce you to Jesse James."

Leah frowned. "The outlaw? I thought he died years ago."

"Not that one. The monkey Jesse James," Grace clarified. "He's a fixture now at the Three Deuces. The cutest thing you ever saw and bringing crowds in by the droves."

"Just ask Harry if *he* thinks Jesse is cute." Deacon's dry tone drew Leah's raised eyebrow as he paid the man stowing her bags into a rented surrey. "Harry came near to quitting." He gave the women a hand into the surrey, the baby in the crook of his arm.

Grace couldn't help but notice how easily Deacon held the baby. He was going to make the gentlest father, and she prayed it was soon. She needed a baby in her arms, didn't matter if it was a boy or a girl.

"I can't wait to see Harry and Sarge again." Leah settled her dress on the seat. "Deacon, do you want me to take Johnny?"

"No, ma'am. I'm going to show him how to maneuver these horses through the streets. You just sit back and take in the changes, little mama."

Winding their way toward the Three Deuces, Grace told Leah about Thurber and rescuing the boys. "They're going to live with us at the ranch, where they can run, ride, and jump to their hearts' content."

"They need that freedom. That's what I loved about the Lone Star." Leah grinned. "I've become quite the horsewoman."

"That's wonderful. I know my parents and Grandpa enjoyed having you there."

"They tried to get me to stay, but this is my home." Leah's voice was quiet.

They turned onto Rusk Street and Leah gasped. "I can't believe this."

Surprise one. Grace watched the pretty young woman's face. Renovation was happening in the Acre. Buildings were being painted or torn down in some instances. Boardwalk fixed. Trash picked up from the street. The houses of ill repute and a handful of saloons had been replaced with reputable businesses.

Then the Three Deuces came into view. "Oh my heavens!" Leah stared at the new whitewash, windows added with pretty blue shutters, blue doors to replace the old.

"Do you like it?" Deacon asked quietly, pulling to a stop.

"It's so pretty. It doesn't look like the same place where I lived and gave birth to Johnny." Leah's voice had a catch in it. Emotion had gotten the best of her.

Grace took her hand. "The place is yours and Harry's to share equally."

"I can't afford to buy anything like this."

Deacon turned around on the front seat. "We're giving it to you, honey."

"I… This is too much. I can't. I didn't earn it."

"Stop." Grace squeezed her fingers. "You notice that we didn't say it would be easy. You'll have to work very hard and put in long hours, be dead on your feet, and still have to take care of little Johnny. We know you can manage though because you have staying power and great determination."

They got out and Leah took the baby. "This is amazing."

Deacon cupped Grace's face, love in his eyes. "I couldn't have said that better."

"You'll always have my undying gratitude." Leah looked up at the sign and laughed. "The Cowboy Café. Miss Grace, you always get the last word."

"I try, and sometimes I win." She met the hunger in her cowboy's gaze and knew that each day he walked beside her she was a winner. "I always knew this place was supposed to be a café."

"Uh, I beg your pardon." Deacon managed a stern frown for all of three seconds. "If my recollection serves, I think you mentioned a mercantile and had me selling combs and mustache cups," he corrected, the sunlight creating a happy glow across his rugged features.

Grace sniffed. "A lady can change her mind."

As well as see a future where none existed.

❧

Deacon stood outside the church with Houston, waiting for the bride's arrival. He'd wakened before dawn to rumbling thunder, its hard edges softened by distance, anxious to make Grace his wife. Waking up next to her each morning was the thought that had kept him going during these two weeks of exhausting, whirlwind activity.

He glanced at Houston, looking rather intimidating in a fitted suit, spit-shined boots, and Stetson. The typical cattleman. "You were right; you do know me."

"Care to say where we met?"

"Medicine Springs. I was on trial for murder; only my name was Blade Reno then." Deacon's heart hammered. The next moments would decide if there would be a wedding or not.

The black slashes of Houston's brows came together as he narrowed his eyes. "Blade Reno. Of course. I remember now. You were very young."

A long moment stretched, the silence broken by the passing

trolley. And Deacon's pounding heart. He held his breath, his mouth bone dry. "I was seventeen and desperately trying to make a life for myself and my sister. Stopped cold by McCreedy. I couldn't let him live for murdering Cass. But I'd have gotten a harsher sentence if not for you standing up for me."

"For the record, I'd have done the same if Cass had been my sister." Houston released a loud sigh. "I wish you'd have told me sooner. Trusted me."

"I was afraid you'd see me as nothing but a convict. A killer." Deacon glanced down and nudged a pebble with the toe of his boot. Then he looked up. Never faltering, he met Houston's gaze. "Grace and I love each other. I hope you don't stop the wedding."

Again, silence with all the noise of a foghorn enveloped Deacon. He'd often thought about the Texas wind. The strength and quality told you where you were and often what you were thinking. Dry wind spoke of the Panhandle and Western plains. Humid air came from the eastern part and down South. But sometimes it was also what blew between two men trying to sort out a past.

"Son, I think you're a fine man, a rancher yourself now." Houston laughed. "I heard you tamed the wildness from a mustang. You're going to need a lot more than luck with Grace."

Deacon chuckled. "Thank goodness I know a few secrets."

Harry arrived in a wagon with Izzy's mother, Anna, and Leah beside him. Boys of all ages spilled out the back. At Izzy's directions, they reached back inside for Davey and gently lifted him to the ground, all smiles. The boy had gotten released from the hospital a week ago but was still recuperating. Shep waited until everyone was out, then leaped down.

"I'm glad you made it." Deacon put an arm around Izzy. "Grace wouldn't have married me if you weren't all going to be here."

"We love Miss Grace." Izzy glanced up, his hair cut short. "And you."

A fancy carriage arrived, bringing with it a flurry of excitement.

The boys made two lines that led to Deacon. His heart stopped at the sight of Grace stepping down and floating toward him through the line of boys. The white satin-and-silk creation had the appearance of frosting, and her golden hair shimmered, kissed by the sun's rays.

Grace glanced up at him, the sweep of her lashes creating a dark frame for her blue eyes. She seemed breathless. "Is this a dream? Are we really going to do this?"

"No dream, princess." He kissed her cheek, a steady grip of her palm. "Ready to make our marriage official?"

"Not so fast, Brannock." The gruff voice belonged to the sheriff. He strode to them wearing a heavy scowl.

Dammit to hell! Deacon couldn't believe this. He couldn't be arrested in front of the boys, his bride, and his new father-in-law. "You have a lot of nerve to arrest me now, Sheriff."

Grace glared. "Haven't you ever heard of decency? There's a time and place for things like this and it's not at a wedding. Deacon has been more than cooperative and answered every one of your numerous, dumb questions. I'm going to write a scathing article about this. You can look for it in the *Gazette*. And furthermore—"

Unruffled, the sheriff looked at her like she was some colorful wind-up toy, waiting for her to run down. Finally, he turned to Deacon. "Brannock, you might like to know we've arrested Pickford's killer. You're cleared."

Sheepish, Grace closed her mouth. "Oh, in that case, can you please forget what I just said?"

"I think he will, darlin'. Won't you, Sheriff?"

"Yes, ma'am." The stocky lawman was trying to hide his laughter.

Deacon shook his hand. "Thank you, Sheriff. Mind telling me who did it?"

"His so-called friend. He broke Pickford out of that shed and shot him during an argument over half a bottle of whiskey and that token for a night at Miss Pearl's."

"Figures." Deacon's gaze followed the lawman down the street before tugging on Grace's hand. "The coast is clear. Let's go."

The words had barely left his mouth when Clyde, Martha, and Jesse James arrived. Shep barked, turning in a circle, tail wagging to beat all.

Jesse appeared awfully sharp in a little black suit, clutching a small box. Giving everyone a big grin, showing his teeth, he leaped on Shep's back.

"Clyde, are you sure he still has Grace's ring?" Deacon asked nervously.

"He's got it." Clyde took Martha's arm and smiled up at her towering over him. "Might be a little bent, though. The rascal tried to eat it and I had to pry it out of his mouth. He bit me for the trouble."

Harry snorted. "Deacon, I told you this was a bad, bad, bad idea."

But Deacon couldn't hear a word. He was occupied by the beautiful woman soon to be his bride.

Love shining from her pretty blue eyes, Grace wound an arm around his. "Come on, cowboy, let's get married before someone else tries to stop the ceremony."

About the Author

Linda Broday resides in the panhandle of Texas on the Llano Estacado. At a young age, she discovered a love for storytelling, history, and anything pertaining to the Old West. Cowboys fascinate her. There's something about Stetsons, boots, and tall, rugged cowboys that get her fired up! A *New York Times* and *USA Today* bestselling author, Linda has won many awards, including the prestigious National Readers' Choice Award and the Texas Gold Award. Visit her at lindabroday.com.

Also by Linda Broday

Bachelors of Battle Creek
Texas Mail Order Bride
Twice a Texas Bride
Forever His Texas Bride

Men of Legend
To Love a Texas Ranger
The Heart of a Texas Cowboy
To Marry a Texas Outlaw

Texas Heroes
Knight on the Texas Plains
The Cowboy Who Came Calling
To Catch a Texas Star

Outlaw Mail Order Brides
The Outlaw's Mail Order Bride
Saving the Mail Order Bride
The Mail Order Bride's Secret
Once Upon a Mail Order Bride

Texas Redemption
Christmas in a Cowboy's Arms anthology
Longing for a Cowboy Christmas anthology

HIGH COUNTRY JUSTICE

The Caleb Marlowe series: Riveting and action-packed
historical westerns from acclaimed author Nik James

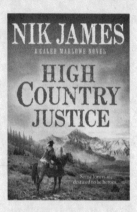

Caleb Marlowe carved out his own legend as a frontier scout and lawman
before arriving in the Colorado boomtown of Elkhorn. Famous for a
lightning-quick draw and nerves of steel, he is mysterious, guarded, and
unpredictable. Now, he wants to leave the past behind. But the past has a
way of dogging a man...

When Doc Burnett, Caleb's only friend in town, goes missing, his
daughter Sheila comes seeking Caleb's help. Newly arrived from the East,
she hotly condemns the bloody frontier justice of the rifle and the six-gun.

Murderous road agents have Doc trapped in their mountain hideaway.
To free him, Marlowe tracks Doc's kidnappers through wild, uncharted
territory, battling animals and bushwhackers. But when Sheila is captured
by the ruthless gunhawks with a score to settle, Marlowe will have to take
them down one by one, until no outlaw remains standing.